January 2012

Dear Friends,

Happy New Year! It's me…again, as you're holding *You…Again.* You're going to enjoy these two stories, and I say that with all humility. Well, I certainly hope you do. The two romances in this volume are especially dear to my writer's heart. The first, *Baby Blessed,* was first published back in 1994, and two of my children were the cover models on the original edition. (If you're interested in seeing that original cover, I've posted it on my website at DebbieMacomber.com.) Jody and Ted met commerical artist John Solie (who did the movie poster for *Romancing the Stone* and the second *Star Wars* movie), and they had the experience of a lifetime. And you know what? The book's not half bad, either.

The second book, *Yesterday Once More,* is one of my earliest, published a quarter of a century ago. My wonderful editor, Paula Eykelhof, and I worked on "refreshing" both books, and editorial assistant Kate Studer helped, as well. It's hard to believe I've been published for more than twenty-five years but, alas, it's true. The world has changed in many ways during that time, but certain things—like the power of romance and the importance of family—endure.

As always, I enjoy hearing from my readers and appreciate your ongoing support. You can visit my website at DebbieMacomber.com or write me at P.O. Box 1458, Port Orchard, WA 98366. And yes, I personally read every website comment and every letter.

Warmest regards,

Debbie Macomber

DEBBIE MACOMBER

You...Again

Recycling programs
for this product may
not exist in your area.

ISBN-13: 978-0-7783-1299-4

YOU...AGAIN

Copyright © 2012 by MIRA Books

The publisher acknowledges the copyright holder of the
individual works as follows:

BABY BLESSED
Copyright © 1994 by Debbie Macomber

YESTERDAY ONCE MORE
Copyright © 1986 by Debbie Macomber

For questions and comments about the quality of this book please contact us
at Customer_eCare@Harlequin.ca.

www.Harlequin.com

Printed in U.S.A.

For
Ann Strauss Hosford,
past president of the Omaha School of Hearing,
for her tireless dedication to
deaf and hard-of-hearing children
and their families

Also by Debbie Macomber

CONTENTS

BABY BLESSED

One

"All right, I'll play your little game," Jordan Larabee said from between gritted teeth. He paced the carpet in front of Ian Houghton's shiny mahogany desk. "Where is she?"

"I presume you mean Molly?"

Ian could be a real smart aleck, and apparently he'd turned that ability into an art form since their last meeting.

"Might I remind you that Molly is *your* wife?"

"She's your daughter," Jordan shot back. "You're the one she went to when she left me."

As Ian relaxed in his high-back leather chair, he seemed to enjoy himself. An insolent half smile curved the edges of his mouth. "It was my understanding that Molly's leaving was a mutual decision."

Jordan snickered. "By the time she moved out, there wasn't anything mutual between us. We hadn't spoken in days." Any communication between them had died with their six-month-old son. The autumn morning they'd lowered Jeffrey's tiny casket into the ground, they'd buried their marriage, as well. For eight months afterward, they'd struggled to hold their lives together. But the grief and the guilt had eaten away at them until there was nothing left but an empty shell, and eventually that had crumbled and scattered like dust.

Ian stood, looking older than Jordan remembered. He walked over to the window and gazed out as if the view was mesmerizing. "Why now?"

"It's been three years," Jordan reminded him.

"I'm well aware of how long it's been," Ian murmured, clasping his hands behind his back.

"It's time I got on with my life," Jordan said coolly. "I want a divorce."

"A divorce," Ian repeated. His shoulders sagged.

"Don't tell me this comes as a shock. I should have filed years ago." Jordan started pacing again, the anger simmering just below the surface. His annoyance was unreasonable, he realized, and directed more at himself than his father-in-law. He'd delayed this confrontation far longer than he should have. The divorce papers were in his briefcase, and all he needed was Molly's signature. After three years, he didn't expect any argument. Actually he was surprised she hadn't initiated this herself.

Ian moved away from the window and glanced at the framed picture on his desk. Jordan knew it was a portrait of him and Molly taken shortly after Jeffrey's birth. He remembered it well. He was standing behind Molly, who held Jeffrey in her arms; his hand was on Molly's shoulder and the two of them were smiling down on their son. They had no way of knowing that their joy would soon turn into the deepest grief they could possibly experience.

"I'd always hoped you two would patch things up," Ian said, his voice tinged with sadness.

Jordan pressed his lips together and thrust his hands inside his pockets. A reconciliation *might* have worked earlier, but it was too late now; the sooner Ian accepted that, the better. "I've met someone else."

Ian nodded. "I guessed as much. Well, you can't blame an old man for hoping."

"Where's Molly?" Jordan wasn't enjoying this any more than Ian was. Time to cut to the chase.

"The East African Republic," Ian told him.

Jordan's head snapped up. *"Africa?"*

Ian nodded. "She's doing volunteer work with some church group. The country's desperately in need of anyone with medical experience, and working there has seemed to help her."

Jordan splayed his fingers through his hair. "How long has she been there?"

"Over two years now."

"Two *years?*" Jordan felt as if he'd taken a blow to the stomach. He slumped into a nearby chair. It was just like Molly to do something that impulsive. The East African Republic had been in the news almost nightly, with accounts of rebel unrest, drought and disease.

"I've done everything I can think of to convince her to come home," Ian said, sitting back down, "but she won't listen to me."

"What's wrong with her?" Jordan demanded.

"The same thing that's wrong with you, I suspect,"

Ian said without rancor. "You buried yourself in your work, and she's dedicated herself to saving the world."

"Any fool would know that place isn't safe," Jordan said heatedly, furious with his soon-to-be ex-wife.

Ian nodded. "She says otherwise. She's working in a hospital in Makua City, the capital, for two weeks of every month. Then she commutes into the backcountry to a medical compound for another two weeks."

"Is she crazy, traveling outside the city?" Jordan wished Molly was there so he could strangle her himself. He was on his feet again, but didn't remember standing. "She needs her head examined."

"I couldn't agree with you more. Something's got to be done." He grinned. "And as far as I'm concerned, you're the man to do it."

"Me? What can *I* do?" Jordan asked, although he was fairly sure he already knew the answer.

For the first time Jordan read a genuine smile in the older man's eyes. "What can you do?" Ian repeated meaningfully. "Why, Jordan, you can go and get her yourself."

It was the evenings Molly loved best, when the compound slept and the night slipped in. She sat outside on the veranda and absorbed the peaceful sounds, allowing them to soothe her exhausted body and spirit. The news from headquarters in the capital had arrived earlier that evening and it hadn't been good. It never was. Each report, no matter where she was in the backcountry, seemed filled with dire warnings and threats. That evening's communication had been no different, with a lengthy account of political unrest and the threat of a rebel attack. Headquarters asked that she and Dr. Morton be prepared to evacuate at a moment's notice. The identical message came through on a regular basis and had long since lost its urgency. At the end of the week they'd return to Makua City, the same way they did every month.

The black stillness of night was filled with animal noises from the water hole outside the compound walls. The savanna was a refuge for the dwindling animal population. The drought had taken a dramatic toll on wildlife, just as it had on the people.

A week earlier Molly had seen a small herd of elephants tramping across the dry plain, stirring up a haze of red dust. They were moving, looking for a more abundant water supply, Molly guessed.

A hyena yipped in the night, and she smiled to herself. Additional sounds drifted toward her as the antelope and other beasts made their way to the water's waning edge. Over time and with patience, Molly had become adept at identifying each species.

Leaning back in the white wicker chair, she stretched her arms and stared up into the heavens. The sky was illuminated with an incredible display of stars, but she would have traded her inheritance for the sight of a rain cloud.

Unfortunately the sky was clear. Molly couldn't look into the night without experiencing a twinge of sadness. Somewhere, in a world far removed from her current life, were the husband she'd abandoned and the son she'd buried.

She tried not to think about either, because the memories produced a dull, throbbing pain. And pain was something she'd spent the past three years running away from. The gold wedding band on her finger felt like an accusation. She wasn't even sure why she continued to wear it. Habit, she supposed, and to ward off anyone who might think she was interested in romance.

She heard familiar footsteps behind her.

"Good evening." Molly greeted her associate. Dr. Richard Morton was well past the age of retirement, short, bald and lovable, but he didn't know how to stop working, not when the need remained so great. Molly, who was too thin, stood nearly a head taller. With her short blond hair and deep blue eyes, she'd caused a minor sensation with the local children.

"Why aren't you asleep?" Molly asked her friend. They both should have fallen into bed exhausted.

"I haven't figured that out myself," he said, settling into the chair next to her. "Something's in the air."

"Oh?"

"I've got a feeling about this last message from Makua City."

"You think we should leave?" Richard couldn't have surprised her more. Her companion had never revealed any sign of being anxious about their safety in the past, even when the radio messages had sounded far more urgent.

Richard shrugged and wiped his face. "I don't know, but something tells me this time is different."

This past week had been hectic with an outbreak of influenza, and they'd both worked grueling hours, often as many as eighteen a day.

"You're just tired," Molly suggested, searching for a plausible reason for his qualms.

"We both are," Richard murmured and gently patted her hand. "Go to bed and we'll talk about this in the morning."

Molly followed his advice, taking a few extra moments to stroll through the pediatric ward. The nurse on duty smiled when she saw her. Molly's walk through the children's ward had become a ritual for her.

Moving silently between cribs, Molly stopped to check that each child was breathing. This was the legacy SIDS had given her. It was as though she was afraid that terrible scene would replay itself with another child in another time and place. That fear never left her.

Once she was assured all was well, Molly made her way into her own tiny room, not bothering to turn on the light. She undressed and climbed into bed, between the cool sheets. Closing her eyes, she dreamed of what her life would've been like if Jeffrey had lived.

"Sorry I'm late," Jordan said, kissing Lesley's cheek before pulling out the chair and sitting down at the restaurant table across from her. Each time Jordan was with Lesley, he was struck by her charm and beauty. "How long did I keep you waiting this time?" he asked as he unfolded the pink linen napkin and placed it on his lap.

"Only a few minutes."

He was half an hour late, and knowing Lesley she'd arrived five minutes early, yet she didn't complain. This was one of the things he liked about her. She understood his preoccupation with work, because as an architect she was often deeply involved in a project herself.

Jordan reached for the menu, scanned it and quickly made his choice, setting it aside.

"Don't keep me in suspense," Lesley said. "Tell me how the meeting with Ian went."

Jordan shrugged, not sure he wanted to talk about Molly or Ian just yet. He found it awkward to be discussing his wife with the woman he intended to marry. There'd been a time he'd hoped he and Molly could salvage their marriage. But as the weeks and months went by and neither of them seemed inclined to end the silence, Jordan lost hope for a reconciliation.

"Everything went fine," he said, picking up the wine list.

"You don't want to talk about it, do you?" Lesley said after a moment.

"Not particularly."

"All right…I can understand that," she said, and although he could hear the disappointment in her voice he knew she wouldn't pursue the issue. This was something else he appreciated about Lesley. He'd known her for years and couldn't remember her so much as raising her voice, even once.

In the past year they'd started working together on a large construction project on Chicago's east side. She was the architect and he was the builder. Heaven knew he wasn't looking for another relationship. Falling in love a second time held no appeal.

Ian was right when he said that Jordan had buried himself in his work after Jeffrey's death. He went from one project to the next with hardly a breath in between. He didn't know what would happen if he ever stopped—didn't *want* to know.

"I realize this is difficult for you," Lesley said, "but you must know what an awkward position this puts me in. I can't continue to date a married man."

"I do understand."

"Nor do I want to force you into a divorce if it's something you don't want."

Jordan frowned. This ground was all too familiar, and he wasn't thrilled to be walking along the same worn path. "The marriage is dead." If he'd said it once, he'd said it a hundred times.

"You told me that in the beginning," Lesley reminded him, "but we've been seeing each other for six months and in all that time you didn't once mention divorcing Molly." This sounded like an accusation.

"I should've filed years ago."

"But you didn't."

Jordan didn't need Lesley to tell him that.

"Do you know why?" she pressed.

"I was too busy," he said, a bit more heatedly than he intended. "Besides, I assumed Molly would see to it."

"She didn't file for a divorce, either," Lesley pointed out. "Have you stopped to consider that?"

He nodded, and motioned for a waiter, who promptly appeared and took their order. Jordan asked for a bottle of chardonnay and for the next few minutes he was preoccupied as the waiter opened the wine. Jordan tasted and approved it, hoping Lesley would drop the subject of Molly and the divorce, but he doubted she would. Her pretty brown eyes were aimed at him, and they held the same gentle persuasion he'd witnessed the night she'd first said she couldn't date a married man. Rather than lose her, he'd agreed to start the divorce proceedings.

"You're still in love with her, aren't you?" Lesley asked. She was rarely angry with him, unlike Molly who seemed to delight in provoking him. Lesley was subtle and concerned, and her methods worked.

"It's perfectly understandable," Lesley added.

"To love Molly?" He couldn't believe she was suggesting such a thing.

"Yes. What happened to the two of you is tragic."

Pain tightened his chest. "She blamed herself," he whispered, his hand gripping the wineglass with unnecessary force. "With all her medical training, she seemed to think there was something she could've done to save him."

He'd argued with her until he had no voice. It hadn't helped that he'd left the house when she and Jeffrey were still asleep. Apparently Jeffrey had stirred and cried out, but it was early and, thinking she'd get a few more minutes of sleep, Molly had ignored his cry. It was the last sound their son ever made. Molly had woken an hour later to discover him dead.

Jordan looked at Lesley and blinked, wondering if what she'd implied was true. *Did* he still love Molly? He'd never blamed her for what happened to Jeffrey, but she'd blamed herself, despite everything he said and did.

But did he love Molly? Jordan asked himself a second time. He didn't know. So much of what he felt toward her was tangled up in his feelings for his son. He'd loved Jeffrey more than he'd believed it was possible for a man to love his child. He'd grieved, in his own way, until he'd nearly killed himself, working all hours of the day and night.

If Jordan had learned anything from his limited experience as a father, it was that he refused to be vulnerable to this kind of pain again. This was Lesley's great appeal. She didn't want children, either. They were perfect for each other.

"I don't mean to pressure you with these uncomfortable questions," Lesley told him in a soft voice.

"You're not," Jordan said. The loss of his son wasn't a subject he'd ever feel comfortable sharing. But if he was going to join his life with Lesley's, they needed to talk about Jeffrey.

The waiter brought their salads, and Lesley, who sensed his mood, left Jordan alone with his thoughts.

At some point this evening he'd have to tell Lesley he was going to Africa to bring Molly back.

Why couldn't Molly have gone to some tropical island and set up a medical clinic? Oh no, she had to throw herself into one of the world's most troubled spots.

Ian hadn't fooled him, either. Molly's father was worried sick about her, and Jordan had fallen right into the old man's hands, coming to see him when he did. Talk about bad timing.

"Molly's in the East African Republic," Jordan told Lesley without warning.

"Africa," Lesley repeated in an astonished gasp. "What on earth is she doing there?"

"She volunteered with some missionary group."

"Doesn't she realize how dangerous it is?" Lesley set her fork aside and reached for her wineglass. Jordan wished now that he'd taken more care in breaking the news to her.

"I'm going after her." He didn't mention that Ian was pulling every string he had to get Jordan a visa. He was going to the East African Republic, even if he had to be smuggled into the country.

"You." Lesley's eyes went wide, and when she set the glass down, wine sloshed over the edge. "Jordan, that's ridiculous! Why should you be the one? If she's in any danger, then the State Department should be notified. Or...or her father should do it."

"Ian's aged considerably in the past three years and his health is too fragile for such a strenuous journey. Someone's got to do something, and soon, before Molly manages to get herself killed."

"But surely there's *someone* else who could go."

"No one Molly would listen to."

"But...what about your work?" He'd rarely seen Lesley so flustered.

"Paul Phelps will take over for me. I shouldn't be gone long—a week at the most."

"What about all the travel documents? No one travels in and out of the East African Republic these days... do they? I mean, from what the media are saying, the country's about to explode."

"Ian's making the arrangements for me. He'd wanted to go himself, against his doctor's advice, but I couldn't let him. Listen, this isn't anything I *want* to do. Trust me, if I was going to take a week away from the job, the East African Republic would be the last place I'd choose to visit."

"I understand, Jordan," she said, her hand resting on his. "This is something you have to do."

Jordan nodded, relieved. He hadn't been able to put his feelings into words, but Lesley had said it for him. It was something he *needed* to do. This one last thing before he said goodbye to Molly and their marriage. He considered going after Molly a moral obligation. To her and to Ian. To the man who'd given him advice and financial backing when he'd started his business. To the man whose daughter he'd loved.

"When do you leave?" Lesley asked, and Jordan noticed that her voice was shaking, although she'd attempted to disguise it. Jordan was grateful that she didn't try to talk him out of it, didn't try to convince him not to put himself in danger for a woman he intended to divorce.

"The first part of the week."

"So soon?"

"The sooner the better, don't you think?"

Lesley nodded, and lowered her eyes. "Just promise me one thing."

"Of course."

"Please be careful. Because I love you, Jordan."

Molly woke to gunfire echoing in the distance. She sat up in bed, but it took her a moment to orient herself. Tossing aside the thin blanket, she climbed out of bed and quickly dressed. The rat-a-tat sounds seemed closer now and propelled her into action.

Dawn had just come over the hills and Molly could see people running in several different directions. Pandemonium reigned.

"What's happening?" Molly demanded, catching an orderly by the shoulders.

He stared at her. "The rebels are coming! You must go...now," he said urgently. "Do not wait."

"Dr. Morton?" Molly pleaded. "Have you seen Dr. Morton?"

He shook his head wildly, then broke away, running toward the row of parked vehicles.

"Richard," Molly shouted. She couldn't, wouldn't, leave without her friend. His sleeping quarters were on the other side of the compound, but crossing the open area was nearly impossible. Sounds came at her from every direction. People were shouting in more languages than she could understand. The pervasive sense of fear nearly immobilized her.

"Molly, Molly." She whirled around to see Richard Morton frantically searching the crowd for her.

"Here!" she shouted, waving her hand.

She had to fight her way to his side. Briefly, they clung to each other.

"We have to leave right away. Mwanda has a truck waiting."

Molly nodded, her hand gripping Richard's. They'd been fools not to heed headquarters' warnings. A coup had seemed like a distant threat that wouldn't affect her, but she was wrong.

"What about the sick?" Molly pleaded. Richard was on one side of her and the six-foot Mwanda on the other.

"We will care for them," Mwanda promised in halting English. "But first you go."

Richard and Molly were thrown in the truck bed, and covered with a tarp. They huddled in the corners, waiting for Mwanda to drive them somewhere else. Somewhere safe.

As the truck fired to life, Molly peered out and saw a tall, thin boy vaulting toward the truck, speaking furiously in his native tongue. Over the past couple of years, Molly had picked up some vocabulary, although she wasn't as fluent as she would have liked. The cold hand of fear settled over her as she translated the frantic words.

Dr. Morton was also peering out from under the canvas tarp, and her gaze met his. She could tell that he understood the message, too.

They couldn't leave now. It was too late. The countryside was swarming with rebel troops, bent on vengeance. Many innocents had already been murdered.

Richard and Molly were trapped inside the compound.

Mwanda turned off the engine and climbed out of the truck. His eyes were empty as he helped them climb down from the back.

"What do we do now?" Molly asked.

Richard shrugged. "Wait."

Wait for what? Molly wanted to ask. For death, and pray that it would be merciful? She doubted there was any real chance of rescue now. If they were captured, her fate—as a woman—didn't bear thinking of.

Surprisingly she wasn't afraid. The fear left her as quickly as it had come, replaced with a sense of calm. If the rebels broke through the compound, they weren't going to find her cowering in some corner. They'd find her doing what she did each and every day, helping her patients.

"I believe I'll do my rounds," Richard announced, his voice quavering slightly.

"I'll come with you," Molly said.

He seemed pleased and offered her a shaky smile.

Mwanda shook his head and, with a resigned shrug of his shoulders, moved away. "I will go back to the kitchen," he said with a wide smile. Molly thought she'd never seen him smile more brightly. Or bravely.

Clinging to routine was of primary importance to them, to their psychological survival. The thread of normalcy was fragile and threatened to break at any moment, but it was all they had to hold on to.

Gunfire continued to sound in the distance, creeping closer, bit by bit. Radio communication with Makua City had been severed, so they had no way of knowing what was happening in the capital. Had the entire country been taken over?

It was not knowing that was the worst. A number of patients left, preferring to take their chances on reaching their families. Richard tended to those who were too sick to walk away from the compound. Some of the fleeing patients had tried to convince Molly and Richard to leave with them, but they refused. This was where they belonged. This was where they'd stay. Molly was shocked to realize that only a handful of people remained in the compound. No one could guess how long they'd be safe behind its protective walls.

Minutes—or maybe hours later—Molly heard the unmistakable sound of a helicopter. It circled the compound, but she couldn't read any markings on it, so she wasn't sure if it was friend or foe.

The chopper hovered, then slowly descended. The

noise was deafening, and the wind strong enough to stir up a layer of dust that cut visibility to practically zero.

From the snatches of color she did manage to glimpse, she saw soldiers leap from the helicopter, dressed in full battle gear.

Molly stayed in the pediatric ward, empty now. The door burst open and she faced a soldier with a machine gun. The man stopped when he saw her, then shouted something over his shoulder. Molly straightened. She waited, not knowing for what.

A few seconds later another man burst into the room. Bracing herself against the rails of a crib, she met the angry eyes and realized they were hazel. And shockingly familiar.

"Jordan?" she whispered, looking up into her husband's face. "What are you doing here?"

Two

"We're getting out of here," Jordan said. His heart rate felt as though it was in excess of ninety miles an hour. From the aerial view he'd gotten from the helicopter, the rebels seemed to be less than three miles outside the medical compound and were quickly gaining territory. They'd likely move in on them at any minute.

"What about Richard?" Molly cried. "I can't leave without him."

"Who?" Jordan gripped her by the upper arm and half lifted, half dragged her toward the door. His friend Zane, a mercenary now, and the men Zane had hired, surrounded the helicopter, their machine guns poised.

"Dr. Morton!" Molly shouted to be heard above the roar of the whirling blades of the helicopter. "I can't leave without Richard."

"We don't have time," Jordan argued.

With surprising strength, Molly tore herself away, her eyes bright as she glared at him. "I refuse to go without him."

"This isn't the time to be worrying about your boyfriend," Jordan snapped, furious that she'd be worried about another man when he was risking his neck to save hers.

"I'll get him," Molly said, surging past. Before Jordan could stop her she was gone. The helicopter blades stirred up a thick fog of dust and smoke, and an ominous crackling noise could be heard in the distance. Bedlam surrounded them. More than once Jordan had asked himself what craziness had possessed his wife to put herself in this situation. Molly wasn't the only one—he was stuck in the East African Republic, too, and wishing he was just about anyplace else.

Jordan's area of expertise lay in constructing high-rise apartments and office buildings. Guerrilla warfare was definitely out of his league and the very reason he'd contacted Zane Halquist.

"Molly!" he shouted urgently. "There isn't time."

Either she didn't hear him, or she chose to ignore his frantic call. It occurred to him that he should leave without her. He would have if he'd known he could live with himself afterward. Jordan had never thought of himself as a coward, but he sure felt like one now.

An explosion rang in his ears, the blast strong enough to knock him off-balance and jar his senses. He staggered a few steps before he caught himself.

Zane shouted something at him, but with his ears ringing, Jordan didn't have a prayer of understanding him. He shook his head to indicate as much, but by that time it wasn't necessary. The man he'd trusted, the man he'd given ten thousand American dollars, raced toward the waiting copter with two or three of the other soldiers.

Jordan's heart slammed against his chest when he realized what was happening. They were leaving him, Molly and a handful of mercenaries behind.

Jordan hadn't finished cursing when he saw Molly with an elderly man on the far side of the compound. She held her hand to her face to protect her eyes from the swirling dust. She stood frozen with shock as she watched the helicopter rise and speed away.

The man who'd found Molly in the nursery grabbed Jordan by the elbow, jerking him out of his momentary paralysis. "Take the woman and hide," he said roughly.

Jordan's instinct was to stay and fight. He wasn't the type to sit on the sidelines and do nothing. "I'll help," Jordan insisted.

"Hide the woman first."

Jordan nodded and ran as if a machine gun were firing at his heels. He raced toward Molly, and she dashed toward him. He caught her just as she stumbled and fell into his arms.

They clung together. Jordan wove his fingers into her hair, pressing her against him. His heart pounded with fear and adrenaline.

Jordan had never been angrier with anyone in his life, and at the same moment he was so grateful she was alive he felt like breaking into tears. It'd been more than three years since he'd last held her and yet she fit perfectly in his embrace.

"Where can I hide you?"

She looked up at him blankly. "I…I don't know. The supply hut, but wouldn't that be the first place anyone would look?"

Jordan agreed. "There isn't a cellar or something?"

"No."

"Then don't worry about it. If the rebels make it into the compound, they'll check every outbuilding. I'll take you and Dr. Morton to the supply hut."

"What about you?" She clutched his arm with a strength he found astonishing.

"I'll be back later."

Her hands framed his face, and she blinked through her tears. "Be careful. Please, be careful."

He nodded. He had no intention of sacrificing his life. Hand in hand they ran for the supply hut. Jordan glanced around for Dr. Morton and saw that the men had taken Molly's friend and were hiding him themselves.

The supply hut was locked, but luckily Molly had the key. Jordan surveyed the grounds, wondering exactly how much protection this ramshackle building would offer her. If the rebels broke into the compound, he needed to be in a position to protect her.

Gunfire rang in the distance, like the soundtrack of a war movie. Only it was real...

"Keep your head down," Jordan said, closing the door behind her. "I'll be back for you as soon as I can." He noticed how pale and frightened she was. He probably didn't look much better himself. His last thought as he left her was that anyone going after Molly would need to kill him first.

Terror gripped Molly at every burst of machine-gun fire. She was huddled in the corner, hunched down, her back against the wall, knees tucked under her chin. She covered her ears and gnawed on her lower lip until she tasted blood. The room was pitch-dark with only a thin ribbon of light that crept in from beneath the door.

Footsteps pounded past, and she stopped breathing for fear the rebels had broken into the compound. The worst part of this ordeal was being alone. She wouldn't be nearly as frightened if Dr. Morton was with her. Or Jordan.

Nothing could have shocked her more than her husband bursting into the nursery, armed with a rifle and dressed as if he were part of Special Forces. He'd briefly served in the military, but that had been years earlier, when he was right out of college.

What had possessed Jordan to risk his life to save her? It might seem ungrateful, but she'd rather he'd stayed in Chicago. He was furious with her, that much she'd read in his eyes, although his anger wasn't anything new. In the end, before she'd moved out, their marriage had deteriorated to the point that they were barely speaking. It hadn't always been like that. Only after Jeffrey had died... She pushed thoughts of their son from her mind. Early in their marriage they'd been so deeply in love that Molly would never have believed anything could come between them.

Death had.

The grim reaper's scythe had struck, and his blade had separated them in the most painful of ways, by claiming their six-month-old child.

Molly had no idea how much time had passed before the door opened. Panic gripped her as she squinted into the light, but she relaxed when she saw that it was Jordan.

"What's happening?" she pleaded, eager for news.

"Don't know." He abruptly pulled the door shut. The room went dark once more and he lit a match that softly illuminated the small space. He leaned his rifle against the wall and sank down onto the dirt floor next to her. His breathing was heavy. His chest heaved as he exhaled. "Knowing Zane, he'll do everything he can to come back for us, but there are no guarantees."

"Who's Zane?"

"An old friend," he said. "You don't know him. We met in the army years ago."

He blew out the match, and the room was pitch-black again. He leaned against her, and some of the terror and loneliness abated at his closeness. "What about the rebels?" She needed to know if there was any chance of getting out alive. Death didn't concern her, but how she died did.

"Apparently Zane and the others have been able to hold them off, for now at least, but there're a thousand unknowns in this. Everything's quiet, but I don't expect that to last."

She nodded, although he couldn't see her. "What are you doing here?" The question had burned in her mind from the moment he'd stormed into the compound.

"Someone had to try to get you out of here. Ian's worried sick. If you want to risk your life, fine, but you might've waited until your father was too senile to know or care. He'd never recover if anything happened to you."

The words were thrown at her, sharp and cutting in their intensity.

"I certainly had no idea anything like this was going to happen," she snapped back defensively.

"You might have opted to volunteer in someplace other than the East African Republic," he said. "Why couldn't you be content with dispensing medication to school kids? Oh, no, that would've been too easy. What'd you do, look for the hottest trouble spot on the world map and aim for it?"

He was stiff and distant. It hurt her to realize that, within five minutes of seeing each other after three years apart, they were arguing.

Molly knew that at some point in the future she'd need to talk to Jordan; she just hadn't suspected it would be *here,* surrounded by rebel troops.

"I'm sorry you're involved in this," she said, and despite her best efforts her voice was hoarse with emotion.

"It isn't your fault I'm here. I agreed to come." The anger had disappeared from his voice, as well, and she sensed regret at his earlier outburst.

"H-how have you been?" she asked. Sitting on the hard dirt floor of a run-down shack, exchanging pleasantries, seemed…odd. Especially when they were in danger of being attacked by rebel soldiers any minute. But Molly sincerely wanted to know how his life had been these past few years.

"Busy."

"Are you still working twelve-hour days?"

"Yeah."

Molly figured as much. Jordan had never allowed himself to grieve openly for Jeffrey. He'd thrown himself into his work, effectively closing himself off from her and from life. Not that she'd handled things any better. After Jeffrey's death, she'd been consumed with guilt and was so emotionally needy a thousand Jordans couldn't have filled the void her son's death had left.

As the weeks and months after the funeral wore on, Molly had become more lethargic, while Jordan took the business world by storm. Within eight months he was Chicago's golden boy, involved in three major construction projects. Meanwhile, Molly had trouble finding the energy to get out of bed in the morning.

A gunshot echoed like cannon fire and Molly jerked instinctively.

"Relax," Jordan said. "Everything's under control."

He couldn't know that, but she appreciated the reassurance. "I feel like such an idiot," she admitted, pressing her forehead to her knee.

Jordan placed his arm around her shoulders and brought her closer to his side. She let herself experience the comfort, wondering how two people who had desperately loved each other had grown so far apart. Molly didn't ever expect to love anyone as much as she'd loved her husband and her son. It seemed vitally important that Jordan know this. She couldn't leave the situation as it was, not when she'd been given the opportunity to make things right. The words felt like a huge lump in her throat. "If...if the worst does happen, I want you to know I'll always love you, Jordan."

He went very still, as if he wasn't sure how to deal with her confession. "I've tried not to love you," he said grudgingly. "Somehow I never quite succeeded."

They heard another gunshot, and she burrowed deeper into the shelter of his arms. As she trembled, Jordan held her tightly against him.

Burying her face in the hollow of his neck, she

breathed in his warm, familiar scent. Jordan said nothing, but continued to hold her as he gently caressed her back.

It had been so long since she'd been in her husband's arms, so long since she'd felt loved and protected. She might never have the chance again. This time together was like a gift. Tears welled in her eyes and spilled down her cheeks.

"Molly, don't cry. It'll be okay, I promise you."

"You've always loved playing the role of hero," she murmured.

That comment was unintentionally sardonic, and she regretted it. She wanted to thank him for being here with her, but couldn't find the words to adequately express her gratitude.

Kissing his neck seemed the natural thing to do. She slid the tip of her tongue over his skin, reveling in his salty taste. She felt him tense, but he didn't stop her, nor did he encourage her.

Her palm was pressed against his heart. His pulse beat strongly and evenly, the tempo increasing when she kissed the hollow of his throat.

"Molly," he warned, his hands gripping her upper arms as if to push her away. He'd done that often enough after Jeffrey's death, as if his desire for her had died with his son. Perhaps not physically, but emotionally.

"I'm sorry…" she whispered, but before she could say any more, his mouth was on hers, hot and compelling. His kiss was so fierce that her breath jammed in her throat and her nails dug into his shoulders.

Molly knew it was risky to get involved in this now,

but that didn't keep her from responding, didn't keep her from moaning in abject surrender. She returned his kisses with a wildness that had been carefully hidden and denied for three long years.

"Molly…"

"Love me," she pleaded softly. "One last time…I need you so much."

"This is crazy." Jordan sighed, but he didn't reveal any signs of putting an end to it.

"The world is crazy," she reminded him and began to undress.

He did the same, his movements hurried. She was well acquainted with his body, and he with hers, and they used that knowledge to drive each other to a fever pitch of need and desire.

Molly gasped with pleasure. Her head fell forward, her hair spilling wildly over her face.

It had been so long, so very long, since they'd made love. She gave a sob of welcome and regret as Jordan set the cadence for their lovemaking.

Danger surrounded them, the threat of death very real, but there wasn't room in her mind for anything more than the wonder of their love, and the need they were satisfying.

She cried out and Jordan clamped his mouth over hers, swallowing her cries of exultation and joy. Pleasure burst gloriously inside her even as the tears rained unheeded down her face.

They didn't speak. There was no need; words would have been superfluous. Gently he kissed her, and then again, not with passion but in thanks. Molly returned his kisses with the same heartfelt gratitude.

Jordan helped her dress and held her close for several moments afterward. When he released her, she felt his reluctance. "I have to go," he told her.

"Where?" she cried, not wanting him to leave her.

"I'll be back soon," he promised, kissing her. "Trust me, Molly, I don't want to leave you, but I've already stayed longer than I should have."

"I understand." She tried to hide, without much success, the panic she felt.

Once she was alone, Molly shut her eyes and prayed God would protect her husband. She'd lost track of time and didn't know if it was afternoon or evening. The light from beneath the door seemed dimmer, but that could be her imagination.

Jordan came back several hours later with blankets and food. Although she hadn't eaten all day, Molly wasn't hungry. Only because he insisted did she manage to down one of the MREs, meals ready to eat, he'd brought with him. Jordan ate ravenously, while she picked at her food.

"What's going on around the compound?" she asked, finishing a piece of dried fruit.

"It's secure for now."

"What about Dr. Morton?"

"He's safe and asking about you." He spread the blanket on the dirt floor. "Try and get some sleep," he advised. "Here." He slid his arm around her shoulders and brought her close to his side, but something was different. His hold wasn't as tight or as personal as it had been earlier.

"Jordan," she asked, nestling close. "Are you sorry about what happened before? Neither of us planned on making love and, well, I thought it might be bothering you."

"No, I'm not sorry." His answer sounded oddly defensive. "But I should be."

"Why? We're married!"

He didn't answer her right away. "It's been three years. A lot can happen in that much time."

"I know."

"I'm not the same person anymore."

"Neither am I."

After the hellish fighting of the day, the night seemed relatively peaceful. For the first time since she and Jordan had made love, she felt safe. Protected.

He bent toward her and kissed her once, then again and again, each kiss gaining in length and intensity. He slid his mouth from her lips across her cheek to her ear, taking the lobe between his teeth and sucking gently. Molly gasped as the sensation rippled down her spine.

Jordan chuckled softly. "I wondered if that had changed."

"Two can play *that* game." She climbed onto his lap and leaned her head against his shoulder. Wrapping her arms around his neck, she spread a series of soft kisses along the underside of his jaw, using her tongue to tease and entice him.

He kissed her then as if he were starving for her, and she met his hunger with her own. Soon their passion became a raging fire that threatened to consume them both. They'd found satisfaction in each other only hours earlier and yet it wasn't enough.

Their desire was urgent and frantic, and they reached

completion with a driving ecstasy she'd never experienced before.

Molly didn't know how much time elapsed before her breathing returned to normal.

"I can't believe this," Jordan said between soft kisses.

"Who would've thought we'd have the most incredible sex of our lives in a supply hut in Africa?" she whispered. If soldiers burst in and gunned her down right then and there, Molly decided she'd die a happy woman. She doubted that either of them could have mustered the strength to put up much of a fight.

And yet… The imminent possibility of death had made her intensely aware of one thing. She wanted to survive.

"You know what?" she murmured. "I just realized I'd like to come out of this mess alive."

"So would I," Jordan said adamantly.

Before tonight, that hadn't been entirely true for Molly. She didn't actively think about death, but she hadn't really cared, either. One way or the other, it hadn't seemed to matter. It did now, and she had Jordan to thank for that.

"Can you sleep for a while?" he asked, his hands stroking her back.

She nodded. "What about you?"

"Yeah, for an hour or two. I've got the second watch. My feeling is we'll know more about what's going to happen in the morning."

Nestled against him, warm and snug, Molly felt herself drifting off.

Sometime later, she felt Jordan leave. He kissed her

before slipping out of the storehouse. She didn't remember anything else until he returned. He crawled beneath the single blanket and lay down beside her, gathering her into his arms. Molly felt his sigh as he relaxed and she smiled to herself. It was almost as if the past three years hadn't happened. It was almost as if they were young and in love all over again. Almost as if Jeffrey hadn't died...

Molly woke to the unmistakable sound of gunfire. It was close. Much closer than before.

Jordan bolted upright and grabbed his weapon. "Stay here," he ordered and was gone before she could protest.

Molly barely had time to collect her wits when the door to the shed was thrown open. Jordan stood framed in the light. "Come on," he shouted, holding out his hand to her. "Zane's coming and this time we're going with the chopper."

Jordan's friend was coming back! She could hear the chopper more distinctly when she moved outside the supply hut. She was greeted with a whirlwind of dust and grit. Trying to protect her eyes, she hunched forward and, with Jordan's arm around her waist, ran toward the deafening sound.

Dr. Morton climbed into the helicopter after her, looking shaken and exhausted. He gave her a weak smile and patted her hand as he moved to the rear of the aircraft. Molly waited for Jordan, but he didn't board with the soldiers.

"Where's my husband?" she demanded.

"He's coming," Dr. Morton said. "Don't worry, Jordan can take care of himself." He guided her firmly out of harm's way.

"Jordan," Molly shouted, near frantic. The chopper was filling up with people and she couldn't find her husband. Pushing her way past the others, Molly was sobbing when she saw him. He was walking backward toward the chopper, his gun raised and firing at what she could only guess.

The chopper started to lift.

"Jordan," she screamed, although he couldn't possibly hear her. "Hurry!"

Despite everything, her voice—or the emotion she felt—must have reached him because he turned abruptly and ran like she'd never seen him run before, sprinting toward the helicopter. The minute his back was turned three rebels appeared from around the corner of the hospital, shooting at him. Two men fired machine guns from the door of the chopper while Zane helped lift Jordan and drag him aboard. He collapsed once he was inside, pale and bleeding heavily from his shoulder. He clutched at the wound and blood oozed between his fingers.

Molly fell to her knees at his side, weeping. "You've been hit."

He smiled weakly up at her, then his eyelids fluttered closed. He'd passed out.

Three

Jordan felt as if his shoulder was on fire. The pain pulled him out of the comfort of the void.

He opened his eyes to find Molly and her physician friend working on him. Bright red blotches of blood covered the front of her blouse and he guessed it was his. She seemed to sense that he was awake and paused to look into his face.

"You're going to be fine," she assured him when she saw that he'd regained consciousness. But Jordan wasn't so out of it that he didn't recognize the cold fear in her eyes.

"Liar," he said. That one word took every ounce of strength he possessed. Even then his voice was little more than a husky whisper.

Molly held his hand between her own, her eyes bright with tears. "Rest if you can. Zane said we'll be in the capital soon. There's an excellent hospital there."

"The capital," he repeated weakly.

"Don't worry, the government's safe. We got a message."

"Good." He attempted a smile.

"I won't let anything more happen to you, Jordan. Do you hear me? It's over now."

He closed his eyes and tried to nod. But the pain in his shoulder increased and he gritted his teeth with the agony. Then, thankfully, everything started to go black. Jordan sighed in relief as he sank into the bottomless void.

When he awoke again, the first things he saw were an IV bottle and stark white walls. The antiseptic scent told him he was in a hospital.

He blinked and rolled his head to one side. Molly was asleep in the chair next to his hospital bed. How she could rest in a molded plastic chair was beyond him. She'd curled up tightly, her feet tucked beneath her. Her head rested against one shoulder and a strand of beautiful golden hair fell across her cheek.

Molly was a natural with children, Jordan remembered as he watched her. Once she forgave herself for what had happened to Jeffrey, there was a chance she'd marry again and have the family she'd always wanted.

A weight settled on his chest. He'd done his stint with this fatherhood business and wasn't willing to take the risk a second time.

Lesley had agreed that there'd be no children. He was convinced they'd find their happiness together.

Molly was a different kind of woman. She loved children, had loved being a mother. Jordan recalled that when they'd first brought Jeffrey home from the hospital, he'd been afraid to hold their son for fear of hurting him.

By contrast Molly had acted as if she'd been around

infants all her life. She'd laughed off his concerns and taught him what he needed to know, insisting he spend part of each day holding and talking to their son. Soon he was as comfortable as she was, and the nightly sessions with Jeffrey had been the highlight of his day. Jeffrey had been a happy baby with an emerging personality.

Then he was gone.

He'd been ripped from their lives, leaving behind a burden of grief and anger that had crippled them both.

Jordan forced himself to look away from Molly. He closed his eyes and with some difficulty brought Lesley's face to mind. Sweet, kind Lesley. A fuzzy image drifted into his consciousness, followed by a deepening sense of guilt.

He'd made love to Molly, not once but twice. One lapse in good judgment he could explain away, but two? Not that he was obliged to explain anything to Lesley. She wasn't the type to ask, and he certainly wasn't going to volunteer any confessions.

"Jordan?" His name came to him softly, tentatively, as if Molly were afraid to wake him.

He turned his head toward her. "Hi," he said, and realized his mouth felt as if someone had stuffed it full of cotton balls.

"How are you feeling?" She stood by his side and stroked his forehead.

"Awful."

"Are you thirsty?"

He nodded, surprised by how well she anticipated his needs.

"Here." She poured a glass of water, which she

brought him with a straw. She held it to his mouth and he drank, letting the cold water quench his thirst.

"All right," he said, relaxing against the pillows. "Let's talk about the bullet. How much damage did it do?"

"There were two and both of them were clean hits. Luckily there's no bone damage. It's going to hurt for a while, but you'll recover. Think of the next few weeks as a long overdue vacation."

"This may come as something of a surprise," Jordan said, "but if I'm going to take a vacation I'd prefer to do it on a nice peaceful Caribbean island instead of someplace where I'm fighting off rebels."

"I couldn't agree with you more. I could arrange for us to fly to the Virgin Islands. A couple of weeks there soaking up the sun would do us both good." Her face brightened with the idea. He could almost see her creating some romantic fantasy....

Jordan closed his eyes. He'd walked into that one all by himself. There was no way on earth he could spend two weeks in some tropical paradise with Molly when he had every intention of going through with the divorce.

"How soon can I travel?" he asked abruptly.

"A couple of days. You're weak now because of the blood loss, but with proper rest you'll regain your strength pretty fast."

"I have to get back to Chicago. I don't have time to hang around on a beach."

"Okay, fine."

Jordan heard the hurt and disappointment in her voice and felt like a jerk. That, together with everything else, left him feeling sick to his stomach. He'd never intended to make love to Molly; of course, he'd never intended to get shot, either.

"How soon can I get out of here?" he asked next. The question sounded gruff and impatient. He felt both. The sooner he broke off with Molly, the better. Unfortunately he'd ruined any chance of making it a clean break.

"You should be released the day after tomorrow," Molly told him. "I've booked a hotel room. I'll arrange the flight back to the States if you want. We'll have to go via London."

Jordan nodded curtly.

Molly walked over to the window and gazed out for a moment. She turned, crossed her arms, then asked, "Why are you so angry?"

"Maybe it's because I've got two bullet holes in my shoulder. Then again, it might be because I was forced to fly halfway around the world to get you when you should've had the common sense to leave on your own. You're the one with the death wish, not me."

"I didn't ask you to come," she flared.

"No, your father did."

"Next time I suggest you stay home," she said heatedly as she walked past the bed.

"Next time I will," he called after her.

Jordan didn't see her again until he was ready to be released from the hospital. Zane stopped by, but Jordan wasn't in the mood for company. They shook hands, and Jordan didn't expect to see his friend again.

Molly was frequently at the hospital. He heard her talking to the doctor outside his room once and she came in to sit with him when he was sleeping. He wasn't sure how he knew this, he just did.

Jordan wasn't a good patient at the best of times. He suspected that the day he left the hospital, the staff was more than happy to be rid of him. Not that he blamed them.

Molly was waiting for him outside the room with a wheelchair.

"I'll walk," he insisted.

"Jordan, for heaven's sake, be sensible."

He threw her a look that said if he had any real sense he would've stayed in Chicago.

The cab ride to the hotel seemed to take hours. By the time they arrived he was exhausted, much too tired to complain that she'd only booked them one room. At least there were twin beds.

Molly ordered lunch from room service and they ate in silence. Jordan fell asleep afterward and woke up two hours later.

Molly was gone, which was just as well. He was uncomfortable around her. If he wasn't such a coward he'd talk to her about the divorce, the way he'd originally planned. Somehow it didn't feel right anymore, not after their night in the supply hut. He didn't know what he was going to do now.

Sitting on the end of the bed, Jordan carefully worked one shoulder. Pain ripped through him and he gritted his teeth. The medication the doctor had given him was in the bathroom and he walked in there without thinking.

He realized his mistake the moment he stepped over the threshold. Molly was in the shower, standing under the spray of warm water. The glass door was fogged with steam, but it did little to hide her lush figure.

Jordan's breath caught in his throat, and he reached out and gripped the sink. He was instantly aroused.

The view of his wife hypnotized him, and for the life of him Jordan couldn't force himself to look away. He could barely control his need to touch her again. He meant to turn and walk out but his feet seemed rooted to the floor.

"Jordan?"

"Sorry," he muttered. "I didn't mean to interrupt you."

"It's no problem." She turned off the water, opened the shower door and grabbed a towel.

Jordan stood transfixed, unable to manage more than the simple breath as she dried herself. Jordan was a strong-willed man, not easily tempted. The past three and a half years of celibacy were testament to that. Despite his recent engagement to Lesley, he'd still considered himself married. He'd taken his vows seriously and hadn't yet made love to his fiancée. Just to his wife... here, in Africa, with gunshots ringing in the night and the threat of death hanging over them.

Somehow he made it back into the other room, fell into a chair and flicked on the television. At least five minutes passed before he realized the broadcast was in French.

A couple of minutes later, Molly strolled barefoot out of the bathroom, dressed in a white terry-cloth robe. She was toweling her hair dry and wore a silly grin as if she was aware of the effect she'd had on him. Apparently she enjoyed seeing him suffer.

"Did you need a pain pill?" she asked ever so sweetly.

Jordan shook his head and concentrated on the TV as though he understood every word.

Jordan had acted strange from the moment they'd left the East African Republic. Things weren't any better now that they were on a flight to London. Afterward, they'd be flying to Chicago.

Molly didn't know what to make of his irrational behavior. One second he was looking at her as if he was counting the minutes before he could charm her into his bed and the next he growled at her. One second he was sullen and sarcastic, the next witty and warm. *Almost* warm, she amended. Jordan had never been all that affable. He was too direct and blunt.

He fidgeted in the cramped airline seat next to hers, trying to find a comfortable position. The pain pills would have helped him relax if he'd agreed to take them. Molly had given up suggesting it. He was a stubborn fool, and if he hadn't risked his life to save hers, she would've told him so.

The newsmagazine Jordan was reading slid from his lap onto the floor. Molly retrieved it for him and he immediately crammed it into the seat pocket in front of him, bending it in half.

"Take it easy," Molly said under her breath.

Jordan muttered something she preferred not to hear, then glanced at his watch, which he did every five minutes or so. She considered reminding him of the old adage about a watched pot never boiling, but strongly suspected he wouldn't appreciate it.

An eternity seemed to pass before the plane touched down at London's Heathrow airport, where they were met by a U.S. Embassy official, who replaced Molly's missing American passport—which was still in her room at the compound. The embassy's assistance had been arranged by Zane, much to her relief. Later that evening they boarded a plane for Chicago and it landed at O'Hare the next morning. She was home, and the joy that swelled in her chest was testament to how glad she was to be back.

Customs took forever. When she was done, she found her father waiting for her, looking older than she remembered. His face lit up with a smile when she appeared and he held his arms open the way he had when she was a little girl.

"Daddy," she said, hugging him close. Unexpected tears welled in her eyes and, embarrassed, she wiped them away. She clung to him, absorbing his love.

"It's about time you came back where you belong," Ian whispered, brushing the tears from his own eyes. He hugged her again, then slipped his arm around her waist.

Jordan shifted his weight from one foot to the other. He hated emotional scenes, Molly knew.

"Thank you," Ian said, breaking away from her and shaking Jordan's uninjured hand. He needed a moment to compose himself before he could continue. "I might have lost my little girl if it hadn't been for you."

Jordan shrugged as if he'd done nothing more than walk her across the street.

A porter walked past with his luggage and Jordan glanced outside, obviously eager to be on his way. His gaze met Molly's and in it she read a multitude of emotions. Relief that they were home and safe. Regret, too, she suspected. His defenses were lower, dulled by pain and fatigue. He couldn't disguise his feelings from her as easily as he had in the past.

"Take care," Molly said, taking a step toward him before she could stop herself. She longed to press her hand to his cheek and thank him herself, although she could never adequately express her gratitude. She longed to kiss him, too, to prove that what they'd experienced had been as real as it was right.

He nodded. "I will. I'll call you later in the week."

He turned abruptly and followed the porter outside.

Molly watched him go. She'd lived apart from Jordan for three years, considered their life together forever gone, destroyed by grief and pain. But this week had proved that Jordan still loved her. Just as she loved him.

He wasn't happy about it, she mused sadly. She doubted that he knew what to do. For now he was as confused and uncertain as she was herself.

Molly woke with the sun rippling across the cherry-wood dresser in the bedroom that had been hers as a girl. She lay on her back, head cradled by pillows, and reveled in the abundant comforts of home.

She wasn't a teenager anymore, but a woman. A married woman. That thought made her frown. There were decisions to make regarding her relationship with Jordan, but neither of them was ready. Three years should've been plenty of time to decide what they were going to do about their marriage, but it wasn't.

Molly put on a sleeveless summer dress she found

in the back of her closet. A pretty white-with-red-dots concoction with a wide belt.

Her father was sitting at the breakfast table with the paper propped up against his glass of freshly squeezed orange juice. Little had changed in the years she'd been away. After her mother's death twenty years earlier, he'd established a routine and never really varied it.

"Morning," she said, kissing him on the cheek and pouring herself a cup of coffee.

"Morning," came his absent response.

"I see you still read the financial section first thing every morning."

"I'm retired, not dead," he said with a chuckle. "Semiretired. I got too bored sitting at home, counting my money."

"So you're working again."

"Don't fuss," he said, his eyes not leaving the paper. "I go into the bank a couple of days a week. The staff there were kind enough to let me keep my office, so I go down and putter around and they pretend I'm important."

Molly smiled, pulled out a chair and sat down. Her father had always been big on formality. Lunch and dinner were served in the dining room on Wedgwood china and Waterford crystal. Breakfast, however, was eaten in the kitchen at the round oak table that sat in a comfortable nook where the sunlight spilled in.

Molly reached for a blueberry muffin and the pitcher of orange juice. "Dad, did Jordan sell the house?"

Her father lowered the paper, folded it in fourths and set it beside his plate. "Not to my knowledge. Why?"

"I was curious, that's all."

He studied her for a long moment. "I take it the two of you didn't get much chance to talk."

Buttering a piece of her muffin, Molly shook her head. "Not really." Her words were followed by a short silence.

"I see." Molly looked at her father. He sounded downright gleeful, as if this small fact was cause for celebration.

"What's the grin about?" she asked.

"What grin?" His eyes went instantly sober, then rounded with innocence.

"Don't tease, Dad. Does Jordan have something to tell me?"

"I wouldn't know," he said, but the edges of his mouth quivered ever so slightly.

Molly stood and set her napkin on the table, frowning. "Something's going on here."

"Oh?"

She'd forgotten what a manipulator her father could be. She walked over to the patio doors, crossing her arms, while she thought about his comments.

"Can I have the car keys?" she asked, whirling back around, her decision made.

Her father held them in the palm of his hand, grinning broadly. "I won't expect you home for lunch," he said and reached for his paper again.

It was ridiculous to show up on Jordan's doorstep before ten. Especially when he'd so recently arrived home from Africa. Unsure how to proceed, Molly drove to their favorite French bakery for croissants. To her surprise and delight, the baker, Pierre, recognized her.

He called to her and hurried around the glass counter to shake her hand.

"I gave up hope of ever seeing you again," he said in a heavy French accent. He got her a cup of coffee and led her to one of the small tables in the corner. "Please sit down."

Molly did, wondering at this unusual greeting. He set the coffee down and his assistant brought a plate of delicate sweet rolls. The aroma was enticing enough to make her gain weight without taking a bite.

"Our daughter's baby died the same way as your son," he said, and his eyes revealed his sadness. "Amanda put her little girl to sleep and Christianne never woke. It's been four months now and still my daughter and her husband grieve, still they ask questions no one can answer."

"The questions never stop," Molly said softly. *Nor does the grief,* but she didn't say that. It grew less sharp with time. The passing years dulled the agony, but it never left, never completely vanished. The pain was there, a constant reminder of the baby who would never grow up.

"Our daughter and son-in-law blame themselves.... They think they did something to cause Christianne's death."

"They didn't." Molly was giving the textbook response, but the medical community had no cut-and-dried answers. Physicians and researchers offered a number of theories, but nothing was proven. There was no one to blame, no one to hold responsible, no one to yell at, or take out their grief on.

With nowhere else to go, the pain, anger and grief

turned inward; it had with Molly. Over the months, the burden of it had maimed her. By the time she separated from Jordan, she was an emotional wreck.

"They need to talk to someone who has lost a child the same way," Pierre said, "before this unfortunate death destroys them both." He stood and took a business card from the display in front of the cash register. Turning it over, he wrote a phone number on the back.

Molly accepted the card, but she wasn't sure she could make the call. There were others this young couple could speak to, others far more qualified to answer their questions.

"Please," Pierre said, folding his much larger hand around hers and the card. "Only someone who has lost a child can understand their pain."

"I…don't know, Pierre."

His eyes boldly met hers. "God will guide you," he said. "Do not worry." He brought her a sack of croissants and wouldn't allow her to pay for them.

Molly left, not knowing what to do. If she hadn't been able to help herself or Jordan, how could she reach another grieving couple?

Jordan's truck was parked outside their home. So he hadn't sold the house; her father had been right about that. Knowing that this one piece of their marriage was intact lifted her spirits. It was just the incentive she needed to propel her up the front steps.

This was the first time she'd been back, and she couldn't decide whether she should knock or simply walk inside. She remembered where they'd always kept the spare key…and it was her home, after all, or at least it had been. No, she'd ring the doorbell, which was the courteous thing to do.

Jordan took an inordinate amount of time to answer. He opened the front door wearing a bathrobe. His hair stood on end and he blinked as if he'd just awakened.

"Before you chew my head off," she said, remembering what a grouch he was in the morning, "I come bearing gifts."

"This better be good," he said, eyeing the white sack.

"Pierre's croissants," she informed him.

He grinned, opening the screen door. "That's good enough."

The house was exactly as she'd left it. Sort of. The furniture was arranged in the identical pattern. Jordan hadn't changed the carpet or the drapes. The only difference was that there were blueprints and files stacked on every surface.

"I see you still bring your work home with you," she commented dryly.

"Listen, if you're here to lecture me, you can go right back out that door. Just leave the croissants."

"Never mind," she said, leading the way into the kitchen. This room wasn't much of an improvement. Luckily she knew where he kept the coffee. She put on a pot, then got two mugs from the cupboard, black mugs embossed with silver lettering—Larabee Construction.

"Hey," she teased, "you're in the big time now. When did you give up the pencils and go for the mugs?"

Jordan frowned at her, and it was obvious that he had no intention of answering her question. Despite herself, Molly found his surly mood entertaining. She waited until the coffee had filtered through, poured him a mug and carried it over to the table, where he'd planted himself.

He wolfed down two croissants before she managed to get hers out of the bag. The return of his appetite encouraged her. She was tempted to ask him about his medication, but she resisted, knowing he'd consider that an invasion of privacy.

"Dad asked me if we'd had a chance to talk," Molly said evenly, carefully broaching the subject.

Jordan stopped eating and his gaze narrowed.

"Was there a particular reason he seemed so curious about us talking?"

He mulled over the question, and Molly didn't press him. She knew Jordan well enough to realize that when and if he offered an explanation it would be in his time, not hers, and certainly not her father's.

The doorbell chimed again. Jordan growled, stood and answered it. Paul Phelps, one of his site superintendents, strolled casually inside, then did a double take when he saw Molly. His face lit up in a broad grin.

"Molly! Hey, it's good to see you." He walked over and gave her a hug.

Molly had always liked Paul, who was as much of a friend as an employee. "How's the family?" she asked.

"Brenda had another girl last year," Paul boasted.

"Congratulations."

He turned to Jordan. "I saw your truck parked outside and wondered if you'd gotten back," he said, helping himself to a cup of coffee. "What happened to your arm?" he asked, gesturing toward the sling.

"Nothing a little time won't fix," Jordan muttered. "If I'm going to have a parade marching through here, I might as well get dressed." He didn't look happy about it, but Molly welcomed the time alone with Paul.

"How's he been?" she asked as soon as Jordan had left the room.

Paul shrugged. "Better in the last year or so since he—" He stopped abruptly and glanced guiltily at Molly. "Since, well, you know, since he hasn't been killing himself working every hour of the day and night."

"If this house is any indication, that's exactly what he *has* been doing."

"What happened to his shoulder?" Paul asked, and Molly wondered if it was a blatant effort to change the subject.

"He was shot," she said, "twice."

"Shot." Paul almost dropped the mug.

"It's a long story," Molly said.

"Longer than either of us has time to explain," Jordan said gruffly, appearing in the doorway. Judging by the frustrated look in his eyes, Molly realized dressing was more than he could handle alone. He needed help, but she doubted he'd ask for it.

Paul glanced from one of them to the other, then set his coffee cup on the counter. "I can see you two have lots to talk about. Great to see you again, Molly. Don't be a stranger now, you hear?"

She nodded and walked him to the door. He seemed anxious to leave, but she stopped him, her hand at his elbow. "What is everyone trying to hide from me?"

Paul looked decidedly uncomfortable. "That's something you need to ask Jordan."

Molly intended to do exactly that. Her husband's

eyes met hers when she returned to the kitchen. "Tell me," she said without emotion.

His eyes briefly left hers. "There was more than one reason I went to Africa," he said. "For one thing, your father asked me to bring you home."

"And?"

"And," he said, taking a deep breath, "I came to ask for a divorce."

Four

Molly felt as if the floor had collapsed beneath her, sending her crashing into space.

Divorce.

Jordan had come to Africa to ask for a divorce.

Since Jeffrey's death, Molly had learned a great deal about emotional pain. The numbness came first, deadening her senses against the rush of unbearable heartache that was guaranteed to follow. Only later would she expect the full impact of Jordan's words to hit her. For now she welcomed the numbness.

"I see," she managed, closing her eyes. She'd made such an idiot of herself, suggesting they vacation together on a tropical island as if they were lovers, as if their marriage had been given a second chance. Her face burned with humiliation, but she resisted the urge to bury her face in her hands. "You might have said something sooner, before I made a fool of myself."

"If anyone's a fool, it's me." Jordan's voice was filled with self-condemnation.

"No wonder you were in such a rush to get back to

the States." It all made sense now, a painful kind of sense.

"I didn't mean to blurt it out like that." He walked to the far side of the room, his shoulders slumped.

"I'm glad you did. Otherwise, who knows how long I would've continued making a complete idiot of myself." Another thought occurred to her. "My father knows, doesn't he?" An answer wasn't necessary. Paul did, as well. That explained the awkward way he'd answered her questions and his hasty exit.

"I know what you're thinking," Jordan muttered.

"I doubt that." How could he when she didn't know herself?

"You're wondering about what happened between us in the supply shed." His mouth tightened as if he dreaded bringing up the subject. "If you're looking for an apology I can't give you one. It shouldn't have happened, but it did, and I'm not sorry."

"I'll admit it was a curious way of saying goodbye," she said with a small laugh. She appreciated his honesty, knowing what it had cost him. "I…I don't regret it, either."

"I never meant to hurt you."

She nodded and turned to leave. Walking to the front door required an incredible effort. She paused, her back to him, when the realization hit her. "You've met another woman, haven't you?"

He didn't answer right away. In fact, it seemed to take him a long time to formulate a reply. Long enough for her to turn around to face him, preferring to hear the truth head-on. His eyes held hers. "Lesley Walker."

The name slid over the surface of Molly's memory and caught. "The architect?"

"We worked together a lot over the past year."

She nodded. Other than the name, Molly had no clear picture of the woman. "She must be very special." Otherwise Jordan wouldn't love her.

"Stop it!" Jordan exploded, his good fist tightly clenched. "You don't need to be so understanding. I should've told you up front. Instead, I left you hanging, thinking there might be a chance for us, when there isn't. You have every right to be angry. Throw something," he shouted, reaching for an empty vase. "You'll feel better."

She smiled and shrugged her shoulders. "You mean, *you'll* feel better." She removed the vase from his hand and set it back down. "Don't look so guilty. I was the one who walked out on you, remember?" Her hand trembled slightly as she opened the front door. "Whatever arrangements you make are fine. Just let me know when you need me to sign the papers."

Jordan would rather have taken another bullet than have Molly look at him the way she had when he'd said he wanted a divorce. First her eyes had widened, as she dealt with the shock his words inflicted, then they'd gone dull and empty. It was all he could do not to reach for her with his uninjured arm, pull her close and comfort her.

He'd never meant to tell her about Lesley like that. He'd wanted to sit down and explain that he hadn't intended to fall in love again. It had simply happened.

But his good intentions had taken the proverbial road straight to hell.

His attempt at following the doctor's instruction— to stay at home and rest—lasted all of an hour. He needed to get down to the job site. He needed to talk to Paul. He needed to escape his own thoughts before he questioned what he was doing. What he really needed, Jordan decided, was to have his head examined.

Lesley met him at the job site. He'd been back nearly twenty-four hours before he'd contacted her. He'd called her cell and left a message without including any details. Hardly appropriate, considering this was the woman he planned to marry. He wanted to blame Molly for his inadequate behavior, but he honestly couldn't. Still, at the moment, he'd rather not see any woman, even Lesley.

"I can't believe you're working," she said, stepping into the construction trailer, looking as wholesome and sunny as a spring day. Her eyes lit up with concern when she saw his arm in the sling. "I went to the house first. Shouldn't you be in a hospital or something?"

"Probably," Jordan muttered, allowing her to kiss his cheek.

Paul took one look at him and made a convenient excuse to leave. Jordan didn't need to ask his friend's opinion; it was there for him to read in Paul's eyes.

Jordan didn't need his best friend in order to feel guilty. After the morning confrontation with Molly, no one could make him feel like more of a jerk than he already did.

"How did everything go in the East African Republic?" Lesley asked.

"Great."

"Molly wasn't hurt?"

"No." He kept his responses brief, hoping she'd realize he wasn't in the mood to talk.

"How did you feel when you saw her? I mean, it's been years, so you must have felt *something.*"

"I did."

The pain in his shoulder grew worse and he slumped into a chair and closed his eyes until the worst of it had passed.

"Jordan, are you okay?" Lesley asked. "In your message, you said it was minor. You've been badly injured."

"It's just a flesh wound." Another understatement, but he didn't want her gushing sympathy all over him. She'd make him sound like some hero, and he wasn't.

"How long will you have to wear the sling?"

"As long as it takes," he answered shortly.

If he wasn't in such a crappy mood, he'd appreciate Lesley more. She understood his need for work and was ambitious herself. They were a perfect match. An ideal couple. It was time to cut the ties that bound him to Molly.

"I realize this probably isn't a good time to ask, but did you mention the divorce to Molly?"

Talking about the divorce left an ugly taste. He ignored the question, stood and pretended to be absorbed in some blueprints.

"Naturally you didn't get a chance to talk to her, not with the country involved in a revolution," Lesley said, answering her own question. "You were lucky to get out with your lives."

"I talked to her about it this morning," he told her

impatiently. "She's agreed. There won't be any problem."

Lesley went still. "I know this was difficult for you, Jordan."

She didn't have a clue, but surprisingly neither had he. A divorce seemed the natural progression for him and Molly. It was the right thing to do, but Jordan hadn't expected the bad feelings that came over him when he told her he planned to formally end their marriage.

"Are you having second thoughts?"

Lesley had a way of reading him that was sometimes unnerving. Was he? "No," he said without a pause. The time for second thoughts was over. "I want the divorce."

Michael Rife wasn't keen on divorce cases. He took them occasionally, generally for a change of pace. He'd met with Jordan Larabee three or four times now and his client had assured him this was a friendly divorce. There was no such thing, but Michael didn't see the point of saying so. Larabee and his wife would discover that soon enough on their own, he suspected.

From what Michael understood, Mrs. Larabee had yet to retain an attorney, and had indicated she saw no need to do so. Apparently she'd read the agreement he'd drawn up and was satisfied with the settlement offer her husband had proposed.

That in itself was highly unusual, but then very little about this divorce was typical. Larabee had bent over backward to make this as easy for his wife as possible. Frankly, Michael couldn't help wondering what had gone wrong in their marriage.

His intercom beeped, and his secretary said, "The Larabees are here to see you."

Michael stood when the couple entered. He exchanged a handshake with Jordan, and everyone was seated. Michael studied Larabee's wife. She was attractive, a bit too thin and fragile-looking. But appearances were often deceiving. A delicate woman wouldn't have spent the past two years as a nurse in an unstable and poverty-ridden African country.

Michael picked up the file and asked Molly, "You've had the opportunity to read the settlement offer?"

"Yes, I have," she answered quietly. "And I found Jordan to be more than generous."

"It's highly unusual for you not to have an attorney look this over on your behalf," Michael felt obliged to explain. He wasn't entirely comfortable with this aspect of the divorce.

"I don't see why. There's nothing here I take exception to, and I see no reason to prolong this."

"As long as you understand the terms of the settlement."

"Everything is perfectly clear to me."

Larabee was unusually quiet. "He's right, Molly. It might be a good idea if you had your own attorney look at it."

"If that's what you want, but I don't see why. You want your freedom, and that's reasonable. You've waited long enough."

Larabee crossed his legs in what seemed a nervous movement. "I don't want you to feel that I've cheated you in any way."

"That's the last thing I'm worried about. You've

been very generous. Why don't we leave matters as
they are?"

"You're sure?"

"Positive."

Michael couldn't remember any couple who were so
caring toward each other about the details of a divorce.
He flipped through the file again, hoping for some indication of what had gone wrong between two decent
people.

"There are no children involved," he muttered to
himself, although he already knew this.

"No children," Jordan repeated.

"There was a child," Mrs. Larabee added, and Michael swore the color of her eyes changed when she
spoke. When she walked in the door, he'd been struck
by their clear shade of blue, but when she mentioned
the child, they darkened. "A son...he died of SIDS. His
name was Jeffrey."

Jordan hadn't spoken of this before, and he said nothing now.

Michael made a notation in the file. It was all
coming together. The divorce wasn't based on the usual
grounds of irreconcilable differences, a couple having
grown apart or infidelity. It was rooted in grief.

"Did you need me to sign something?" Molly Larabee asked, breaking into his thoughts. She sounded
eager, wanting this over as quickly as possible.

"Yes, of course." Michael took out the papers and
handed her a pen. "I'll file these papers this afternoon.
The divorce will be final in sixty days."

"That soon?" Jordan asked.

"That long?" was his wife's question.

Michael studied the couple sitting across from him. Over the years, in most of the divorces he'd seen, the couple hated each other by the time they filed the final papers. It was disconcerting to represent two people who continued to love each other.

Sitting beneath the weeping willow tree in her father's yard seemed the thing to do after meeting with the attorney. Molly hadn't anticipated the emotional toll the appointment would take. She was grateful her father was away for the afternoon, because she needed time alone to sort through her feelings.

She expected tears. None came. How could she weep for a marriage that had been dead all these years?

The spindly branches of the willow danced in the wind about her feet. With her back against the trunk, she stared at the meticulously kept gardens that had been her mother's pride and joy. But her mother, like Jeffrey, like her marriage, was dead and forever gone.

In the week since Jordan had asked for the divorce, Molly had made discreet inquiries about Lesley Walker. Everything she learned about the other woman was positive. Lesley was a talented architect with a promising future. She was energetic and well-liked. Difficult though it was for Molly to stomach, Lesley was exactly the type of wife Jordan needed.

Admitting that produced a sharp pain, and the tears that had refused to come earlier now rolled down her face.

"I wondered if this was where I'd find you." She heard her father's voice behind her.

Molly hastily wiped the tears from her face. "I thought you were going to be away for the afternoon."

"I was," Ian Houghton said, awkwardly sitting down on the grass beside her. He looked out of place in his expensive suit. "But I thought you might be feeling a little blue after signing the final papers."

"I'm fine."

Ian handed her his crisp white handkerchief. "So I noticed." He placed his arm around her shoulders. "You used to come here when you were a little girl. The gardener's been telling me for years I should have this old tree cut down, but I could never do it."

"I'm glad you didn't."

"Things aren't as bleak as they seem, sweetheart. I know that from experience, from losing your mother. Someday you'll look back on all this and the pain won't be as deep."

Her father had said something similar after Jeffrey died and she hadn't found it to be true. The ache would never leave her.

"Would you rather Jordan had never been a part of your life?" Ian asked.

Her immediate instinct was to tell him yes, she wished she'd never met Jordan, never loved him, never given birth to his son. But it would've been a lie. Jordan was her first love, her only love, and how could she ever regret having had Jeffrey? It wasn't in her to lie, even to herself.

She'd failed Jordan, Molly realized, and he'd failed her. They'd been equal partners in the destruction of their marriage. It occurred to her, not for the first time, that she should have pursued counseling, even if Jordan refused. He'd believed, or claimed to believe, that talking about their loss would only perpetuate it.

And yet, he was the first one to recognize that their marriage was over. He was the first one to make a new life for himself.

"I remember when Jeffrey died," her father said with some difficulty. She knew it was hard for him to talk about his only grandchild. "Grief leaves you feeling hopeless. It turns you hollow inside and makes you wonder about God."

Molly was well acquainted with the toll grief demanded. "Whenever I'm hurting that badly, I ask myself why God doesn't do something," she said.

"He does, but we're in too much pain to see it."

Molly knew that, as well.

Now, nearly four years after losing their son, Jordan was moving ahead and she needed to take that first tentative step herself. "I'm going to find myself an apartment," she announced.

"There's no rush," Ian told her.

"It's time I got on with my life."

"Like Jordan?"

"He's right, Dad. I shouldn't have buried my pain. Heaven only knows how long I would've stayed in Africa if it hadn't been for the rebels. I was hiding from life and it got to be downright comfortable."

"I realize I'm being selfish, but I hate to see you move out so soon."

Molly hugged her father, grateful for his love and support. He was all she had left in the world now. It was the same way it'd been from the time she was eleven, just the two of them.

Once Molly decided what she was going to do, it didn't take her more than a week to find a nursing job and an apartment. She moved several pieces of furniture from Jordan's, along with a number of personal items.

She made sure she went to the house when there wasn't any chance of running into him. For courtesy's sake, she left him notes, listing what she'd taken. She also gave him her new address.

The duplex she'd rented was in a friendly neighborhood and included a small yard. Molly loved roses and was looking forward to planting some once she was completely settled.

The apartment was roomy with two large bedrooms, a good-sized kitchen and a comfortable living room. It wasn't home yet, but it would be once she'd arranged everything the way she wanted. Compared to her quarters in Africa, the duplex was a mansion. The best thing about her new home was that she wasn't far from either Lake Michigan or her work at Sinai Hospital.

Molly was dressed in cutoffs and a sleeveless T-shirt, placing books inside the bookcase, when the doorbell rang. She wiped the perspiration from her forehead with the back of her arm and got to her feet.

She suddenly felt dizzy and collapsed onto the sofa, taking deep, even breaths. A moment passed before the world righted itself once more.

Whoever was at the door punched the bell again, this time in short, impatient bursts. No one she knew rang a bell like that except Jordan Larabee.

Standing, she composed herself and walked over to the front door. Jordan had a box braced against the side of the duplex, holding it beneath his good arm and having difficulty doing so. "It took you long enough," he said gruffly.

"Sorry," she said, opening the screen door. Jordan walked in and dropped the box on the carpet next to the one she was unloading into the bookcase.

"You forgot this," he said.

The dizziness returned and Molly slumped onto the arm of the sofa and pressed her hands against her face.

"Are you all right?" Jordan asked, his expression concerned. "You're as pale as a sheet."

"I…don't know. I must've gotten up too quickly. Everything started to spin for a minute there… I'm fine now."

"You're sure?"

"Listen, Jordan, I'm a registered nurse. I may not know a lot about *some* things, but I do know when I'm healthy—and I tell you I'm fine."

"Good." He shoved his hand into his pants pocket and walked around the room, surveying the duplex. "What does Ian think about all this?"

"My moving? Well, he'd rather I stayed with him for the rest of my life, but I'd prefer to live on my own." She surveyed the contents of what he'd brought and didn't find anything that warranted his visit. She could have picked it up the following day, or whenever she made her next trip to the house.

Jordan strolled into the kitchen. "Do you mind if I get myself something to drink?"

"Go ahead." Apparently there was more on his mind than helping her move, otherwise he wouldn't be making excuses to stay. "There's lemonade in the refrigerator. I'm afraid I don't have anything stronger."

"Lemonade's fine." He got a glass from the cupboard, a beautiful crystal one they'd received as a wedding gift from her aunt Catherine a thousand years ago. He paused, his hand cupped around the base of the glass.

Molly moved one step forward. "I hope you don't mind that I took those glasses... They weren't specifically listed in the agreement. I didn't think it'd matter."

"Why should I care about a few glasses?"

"You looked as if you might object."

"I don't," he said. "I was just thinking about the last time we used them—Christmas, wasn't it?" He stopped abruptly and shook his head. "Never mind, it isn't important." He filled the glass with lemonade and carried it into the living room, where he sat down on the sofa, balancing his ankle on the opposite knee. He stretched his arm across the back of the sofa and appeared to be at ease.

Molly felt anything but relaxed. She sat on the ottoman facing him, hands pressed between her knees, waiting. Clearly there was something he wanted to say.

He took a sip of the lemonade. "How have you been?"

"Fine, and you?"

"Can't complain."

"How's the arm?"

The sling moved against his chest. "It's getting better every day. I should be able to get rid of this by the end of the month."

"Good."

Silence.

Briefly she wondered how long it would take him to get to the point of this conversation.

"Was there some reason you wanted to talk to me?" she finally asked when she couldn't tolerate the quiet for another second.

He dropped his leg and leaned forward, leaning his good arm against his elbow. "The divorce will be final soon."

Molly knew that as well as he did. "So?" She didn't mean to sound flippant, but she didn't understand what he was getting at.

"Are you happy?" He rubbed his face, as if he wanted to start the conversation over again. Sighing, he said, "I'm making a mess of this. Listen." He vaulted to his feet. Jordan had never been able to sit in one place when something was troubling him.

"You want to know if I'm happy?" she asked. "Do you mean, am I happy about the divorce?"

"I don't know what I mean. I just have this incredible sense of guilt over I don't know what. Coming here like this doesn't make a bit of sense, but somehow I'm not comfortable ending our marriage without...without what?"

Jordan turned and their eyes met. She read his bewilderment and knew she'd experienced those same feelings herself, and like him, had been unable to put them into words.

"I guess in some ways I'm asking you to absolve me," he said with a short, mocking laugh. "The problem is I don't know what it is I want you to forgive."

"The divorce makes me very sad," she admitted in a

whisper. "I don't blame you, Jordan, and I'm not angry with you if that's what you're wondering."

"Maybe you should be. Did you ever think of that?"

Molly took a moment to carefully examine her feelings. She wasn't angry now, but that didn't guarantee she wouldn't be in the future. All the emotions tied into the divorce and their time together in Africa hadn't been fully processed.

"Give me a few weeks," she suggested with a weak smile.

"There's something you should know," Jordan said, his shoulders heaving. "Lesley and I have never been lovers."

"Jordan, please, that's none of my business." She stood and walked over to the bookcase, examining the even spines of the volumes she'd placed inside.

"I know that. The fact is, it embarrasses me to be talking to you about my relationship with another woman. However, I want you to know that while I've committed my share of sins, adultery isn't one of them."

Their conversation was growing decidedly uncomfortable. "You asked me if I was happy," she said, throwing his question back at him. "That's what you really came to find out, and I'll tell you." She brushed the hair away from her face and held it there. "I'm ready to resume my life. I'm completely on my own for the first time.... Africa didn't really count. I have a new job I start Monday morning. Am I happy? Yes, I suppose I am, but I'm not sure what happy means anymore. I haven't known since Jeffrey died."

Jordan's jaw tensed. He seemed to need time to compose himself. "Why does every conversation we have come down to Jeffrey?"

"He was our son."

"He's dead!" Jordan shouted.

"And that's the problem," she shouted back, her voice trembling. "You want to pretend Jeffrey never lived. You wanted to destroy his pictures and ignore the fact that we had a child. I can't do that. I'll never be able to do that. Jeffrey was a part of you and a part of me and I refuse to deny he lived." She was sobbing now and made no effort to disguise her tears.

"How long will it take you to forget?" Jordan demanded furiously. "Five years? Ten? When will it ever end? Tell me."

His words exploded like firecrackers dropped into the middle of the room. "How long will you continue to grieve?"

Squaring her shoulders, Molly met his angry glare, her fists clenched at her sides.

"When are you going to *start?* When will you stop denying we had a son? When will you be willing to own up to the fact that Jeffrey existed?"

Jordan didn't answer, not that she expected he would. He headed for the door, threw it open and stalked outside.

Molly was shaking so badly she had to sit down. She held one hand over her mouth to hold back the anguish. Her stomach cramped and she knew she was going to vomit. She barely made it to the bathroom in time.

Her queasy stomach didn't go away. The following morning, she woke with a headache and had to force herself out of bed. By noon she felt well enough to meet her father for lunch.

She arrived at the restaurant to find him seated and waiting for her.

"Molly, sweetheart, I'm so pleased you're feeling better. Is it the flu?"

"No," she said, wrinkling her nose. She reached for the menu. "It's Jordan. We argued and, well, it upset me. I'm fine now."

"What did Jordan say that troubled you so much?"

"Dad," Molly chided, loving the way his voice rose with indignation. "It's over and forgotten. The divorce will be final soon and then we'll never have anything to do with each other again." She made a pretense of studying the menu.

The waiter appeared before she could make her selection. Her father, however, had already decided. "I'll have a bowl of the French onion soup," he said, spreading the napkin across his lap.

The waiter looked at her expectantly. Molly's stomach heaved and she placed her hand on her abdomen. "I'll...I'll have a salad...a spinach salad." Her voice quavered and a paralyzing numbness settled over her. She closed her eyes. There'd only been one other time that the mere mention of French onion soup had made her instantly ill. And with her various other symptoms—the dizziness, the exhaustion—she should've figured it out much sooner. She was a nurse, after all.

"Molly?" Her father's concerned voice sounded as if it came from a long way off. "Is something wrong?"

She managed a weak nod. "Something's very wrong.

Oh, Dad, I don't know what I'm going to do." Tears flooded her eyes and she hid her face in her hands.

"Sweetheart, tell me." He gently patted her arm.

When she could, Molly lowered her hands from her face. "I'm...pregnant."

Five

Dr. Doug Anderson, her obstetrician, walked into the cubicle, reading Molly's chart. She scrutinized him carefully, although she already knew what he was going to say. She was pregnant. Not a shred of doubt lingered in her mind.

"Well, Molly," Doug Anderson said cheerfully, smiling at her. "Congratulations are in order. Your test is positive."

"I guessed as much." She glanced away, fighting back her emotions. Tears were close to the surface, along with the almost irresistible urge to laugh. She knew this hysteria was caused by her growing sense of fear.

"Molly, are you all right?"

She gestured with her hands, not knowing how to answer him. "I'm afraid, Doug, more afraid than I can ever remember being." She'd lost her son; she didn't know if she could survive that nightmare a second time.

Doug pulled out a chair and sat down. "You aren't

going to lose this baby to SIDS," he said, sounding remarkably confident.

"You can't guarantee that." She was a medical professional herself and knew the statistics well. Crib death was a major cause of infant death in the United States. One out of every five hundred babies died mysteriously, for no apparent reason. She was also aware that the chances of losing a second child to SIDS were so infinitesimally small it shouldn't warrant her concern. But it did.

How could she *not* worry?

"It's more than that," she whispered, fighting hard to keep her voice from shaking. "Jordan and I are getting a divorce. It'll be final very soon."

Doug looked as if he wasn't sure what to say. "I didn't know."

Molly didn't want to discuss her marital troubles, especially with someone who knew Jordan. "I realize I'll need to tell him about the baby." The prospect filled her with dread.

"He'll want to know," Doug agreed. "It could make a difference."

Molly nodded. Doug seemed to think the news might have some effect on the divorce proceedings, but Molly doubted that. Jordan was involved with Lesley. He was the one who wanted out of the marriage.

This complicated everything.

Doug patted her hand and asked, "Is there anything I can do for you?"

"No, but thanks for asking."

"I'd like you to make an appointment for two weeks from now."

"Okay," she said mechanically.

For some time after Doug left the cubicle, Molly didn't have the energy to move. Although a part of her had accepted the information that she was indeed pregnant, another equally strong part of her had found comfort in denial. That luxury had been taken away from her. She was carrying Jordan's child; there was no longer any question.

Naturally she had no choice but to tell Jordan. The task, however, held no appeal.

She returned to her apartment, changed into shorts and a sleeveless top, poured herself a glass of juice and sank into her chaise longue on the sunlit patio. She needed to review her options, but she couldn't seem to get past the nearly suffocating fear of losing a second child.

She'd barely had time to assimilate all the changes a baby would bring into her life when the doorbell rang, scattering her thoughts.

She opened the front door to see Jordan, dressed as if he'd just walked off the job site, still wearing his hard hat. He frowned, obviously worried or displeased.

"Hello, Jordan." For one wild moment, she panicked, fearing he'd somehow learned about the pregnancy. It didn't take her long to realize he wouldn't be nearly this calm if that had been the case.

"Could I come in?" he asked.

"Of course." She held open the screen door for him, wondering about the purpose of his visit.

"Would you like a glass of juice? Or iced tea?" she asked.

He looked tempted, then shook his head. "Listen, I thought I should clear something with you."

"About what?"

"Kati's wedding."

Her cousin's wedding was scheduled for that Saturday.

"She sent me an invitation," Jordan went on to say. "I'm fond of Kati and, frankly, I'd like to go. But I won't. Not if it'll be awkward for you."

"Jordan, for heaven's sake, don't be ridiculous! Of course you should. Kati's been half in love with you for years. There's no reason you shouldn't go."

He lowered his gaze. "I was thinking of asking Lesley to join me."

Hearing the other woman's name bothered her, but Molly refused to let Jordan know. "Are you asking my permission?"

"In a way, yes," he said, which was a concession coming from him.

"We're getting divorced, remember?"

"I'm trying to be as honest and up-front with you as possible," Jordan said, his voice raised as though he was struggling to maintain his composure. "The situation might be awkward, and it seemed only fair to give you notice."

"My family will find out about the divorce eventually. Now is as good a time as any to get it out in the open."

"If you'd rather I didn't invite Lesley, then—"

"Jordan, please, you've got to make that decision yourself. Don't ask me to do it for you."

"I don't want the wedding to be uncomfortable for you."

"Stop worrying about me."

"It's your family."

"Do you think the divorce will come as a shock to my relatives?" she asked, forcing a laugh. "We've been separated for three years."

He nodded, but he clearly wasn't happy with what she'd had to say. It occurred to her that she should tell him about the baby right now. The sooner she did, the better for everyone involved.

Jordan walked back to the front door. "I'll see you Saturday afternoon, then."

"Jordan." Even to her own ears, his name had a frantic edge, and he turned around immediately.

"Yes?"

She looked at him, debating whether to tell him, and instinctively knew she couldn't. Not yet. She needed time to come to grips with the news herself before she confronted him. When she told Jordan, she'd need to be strong and confident, and right then she was neither.

"Nothing," she said, offering him an apologetic smile. "I'll see you Saturday."

As he'd said, Jordan was fond of Kati. She was by far his favorite of Molly's cousins, and since she'd specifically sent him a wedding invitation he felt honor-bound to attend.

But there was more to his determination to attend this family event than sharing in Kati's happiness, Jordan had to admit.

True, this wedding was an excellent way of broadcasting his divorce from Molly. He would use it to introduce the woman he intended to marry, but it was also his way of proving to himself that the marriage was completely over.

Inviting Lesley had been a calculated risk on his part and Jordan had weighed the decision carefully. If he attended the wedding alone, it was a foregone conclusion that at least one of Molly's aunts would take it upon herself to speak to him and possibly Molly about the breakup of their marriage.

By bringing Lesley with him, he was making a statement to all concerned that the divorce was imminent. Any well-meaning advice at this point would be irrelevant.

Decision made, he invited Lesley. When he picked her up on Saturday, he thought she'd never looked lovelier. She was a wonderful person and she cared deeply for him. They would make a good life together. Jordan didn't know why he found it necessary to remind himself of that so often. He'd be glad when this divorce was over and done with.

And yet…he couldn't make himself stop feeling guilty. Not that he knew what he had to feel guilty about. Molly was the one who'd abandoned *him*. She'd been away for three years.

All right, so he'd made an idiot of himself in Africa, but under the circumstances, that seemed forgivable. As for the divorce, he'd bent over backward to be fair in his settlement offer. More than fair. All he was asking for was his freedom. There wasn't a single reason he should feel the way he did.

"You seem very absorbed," Lesley commented as they drove to the church.

Lesley often sensed his mood. He reached over and squeezed her hand. "I was just doing a little thinking."

"About what?"

"Our wedding," he lied, and the words nearly caught in his throat. "We should start making the arrangements soon."

"I'm not in any rush and I don't think you should be, either."

Her hesitation surprised him.

"Why not?"

"Jordan, a divorce takes time."

"It's just a few more weeks!"

"I don't mean legally, I mean personally. You'll need to grieve the loss of your marriage before we can make any wedding plans ourselves."

"Grieve the loss of my marriage," he repeated impatiently. What did she think he'd been doing for the past three years?

"You'll understand more once it's final," Lesley added with a sigh.

He didn't know what had made her such an expert and bit his tongue to keep from saying so. The last thing he wanted to do was argue, especially now.

"Fine, whatever you say," he muttered as they approached the church.

Finding a parking place was a struggle, and his mood hadn't improved by the time the ushers seated them on the bride's side of the church. The first person he saw, two rows up from him and Lesley, was Molly, sitting beside her father. She was wearing a pretty outfit with a red blazer and a pleated red-and-white flow-ered skirt. He remembered it from years earlier and how she'd had trouble fitting back into it after Jeffrey was born. It fit her just fine now. Just fine.

Thankfully they didn't need to wait long before the organ music swelled and the bridesmaids marched cer-emonially down the center aisle. Jordan stood with the others when Kati appeared on her father's arm.

Uncomfortable emotions began to stir memories of his and Molly's wedding. They'd been so much in love. They were young, younger than they should've been, and crazy about each other.

Jordan vividly recalled the moment Ian had escorted Molly down the same church aisle and how he'd stood at the altar waiting for her, thinking he'd never seen a more beautiful woman in his life. He remembered the vows he'd spoken that day and how his voice had shaken with the intensity of what he was feeling. He'd meant every word.

Molly had looked up at him, her eyes filled with de-votion as she'd repeated her own vows. Jordan could remember thinking he'd rather die than stop loving her.

The years hadn't changed that. He did love Molly. Not in the same way he had the day he married her. Over time his love had matured, just as he had. He re-membered when Jeffrey was born—

His thoughts came to a grinding halt, and he gave himself a mental shake, refusing to drag his son into this.

Everyone sat back down and Jordan was grateful. Not because standing had become a burden, but the change gave him the opportunity to focus his attention on the bride and groom and push the memories of his own long-ago wedding out of his mind.

That, however, proved to be impossible. Kati and Matt seemed intent on having everyone join in as they exchanged their vows. Lesley reached for his hand, and for the briefest of moments he was surprised to realize she was with him. It shocked him to look down and find a woman other than Molly standing at his side. To his credit, he recovered quickly.

Jordan tucked Lesley's hand in his elbow and patted it, hoping to assure her of his devotion. He did care for her, but he didn't love her, not the way he'd loved Molly.

But that stood to reason, he told himself. Of course he loved Molly. They'd been married—and would be for several more weeks. They had a history together. What Lesley had said earlier about needing to grieve for their marriage made sense. He didn't have to wear sackcloth and ashes, but he needed to accept that an important part of his life had ended. A *defining* part of his life.

Before he knew it, Kati and Matt were kissing, to the approval of their guests. Smiling, they hurried down the aisle, arm in arm, their happiness glowing. He and Molly had been that happy once.

The reception was being held at the country club, the same one where he and Molly had held theirs. Jordan hadn't made the connection until they arrived. He wished now that he'd mailed Kati her gift and left it at that.

The valet parked his car, and Jordan and Lesley walked through the clubhouse and onto the lush green grass where the dinner and dance would take place. The yard was beautifully decorated with Chinese lanterns and round tables and white wooden chairs. The food was exquisitely displayed on long linen-covered tables beneath the canopies.

It all looked far too familiar....

By then he was beginning to have second thoughts about the wisdom of following through with this. He decided to drop off his gift, congratulate the newly-weds, make his excuses and leave. He felt sure that Lesley would understand.

"Jordan Larabee, my goodness, is that you?"

He found himself face-to-face with Molly's aunt Johanna. He loved her dearly, but the woman was a born meddler. "Aunt Johanna," he said, hugging her. When he finished, he placed his arm around Lesley's shoulders. "I'd like to introduce you to Lesley Walker, my fiancée."

Aunt Johanna giggled as if she'd heard a joke. "How can you be engaged when you're married to Molly? You'd think it was April Fool's instead of May."

Jordan wished he'd warned Lesley. "Molly and I are getting divorced," he explained. "And I've asked Lesley to be my wife."

Aunt Johanna's face turned a bright shade of pink. "Oh, Jordan, I'm so sorry to hear that. I mean, it's sad for Molly, but good for... Oh, dear," she said, pressing her hands to her face. "I'm doing this all wrong."

"There's no need to apologize," Lesley said, her natural graciousness taking over. "It was an honest mistake."

Jordan was grateful for her handling of the uncomfortable scene.

"It was, uh, good to see you again," Molly's aunt said, making a hasty exit.

"I'm sorry," Jordan whispered. And he was. He should have told her what to expect and wanted to kick himself for being so insensitive to her feelings.

"Jordan, it wasn't that big a deal."

"We'll make our excuses and leave."

Lesley rested her hand on his arm. "We most certainly will not. Leaving now will embarrass poor Aunt Johanna and leave Molly to make lengthy explanations. The last thing she needs is to explain what you were doing here with another woman."

Lesley was right. "We'll stay no more than an hour, though. Agreed?"

"Perfect," Lesley said, smiling up at him. "It's going to be all right, darling, I promise."

Lesley didn't often use affectionate terms and the fact that she did now came as a surprise. Not until later did he realize she was staking her claim. That pleased him. Lesley wasn't immune to a few pangs of jealousy.

Jordan was even more surprised to realize he wasn't exempt from being visited by the green-eyed monster himself. Only the source was Molly. Once the meal had been served, the band struck up and space was cleared for dancing.

Jordan had originally intended to stay only for the first few dances, the traditional ones between bride and groom, but before he knew it he was on the dance floor, enjoying himself with Lesley.

He couldn't remember the last time he'd let go like this. He was shocked by how good it felt to throw back his head and laugh.

Then he saw Molly, dancing.

The sight of her in the arms of another man had a curious effect on him. He felt like he'd been punched in the head.

He didn't give any outward indication of what he felt, although he made an excuse to leave the dance floor soon afterward.

"Don't tell me you're tired already," Lesley said. "We were just getting started."

"I need something to drink." Jordan grabbed a glass of champagne from a waiter's tray as he walked past. He preferred red wine to champagne, but it was any port in a storm, so to speak, and he felt as if he'd been hit by hurricane-force winds.

It took some doing to divert his gaze from Molly and her partner, and focus his attention on Lesley instead. He didn't recognize the tall, good-looking man with his soon-to-be ex-wife. He held her in a possessive way that incensed Jordan—even if he had no right to feel that way.

Thankfully there were plenty of acquaintances to renew, plenty of people to occupy him until he decided what he was going to do. If anything.

Carrying his champagne glass, Jordan circulated, introducing Lesley and doing his best to ignore the fact that his wife was in the arms of another man.

"Hello, Jordan, it's good to see you."

"Ian," Jordan said, courteously inclining his head. "Have you met Lesley Walker?"

"Hello, Lesley," Ian said, taking her hand and holding it in both of his. His father-in-law had always been

a consummate charmer, and Lesley responded immediately, laughing and chatting.

However, she must have guessed that Ian wanted to
speak privately to Jordan because a few minutes later,
she quietly slipped away.

"You're looking good," Ian said and slapped him on
the back. "Recovered from your little adventure, I see."

Jordan frowned. "I'm fine. Get to it, Ian."

"Get to it?" The old man raised his eyebrows, doing
a fair job of pretending.

"Just say what you want to say," Jordan told him.

Ian seemed amused. "I don't have anything important to say," Ian murmured, but his mouth quivered.
"That might not be the case with my daughter, however. When was the last time you talked to her?"

"This week, why?"

"Why?" Ian said, breaking into a smile. "You'll need
to ask her that."

"I will." This was just the excuse Jordan had been
looking for. He set his champagne glass aside and
walked onto the dance floor. Molly's eyes widened with
surprise when he tapped her partner on the shoulder.
"I'm cutting in," he said without apology. And pro-
ceeded to do exactly that.

"Jordan," she said, staring up at him, "that was
downright rude."

He didn't have a word to say in his own defense, so
he let the comment drop. "What's your father grinning
about?" he demanded.

Molly's gaze darted away from his. "Nothing," she
answered smoothly. "You know my how my dad gets

sometimes. If...he's bothering you, I'll be happy to say something to him."

She did a commendable job of disguising whatever she was feeling. Jordan might have believed her if he hadn't felt her stiffen in his arms the moment he mentioned Ian.

"Tell me."

"There's nothing to tell."

"You're sure?"

"What could I possibly have to say at this point?"

She felt good there, in his embrace, and after a couple of minutes he forgot why he'd asked her to dance and enjoyed the simple pleasure of holding her.

"It was a beautiful wedding," he said. His remark was merely a way to continue the conversation.

"It reminded me of our own." As soon as Molly admitted that, he knew she regretted it. "The comparison is inevitable, really. The same church—and our reception was held here, too, remember? We also invited a lot of the same guests."

"Don't worry, I know what you're saying." Of course she'd noticed the things he had, felt the same brooding emotions.

Jordan wondered what she'd been thinking while Kati and Matt exchanged their wedding vows. He wondered if she remembered how his voice had shaken or how her eyes had filled with tears. Did the memory of how desperately they'd been in love come back to her, too?

The music stopped and he had a difficult time dropping his arms and stepping away from her.

"You'd better get back to Lesley," she whispered.

Lesley. He'd nearly forgotten her. "Yeah. Your dance partner's throwing daggers my way, as well." It was a weak attempt at a joke. A weak attempt at getting the information he wanted about the other man.

Molly was kind enough to smile. "David's not like that."

"Who is he?" Jordan asked, hoping to sound casual and approving.

"David Stern. Dr. David Stern. He works at Sinai. We met last week."

"He's your date," Jordan said, stunned by the realization. He hadn't been aware of Stern at the church, but that was understandable. His gaze hadn't moved past Molly in her cheery red suit and broad-rimmed white hat. It hadn't occurred to him to notice the man who was standing next to her.

"Not really," Molly was quick to tell him. "David's a family friend of Matt's. I didn't realize he knew Matt, and David didn't know Kati was my cousin. We'd both talked about attending a wedding on Saturday without realizing it was the same one."

"I see," Jordan said stiffly. He didn't like Stern. *Dr.* Stern, he corrected.

"Lesley looks very nice," Molly said, glancing behind him.

"Have you talked to your aunt Johanna lately?" Jordan said as they walked off the dance floor. He was making excuses to linger and knew it, although he didn't understand why. Nor did he want to know.

"Apparently she wasn't aware we're getting a divorce," Molly said, answering his unspoken question. "You needn't worry. Word will get around fast now.

Aunt Johanna is the family gossip. Everyone who's even distantly related will hear the news by nightfall." Her smile was forced, but only someone who knew Molly well would see that. "I hope she didn't embarrass you."

"No," Jordan muttered. "What about you?"

"Not in the least. It's better if people know as soon as possible, don't you think?" She seemed eager to leave now, looking around as if she was trying to locate her precious David.

"I'd better get back to Lesley," he said, making his own excuses. "It was good dancing with you again."

"You, too." How polite they sounded, as though they were little more than strangers. That was the way it would have to be, he told himself. They had no future, only a painful past.

Jordan watched as she moved across the dance floor. Instead of finding David Stern, she took the most direct route to her father's side. Even from this distance he could see that she was irritated with Ian. His father-in-law didn't seem upset by her chastisement, reaching for a glass of champagne halfway through her tirade.

Apparently there was some basis to Ian's I-know-something-you-don't smile. Jordan wondered what it was, but he supposed he'd find out soon enough.

Monday morning Jordan received a call from Michael Rife. "I just got the court docket, and the final hearing is set for Thursday afternoon."

"That soon?"

"Count your blessings," Rife went on to say. "If

Molly had wanted to, she could've tied you up in court for years."

"But it hasn't been the full sixty days."

His lawyer hesitated. "Are you sure you want to go through with this?"

"Yes, I'm sure," Jordan snapped. "Fine, I'll be in court Thursday afternoon. What time?"

Michael told him. Jordan stared at the receiver for long minutes afterward. Thursday afternoon would be the end of his marriage. Thursday afternoon some judge he'd never seen before would pound his gavel and his life with Molly would end.

He waited until he suspected she'd be home from work before he called her. She answered on the third ring; her voice was thin as if she were ill and trying not to show it.

"It's Jordan," he announced. "What's wrong? Are you sick?"

"I'm fine."

She sure didn't sound like it. "Have you got the flu?"

"Something like that."

He would've liked to question her more, but didn't know how to pursue it. "I got a call from Michael Rife this afternoon," he said, moving on to the purpose of his call. "The divorce will be final on Thursday."

"Will I need to be in court?"

"No. Not unless you want to be."

"I don't."

"I was the one who filed, so I'll go. Do you want me to call you afterward?"

She hesitated as if this was a momentous decision.

"That won't be necessary. Thursday it is, then. Thank you for letting me know."

It seemed crass to tell her she was welcome. Crass to thank her for the good years they'd shared. Now didn't seem the time to tell her how sorry he was about Jeffrey, either, or to apologize for failing them both.

He'd assumed getting the divorce was a formality. All that was required of him was his signature. No one had told him it would be like having his arms torn off and that it would leave him feeling as if he were sitting on a pile of rotting garbage. It wasn't supposed to be like this, was it?

"Goodbye, Molly," he said after a moment.

"Goodbye, Jordan." Her voice quavered and he knew she was experiencing the same things he was. The same pain, the same sense of loss.

From Thursday onward it would be like that song Molly sometimes sang. He'd be someone she used to love.

"Jordan," she said quickly. He heard a note of panic in her voice.

"Yes?" he said softly.

"Nothing."

"Molly, listen, I know we're divorcing, but if you ever need me for anything…"

"Thank you, but that won't be necessary."

"I see." He shouldn't be hurt by her words, but he was.

"I'm sorry. I didn't mean that the way it sounded," she said. "Thank you for the offer, Jordan, I appreciate it. If you ever need *me* for anything, please call."

"I will." Although he doubted he would. "Goodbye,"

he said again and replaced the receiver before she could echo the word.

For reasons Jordan didn't want to analyze, he didn't have the heart to hear her say it a second time.

Six

"If you don't tell Jordan before Thursday afternoon, I swear I will."

"Dad!" Molly argued, so frustrated she wanted to weep. "This is none of your business."

"I'm making it my business!" He got up and walked around his desk until he stood a few feet from where she was sitting. They rarely disagreed, and when they did Molly could generally reason with her father. Not this time.

"Jordan has a right to know he's going to be a father."

"I'll tell him in my own time," Molly insisted.

"You'll tell him before Thursday," Ian said.

"Do you seriously believe Jordan will call off the divorce?"

"Yes."

"The baby isn't going to affect how he feels about Lesley. He wants his freedom, and my pregnancy isn't going to stand in his way."

"We'll see, won't we?"

Ian was serious; if she didn't tell Jordan she was

pregnant, he'd do it himself. She almost wished she could let him. Walking over to the phone she punched out the number she knew so well. Jordan answered immediately.

"Are you alone?" she asked.

"Yes, why?"

"I'm coming over."

"Now?"

"Yes, I'll be there in ten minutes," she said and banged down the receiver. Her father smiled approvingly until she walked over to the liquor cabinet and took out a full bottle of his favorite Kentucky bourbon.

"Where are you taking that?" he demanded.

"To Jordan. He's going to need it."

Her father chuckled and escorted her to the front door, opening it for her. "Give me a call later."

"You're a conniving old man."

"I know," Ian Houghton said, beaming her a wide smile. "How do you think I got to be bank president?" The sound of his amusement followed her out the front door.

By the time Molly pulled into the driveway of the home she'd once shared with Jordan, she'd changed her mind no fewer than three times. She might have done so again if he hadn't already opened the door and stood on the porch waiting for her.

"What's going on?" he asked.

Molly didn't answer him. Instead she walked into the house and headed straight for the kitchen and took a thick glass tumbler from the cupboard. Next she walked over to the refrigerator, opened the freezer door and filled the glass with ice. Then she poured Jordan a stiff drink and handed it to him.

"What's that for?" he asked, frowning.

"You might want to sit down."

"What's going on?"

Molly had thought she could do this unemotionally, but she was wrong. She was shaking like the proverbial reed.

"If you won't sit down I will," she said, slumping into a chair. She set the whiskey bottle on the table, and it made a loud clanking noise that echoed through the kitchen.

"What's gotten into you?" Jordan asked. He pulled out the chair across from her. "I realize this divorce thing is more emotionally wrenching than either of us expected, but..." His voice trailed off.

Her eyes started to water. "This doesn't have to do with the divorce."

"Then why are you here?"

"Oh, honestly, Jordan," she said impatiently, "don't be so obtuse."

"Obtuse? About what?"

She had an aversion to coming right out and telling him. "Think about it," she told him, gesturing wildly with her free hand. The other continued to hold the bottle.

"I am thinking."

She felt like having a stiff drink of that bourbon herself, but she couldn't, not when she was pregnant.

"Care to join me?" Jordan asked, bringing down a second tumbler.

"Not a good idea for me right now. Trust me, it's tempting, I could use the courage."

"It's probably better if you don't. You never could hold your liquor."

"Great, insult me."

He stared at her as if he hadn't seen her in a long while, as if studying her would tell him what it was he didn't know.

"We made love in Africa, remember?" She waved the whiskey bottle at him, hoping to jolt his memory.

"Yeah, but why bring it up now?" As soon as the words left his lips, he made the connection, falling back into the wooden chair. Slowly his eyes met hers. They grew wide, then narrowed as he reached for the tumbler and drank down a big gulp. He pressed the back of his hand to his mouth and briefly closed his eyes. "You're pregnant."

"Nothing gets past you, does it?" she said mockingly.

"How long have you known?" Why he found that so important, she could only guess.

"A couple of weeks."

"It's taken you until now to tell me?"

Outwardly he was as calm and collected as the next man, but his anger simmered below the surface. The inflection of his voice gave him away.

"Sure," she cried, "blame me! I didn't get pregnant all by myself, you know. Oh, no, you had to come after me like…like Indiana Jones, sweep me into your arms and—"

"Our making love was…unexpected," he said. "I didn't plan for that to happen."

"Are you saying I did?"

"No," he shouted and wiped one hand down his pale face. He picked up the bottle and refilled his glass. "What are you going to do?" he asked, not looking at her.

"About what?"

"The pregnancy?"

"That's a stupid question. I'm going to have this baby, raise him or her and live long enough to be a problem to my grandchildren. What else is there to do?"

Jordan propped his elbows on the table. "What about the divorce?"

"I don't see how this pregnancy should make any difference. Lesley will understand." Although Molly would have enjoyed being a bug on the wall when he broke this news to his fiancée.

"You might have said something sooner, don't you think?" He glared at her accusingly. "You knew on Saturday, didn't you? That's what your father was hinting at. Who else did you tell—your good friend Dr. Stern?"

"David has nothing to do with this."

"But you—"

"Listen, Jordan," she broke in. "I've done my duty and told you about the baby. I realize it's a shock—it was a shock to me, too. But this doesn't change anything. You can go on your merry way and do whatever you please."

Jordan scowled at her. "You might have given me some warning. I don't know *what* I'm going to do."

"Might I suggest—nothing?"

"No," he growled.

"Here," she said, handing him the bottle. "When

you've had time to think this through, give me a call and we can talk about it in a more reasonable fashion."

Reasonable fashion!

It was just like Molly to waltz into his home, the night before their divorce was final, and casually announce she was pregnant.

Jordan was furious. He reached for the tumbler, and brought it to his mouth. At least she'd had the foresight to realize he was going to need a drink to help him deal with this.

Pregnant.

A baby.

Jordan's hand tightened around his drink. How could this have happened? If he wasn't so shocked, he'd laugh. Weeping, however, seemed far more appropriate.

Molly had had time to adjust to the news. He hadn't. Frankly, he didn't know that he ever would. Dealing with the possibility of losing a second child was beyond his endurance.

His hand was shaking, and Jordan realized it had nothing to do with the amount of alcohol he'd consumed.

He was frightened. So frightened he shook with it. Give him a band of gun-toting rebels any day of the week. Another gunshot wound was preferable to the risks involved in loving another child.

The grandfather clock in the living room signaled the time, reminding him that in a matter of hours he'd be standing before a judge.

"Thank you so much for meeting with me," Amanda Clayton said on Thursday, when Molly joined her on the wooden bench in Lincoln Park. She was a petite young woman with thick dark hair that curled naturally.

Pierre had given Molly dozens of croissants over the past few weeks in an effort to encourage her to meet his daughter. Molly had finally agreed, but she wasn't sure she'd be able to say anything that would help.

Although the day was cloudy and overcast, Amanda wore sunglasses. Molly wasn't fooled; the glasses were an effort to disguise her blotchy red eyes.

"How long has it been?" Molly asked gently.

"Christianne died six months ago yesterday. How... how about you?"

"Jeffrey's been gone almost four years now."

"Four years," Amanda echoed, then added softly. "Does it ever get any better? Does the pain ever go away?"

"I don't know." Molly had been uncomfortable about this meeting from the first. How could she possibly help someone else when she hadn't been able to help herself? "I can get through a day without crying now," Molly told her.

"How... how long did that take?"

"Two years."

"What about your husband?"

"How do you mean?"

"This seems so much harder for me than it does for Tommy. I can't even talk about Christi with him because he thinks we should forget. But how am I supposed to forget her?"

"You can't and you won't. Your husband's hurting, too, but men often have a more difficult time expressing their grief. My husband never cried, at least not when

I could see him." She knew Jordan had grieved in his own way, but never openly and never with her.

"What…what did you do with Jeffrey's things? I know this must sound stupid, but what am I supposed to do with Christi's clothes and her toys and the special things we bought for her? Do I just pack those up as if she'd never lived? Do I give them away? Or do I leave them out?"

"I don't know," Molly answered sadly.

"What did you do?"

Molly clenched her hands into tight fists. "A few days after we buried Jeffrey, my…husband went into our son's room, closed the door and packed up all his things to give to a charitable organization."

Molly vividly remembered the terrible argument that had followed as she fanatically sorted through the boxes, removing the precious items that had marked Jeffrey's too-short life. She'd managed to salvage his baby book, a hand-knit blanket and his baptismal gown. A rattle, too, and a few other things that were important to her.

Their argument had scarred their marriage. It was as though Jordan believed that if he could get rid of every piece of evidence that Jeffrey had lived, the pain would stop. They'd each dealt with their grief in different ways. Molly had clung to every memory of Jeffrey, while Jordan had systematically pushed their son out of his life.

This was what had driven them apart. In looking at Molly, Jordan was forced to remember his son. In looking at Jordan, Molly was forced to cope with Jeffrey's death.

"Tommy thinks we should sell the house."

"Do you want to move?" Molly asked.

"No. Tommy has some bizarre theory that there was something in the air that caused Christi to die. He believes the same thing will happen if we have another baby, but I love our home, and the neighbors have been wonderful. I don't want to move someplace where I don't know anyone. I talked to the doctor about it and he's assured me nothing in the environment was responsible. Besides," Amanda said, "I don't have the energy it would take to find a new home and then pack up everything we own. It's all I can do to get from one day to the next."

Molly understood that. For weeks after Jeffrey died, she could hardly manage to get out of bed in the morning and dress. By contrast, Jordan was up at dawn and didn't return until long after dinner.

Work had been his release, his salvation. There hadn't been any such relief for Molly, not until she realized she couldn't continue to live with Jordan.

"Eventually I went back to work," Molly said, remembering that it had taken eight months for her to function again. "That helped me more than anything. At least when I was working I didn't dwell on 'if only.'" She dragged in a deep breath, knowing that only someone who'd suffered these kinds of regrets would understand. "You see, I'm a nurse, and as a medical professional I couldn't keep from blaming myself. I should have known.... I kept telling myself I should have been able to do something. Jeffrey woke that morning and cried. I...I wanted to catch a few minutes'

extra sleep, so I stayed in bed. By the time I got up..."
It wasn't necessary to finish.

"Tommy and I woke before Christi and he wanted to go in and get her up, but I told him to let her sleep while I took a shower. Only she wasn't sleeping," Amanda said, her voice cracking, "she was dead."

Molly reached for her hand and gently squeezed her fingers.

"I lost more than my baby when Christi died," Amanda whispered brokenly. "I lost my faith, too. I don't attend church anymore. I don't want to believe in a God who allows children to die."

Molly had made her peace with God early in the grieving process. She'd felt so terribly alone and needed Him so desperately. "I can't believe God caused Jeffrey's death, but I know He allowed it. I don't understand why. I just have to accept it."

Amanda reached for her purse. "Would you like to see Christi's picture?"

"Very much," Molly said.

Amanda opened her purse and handed her a small padded photo album. Christi had been a beautiful baby with a head full of dark, curly hair and bright blue eyes. "She looks like such a happy baby."

"She was. I sometimes wonder..." Amanda didn't finish. She didn't need to; Molly understood. She'd wondered herself what Jeffrey's life would've been like if he'd lived. Her own life, and Jordan's, too, would have been drastically different.

"I have to get back to the hospital," Molly said. They'd already talked much longer than she'd expected. "I'm glad we met."

"I am, too. Although I don't know that I helped you."

"But you have," Amanda assured her. "More than you realize. Would it be all right if we got together again sometime? I know it'd help my husband if he could talk to yours."

"I'm sorry," Molly said, struggling now to keep her voice even. "I'd be happy to meet with you again, but Jordan and I are getting divorced." It was the first time she'd ever spoken the words aloud. She didn't add that their divorce was effective that very day.

"Oh, I'm so sorry."

Molly stared into the distance until she'd composed herself enough to respond. "So am I."

She should probably do something wild and expensive, Molly decided when she got off work that afternoon. It wasn't every day a woman got divorced. Surely the occasion called for a shopping spree or a lengthy appointment at a spa.

Molly had almost reached her car when she heard someone calling her name. She turned to find Dr. David Stern walking briskly toward her.

"Hi," he greeted her breathlessly. "I was beginning to think I wasn't going to catch you."

"Hello again." She was mildly surprised that he'd been looking for her. They'd danced a few times at Kati and Matt's wedding, and had eaten together on the lush green lawn, but she hadn't talked to him after Jordan had been so rude.

"I was hoping I could convince you to go out to dinner with me tonight," David said. He was tall and burly. A few of the staff members referred to him as

Dr. Bear, not because of his temperament, but because of his size.

"Tonight," she repeated.

"I realize it's short notice, but I'm on call the rest of the week. We could make it another evening if that's more convenient, but it never fails—if I've got a date, someone decides this is the night they're going to hurl themselves off a cliff." His grin was wide and boyish.

Molly had liked him from the moment she'd watched him comforting an elderly patient. She liked his compassion, his gentleness, his sense of humor.

"I'd enjoy dinner with you very much," she told him. "But not tonight."

"You've got other plans?"

"In a way. My divorce was final this afternoon and, well, I was thinking I should do something…extravagant. I don't know what. Something reckless."

"Hey, some would say having dinner with me is pretty daring."

Molly was tempted to accept his invitation, but she wasn't ready to date again, not so soon. In addition, there was the baby. Not every man would be thrilled to date a pregnant woman. "I don't think I'd be very good company."

"I understand," he said, and although he sounded disappointed he offered her a warm smile. "If you need to talk to someone, give me a call." He pulled a prescription pad from his pocket, wrote out his home phone number, peeled off the sheet and handed it to her.

"Promise me one thing," he said, "don't sit around alone and mope. I'll be in all evening if you want to talk. If nothing else, I've got this great joke book and I can read it to you over the phone."

Impulsively Molly hugged him. She could use a friend just now.

A few minutes later, she walked into her apartment and closed the door. The sun had broken through the afternoon clouds and the sky was a shimmering blue. Funny how bright everything was outside while she was living through a fierce emotional storm. The least it could do was drizzle. A downpour would have been more appropriate.

The phone rang, and Molly swerved around to look at it. Perhaps it was fanciful thinking on her part, but she half hoped it was Jordan calling to tell her how the final divorce proceedings had gone. That wasn't likely, however, and call display confirmed it.

"Hello, Dad."

"How are you?"

"Fine."

"You didn't call me," he said. "How did your talk with Jordan go yesterday?"

"It went. He wasn't too pleased, as you might imagine."

"Did he change his mind about the divorce?"

"No." Some small part of her had hoped he would, although she'd never have said as much to her father. In fact, she'd only now admitted it to herself.

Ian's talk had ignited a spark of hope, however futile, that her marriage could be saved. But Jordan was engaged to Lesley now. Naturally he wanted to sever his ties with her.

"You told him about the baby, didn't you?"

"Yes."

"And he still went through with the divorce?" Ian's voice revealed his shock. "I thought..." He hesitated, recovered quickly and when he spoke again he sounded calm. "How are you taking all this?"

"I'm fine." If it wasn't for the baby, Molly would make a point of getting good and drunk, which would take, at most, one margarita. But despite everything, she was mildly surprised to discover it was true—she was going to be all right.

"What are you doing?"

"You mean this very minute?"

"I don't think it's a good idea for you to be alone at a time like this."

Molly smiled, loving him for his concern. "I've already turned down one invitation for dinner. I prefer my own company tonight. I was going to order myself a decadent pizza, soak in a hot bubble bath and be especially self-indulgent for the next few hours."

"I can come over, if you want."

"Dad, I'm a big girl. I'll be fine."

It took her another five minutes to persuade him of that. When she hung up, Molly stood there for a few moments, attempting to connect with her feelings. The afternoon had been spent assuring everyone how well she was taking this divorce.

Really, what else was there for her to do? Pound the walls? Weep with frustration? Wallowing in regrets and recriminations was draining. She'd spent the past eight hours on her feet and lacked the energy for a pity party, especially when it would be so sparsely attended.

In the end, Molly changed into her most comfortable pair of shorts and propped her bare feet on the ottoman. She sat in front of the television and watched the evening news.

The tears that crept silently from the corners of her eyes were unexpected and unwelcome. She reached for a tissue and wiped her face. Her emotions were unpredictable when she was pregnant, and this was an emotional day.

She certainly wasn't going to beat herself up over a few maverick tears. If she needed to cry about the divorce, then she should be able to do so.

Apparently she needed to cry.

"Oh, damn," she said, angry with herself, and grabbed another tissue. It hurt, far more than she'd thought it would. Jordan was free to marry Lesley and live happily ever after with someone else.

She closed her eyes. At least she wasn't walking out of her marriage empty-handed. This pregnancy was Jordan's final gift to her.

Determined to ignore her need to weep, she called her favorite take-out place and ordered a deep-dish sausage pizza with extra cheese. She'd discovered she was ravenous. Crying took a lot of energy and if she needed to fuel those tears, what better way than with a Chicago pizza?

Her doorbell chimed forty-five minutes later. Carrying a twenty-dollar bill, Molly opened the front door to find Jordan standing on the other side.

His hands were deep in his pockets and he looked as if he wanted to be anyplace else. "You're crying."

She mocked him with a smile. "I never understood

why you wanted to be a builder when it's obvious you would've made a great detective."

He ignored her sarcasm. "Are you going to invite me in or are you going to make me stand on your porch all evening?"

She held open the screen door.

He stared at the twenty-dollar bill in her hand. "What's the money for?"

"I thought you were the pizza delivery guy."

Jordan's frown deepened. "Pizza gives you heartburn."

Molly found it ironic that he could remember something like that, but not her birthday. "I take it there's a reason you wanted to see me?"

He nodded and walked over to the sofa. "What's been going on in here?" he asked, gesturing at the discarded tissues. It did look as if she'd held a wake, and in a manner of speaking she had, but that wasn't something she wanted to share with her husband.

Ex-husband, she reminded herself.

"I've got a cold," she lied, grabbing the tissues, wadding them up into a clump and holding it with both hands.

"Sit down," he ordered.

"Is there a reason I should?"

"Yeah, I think we should discuss the…pregnancy."

"The word isn't all that hard to say," she muttered under her breath, just loudly enough for him to hear.

A long uncomfortable moment passed before he spoke. "You're making this very difficult."

She knew she was being unpleasant to him, but he'd

interrupted her grieving. That didn't seem fair. Especially now, when her pizza was about to be delivered.

No sooner had that thought skipped through her mind than the doorbell chimed. This time it was her pizza.

"Do you mind if I eat while you talk?" she asked. She couldn't see any reason to let her pizza get cold.

Jordan didn't seem thrilled by her request, but he agreed with a nod of his head. Molly brought out a plate and dished herself up a piece. She was about to offer him one, when he spoke.

"Do you plan on eating that all by yourself?"

"That was my original intention. You're welcome to some, if you'd like."

Apparently he did, because he got himself a plate and joined her on the living room floor. They sat cross-legged, with the pizza between them.

"You were saying?" she prodded when he didn't immediately resume their discussion.

"I talked to Michael Rife this morning about the pregnancy."

"I bet that surprised good ol' Mike."

"Mike, nothing," Jordan muttered. "I wish you'd said something to me a little earlier."

"Come on, Jordan. You can't tell me the possibility never crossed your mind." Although she had to admit it hadn't crossed hers... At the time, she hadn't been rational, hadn't thought about possible consequences. Hadn't *thought* at all. She'd only felt, and those emotions had been desperate. Urgent. Compelling.

He glared at her. "No, it never crossed my mind. I assumed you were on the pill."

Molly laughed. "Why would I be taking birth-control pills? I hadn't slept with a man in years."

"All right, you've made your point." He picked up a napkin, wiped his hands clean and set his plate aside. "It was stupid of us both, and now we're stuck with the consequences."

Molly set her own pizza aside, her appetite gone. Jordan spoke as if her pregnancy was something unpleasant, something that had to be *dealt* with. A problem. That irritated her. In fact, it infuriated her.

"Michael's arranging for child-support payments to be sent on a monthly basis."

"I don't want anything from you, especially your money."

"That's too bad, because it's already been arranged."

"Fine." She'd let his money accumulate interest in the bank.

"You'll need to tell me who your physician is, too."

"Why?"

"I changed medical insurance a couple of years back and the physician has to be on their approved list."

"I went back to Doug Anderson. I always liked him despite what you said about his golf game. Besides, he spent a lot of time with me after Jeffrey died."

Jordan flinched at the mention of their son's name, and her heart softened. The tears returned and she grabbed a paper napkin and held it to her mouth.

Jordan reached out as though to comfort her, but stopped himself. Slowly he lowered his arms to his sides. "I'm sorry, Molly, more sorry than I can say."

"Just be quiet," she sobbed. "You aren't supposed to be nice to me."

He put his arms around her then, holding her against him, letting his body absorb her weeping. She knew she should break away, but couldn't make herself do it.

"I've hardly slept since you told me about the pregnancy," he whispered.

"You're right.... I should've said something right away."

"I can't go through this again, Molly. I'm sorry, but I just can't. I'll try to help you through the pregnancy, but I don't ever want anything to do with the child."

His words hurt, and she jerked herself out of his arms. "Don't worry, you're free now," she said bitterly. "You've taken care of your responsibilities. I'm sure Lesley's been waiting for this day for a long time." That was an incredibly mean thing to say, but she didn't care.

"What's Lesley got to do with this?"

"You're free," she said, dramatically throwing her arms in the air.

"No, not really."

"What are you talking about? You went before the judge, didn't you?"

It took him far longer to answer than it should have. "As a matter of fact, I didn't."

Seven

"You mean to tell me we're not divorced?" Molly cried, vaulting to her feet.

"We aren't divorced," Jordan said as if he regretted his decision.

"Why aren't we?"

"Because you're pregnant," Jordan returned forcefully.

"So? You just finished saying you don't want anything to do with the baby."

Jordan thrust his hands in his pockets, and his gaze avoided hers. "The pregnancy makes a difference. It's reasonable to wait and refile the papers after the baby's born. Another few months won't matter one way or another, will it?"

Molly didn't answer him. She doubted Lesley would agree with him, but it wasn't her place to point that out.

An awkward silence fell between them. "How are you feeling?" Jordan eventually asked.

"I'm fine."

"Morning sickness?"

She shrugged. "A little."

"What about the afternoons?"

So he remembered the afternoon bouts of nausea she'd suffered when she was pregnant with Jeffrey. "Some, but not as bad as it was…the first time."

He nodded and took his hands out of his pockets.

Molly pushed the hair away from her face. The muggy heat felt stifling. It didn't seem right for them to be sitting in her living room, discussing her pregnancy.

"I don't know how to act around you anymore," she whispered. "You aren't my husband, and yet we're still married. I'd made my peace with the divorce and now we aren't divorced. What exactly *are* we, Jordan?"

The question seemed to cause some deliberation. "Couldn't we be friends?" he finally asked.

Molly didn't know how to answer him. Friendship implied camaraderie and rapport, and she wasn't sure they had that anymore. It also implied an ongoing relationship.

"Remember how we told Michael this was going to be a friendly divorce?" Jordan prompted.

"That's the problem," Molly said, laughing softly. "The divorce is friendlier than the marriage."

Jordan laughed, too, and it helped ease the tension between them. He sat down at the other end of the sofa.

"A few months won't make any difference," he said again, almost as if he was speaking to himself. "Lesley won't mind."

"You're probably right," Molly said, although if she were Lesley she'd have a lot more to say on the subject.

"When will you be seeing Doug again?"

"Late Monday afternoon."

"So soon?"

"He wants to monitor this pregnancy closely because I've just come back from Africa." That, plus the fact they'd lost Jeffrey, which was obvious.

"I see," Jordan commented. "Is his office still downtown?"

Molly nodded.

"That's my project going up, two blocks over. I'll be there on-site Monday afternoon. Why don't you stop by afterward and let me know what the doctor has to say."

"All right," Molly agreed, "I will."

Jordan tried not to think about Molly all morning, but she kept turning up in his thoughts, plaguing him with memories of how good their lives together had once been. All that had changed with Jeffrey.

He couldn't think about his son and not experience anger. An anger so intense it bordered on rage. Over time Jordan had focused that anger in just about every direction. At first he blamed the medical profession, Jeffrey's pediatrician, Molly and finally himself.

If only he'd gone into Jeffrey's bedroom that morning. Instead he'd left the house and damned Molly to the agony of finding their lifeless son.

Jordan's fists clenched as the fury surged through him. His breathing was heavy, and his heart felt like a rock pounding against his ribs. Within a few minutes the anger passed, the way it always did, and his tension eased away.

Now Molly was pregnant again.

Jordan had delayed the divorce, and even now he

wasn't sure why. Molly was right; the baby wasn't going to change anything. Seven, eight months from now it would be born.

It.

He was more comfortable thinking of the baby as an it. Dealing with a tiny human being who cried and laughed and smiled when he recognized his daddy was beyond Jordan's capabilities. He'd keep his distance, Jordan promised himself. He planned never to see this baby, never to hold it, never to love it. But for Molly's sake and perhaps his own, he'd do what he considered best for now—wait until after the birth to pursue the divorce.

Once the baby was born, Jordan fully intended to have the final papers processed. Then he'd marry Lesley.

He felt better. His life was neatly arranged. He was in control again.

He glanced at his watch and exhaled slowly. He was meeting Lesley briefly, returning some blueprints to her office. He wasn't looking forward to this because he knew she was going to ask about the divorce.

When he hadn't been obsessed with thoughts of Molly, Jordan had been worrying about what he'd tell Lesley. The truth, of course. But he needed to couch it in a way that assured her of his commitment. Doing it now, however, felt wrong. He'd prefer to give it a few days and sort through his feelings.

If luck was with him, Lesley would be busy and he could simply hand over the papers to her assistant. But as it happened, Lesley had stepped outside her office and was talking to a colleague when Jordan arrived. He was cursing his fate when she looked up and beamed him a delectable smile.

"Jordan, come and have a coffee with me."

"Sure." For show he looked at his watch, hoping to give the impression that he had another appointment and could only manage a few minutes. He followed her into her office, his heart heavy. This could well be the most difficult conversation of his life.

He liked the way Lesley had decorated her office with oak bookcases and an oak drafting table. One thing he could say about her, she had exquisite taste.

"So," she said, automatically pouring him a cup of coffee. "How did everything go in court yesterday?"

He'd assumed there was no way to say it other than directly, but perhaps he should reconsider his tactic. He borrowed a trick from Molly instead. "You'd better sit down."

"Sit down?" She raised her eyes from the glass coffeepot until they connected with his. "Something's wrong?" she asked and walked around to her side of the desk.

"Not exactly wrong." For all his advice about sitting, he found it necessary to stand himself. "I got a bit of a shock the other night."

"Oh?"

He paused, then decided the only way to say it was straight out. "Molly's pregnant."

"Pregnant?" Lesley sounded as if she'd never heard the word before. "That must have been a surprise. Who's the father?"

"Ah…" He would have told her then if she'd given him the chance.

"I imagine it's that doctor friend of hers you mentioned. The one who was with her in east Africa?"

He stiffened and met her gaze. "No. I am."

The mug in Lesley's hand started to shake and coffee splashed over the sides until she managed to set it down on her desk. She sank into her chair.

"I know this is a blow, Lesley, and I can't tell you how sorry I am."

"You and Molly—I see."

Witnessing the pain in her eyes was almost more than Jordan could bear. "I don't have any excuses. It happened while we were in Africa, while we were held down by the rebel gunfire. We hid in a supply shed and for a while I didn't know if we were going to make it out alive."

"That's your excuse?" she asked, and her voice quavered with indignation.

"Lesley, I couldn't be more sorry. I wouldn't hurt you for the world."

"Funny that you've done such a good job of it." She reached for her coffee in an effort to mask the tears that brimmed in her dark eyes.

Jordan had never felt like more of a jerk. Without trying, he'd managed to offend the woman he cared about and wanted to marry.

"You didn't go through with the divorce, did you?"

He shouldn't be surprised by how well Lesley knew him. "No, not yet. I felt it was better to wait until the baby was born."

"I see."

"I don't blame you for being upset," Jordan said, leaning toward her, his hands clasped. "I wouldn't blame you if you threw me out the door and said you never wanted to see me again, but I hope you won't. My marriage is dead—"

"Apparently not as dead as I once believed," Lesley broke in, her voice trembling.

"A baby isn't going to solve the problems between Molly and me. If anything, this pregnancy complicates the issues."

"What about the child?" Lesley wanted to know. "How do you feel about...having a child?"

His hands tightened until his fingers ached. "I never wanted another family. It was understood from the moment you and I discussed marriage that there wouldn't be children. My feelings about that haven't changed. Molly seems to have adjusted to the news without too much trouble, but I...frankly, I don't ever plan on seeing the baby. Naturally I'll support the child financially, but I refuse to have any emotional involvement."

Lesley's lips quirked upward in a brief smile; at least, Jordan thought it was a smile. "Jordan, it would be impossible for you not to love this child."

His spine stiffened. Another Jeffrey? Never. "You can't love what you don't see," he told her.

"You already love this child. Otherwise you would've gone through with the divorce," Lesley said. "A pregnancy wouldn't have mattered if you honestly believed you could turn your back on the child."

"It was Molly I couldn't walk away from," he countered. As soon as the words escaped, he realized the profound truth of them, and how deeply they'd wounded Lesley. "She had a difficult pregnancy the first time," he added quickly, wanting to undo the damage, knowing it was too late.

Lesley stood and walked to the window, her back to him. He noticed how rigidly she stood, as if she were fighting back the pain. She crossed her arms. "You still love her."

"No," he denied, then said, "Yes, I suppose I do." He waited, hoping Lesley would turn around, but she didn't. "Don't condemn me for that. Molly was...is my wife. A man doesn't forget his first love."

He saw Lesley's hand move to her face and he realized she was wiping the tears away. It pained him to know he'd hurt her so deeply.

"You might think this an asinine question, but would you be willing to wait for me to divorce Molly?" he asked. "It shouldn't be more than a few months. Nothing has to change for us unless you want it to." He'd been as honest with her as he could be, and he hoped she'd take that into consideration.

"I ought to throw you out that door, just like you suggested."

"But you won't," he said, confident that she would have by now, if that had been her intention.

"I...don't know what I should do. Then again, it should be crystal clear," she said with a laugh that sounded more like a sob. "I need time to think this through."

"All right. How long?" They were supposed to attend a cocktail party with a group of investors over the weekend. Important investors. Even if they didn't arrive together, avoiding each other would be impossible.

"I can't give you an answer yet," Lesley said. "But I promise to call you once I make up my mind."

Molly stood in line at the hospital cafeteria, deciding between the egg-salad sandwich and the chicken salad, when David Stern cut in front of her.

"Hello again," he said, grinning as he slipped his orange plastic tray next to hers. "I've been waiting to hear from you."

Molly felt mildly guilty for not seeking him out, knowing that was what he'd expected. She liked David, but she didn't want to mislead him into believing they could become involved.

"Care to join me for lunch?" he asked.

"I'd care a whole lot," she joked.

He paid the cashier for her sandwich and milk, plus his own much larger lunch, then wove his way between crowded tables to the patio outside.

Molly followed him, grateful he'd chosen to eat outdoors. She set her tray down on the round glass table, under the sheltering shade of the blue-and-yellow umbrella.

"What decadence did you fall into the other night?" David asked.

"A sausage and extra-cheese pizza," she said, opening the milk carton and pouring it into a glass.

"That sounds pretty tame to me. Surely a divorce rated a double Scotch on the rocks."

"I can't drink now," she returned automatically. Her hands froze on the milk carton as she raised her eyes to David's. She might as well tell him. Her pregnancy wasn't a secret. "I'm pregnant."

David took the information in stride. "Does your ex know?"

"Yes. It was a shock for us both, but he paid me back in spades."

"How's that?" David asked as he dumped half the pepper shaker on his tuna salad.

"He had his attorney withdraw the divorce petition. I drowned my sorrows in pizza, only to discover we're still married."

"He wants to reconcile?"

It wasn't polite to laugh, but Molly couldn't help it. "Nothing that drastic. He felt, for whatever reason, that we should wait until after the baby's born. I don't know how his fiancée is going to take this, but that's his problem."

"He's engaged?"

Her life sounded like a soap opera. "From what I understand, she's perfect for Jordan." Molly raised her sandwich to her mouth. "As you can see, I'm not exactly a prime candidate for a relationship. I'd suggest counseling for any man who wanted to become involved with me."

David laughed. "You sound like you might need a friend."

That was the word Jordan had used, too. Why was it that every man in her life suddenly wanted to be her friend? She might as well get used to it. There was only one thing about which Molly was completely certain. She never intended to marry again.

"You're right," she admitted, "I could use a friend."

"So could I," David said, centering his attention on

his lunch. "My wife died in the first part of January. We'd been married for fifteen years."

"David, I'm sorry, I didn't know."

"She'd been sick with cancer for several years. In the end death was a blessing. We both had plenty of time to adjust to the inevitable."

"Can you ever prepare yourself for the death of a loved one?" Molly asked. As a nurse, she'd seen death countless times. She'd watched some patients struggle and hold on to life. Yet others slipped gracefully from one life into the next.

"I thought I was prepared," David said quietly, "but I wasn't. Certainly I didn't want Karen to suffer any longer. What surprised me was the desperate loneliness I experienced afterward. That lack of connection with one other human being." He stopped eating and reached for his glass of iced tea.

David had walked through the same valley she had, where death cast its desolate shadow. That was what had attracted her to him and why she'd felt an instant kinship.

"It's taken me months to come to terms with Karen's death. I'm not expecting to get involved in another relationship, if that concerns you. All I want is a little companionship, and it seems to me we're really after the same thing. Maybe we could help each other."

Molly's eyes met his. "Maybe we could."

Jordan's pickup was parked outside the house when Molly pulled in behind it. It might have been better if she'd phoned, but she'd agreed to see him following her appointment with Doug Anderson. Only it was much later than she'd told him.

It felt strange to ring the doorbell at the home that had once been hers, then stand outside and wait for Jordan to answer. She wished now that she'd phoned. She couldn't be friends with Jordan. Cordial, yes, but their pain-filled history precluded friendship. She appreciated his concern, but it would probably be best if they kept their distance.

When he answered the door, Jordan's eyes revealed his surprise at seeing her. The first thing Molly thought was that Lesley was with him and her unannounced arrival would embarrass them all.

"Have I come at an inconvenient time?" she asked. "Because I can leave."

"Don't be ridiculous," Jordan said. He must have recently gotten home himself because he was still dressed in his work clothes—khaki pants and a short-sleeved shirt.

"I can leave if…someone's with you."

"I'm alone," he said, drawing her into the house. "What happened? When you didn't show, I contacted Doug's office and got his answering service."

"He was called into the hospital for a delivery. I had to reschedule my appointment. I tried to reach you, but you've got a different cell number now."

"That's right. Here, let me give it to you."

"No," she said, holding up one hand. "It isn't necessary." Having his cell number seemed too intimate, too familiar.

Jordan looked surprised by her refusal. "You might need it."

"I…I can always contact your office. They should be able to reach you, shouldn't they?"

He shrugged as if it made no difference to him one way or the other. But it did, and she could tell that her refusal had offended him.

"How are you?" he asked, after a short delay.

He wasn't comfortable asking about the baby, she realized, but his question implied his concern. "Perfectly healthy. The morning sickness isn't nearly as severe this time."

He didn't respond, but opened the refrigerator and brought out a pitcher of ice water. Without asking, he poured her a glass.

"I thought I'd stop by and explain why I didn't call you earlier," Molly said, positioning herself so that the breakfast counter stood between them. "I…won't stay."

"Fine. If that's what you want."

Her stomach rolled and pitched, and she suddenly felt ill. "Would it be all right if I sat down for a minute?"

"Of course." Something in her voice must have told him how sick she was feeling, because he took her by the elbow and guided her into the family room.

Sitting helped slightly, and she took in several deep breaths. Unfortunately it wasn't enough. She shot up and raced for the bathroom and promptly lost her lunch.

When she finished, Jordan was there with a wet washcloth.

"I'm sorry," she whispered, feeling weak and close to tears.

"You don't need to apologize," Jordan told her, gently guiding her back to the upholstered chair. He brought her a glass of water and she drank thirstily. Jordan stayed by her side.

Resting her head against the back of the chair, Molly closed her eyes. "I'll be all right in a minute," she said.

"Relax," Jordan told her.

Molly felt him place a thin blanket over her. Her mind was drifting into a lazy slumber. She tried to tell herself it wasn't a good idea to fall asleep while she was at Jordan's house, but that demanded far more effort than she could muster....

Jordan sat across from Molly, watching her while she napped. His heart ached as he studied her, hoping she could rest.

The awkwardness between them troubled him. He knew he was to blame and that Molly was protecting herself from any further heartache.

He'd acted like an idiot about the pregnancy. Over the past week he'd made several attempts to reconcile himself to the fact he was going to be a father again. It hadn't worked. His instincts told him to run as fast as he could in the opposite direction.

He admired Molly's courage and wished he could be different. He wished he could feel the elation he'd experienced when they'd first learned she was pregnant with Jeffrey. But that wasn't possible. Not anymore.

From the moment Molly told him she was going to have another child, all he'd known was fear. It clung to his every thought, dictated his actions and taunted him with the feeling that nothing in his life would ever be right again.

He longed to give Molly the emotional support she

needed and deserved through this pregnancy. But he didn't know if he could. This child, innocent and fragile, left him weak with anxiety.

A strand of blond hair fell across her pale skin. Jordan yearned to tuck it behind her ear, to hold her in his arms. He didn't examine his feelings too closely because if he did he might remember their night together in Africa....

It'd been like that in the beginning, when they were first married. Their need for each other had been insatiable, and their happiness had brimmed over into every aspect of their lives.

He needed to move away from Molly, Jordan decided, otherwise he'd become trapped in the maze of happy memories.

Making dinner seemed the solution, so he went into the kitchen and brought out a package of steaks. His culinary skill was limited, but he could barbecue a decent steak. Salads weren't that difficult, either. He took the lettuce from the refrigerator, plus a tomato and a green pepper. He chopped the vegetables, feeling especially creative. Every now and again, his gaze involuntarily drifted to Molly.

He must have been glancing at her more frequently than he realized, because the knife sliced the end of his index finger. A rush of bright red blood followed.

"Damn," he muttered at the unexpected pain. The cut was deep and bled freely. Turning on the faucet, he held his finger beneath the running water.

"What happened?" a groggy Molly asked.

"Nothing."

"You cut yourself." She was standing next to him. "Let me see."

He jerked his hand away from her. "I told you it's nothing."

"Then let me take a look at it," she insisted. She turned off the water and held his wrist, then wrapped his hand in a clean kitchen towel.

"It's not that bad," Jordan said, feeling foolish. It was his own fault for being careless.

"You'll live," she agreed. "I'll put a bandage on it and you'll be good as new within a week." She opened the cupboard by the kitchen sink and removed the bandages, carefully wrapping his index finger in gauze and tape. When she'd finished, she kissed the back of his hand.

The kiss, simple as it was, rippled through him. Unprepared for the impact of her touch, he drew in his breath sharply. Somewhere in the farthest reaches of his mind, the pleasure took hold of him and refused to let go. It had been like this in Africa when she'd put her arms around his neck and her breath came hot against his throat.

When he dared, he lowered his eyes to Molly's and found that she was staring at him. Hers were a reflection of his own, filled with doubt and wonder.

Neither of them moved, neither breathed. He needed to kiss her. Not wanted. *Needed.* He couldn't think about this feeling, couldn't analyze it, knowing that if he did he'd lose courage.

He reached for her and she came into his arms. She parted her lips to him and trembled as her body adjusted to his.

He kissed her again. What had started out gentle and exploratory had become a frenzy of need.

"Jordan?" She whispered his name, breathless and needy. The only time she said it in just that way was when she wanted to make love. It hadn't been so long ago that he'd forgotten.

He moved his hands to her hips and held himself against her, letting her feel the strength of his need. She moaned and met his kiss with a desperation and insistence that was as powerful as his.

Where he found the strength to break away, Jordan didn't know. "Not in the kitchen," he muttered. He lifted her in his arms and carried her into the family room and placed her on the sofa. His breath was thin and his heart pounded wildly. They were crazy, the pair of them together like this, but he didn't care.

"I want you," he said.

"I know." The words were slow. "I want you, too."

Her arms circled his neck and he felt the wetness of her tears. He wanted to tell her how sorry he was, and couldn't. Instead he kissed her again, gently, lovingly.

"I love you," Jordan whispered. "I never stopped."

"What about the baby?"

His world crashed at his feet and shattered. "I don't know…I just don't know."

The phone rang then, ending the moment, tearing them apart.

"Ignore it," Jordan said.

"No." She shook her head. "It might be important."

Nothing was more important than having her in his arms, but the phone rang again. "Answer it," she said urgently. Against his better judgment, he moved away from Molly and grabbed the receiver.

"Hello," he barked, irritated at the intrusion.

"Jordan." It was Lesley.

Jordan closed his eyes.

"Jordan, are you there?"

"Yes."

"Is something wrong? You don't sound like yourself."

Eight

"Lesley," Jordan said. Out of his peripheral vision he caught a glimpse of Molly leaping off the sofa. Quickly she righted her clothes, her movements filled with righteous indignation.

"I thought you'd want to know," Lesley said when he didn't continue.

"Know?"

"What I've decided."

"Yes, of course." Jordan cupped his hand over the mouthpiece. "Molly, wait," he pleaded. They needed to talk, needed to discuss what had happened.

Molly hesitated.

"Molly's there now?" Lesley asked.

"Yes. Listen, could we talk later?"

"That sounds like it'd be best. Tomorrow morning?"

"Ah, sure." All he wanted to do was get off the phone. His main concern was keeping Molly with him, until they'd had a chance to talk. It was just like her to run. Just like her to leave him grappling with regrets.

"At ten?"

"Fine. I'll see you then." Jordan replaced the receiver just as Molly hurried past him on her way to the front door. "Molly, please wait," he called, nearly stumbling in his rush to reach her before she escaped.

She stopped, her purse clutched against her stomach.

"Please don't go. Not until we've talked."

"No," she answered stiffly. Her eyes, which only moments earlier had been warm with passion, stared back at him, bleak and empty now.

"Molly, don't do this."

"*Me?* I'm not the one with both a fiancée and a wife. As far as I'm concerned, you've got one woman too many. I don't want to see you again, Jordan. I'll have my father notify you when the baby's born and you can have Michael petition the court. All I ask is that you notify me when the divorce is final."

"How can you walk away after what happened? What nearly happened," he corrected.

"Easy. We've been married and, well, I guess you could say we fell back into an old habit. It didn't mean anything. How could it, when you're marrying Lesley? It was just one of those things."

"Habit?" Jordan repeated. "You don't honestly believe that."

"Come on, Jordan," she said and laughed, but the sound of her laughter was hollow. "We used to make love on that old couch more often than we ever did on the bed upstairs."

Jordan couldn't disagree with Molly. But kissing her wasn't habit. It had been a rediscovery, a reawakening. He wasn't ready to dismiss it, nor was he willing to leave the situation between them so unsettled.

"It was far more than habit and you know it," he argued.

Molly sighed. "I'm not going to fight with you. If you don't buy my explanation, then make up one of your own." She met his gaze steadily, conviction flashing from her beautiful blue eyes. "What I said stands. I don't want to see you again. Please don't make this any more difficult than it already is."

"If you're worried about Lesley, then—"

"I'm not going to discuss Lesley with you."

"It's over between Lesley and me," he said, then realized Molly had walked away. He debated whether he should run outside and try one last time to reason with her.

His relationship with Lesley had been a mistake. Jordan didn't know why it had taken him so long to understand that. He wasn't entirely sure why he'd gotten involved with her. Loneliness, he suspected. He'd been separated from Molly for three years and his life was empty.

One night, after a couple of drinks, he'd done some two-bit self-analysis and decided he was over Molly, over Jeffrey, and wanted out of the marriage. He'd wanted a new relationship, one that wasn't weighed down with grief.

Jordan felt tired and old, and the emotional resilience he'd once prided himself on was long gone. The truth was he'd never stopped loving Molly. As hard as he tried, he couldn't make himself not care about her. Oh, he'd managed to convince himself he had for a while, when he'd first started dating Lesley. That theory had been blown apart in a supply hut in east Africa.

The situation might have righted itself naturally if it weren't for the pregnancy. The icy cold fear he experienced each time he thought about this new life they'd created left him trembling. But he'd be divorced by now if Molly wasn't pregnant. He didn't know if this baby was a blessing or a curse.

One thing he did know. He wasn't ready to be a father again.

He didn't know if he'd ever be ready. Or if he wanted to be.

Jordan walked outside, hands in his pockets as he strolled toward Molly. He was willing to swallow his pride in order to keep her with him until they could settle this.

"You're running away again," he said. It was what Molly had done after Jeffrey died and now she was doing it again.

"I'm running away *again?*" Her eyes filled with fury. "Are you seriously suggesting I was running away when I moved out? Did it ever occur to you, Jordan Larabee, that you all but *pushed* me out?"

"That's not true," he said heatedly, struggling to hold on to his temper.

"You couldn't stand to look at me because every time you did…"

"You cried and cried and cried. All you did was mope around the house, sobbing from one room to the next for weeks on end. Jeffrey was the center of every thought, every conversation. Did you think that if you cried long enough and hard enough it would bring him back?"

"I was in mourning."

"You didn't even have the decency to tell me you were leaving. I walked in the house and found a stupid note on the refrigerator. You couldn't have told me face-to-face?"

"Why should I? We hadn't talked in weeks. The only reason I left a note," she said, throwing back her head and glaring at him, "was because I figured that otherwise it'd take a month for you to notice I'd moved out."

"I handled Jeffrey's death in my own way," Jordan shouted.

"You handled nothing! You wanted me to pretend he'd never lived...you wanted me to continue as if nothing was wrong. I couldn't do it then and I refuse to do it now."

"You're throwing Jeffrey in my face again. You're using him as a weapon to beat me up, to tell me how wrong I've been."

"You're the one who's guilty of repeating the same mistakes," she said. "You want to pretend this baby isn't alive, either." She flattened her hand over her stomach and her eyes brimmed with tears. "I find it ironic that you accuse *me* of running away when that's what *you've* been doing for nearly four years."

Jordan clenched his fists, fighting down his rage. "For once you're right. We have no business seeing each other. By all means, let's not make the same mistakes again."

"That's perfectly fine with me. Go back to Lesley," Molly suggested, reaching her car. "I'm sure you're exactly right for each other."

The next morning, Jordan met with Lesley. He wanted to be kind to her, and hoped he could break off their unofficial engagement in a way that left her with her pride intact.

Following his argument with Molly, his nerves were raw. He felt edgy, impatient and so weary. He'd sat up most of the night thinking, not that it had done any good. In the morning, he felt as if he were walking in a haze, and the sensation reminded him of when he'd woken in the hospital after being shot.

"This time hasn't been easy on either of us, has it?" Lesley commented, bringing him a cup of coffee. He sat in the leather chair across from her desk and thanked her with a smile. It was going to take a lot more than caffeine to get him through this ordeal.

"I've done some soul-searching in the past couple of days," Lesley said evenly, taking the seat behind her desk. He saw that she avoided looking directly at him, and guessed she was as uncomfortable as he was.

"What did you come up with?" Jordan asked, sipping his coffee.

"Mostly, I realized that I've been playing a fool's game," she said nervously. "You're in love with Molly. I should've realized it when you decided to go after her in Africa yourself. As soon as you came back, I knew immediately that things were different between us, but I didn't want to admit it. Then...then at her cousin's wedding, I saw the two of you dancing. It should've been clear then. You might have said something, Jordan, and spared me this."

She had every right to be angry. Jordan had no defense.

"When I learned Molly was pregnant and you decided to hold up the divorce…well, that speaks for itself, doesn't it?"

"I didn't mean to hurt you." How weak that sounded. Her hands cradled her coffee mug and she lowered her gaze, taking a moment to compose herself before she continued.

"I understand now that I was willing to marry you for all the wrong reasons. We'd worked together for several years and were comfortable with each other, but there's never been any great passion between us. The fact that we've never done more than kiss should've told me that. I was willing to marry you, Jordan, because I so badly want to be married. For years I've struggled to build my career and then I woke up one morning and realized how lonely I was. I wanted a loving relationship. Needed one."

"We were both lost and lonely," Jordan interjected.

"I…know I agreed there wouldn't be any children, but I was hoping you'd change your mind later. Talk about living in a fool's paradise."

"I'd like it if we could find a way to remain friends."

Lesley nodded. "Of course. I'm not angry—at least, not at you. You're a good man, Jordan, and I'm hoping you and Molly can work things out."

"I'm hoping we can, too." But it wasn't likely, not now. He stood and set down his coffee mug. "There's someone out there for you, Lesley. You'll meet him, and when you do, you'll know."

October was Molly's favorite month of year. The winds off Lake Michigan were still warm, swirling up orange and brown autumn leaves as she walked along the redbrick pathways of the neighborhood park.

At four and a half months, her baby was actively making himself known, stretching, exploring his floating world. Despite the ultrasound she'd recently had, she didn't know if her baby was a boy or a girl. She used masculine references just because she was so used to doing that, she supposed. Boy or girl, it didn't matter.

Molly hadn't seen Jordan since that afternoon six weeks earlier. He hadn't made an effort to contact her, and she certainly had no plans to see him. Not after the terrible things they'd said to each other.

In the intervening weeks, Molly was struck by how different she felt. About herself. About life.

The years she'd spent in Africa, she'd been hiding in the shadows of the past. Her loss had become almost comfortable. It had defined her life. Ever since she'd discovered her son dead in his crib, she'd examined those final hours, those final words, those final acts, until the darkness took over and her life had narrowed down to one single point of light. She hadn't moved forward since.

Until now.

She'd stepped forward into the sunlight. She'd leaped back into life and felt joy once more. Only now could she look with gratitude at the happiness Jeffrey's short life had given her. The innocence of those few months they'd shared would always be with her. The memories of holding him and nursing him, so pure and perfect. And loving him with all her heart.

Now she was going to have another child to love. She wanted to laugh when she recalled how shocked and unhappy she'd been when she first realized she was pregnant. She wasn't unhappy now. This baby had given her life purpose—a reason to look forward to each new tomorrow.

"I thought you were going to wait for me," David said breathlessly, running up to her, wearing his new jogging outfit. He slowed his steps to match hers, stopped and braced his hands on his knees while he caught his breath. "How do I look?" he asked.

"Like an Olympic athlete," she said.

David would have laughed if he'd had the energy, Molly guessed. "That's what I like about you," he said, gasping for breath, "your ability to lie so convincingly."

Molly smiled, squinting into the sunlight.

"How about something to drink," he suggested.

"Sure."

He walked her to a café across the street from the park and ordered lattes for both of them. They sat at one of the outside tables.

"I've got two tickets for the gala production of *Les Miserables* for Saturday evening," David said casually.

It wasn't the first time he'd hinted that he'd like to take her out. Until now, Molly had declined, but the expectant look in his eyes stopped her. She hated to disappoint him.

David had become a good friend in the past six weeks. They'd never officially dated—Molly was uncomfortable with that—but they often walked in the park and occasionally their schedules coincided so they ate lunch together in the hospital cafeteria. But that had been the extent of it.

Molly feared that if she openly dated David, the hospital staff might assume he was her baby's father, and she didn't want to burden him with gossip.

"I'm starting to show a little," she said, answering his suggestion with a comment.

"Does it bother you to be seen with me in public?"

She shook her head. "No, of course not."

"Then why the hesitation? These are great tickets."

David deserved her honesty. "I'm afraid someone might think you're the father and I don't want to do anything to taint your reputation."

David laughed outright at that. "I've been waiting years for someone to taint my pristine reputation. Come on, Molly, let's live dangerously. You'll love the play, and we could both use a night out."

"Well…"

"I just finished a seven-minute mile, and I told myself when I could do that I was going to treat myself to something special."

"You mean the play?"

"No," he said, taking her hand. "A date with you. You'll go with me, won't you?"

Although she wasn't convinced she was doing the right thing, Molly agreed. She was lonely, and David was her friend.

Jordan wasn't really interested in attending this play. He'd purchased the tickets six months earlier because Lesley had told him how badly she wanted to see *Les Miserables*.

He'd phoned and reminded her about the tickets, planning to ask if she wanted the pair herself. It was the first time they'd talked, outside of business, in six weeks. She was the one who'd suggested they attend the play together, and Jordan figured he owed her that much. Perhaps he'd agreed because he was lonely.

The past six weeks had been difficult. Molly hadn't wanted to see him, and he'd abided by her wishes. And yet…he continually toyed with the idea of making one last-ditch effort to settle their differences.

He hadn't done it, for a number of excellent reasons. All right, one excellent reason.

Molly was right.

He'd been running, just the way she claimed. He'd submerged himself in denial, refusing to deal with Jeffrey's death or accept this new life Molly's body was nurturing.

He picked Lesley up at seven and whistled appreciatively when he saw her. She was dressed in a beautiful dark blue full-length silk dress that outlined her trim figure.

"You look fabulous," he said, but even while he was speaking his mind drifted to Molly. She was nearly five months pregnant now. Her stomach would be swelling, and the pregnancy would be apparent.

He shook his head in an effort to free himself from thoughts of his wife. He was going to enjoy himself this evening, put his troubles behind him and remember there was a lovely woman on his arm, a woman who was his friend.

They arrived at the Shubert Theater in plenty of time. Jordan was buying a program when he spotted Molly in the lobby.

His heart skidded to a sudden halt. She was laughing, her eyes bright with happiness, and Jordan swore he'd never seen anyone, anything, quite so beautiful. She wore a simple white dress with a high waist. The gown hinted at her pregnancy, and she looked elegant and—in a word—stunning.

Her hair was longer than he remembered. She'd tucked it behind her ears, and it bounced against her bare shoulders. Her earrings were a dangly gold pair he'd given her the first Christmas they were married.

Jordan didn't know how long he stared at her. Several minutes, he suspected. It took that long for him to notice Molly wasn't alone; a tall sturdy man stood at her side. Recognition seized Jordan. Molly was with the same man she'd danced with at Kati's wedding. That doctor—David Stern.

She'd had the gall to hurl Lesley in his face while she herself was involved with someone else! It took every shred of decorum he possessed not to storm over and cause a scene.

Getting a grip on himself proved difficult, but eventually he returned to his seat, where Lesley was waiting for him.

A few minutes later, Lesley turned to him, whispering, "Jordan, what's wrong?"

"Nothing."

"Then why are you so tense?"

"I'm not," he said sharply. It was apparent he wasn't going to be able to disguise his irritation. "Excuse me a moment," he said as he jerked himself out of his seat.

"Jordan," Lesley said anxiously, "the play's about to start."

Jordan ignored her comment. Thankful he was in

the aisle seat, he dashed back to the lobby. Not that he had any idea what he intended to do once he got there.

The minute he entered the lobby, Jordan realized his mistake. Molly was still there with her doctor friend.

She glanced up just then and their eyes met. The shock was enough to sweep the breath from his lungs. He felt sure that Molly had experienced the same phenomenon. She looked up at her date, placed her hand on his forearm and excused herself.

David Stern's eyes sought Jordan out, but he refused to meet the other man's gaze. Instead he focused on Molly, who was coming toward him. Her fingers nervously adjusted the strap of her evening bag.

Within seconds they faced each other. Silence followed.

"Hello." It was Molly who spoke first.

"Molly." Slipping his hands in his tuxedo pockets became necessary, otherwise he feared he'd drag her into his arms.

Silence again, as he absorbed the sight of her. "How are you feeling?"

"Very well," she told him. She flattened her hand over her stomach; the pregnancy wasn't obvious, but noticeable. "How about you?"

"Okay." He shrugged. "You look great."

She smiled, lowering her lashes, clearly ill-at-ease with his compliment.

"You seeing much of the good doctor?" His gaze briefly left her to rest on the man waiting impatiently for Molly to return to him. He clenched his back teeth to keep from saying something he shouldn't.

"Not that much. How's Lesley?"

Jordan wondered if she'd seen them together. "She's fine."

The orchestra started to play and again Molly lowered her lashes. "David and I had better find our seats. It was nice to see you again."

His hands remained in his pockets and hardened into fists as he made another desperate effort not to behave like an idiot. "Nice to see you, too," he murmured.

"I hope you enjoy the play," she added softly and turned away from him.

He waited until his wife and Dr. Stern had disappeared from his line of vision before he returned to his seat. The play was exceptionally well performed, but it couldn't hold Jordan's attention. He doubted that anything could have.

Somehow, through the course of the evening, he managed to say all the right things, comment on the play, even laugh at a joke Lesley made. At intermission he slipped away on the pretext of making a call, but in reality he stood in a corner and waited, hoping for another glimpse of Molly.

He didn't find her again in the crowded lobby. Disappointed, he went back to his seat. The strength of his feelings for her frightened him. The last time they were together they'd come within a heartbeat of making love. He wanted her, *needed* her, nestled against him in sleep. He wanted to watch her wake up and smile that dulcet smile of hers when she found him looking down at her. He wanted her to raise her arms to him and welcome him into her heart.

How Jordan managed to sit through the remainder of the play, he didn't know. A hundred times, possibly more, he considered seeking Molly out and insisting she leave with him, right then and there.

He drove Lesley home, feeling guilty because he couldn't get away from her fast enough. As always, she was warm and generous and understanding.

Jordan had never viewed himself as an obstinate man, but he had no other way of accounting for the length of their separation. He should have approached her earlier. Now it might be too late; he might have lost her to another man. The thought flashed through his mind, torturing him with the unknown.

There was only one way to find out.

He'd ask.

Two days later, Jordan walked into Ian Houghton's home office and shook hands with his father-in-law.

"Please, sit down." Ian gestured toward the high-back leather chair across from his desk. "To what do I owe this unexpected pleasure?"

Ian was always the gentleman, but Jordan knew the old man well enough to recognize the glee in his eyes. Ian had been waiting for this day.

Jordan couldn't see any reason not to cut to the chase. "I want Molly back. Is it too late?"

"Too late?" Ian repeated. "I don't know. You'll have to ask Molly that, not me."

"I saw her Saturday night."

"She was with David?"

Jordan nodded. He almost commented on how beautiful she'd looked, but knew if he did he'd be playing right into Ian's hands. His father-in-law already had the advantage, and Jordan wasn't willing to add to it.

"Has she been seeing a lot of him?"

Ian toyed with a gold pen. "Not to my knowledge, but my daughter doesn't discuss these things with me."

Jordan was disappointed. He'd hoped Ian could tell him more about Molly's relationship with the other man. If he was too late and she was in love with David, he'd have to make his peace with that. But if he stood a chance with her again, even a small one, he'd do everything he could to make their marriage work.

"What about the baby?" Ian asked. "From what Molly said, you don't want anything to do with the child."

Jordan didn't respond. He didn't have an answer to give the older man. He rubbed his face and relaxed against the leather cushion. "I don't know."

Ian was quiet for a moment before he spoke again. "Did you come here looking for advice?"

"No," Jordan said stiffly, then realized his pride hadn't served him well thus far. "But if you want to offer me some, I'll listen."

Ian raised his eyebrows and grinned. "I suggest you make up your mind about the baby before you approach Molly. What you've got here, son, is a package deal. Nothing on this earth will ever separate my daughter from her child. Not even you, and God knows she loves you."

That tidbit of information should have encouraged Jordan, but it didn't.

He stood, his thoughts more tangled and confused than ever. He desperately wanted Molly. Yet he couldn't bear the thought of loving—and the risk of losing—another child.

He left the office without a word to Ian and stepped outside. He walked past his car and kept on walking, block after block, mile after mile. Each step moved him forward, but did nothing to solve the dilemma of his heart.

He needed Molly.

But not the child.]

Jordan knew the truth of what Ian had told him. Molly and the baby were a package deal.

Jeffrey's chubby happy face, smiling cheerfully at him, returned to haunt Jordan. The pain that cut through him with the memory was sharper than any physical agony he'd experienced. Physical pain he could handle, but not this unending emotional torment.

All at once Jordan was tired. Overwhelmed. He felt as if nothing was real anymore. He continued to walk, but he moved in a haze from one block to the next with no real destination in mind. At least, he didn't realize he'd set his course until he stepped off the curb and crossed the street. Molly's duplex was three doors down.

"Make up your mind about the baby before you approach Molly." Ian's words echoed in his heart as he walked up to her porch.

He didn't have anything to offer Molly, nothing he could say—only that he wanted her, needed her back in his life. Other than that, he was as lost now as he had been when he'd talked to Ian.

He had to see her or go insane. Had to know if she still loved him. Had to know if there was any chance they could mend the rift between them.

He didn't remember ringing the doorbell, but he

must have, because the next thing he knew Molly was standing directly in front of him. The screen door was all that separated them.

"Jordan, what are you doing here?"

She was shocked to see him and it showed in her eyes. She was dressed in jeans and a loose-fitting shirt. His gaze fell to her waist and he saw that the snap of the jeans was undone to make room for the baby.

The baby.

"Come in," she said, holding open the door for him.

"Are you alone?" he asked, psychologically distancing himself from her because of the power she wielded. One look, one word, could devastate him.

Molly's eyes widened. "Yes."

He entered the duplex and closed the door. He studied her, wondering what he could possibly say that would make a difference.

"Why are you here?" she asked a second time.

"Are you in love with him?" Jordan blurted out.

"With David? No, not that it's any of your business." His heart raced and he briefly closed his eyes.

"Why?"

"Why what?" she asked, but he couldn't explain.

"Jordan," she whispered, her face revealing her confusion.

For hours he'd been numb, walking, thinking, lost in a maze of impossible emotions. Now Molly was standing within touching distance and he could feel again.

His eyes held hers. "I'm sorry, Molly," he said. "So sorry." The words barely made it past the lump in his throat. There was more he wanted to say, needed to say, but couldn't.

He watched the tears fill her eyes and her bottom lip start to tremble.

Jordan wasn't sure who moved first, him or her. It didn't matter. Within a single heartbeat they were in each other's arms. He felt the tears that coursed unheeded down her face, then wondered if they were his.

With a deep-seated groan, Jordan kissed her.

The kiss was like fire, a spontaneous combustion. He wanted it never to end, but by some miracle he found the strength to tear his mouth from hers. His chest was heaving; hers was, too. Her hands clutched his shirt and she stared up at him.

"Tell me to leave, Molly. Order me out of here, otherwise I won't be able to keep from touching you. I need you too much."

He watched her carefully, knowing the impossibility of what he was asking, praying she wanted him as urgently as he wanted her.

Gradually a smile formed, starting at the corners of her mouth and working its way to her eyes.

"Are you going to make love to me?" she asked.

He closed his eyes and groaned. "Yes. Yes."

"What about Lesley?"

He was tugging the shirt over her head, fingers shaking in his need to hurry. "I broke it off six weeks ago."

"You did?"

"Yes." He tossed the shirt aside. Next his hands were at the zipper of her jeans. She laughed softly and kissed him, using her tongue in ways that caused his knees to buckle.

"What took you so long to come back to me?" she whispered, as he lifted her into his arms and carried her to the bedroom.

Nine

Jordan woke some time later, with Molly asleep in his arms. He moved onto his side so he could study her, but he kept her within the circle of his arms, unwilling to be separated from her.

Never again would he try to convince himself that he could live without her. He knew it was a hopeless endeavor, one at which he was destined to fail.

He brushed a strand of hair away from her cheek and noted the track her tears had taken.

Unable to stop himself, he leaned forward and ever so lightly kissed her temple. She stirred, smiling, before she reluctantly opened her eyes.

The smile was what did it, that sexy, womanly smile of hers. He kissed her.

"Mmm, that feels good," she whispered, slipping her arms around his neck.

He gathered her close, cradling her in his arms. "You were crying," he said close to her ear, not understanding her tears. Then again, he did. He experienced a deep gratitude for this second chance and he could tell that she felt the same thing.

"I...never thought we'd make love again," she said, brushing the hair away from his face. Her hands trembled.

Like Molly, Jordan was caught in the force of an emotional upheaval. His arms circled her waist and they clung to each other.

He could account for every minute they'd spent apart in the past few years. He didn't know what it meant to waste an afternoon, or even an hour. He'd driven himself and his employees hard, ignoring the emotional and physical cost. Anything that would allow him to escape the crippling sense of loss that overwhelmed him....

He needed this marriage. Needed Molly and the healing touch of her love. Her touch, her kiss, her generosity, had given him a fresh breath of life. A taste of what their marriage had once been.

Jordan wanted it back. All of it.

He could think of no way to tell her this, so he kissed her. She made a soft, womanly sound that was half whimper, half moan as he reached for her....

When Jordan woke again, the room was pitch-dark. He felt utterly content, satisfied. After three long, love-starved years, they had a lot to make up for.

Jordan eased himself out of Molly's arms, intent on finding himself something to eat. Some cheese, a peanut butter and jelly sandwich, anything.

"Jordan?" Molly's whisper followed him to the bedroom doorway.

His heart nearly broke at the dread he heard in her

voice, as if she was afraid he was leaving her, sneaking away while she slept. Nothing could be further from his mind.

"I'm hungry."

He heard her soft laugh. "No wonder." The bed creaked as she climbed off, reached for something to cover herself and joined him. Jordan had felt no compulsion to dress and stalked naked into the kitchen. It was dim, the moon the only source of light, but when he opened the refrigerator the glow filled the room.

Jordan noticed that Molly had chosen to wear a long T-shirt that hung to her thighs. She looked very much as though she'd spent the past four hours in bed, her eyes hazy with satisfaction, her smile seductive and wanton.

"What are you looking at?" she muttered.

"You."

"I…I'm a mess."

"No," he said. "I was just trying to decide if I had enough stamina to make love to you again, right here in the kitchen."

Her smile widened, and she blushed prettily. "It wouldn't be the first time we did it in a kitchen."

Jordan remembered the early days of their marriage when they'd made love in every room of the house, and he grinned broadly.

"Let's eat," she said. "I'm hungry, too."

"There's nothing here," Jordan complained, glancing at the refrigerator's contents.

"I've been so tired lately that it's easier to open a can, or pop something in the microwave." She lifted one shoulder. "I was planning to get some groceries tomorrow."

Jordan knew Molly had a grueling schedule at the hospital and he wanted to ask her to quit, but had no right to do that. Soon, once they'd settled everything, he'd persuade her to work part-time, preferably on a volunteer basis. He was a wealthy man and there was no reason for her to put in such long hours.

He searched the cupboard next and found a can of peaches.

"I'll scramble us some eggs," Molly offered.

"Nice idea, but I didn't see any eggs," Jordan said as he ran the peaches under the can opener. He tossed the lid in the garbage, dug into the can with his fingers and produced a slice of peach that he fed her.

He fed himself the next slice.

"Jordan," Molly said excitedly. "Feel!" She grabbed his free hand and pressed it against her stomach. "The baby just kicked."

Jordan felt as though she'd thrown ice water in his face. The shock of it rippled over him, and his breath froze in his lungs.

The baby.

For these few idyllic hours he'd managed to push his awareness of this child from his mind.

"Here's your daddy," Molly was chirping softly, unaware of Jordan's downward spiral of emotion. He knew he wouldn't be able to hide it much longer. He wanted to jerk his hand away, but she held it flat against her abdomen.

"Molly."

"Did you feel the baby?" she asked, looking up at him expectantly. The joy disappeared from her eyes the second they connected with his.

She released his hand and without another word, she turned and marched down the hall.

"Molly," Jordan pleaded, following her, although he didn't know what he'd say if she did decide to listen to him.

She gathered his clothes from the floor, wadded them tightly and thrust them into his arms.

"I'd like to talk about this," he said calmly.

"Go ahead."

"I'm afraid, Molly."

"Do you think I'm not?"

"It's different for you. The baby's a part of you. It's not the same for a man."

"A lot of things are different for a man, aren't they?"

Jordan didn't have an answer for that. He didn't want to argue with her, didn't want this beautiful time to end with them hurling ugly words at each other.

"I'm trying, Molly. Give me credit for that."

She, too, must have felt the need to preserve what they'd shared. Their peace was fragile and easily destroyed; Molly was as aware of that as he was and seemed equally reluctant to ruin it with another argument.

"Be angry with me in the morning," he said. "Hate me then, if you must, but for now let me hold you and love you." He dropped his clothes on the floor and stepped toward her. He was afraid to reach for her, convinced she'd push him away. When he clasped her in his arms, she held herself still, arms hanging lifelessly at her sides. But gradually he felt the tension ease from her body.

"Wait until morning to be angry," he urged softly.

Eventually they returned to the bed and lay together silently. She cuddled close to his side.

"What time is it?" she asked.

Jordan glanced at the illuminated dial of his watch. "A little after midnight. You'd better get some sleep." One of them should, he mused. For his own part, he didn't want to waste a single minute on sleep.

Molly covered them with a blanket. It looked for an instant as if she meant to roll away from him, but he brought her back to his side.

"I have tonight," he reminded her. "You can regret it in the morning if you want, but for the rest of the night let's pretend it doesn't matter."

Molly said nothing.

"If you're going to regret tonight," he murmured, "let's make it worth your while."

And then he slowly made love to her, over and over again.

Molly waited for Amanda Clayton outside a secondhand furniture shop early Saturday afternoon. Amanda parked her truck next to Molly's car and they both opened their doors and got out simultaneously.

When she stepped onto the sidewalk, Amanda's eyes beamed with pleasure. "My goodness, you're showing."

"You can tell?" Molly cradled her slightly enlarged abdomen, making the swelling more pronounced. She looked up at Amanda. "I'm nearly five months now."

"You look wonderful," Amanda said, smiling. "I could be jealous. You're obviously one of those women who positively glow when they're pregnant. Not me. I went through the entire nine months looking like I needed a blood transfusion. If I had any color at all, it was a faint tinge of green."

Molly laughed.

"How are you feeling?" Amanda asked.

Molly shrugged. "I've felt better." She hadn't been sleeping well, but she couldn't blame the baby for that. It'd been five days since she'd seen Jordan, and she had yet to decide how she felt about their interlude. She wanted to deny she'd enjoyed their lovemaking, but couldn't.

When Jordan did contact her again, her reaction would depend on the mood she was in. Either she'd slam the door in his face, or throw her arms around his neck and drag him back to her bedroom.

He must have intuitively known how ambivalent she felt because he'd completely avoided her. One thing was certain; she wasn't going to seek him out.

"I appreciate your helping me with this," Molly said, leading her into the shop. She'd purchased the crib a week before, but didn't have any way of getting it to her duplex. Amanda had kindly offered the use of her truck.

"I'm happy to do it," Amanda returned graciously. "You've helped me more than you'll ever know. It feels good to be able to lend you a hand."

With the shopkeeper's assistance, they loaded the crib into the bed of Amanda's truck. Molly drove to her apartment and together they set it up in the spare bedroom. Since Molly intended to paint the crib, she'd spread newspapers and plastic over the carpet.

"Stay and have some tea with me," Molly said when

they'd finished. "I'm having a glass of milk myself but I'll make a pot of tea."

"You're sure you've got the time?"

"Of course."

"I talked to Tommy about having another baby," Amanda said, while Molly filled the teakettle and set it on the burner.

"What did he say?" she asked, wondering if Amanda's husband felt the same way as Jordan.

"He wants to wait."

"How long?"

"Another six months."

"How do you feel about that?" Molly asked.

Amanda lowered her gaze, then shrugged. "In my heart I know another baby will never take Christi's place, but my arms feel so empty."

Molly understood what her friend was saying. Her arms had felt empty, too. Her arms and her life. That was why she'd volunteered to work in east Africa. She'd been willing to travel anywhere in the world, endure any hardship, if only it would ease the ache in her soul.

"Do you think that's what concerns Tommy?"

"I don't know. He's afraid we'll lose a second baby, too, and I don't think either of us would survive that."

"I...didn't think I'd survive losing Jeffrey," Molly said, and in some ways she continued the struggle and would for a very long time.

"We agreed that I'd go off the pill in three months. It took me six months to get pregnant with Christianne. The way we figure it, the timing should be about right."

The kettle whistled and Molly removed it from the burner.

"How's Jordan?" Amanda asked timidly. "Listen, you don't have to talk about your husband if you don't want to. It's just that…well, I can't help being curious, especially since he's decided to delay the divorce until after the baby's born."

"He's fine, I guess. I—he stopped by last week."

"He did?" Amanda asked excitedly. "Remember when you told me about seeing him at the play? Something about the look on your face when you mentioned him struck me. You're still in love with Jordan, aren't you?"

There wasn't any use in denying it, so she nodded.

"I knew it," Amanda said triumphantly. "What did he want?" She edged closer to the table, then seemed to realize Molly and Jordan's relationship was none of her business. "You don't need to answer that."

"Apparently he's broken off his relationship with Lesley," Molly said.

"Hot damn!"

"He'd like a reconciliation…I think."

"Double hot damn!"

"But he's still having trouble dealing with my pregnancy."

Amanda's shoulders slumped dramatically. "He's afraid. Tommy and I are, too. It's only natural, don't you think?"

"Perhaps, but it's more than just fear with Jordan. He's terrified." Molly didn't know what he expected of her anymore. It wasn't as though she could ignore their child. "He doesn't want to have any feelings for this child," Molly continued. "I think he's convinced the minute he does, something will happen. He keeps everything bottled up inside. He always has...even with Jeffrey."

"I feel sorry for him," Amanda said thoughtfully. "He must be miserable, loving you the way he does."

They were both miserable.

Molly poured tea for Amanda and milk for herself, and the two women chatted for fifteen more minutes. Although they were very different, they'd become friends, bonding over the heart-wrenching tragedy of losing a child to SIDS.

As soon as Amanda left, Molly changed clothes and got out the paint she'd purchased earlier in the day. She'd put on an old dress shirt of Jordan's, rolled up the sleeves and paused to study herself in the mirror.

"Stop kidding yourself," she muttered. Choosing to paint in Jordan's shirt had been a deliberate act. Illogical though it was, she felt close to him in this shirt. Years earlier, before they knew what was to befall them, it had been a favorite of hers.

She'd stolen it from his closet when she'd picked up her things at the house and moved them into the apartment. For a short time afterward, she was afraid he'd ask her about it. As the weeks passed, she realized he had so many shirts he wouldn't miss this one.

Wearing it now, while she painted the baby's crib, had been an effort to bring him closer to her and their baby. In this shirt, she could pretend his arms were around her.

She was stirring the paint when the doorbell chimed. She hurried impatiently into the living room.

The last person she expected to find at her door was

Jordan. His arms were filled with two heavy brown sacks, and his eyes met hers with a beguiling smile.

"I come bearing gifts," he said.

"What kind of gifts?" she asked, crossing her arms, trying to decide what to do. Let him in? Or shut the door?

"Dinner, with all the fixings," he said. "All your favorites."

"Southern-fried chicken, potatoes and giblet gravy?"

"Or a variation thereof."

Molly threw open the screen door. "Come on in."

Jordan chuckled. "You always could be bought with food."

"If you plan on staying more than five minutes," she warned, "then I suggest you start cooking."

His grin grew broader. Molly followed him into the kitchen and quickly discovered he'd brought far more groceries than were necessary for a single meal. He made two additional trips to his car.

"I don't mean to be nosy," he said, placing fresh vegetables in her fridge, "but where'd you get that shirt?"

Molly's eyes grew round with feigned innocence. "This old thing?"

"It looks a lot like one of mine."

She fluttered her long lashes. "Are you suggesting I stole it?"

He turned and faced her, hands on his hips. "I am."

She lowered her gaze demurely. "Did you miss it?"

"No, but I've got to tell you, it never looked that good on me."

Molly laughed and, turning on her heel, left him and resumed her task in the baby's bedroom. She could hear

Jordan working in the kitchen, as he went about preparing their dinner. Not that it would require any great skill. The deli had already roasted the chicken, which he was attempting to pass off as southern fried, and the mashed potatoes and gravy looked suspiciously as if they'd come from a restaurant.

Fifteen minutes later, he joined her, watching her dip the brush in the paint and spread it evenly over the wood. Molly waited for him to say something, but he didn't for the longest time. She paused to glance up at him.

"Is it a good idea for you to be painting in your condition?" he asked.

"It's perfectly safe. This is latex paint, not oil-based. I checked on the internet *and* I asked the doctor." If he was so concerned, she had an extra brush. She waited, but he didn't volunteer and she didn't ask.

"How was your week?" he asked, and the question was full of meaning.

Not sure how to respond, Molly reviewed her options. She could lie and tell him everything was just great, although she'd been restless and miserable. Or she could admit she hadn't slept through a single night because each time she closed her eyes she remembered how good she'd felt in his arms.

"I don't know how to answer that, Jordan," she finally said.

"Did you think about me?"

She dipped the brush in the paint and hesitated. "Yes." Turnabout was fair play. "Did you think about me?"

"Every minute of every day. It took me until this afternoon to work up the courage to come back and try again. I never know what to expect from you."

She couldn't deny what he was saying, but the reverse was also true. "We've both been hurt so badly. Why do we say such terrible things to each other?"

"I don't know, Molly. All I know is that I love you."

Under other circumstances that would've been enough. But she was no longer the only one involved. A new life grew inside her. A new life that couldn't be ignored.

"Say something," Jordan urged, walking toward her.

She hung her head, knowing the instant she mentioned the pregnancy she'd erect a wall between them.

Jordan placed his index finger beneath her chin and raised her head until their eyes met. Then, ever so gently, he lowered his mouth to hers. The kiss was long and sweet.

Jordan kissed her again and reached for the snap of her jeans. "I didn't stop thinking about us, and how badly I want to make love to you every night for the rest of our lives."

"I…I don't know if this is a good idea," she said, making an attempt to offer some resistance, even if it was only token.

"I know what you're thinking," Jordan countered. "You're wondering if all we share is fabulous sex."

Molly's eyes flew open. That wasn't remotely close to what she was thinking.

She pushed herself out of his arms. "You believe all we share is sex?" she repeated, outraged that he'd suggest such a thing. "What about our son, several years of marriage and this pregnancy?" she cried.

Molly didn't give him time to answer. She'd forgotten the paintbrush in her hand, but she remembered it now. Stepping forward, she slapped the paint-soaked bristles across the front of his shirt.

"Here's what I think of that," she said.

Ten

Molly clamped her hand over her mouth, unable to believe she'd actually painted Jordan's shirt. He held up his arms and stared down at his shirtfront with a look of horrified surprise.

"Oh, Jordan, I'm sorry," she muttered, setting the paintbrush aside. She dabbed at him with a rag, but it soon became apparent that her efforts were doing more harm than good.

"You...painted me."

"You deserved it," she said, smothering a laugh. In her opinion, Jordan Larabee should count his blessings. He was lucky she hadn't taken the brush to his face.

"You might apologize yourself," she suggested while he peeled off the shirt, being careful to avoid spreading the wet paint across his arms and chest.

"All right," he agreed, handing her the damaged shirt, "perhaps I was wrong."

"Perhaps?" She put her hand on her hip and glared at him. *"Perhaps?"*

Jordan swallowed visibly, holding back a laugh.

Apologies had never come easily to him, she realized, and he usually disguised them with humor.

"Fine. I was wrong," he muttered, his eyes growing serious, but only for a moment.

She rewarded him with a smile and carried his shirt to the compact washing machine, tucked neatly away in a kitchen closet, with the dryer stacked above.

"Don't worry, it's washable," she told him, setting the dial. At the sound of water filling the machine, she turned to him. True, her reaction to his outrageous suggestion had been instinctive, but it was also funny.

Their eyes met and held.

Having her estranged—and very attractive—husband walking around her home bare-chested offered more of a temptation than Molly was willing to admit.

"Wait here," she said, returning to her bedroom, taking off his old shirt and replacing it with a short-sleeved cotton top. She delivered the shirt to him minutes later, hating to part with it.

"Thanks," he mumbled, pulling it on.

While he was buttoning it up, Molly lowered her eyes. She couldn't look at him and not remember their recent night together. She recalled how she'd felt lying next to him, her ear pressed against his chest. The even, rhythmic beat of his heart had lulled her to sleep, lulled her into believing that there was hope for them, for their wounded marriage.

Molly was well aware of the mistakes she'd made. She regretted them and wanted to right the wrongs she'd done to Jordan, if that was possible. Molly was convinced their relationship would always be strained until Jordan had grieved for Jeffrey properly.

Molly waited until they were seated across the dining table from each other, their plates piled high with the food Jordan had brought.

Molly dipped her fork in the steaming mashed potatoes and gravy. "I'd like us to talk, Jordan. Really talk."

"All right," he agreed, but she heard the hesitation in his voice.

"I love you, and this...this awkwardness between us is hurting us both."

Jordan set his fork on the plate. His eyes shone with tenderness. "I love *you*, Molly, so much. I can't believe I allowed all this time to pass. I should've gone after you the day you moved out. My foolish pride wouldn't let me."

"I should never have left the way I did. Those days after we buried Jeffrey were so bleak. I wasn't myself, and I didn't know if I'd ever be again.

"I felt like I was walking around in a haze. I was insane with grief and couldn't make myself snap out of it. You were right when you said all I did was cry."

She waited a moment, then continued. "I realize now how depressed I was, but I didn't know it then. I don't think even my doctor did. He wanted me to see a counselor, but I couldn't make myself go. That was a mistake."

"I should have helped you."

"You tried," Molly whispered, fighting back tears. "But you couldn't help me." In retrospect, Molly believed she'd probably been close to a breakdown.

They made the pretense of eating, but neither appeared to have much of an appetite. They didn't speak again, each trapped in the memories of those painful months following Jeffrey's death.

Molly finished her dinner first, dumping her leftovers in the compost bin beneath the sink. "Thank you, Jordan, you're a fabulous cook," she said in an effort to cut through the tension.

"Anytime." He smiled, but his eyes were devoid of any real amusement. He stood and carried his plate to the sink, as well.

"Would you like a cup of coffee?" she asked.

"Please."

"Decaf okay?"

He nodded.

Her back was to him as she reached for the canister and scooped the grounds into the paper-lined receptacle. The coffee had dripped into the pot before she broached the subject of their son a second time.

"We need to talk about Jeffrey."

Her words were followed by silence.

"Why?" he finally asked.

"I believe it'll help us." She turned to face Jordan.

He was standing not far from her. Two mugs sat on the kitchen counter where he'd placed them. His hands were clenched at his sides, the knuckles white.

Pretending they were having a normal, everyday conversation, she reached for the mugs and filled them. Jordan took a seat across from her at the table. She sipped her coffee, then slowly brought her gaze to his, waiting for him to respond.

Five minutes passed.

"We had the same problem before," he said, sounding perfectly natural. "Jeffrey is dead—talking about him won't bring him back."

"That's true," she said evenly. Molly wasn't fooled. Jordan's back was ramrod straight, and he held the mug tightly between his hands. She knew the heat from the coffee must be burning his palms, but he seemed unaware of it. "No amount of discussion will resurrect our son," she said, even as the pain sliced open her heart. It still hurt to talk about Jeffrey, especially with Jordan.

"Then why insist on dragging him into our conversation? Into our lives? He's gone, Molly. As painful as that is to accept, he's never coming back."

"Do you think I don't know that?"

"I have no idea anymore."

She needed to tread carefully, Molly realized, otherwise they'd fall into the same trap and their discussion would disintegrate into a bitter shouting match. That had been their pattern almost four years earlier, until they'd blocked each other completely out.

She rested her hand on the bulge created by her baby. As she guessed he would, Jordan followed the movement of her arm. He quickly looked away.

"I'm pregnant with another child," she said softly.

Jordan trained his eyes across the room as if he couldn't bear to be reminded of her pregnancy. "This child has nothing to do with Jeffrey."

"That's where you're wrong. This baby has *everything* to do with Jeffrey. For nearly four years you've tried to pretend our son didn't exist. You don't want to talk about him. You tried to destroy every piece of evidence he lived. It isn't as easy as that, Jordan. Jeffrey was our son and he's indelibly marked our lives, the same way this baby will."

"Listen, Molly, I'm not going to let you force this baby on me," he said, his control snapping. "The pregnancy was a mistake. It should never have happened."

"I refuse to believe that," Molly said as unemotionally as she could, despite her pain and anger. "If it hadn't been for this baby, we'd be divorced by now. This child is a blessing."

The truth hit her then with as much shock as when she'd walked into Jeffrey's bedroom that fateful morning. She raised her eyes to Jordan and stared at him. "Maybe I *am* nothing more to you than a good lay," she choked out. "Maybe there's nothing between us except sex—just like you said."

"No." Jordan's response was immediate and strong. "That's not true. I love you, Molly. I've never been able to stop loving you."

How she managed to hold on to her composure she didn't know. "My baby isn't a mistake, Jordan, not to me."

He didn't say anything.

Her hand trembled as she raised it to her face, to brush away a strand of hair that had fallen over her eye. "I'm hoping we can both be mature enough to accept each other's opinion."

"I didn't mean to hurt you," he said.

She lowered her head and a tear fell onto the table. "I know."

His hand reached for hers. "I'd better go."

Just the way he said it made her suspect he wouldn't

be back anytime soon. Even knowing that, she couldn't bring herself to suggest he stay.

Jordan was about to walk out of her life and she was about to let him. Another tear fell, followed by another and then another.

Jordan got up and made his way out of the room. He paused abruptly in the doorway, his hands knotted at his sides. He stood there for so long that Molly looked up at him. His back was stiff, his shoulders tense.

"Can I come and see you again?"

Tightness gripped her throat and when she spoke her voice squeaked. "All right."

He left then, and Molly wondered if they were simply prolonging the inevitable.

Sometimes loving each other wasn't enough.

Perhaps the kindest thing she could do was cut her losses now and set them both free.

Jordan sat in front of a set of blueprints, drinking a beer. His mind wasn't on his construction company and hadn't been from the moment Molly came back into his life.

He'd left her apartment barely two hours ago and already he was wondering how soon he could manufacture an excuse to see her again.

He'd managed to hold off for a week and it'd nearly killed him to stay away that long. He doubted he'd last another seven-day stretch without seeing her, without holding and kissing her again. He could live without lovemaking, but he couldn't live without her.

Jordan wasn't a man who felt inept around women.

He knew he was reasonably good-looking and that women generally considered him attractive.

It wasn't anything he wanted to brag to Molly about, but he could have found plenty of solace after she'd moved out on him, if he'd wanted.

He hadn't.

That was the crux of the problem. He'd never wanted another woman from the day he'd met Molly Houghton, fresh out of college. He knew the moment they were introduced that this woman with eyes the color of a summer sky would change his life.

For a while he'd convinced himself that he cared for Lesley, and he did, as a friend. But they'd never been lovers, never shared the deep love and intimacy that had been so much a part of his relationship with Molly. He'd attempted to fool himself into thinking he could put his marriage behind him and make a new life. Lesley had fallen in with his scheme, eager to get married. She'd admitted it herself.

Jordan sipped his beer, wrinkled his nose and set the bottle aside. He didn't like beer, had never liked beer. The only reason he kept it on hand was for his project superintendent, Paul Phelps, who sometimes dropped by the house.

Come to think of it, the last time Jordan had indulged in a beer had been when he and Molly had last lived together and had disagreed about something. He emptied the bottle into the sink.

Maybe Molly was right.

She seemed to think that all they needed was for him to feel the pain of losing Jeffrey. Which left him to wonder what he'd been doing for the past four years.

No, Molly was wrong. He *hadn't* denied Jeffrey's existence. He couldn't. True, he'd disposed of Jeffrey's personal things, but he'd done so in an agony of grief, believing it would be easier for them to deal with their son's death if they weren't constantly reminded of what they'd lost. In retrospect he could understand why it had been a mistake. They'd both made blunders in the frantic days after their son's funeral.

For all the unknowns Jordan faced, there were an equal number of facts he did recognize. Molly's pregnancy leaped to mind, bright as the noonday sun, blinding him with the glare of truth.

He'd longed to push all thoughts of this baby from his mind, and to some extent he'd succeeded. But he was well aware that his marriage was doomed if his attitude didn't change, and change fast.

Until tonight, he hadn't seen Molly in a week, and even in that short time he noticed the subtle changes in her body. It was easy to deny the baby when the evidence was quietly hidden from view. But the baby was making itself more and more evident as time progressed. Soon Molly would be wearing maternity clothes, and every time he looked at her he'd be reminded of the child.

He rubbed a hand down his face. Despite what Molly felt, what she wanted, he couldn't force himself to believe this pregnancy was anything but a mistake.

The thought of Molly pregnant depressed him. Needing to escape, Jordan reached for his jacket and left the house. He was in his truck, driving with no destination in mind, before he pulled onto the side of the road and parked. There was no place he could run. No place he could hide.

Gripping the steering wheel, he closed his eyes and desperately sought a solution. He waited several minutes for his breathing to relax and his racing heart to return to its normal pace.

The temptation to turn his back on the whole situation was strong. He could move his company to another city. The Pacific Northwest appealed to him. In a few years he could establish himself in Seattle, or maybe Portland. Molly could continue to live here in Chicago and come visit him on weekends. He'd find someone she trusted to leave the baby with. Molly might object, but—

The sheer idiocy of the idea struck him and he expelled a sigh and restarted the truck. His thoughts as troubled as when he'd left, Jordan returned to the house.

He sat down in front of the television, and it was a long time before he moved. When he did, it was to turn off the set and go to bed, knowing he'd solved nothing.

"Dad," Molly said as he led her by the hand into her childhood room. "What did you do, buy out the store?" Her bed was heaped with every piece of clothing the baby could possibly need, in addition to a car seat, stroller and high chair.

"You said you didn't have anything other than the crib."

"I certainly didn't expect you to go out and buy it."

"Why not? I'm a wealthy old man, and if I can't indulge my grandchild, what's the use of having all this money?"

"Oh, Daddy," she said, throwing her arms around his neck. He, at least, shared her excitement about the baby. It was all becoming so much more real now that she could feel the baby's movements. "Thank you."

"It's my pleasure."

Molly and her father spent the next hour examining each and every item he'd purchased. She held up a newborn-size T-shirt and nearly laughed out loud. "Can you imagine anybody this tiny?"

"That's what I said to the salesclerk."

There were several blankets, all in pastel colors.

"Have you had an ultrasound yet?" her father asked, sounding eager.

"I've had two." Dr. Anderson was being extra cautious with this pregnancy, trying to reassure her as much as possible.

"And?" her father prompted.

"If you're hoping I'll reveal the baby's sex, I can't. I told Dr. Anderson not to tell me. I don't care if the baby's a boy or a girl." She realized that in all this time Jordan hadn't once inquired about the baby's sex, although she'd mentioned the ultrasounds. He didn't want to know—because he wanted nothing to do with their child.

She tried not to think about Jordan in connection with the baby since that resulted in a lengthy bout of unhappiness.

"From that frown, I'd say you're thinking about Jordan," her father said, breaking into her thoughts.

Molly nodded.

"How are things between the two of you?"

"I'm not sure." Rather than raise Ian's hopes for a reconciliation, Molly had decided to play it safe.

"You're seeing him on a regular basis now, aren't you?"

Molly nodded, holding one of the receiving blankets against her before refolding it and placing it inside the protective covering. "At first he made a point of stopping by once a week, but it's more often now."

She wouldn't be surprised if Jordan showed up at her apartment after she got home. She hoped he would because she was going to need help carrying all the things her father had bought into the house.

"Come downstairs and have a cup of tea with me before you drive home," Ian coaxed.

Molly followed him down the stairs. As she did, she could barely see her toes. She wasn't fully six months pregnant and already she was experiencing some of the minor discomforts of the third trimester. Her feet swelled almost every day now and she'd decided to request a schedule change for part-time employment after Thanksgiving.

"You haven't mentioned your friend Dr. Stern lately," her father said casually. "How's he doing?"

"Just great. We had lunch together last week, and he was telling me about a woman he recently met through a colleague of his. They seemed to hit it off and he's taking her to dinner this week." Molly smiled to herself as she recalled their conversation. David had sounded as excited as a teenage boy about to borrow his father's car for the first time. Molly was pleased for him.

David had been a good friend and exactly what she'd needed those first few weeks. They'd had plenty of in-depth discussions since the day they'd bumped into each other at her cousin's wedding. He still called her occasionally, but he no longer had any romantic expectations, which was just as well.

"He's a good man," her father commented, carrying his cup of tea and her glass of milk to the kitchen table. He chuckled softly. "Jordan came to see me, you know."

"No, I didn't."

Her father gave her a sly smile. "He was afraid it was too late and you and David were already in love."

"When was that?"

Ian cocked his head as he mulled over his answer. "I can't precisely remember, but it was a number of weeks back. Don't get me wrong—I think of Jordan as a son— but there are times I'd like to slap that boy silly."

"I'll hold him down for you," Molly volunteered, and Ian chuckled.

"How's he treating you?" her father asked.

"With kid gloves." She didn't want to say too much for fear Ian might decide to take matters into his own hands. Jordan had made progress. Not much, but he was trying. She had to believe that or she wouldn't be able to continue seeing him.

"I love him, Dad."

"I know, sweetheart, and he loves you. Somehow I don't think he even realizes how much." Deep in thought, her father sipped his tea. "Be patient with him, Molly."

"I'm trying, Dad. So is Jordan."

"Good."

Ian helped her load the car, and before she left his house Molly phoned Jordan's home number.

"Hello," he answered gruffly on the second ring.

"Hi," she said. It was the first time she'd called him, preferring to let him set the course of their relationship, at least at this stage. She felt self-conscious now, with her father blatantly listening in, and wished she'd waited to contact Jordan until after she'd arrived home.

"Molly. I came by earlier and you weren't home. And you didn't answer your cell."

"I'm still not home. And I turned my cell off." So she'd guessed right. Jordan had sought her out. He'd taken her to a movie on Saturday and brought Chinese takeout when he stopped by the house Sunday afternoon. Monday he was going out of town for a brief business trip, and he told her not to expect to hear from him.

"According to call display, you're at your dad's."

"Yeah. Listen, he went on a shopping spree and I'm going to need some help unloading my car. Can I bribe you with the offer of dinner?"

"I'll be there in five minutes."

"Jordan, your house is a good ten minutes from mine, and that's in light traffic."

"I know that. I intend to speed. I've missed you. In fact, I think we should give serious consideration to moving in together. This going back and forth is ridiculous."

Molly's heart cheered at the news, but she didn't say anything one way or the other. It was too soon, but the suggestion was tempting.

Jordan was waiting for her in front of her duplex

when she drove up. She'd barely had time to put the car in Park when he opened the driver's door and all but lifted her out of the car.

Not giving her time to protest, he hauled her into his arms and kissed her as if they'd been apart for months instead of days. When he'd finished Molly clung breathlessly to him.

Jordan buried his face in her neck. "I don't think it's a good idea for you to look at me like that."

"Like what?"

"Like you can hardly wait for me to take you to bed."

Molly blushed profusely, because that was exactly the way she felt. They hadn't made love in weeks, not since the night they'd spent together. The night they'd argued. . . .

The subject had been on both their minds since then. Molly couldn't have Jordan touch her and not want him to continue. She was certain he felt the same physical pull she did.

The lovemaking had always been good between them, and Molly knew it could easily become addictive, again.

Reluctantly she stepped out of his arms. "I'll unlock the door," she said, hurrying away from him.

Jordan opened the back door of her car and piled his arms full of sacks. "What is all this stuff?" he asked, following her up the brick walkway that led to her half of the duplex. "Why did he buy so much?"

Molly didn't answer right away and entered the apartment, turning on light switches as she went. She paused in the baby's bedroom. She'd decorated it with love and care, eager for his or her arrival.

"Dad's looking forward to being a grandfather again" was the only explanation she gave.

Jordan stood in the nursery doorway, his arms loaded down. For a long moment he didn't step beyond the threshold. Molly turned and waited, her heart pounding, echoing in her ears. After what seemed like an eternity, he came into the room and dropped the packages in the crib, then hurried back out.

Together they must have made five more trips.

"It looks like he bought out the store," Jordan complained as he brought in the box that contained the high chair.

"I said the same thing." Molly laughed. She was hoping Jordan would agree to assemble the chair for her, but she'd suggest it later.

"Like I told you, Dad's getting excited." So was she, but she found no such enthusiasm in her husband.

Jordan nodded, and decisively closed the door to the nursery.

Discouraged, Molly went into the kitchen. She didn't want to argue, not tonight. She was tired and she'd missed him.

"Do you need help with dinner?" he asked.

Molly shook her head. Hoping inspiration would strike as to what she'd make for dinner, she opened the refrigerator and gazed inside.

"I meant what I said earlier," Jordan said. His arms came around her from behind. "It's crazy for us to live apart when we're husband and wife. I want you in my home and in my bed. I love you, Molly, and you love me."

"I...don't think it's a good idea. Not yet."

Jordan turned her around and kissed her, backing her against the refrigerator door.

"I...was going to cook dinner."

"Later," he said between kisses.

Molly was having trouble keeping a clear head. When she found the strength, she pulled her mouth from his. "You must be starved by now," she gasped.

Jordan directed her lips back to his. "You haven't got a clue how hungry I am." He slipped his arms around her waist, or what remained of her waist, and started to slide them up.

She knew what he intended to do, and she was intent on letting him, when the baby kicked hard. Jordan obviously felt it, too.

He went still and then expelled his breath loudly. His head fell forward until he'd braced his forehead against her shoulder.

"Jeffrey used to do that, too, remember?" It was risky mentioning their son.

Jordan nodded. Moving away from her, he managed to offer her a shaky smile.

"What was that you were saying about dinner?"

Eleven

Dipping the crisp dill pickle into the butter-brickle ice cream, Molly swirled it around and brought the coated pickle to her mouth. After she sucked off the ice cream, she repeated the process. Pregnant women craving pickles and ice cream—it might be a cliché, but like most clichés it had some basis in truth.

Wearing her robe and black silk pajamas, she stood in the kitchen, depressed and miserable. She hadn't heard from Jordan in three days. Three of the longest days of her life.

He'd helped her unload her car and stayed for dinner, but quickly made an excuse to leave immediately afterward. She hadn't seen him since. Hadn't received so much as a phone call.

Something had been bothering him from the moment he'd held her and felt the baby kick. He'd tried to hide his distress, but Molly knew. Until that evening, he'd ignored the fact that she was pregnant. He couldn't do that anymore. Not with the evidence so…evident.

Molly patted her swollen abdomen. The time had

come for Jordan to make his decision about her and the baby. Perhaps that was what had kept him away.

The countdown had started for them and their marriage. Jordan had to decide what he wanted. It was either love and accept this child or—God, please, no— go through with the divorce.

Glancing at the phone, Molly wavered as she thought about calling him herself. She didn't want to lose Jordan, and she refused to give up without making one last effort.

Swallowing her pride was difficult, but too much was at stake to let her ego stand in the way. If she lost Jordan, she didn't want to look back and wish she'd made one simple phone call.

Her hand tightened around the receiver as she punched in his number.

Jordan answered almost immediately as if he'd been sitting next to the phone, anticipating her call.

"Hello," she said softly.

"Molly." He seemed surprised to hear from her, but the inflection in his voice told her he was pleased.

"I hadn't heard from you in a few days," she said.

"I've been busy."

"I thought that must be it."

He hesitated as though he planned to say more, then changed his mind.

"How are you?" she asked when there didn't seem anything else to say.

"Fine. You?"

Molly decided to plunge right in. "The baby and I are doing great."

"I'm glad to hear that."

"I've gotten everything put away in the nursery now. It's organized and ready for when I come home from the hospital." *Enough,* she told herself. She hadn't meant to shove the subject down his throat.

"So you've been busy, too."

"Yeah," she said. Closing her eyes, she leaned her shoulder against the wall. "I miss you, Jordan."

He expelled his breath in a lengthy sigh. "I miss you, too."

"Come and see me," she whispered, closing her eyes. She needed him with her, yearned for the feel of his arms around her.

"You want me to drive over now?" He sounded reluctant, and she decided he needed a bit of incentive.

"I'm wearing my baby-doll pajamas." At one time the silky black outfit had been Jordan's favorite. It seemed they made love whenever she wore them. She'd put them on that evening, wanting to feel close to him, to remember that love.

He hesitated. "Molly, I don't think my coming over is such a good idea."

Her eyes flew open with hurt and disappointment. "Why not?"

It took him a long time to respond. "If I do, we're going to end up making love."

The time to be coy had passed and Molly smiled softly to herself. "I know."

"You're sure about this?" His voice trembled slightly.

"I'm sure I love you. Is that answer enough?"

Her words seemed to convince him. "I'll be there before you know it."

Molly barely had time to put away the pickles and

the ice cream when the doorbell chimed. She hurried to the front door, checked to be sure it was Jordan and then, hands trembling with eagerness, let him in.

"Hello," she said, smiling up at him. "You got here fast."

"Any man would with the invitation you just offered."

She laughed and lowered her gaze. "I suppose you're right." She was hoping he'd take her in his arms, kiss her and then carry her into the bedroom and make love to her. His lack of response did little for her self-confidence.

"You've got something on your chin," he said, rubbing his thumb over the offending spot. He frowned. "What is that?"

"Ice cream... I was eating it with a pickle and I guess it was messier than I realized." She glanced down at her top and found a couple of spots where the ice cream had dripped.

"How do you eat ice cream with a pickle?" Jordan asked, as if he'd come here specifically for a demonstration.

"I'll show you." She walked back into the kitchen, removed both containers from the refrigerator and scooped up a dollop of ice cream on the end of a pickle. "You need to soften the ice cream first, but once you do that it works great. Do you want to give it a try?"

"Why not?" he asked, his eyes smiling.

If she didn't know better, Molly would think he was stalling for time. Her choice of dessert had never particularly interested him before.

She swirled the pickle around the edge of the ice-cream container and fed it to Jordan. His brows arched upward with surprise. "Hey, it isn't bad. This isn't butter brickle, is it? You hate butter brickle."

"I used to. About a week ago I got this craving for it. I've always heard about pregnant woman getting cravings, but this is the first time it's happened to me."

Jordan looked down at her protruding stomach. Feeling self-conscious, Molly tugged the silk robe closed and tied the loop around what had once been her trim waist.

"It wasn't your work that kept you away for the past three days, was it, Jordan?" she asked softly.

"No."

At least he was honest about it.

"I've been doing some thinking," he admitted.

"And?" she prompted when he didn't immediately continue, eager to hear if he'd found any solutions.

"Would you mind if we sat down?" he asked, nodding at her sofa.

"Of course not." She followed him into the other room, and they sat together. Curling her feet beneath her, she leaned against him and smiled when he raised his arm and placed it lovingly around her shoulders. Molly sighed at the comfort she felt in his embrace.

He kissed her hair. "I've missed you," he murmured.

"Why did you stay away?" The last time they'd met, he'd asked her to move back into the house; now she had to call and almost plead to see him.

"I can't think when we're together," he said, then added, "I needed time to give some thought to us—and the baby."

"I assumed as much. Did you come up with any solutions?"

"No."

"I haven't, either." She slid her arms around his neck, bringing her lips to the hollow of his throat, kissing him there.

"Molly." Her name was more like a whispered plea.

"Hmm?"

"This isn't going to solve anything," Jordan whispered huskily.

"I'm tired of looking for solutions. I want to make love." She seldom played the role of aggressor, but when she had in the past, Jordan had enjoyed it as much as she did.

Kissing him in the ways she knew he loved, she crawled onto his lap. She freed his tie, then pulled it loose and tossed it aside. Next she unfastened his shirt buttons. The entire procedure had been accomplished with her mouth on his.

Jordan stretched out an arm for the lamp and fumbled until he found the switch. Shadows filled the room and the only sound that could be heard was the mingling of their sighs and moans.

It was while she was on her husband's lap, kissing him and removing his clothes, that their baby decided to make his presence known. The first fluttering movement they both ignored, but that quickly became impossible as he kicked against Jordan's chest.

Smiling, Molly eased her mouth from Jordan's. "Isn't he strong?" she said proudly. "Or she, of course."

Jordan closed his eyes and rested his head against the sofa.

Molly reached for his hand and pressed it against her stomach. He didn't offer any resistance, which encouraged her. Gradually he opened his eyes and straightened.

"You're going to love him, Jordan," she said, wanting to reassure him. "You won't be able to stop yourself."

Again he didn't respond.

"I love you," she whispered, speaking to both father and child.

Jordan slid her carefully off his lap, stood and paced the room. His steps grew quick, his distress more obvious with every stride. "This isn't going to work."

"What isn't?" she asked, her gaze following him as he moved from one end of the room to the other. Turn, pace, turn, until it was all she could do not to yell at him to stop.

He paused and looked at her in the dim light. "I can't make love to you."

Molly settled back in her seat and wrapped her dignity around her. "Why not?"

"I don't mean to hurt you, Molly." He avoided looking at her as he repeatedly rubbed the back of his neck. Much to her irritation, he resumed his incessant walking.

"Tell me," she insisted. Any other woman might have left it at that, saved herself the humiliation, but she had to know.

"This embarrasses me. It happened the other night, too," he said, as if making a confession. "I can't look at you and not want to make love, but the minute I feel the baby move, my desire is gone. It's the same way now. I love you, Molly, but right now I'm physically incapable of making love to you."

Molly wasn't sure what she'd expected, but not this. He was telling her he found her unattractive. His words hurt her badly.

Silence fell as he waited for her to respond.

It took Molly several minutes to recover. "Well, that answers that, doesn't it," she said, hoping to hide the extent of her pain. "I don't have a single argument, do I? My figure certainly isn't what it used to be."

Climbing off the sofa, she reached for the lamp and turned the switch. Light spilled into the room. Molly would've given anything not to be wearing these sexy pajamas. She felt like an elephant who'd, by some miracle, managed to stuff itself into a bikini.

Gripping the front of her robe, she walked over to the door and opened it for Jordan. "I'm sorry you have to leave so soon."

"Molly, don't send me away. Not like this."

In her opinion, she should be awarded a medal for keeping the tears at bay. Holding her chin high, she slowly turned her head so their eyes met. "Please, Jordan, just go."

"The problem's mine, Molly, not yours. You're beautiful. I'm the one who needs help. Let's talk about this."

"Everything's been said a thousand times," she whispered. "I believe you put it best. This isn't going to work."

Jordan rammed his fingers through his hair. "I shouldn't have said anything, but sooner or later you were going to suspect something was wrong."

Molly could sympathize with him. He'd backed himself into a corner, but that didn't make any difference. It would always be like this with him. Jordan wasn't going to change and she was living in a dream world if she believed otherwise.

"You once suggested that the only good thing between us was the sex... I was quick to take offense," she reminded him, "but now I realize you could be right." This last part was the most painful. "Now that I don't... arouse you, there really isn't anything left, is there?"

"Molly, that's not true!"

"Maybe," she said. "But then again, maybe not." All she could be sure of at the moment was that she wanted Jordan out of her home. If he didn't leave soon, she'd be in serious danger of an emotional breakdown. Her pride was already in shreds, and she didn't relish the thought of humiliating herself further.

"You'll give me a call?" he asked when he realized she wasn't going to change her mind. She stood holding open the front door, waiting for him to vacate her apartment.

"I don't know," she whispered, although she doubted she would. It probably would've been best to tell him that, but she didn't want to invite additional arguments.

His eyes connected with hers before he left. In his she saw regret and pain and several other emotions. She forced herself to stare straight through him, hoping he'd read her lack of emotion as blatant indifference.

Of one thing Molly was certain—she'd never be indifferent to Jordan Larabee.

A week passed, and Jordan still couldn't decide what he expected from Molly. He'd insulted her, wounded her pride and just about ruined whatever hope there was of salvaging their marriage. Whoever said honesty was the best policy had never been married, he thought ruefully.

He'd phoned her countless times in an effort to undo the damage, but Molly screened her calls. He'd stopped by her apartment so often the neighbors had started waving when they saw him. But he hadn't found the courage to confront her, especially when she'd made it plain she didn't want to see him again.

Nothing short of a blowup with Molly would have led him to visit his father-in-law. Ian Houghton would delight in knowing Jordan had made a fool of himself for the umpteenth time. But then Jordan should be accustomed to Ian's attitude by now.

His father-in-law was looking pleased with himself when Jordan joined him in his den, with the book-lined walls behind him. The scent of lemon oil permeated the air.

"Jordan, good to see you," Ian said as he stood to greet him. The two men exchanged handshakes.

"You, too." Jordan sat down and rested his ankle on his knee, hoping to give a carefree, relaxed impression.

"My guess is that you're here to inquire about my daughter?"

"What makes you think this isn't a friendly social call?" Jordan asked.

Ian laughed. "I know you too well for that. You don't make social calls. If you've taken the time and the trouble to come and see me, it has something to do with Molly."

"Don't be so sure. I might be here about money." He'd come to Ian to discuss financing often enough when he was starting his construction company. The older man's assistance had been invaluable. He and Molly had spent many an evening with Ian going over the details of a construction project. Molly had never complained and often curled up with a book in this very room while the two men talked business. Jordan missed those times and the closeness the three of them shared.

Jordan met Ian's look. With a knowing smile, his father-in-law said, "You've got more money than you know what to do with these days. It's not money you're after, it's Molly."

Obviously, there was no point in being subtle. "All right," he said decisively, "if you must know, this does have to do with Molly. We had a falling-out."

"About what?"

He felt foolish enough already without explaining the details. "I insulted her."

Ian relaxed in his leather chair and smiled broadly. "Hell hath no fury like a woman scorned."

"If I wanted to listen to proverbs I'd be reading *Poor Richard's Almanac*. I'm here for advice. I don't want to lose Molly. I love her."

"And the baby?"

Jordan had wondered how long it would take Ian to bring up the pregnancy. "I'll grow accustomed to the baby."

Ian's eyes were dark and serious. The smile Jordan had found irritating seconds earlier disappeared. "My daughter isn't having just any baby, Jordan Larabee, she's having yours. It's time you accepted some responsibility."

Jordan stiffened, disliking Ian's tone. "I told Molly

from the first that I'd assume complete financial responsibility for the child."

Ian's eyes narrowed as he directed the full force of
his outrage on him. "I'm talking about *emotional* responsibility. Do you think you're the only one who's
ever lost a baby? Enough is enough. No wonder Molly's
having medical problems."

Immediate fear stabbed him. "Molly's having problems?"

"She hasn't been at work all week."

"What's wrong?" Jordan was on his feet by now.

"Don't worry, it's under control."

"What's wrong with her?" Jordan demanded, more
strenuously this time.

"You'll have to ask my daughter. She tends to get
feisty when I do her talking for her," Ian said nonchalantly. Jordan swore the old man was hiding a smile.

Jordan paced to the other side of the room. "She
doesn't answer my calls."

"You might want to visit her."

"Has she been in to see Doug Anderson?" Jordan
demanded. The physician was a friend of his, although
they hadn't seen each other in several years—not since
Jeffrey died. Jordan's company had been involved in
constructing the medical building where Anderson
practiced.

"I don't know, Jordan. You'll have to ask Molly that
yourself."

Jordan glared at his father-in-law and his blatant
effort to get him to visit Molly.

"She only tells me a little about what's going on in
her life," Ian said. "My guess is that she has seen the

doctor. I'm sure she's got regular appointments. I know she wasn't feeling well, but…"

Jordan was tempted to drive over to her apartment and find out for himself exactly what was wrong. He would have if he believed it'd do any good. The minute Molly knew it was him, she simply wouldn't open the door. She had a stubborn streak that rivaled his own.

Before he jumped to conclusions, Jordan decided to call Doug Anderson himself and find out what he could. He left Ian, and sat in his truck and called Doug on his cell.

"Jordan Larabee. Hey, how long has it been?"

"Too long," Jordan answered. "I understand Molly's still your patient?"

"Yes. I know this bout of flu has been difficult for her, but it's nothing to worry about. She just needs to get lots of rest."

"You're *sure* it's just the flu?"

"Fairly certain. I've treated a number of patients in the past couple of weeks with the same symptoms."

"Do you want to get together for a drink?" Jordan asked. "I know it's short notice, but there are a few things I'd like to talk over with you."

"Sounds like a good idea. Why don't you come by the house. Mary would love to see you. In fact, she's been wanting to ask you about a contractor. We're planning to have an extension built."

Forty minutes later Jordan pulled up in front of Doug and Mary Anderson's three-story brick home.

Mary answered the door and greeted him like a long-lost relative. Jordan regretted having allowed their friendship to lapse. He'd always liked Doug and

Mary and couldn't remember the last time he'd talked to them. After Jeffrey died, and Molly moved out, there hadn't been room in his life for anything other than work.

Mary insisted on giving him dinner. Jordan had forgotten how good it was to sit down at a table with friends. The Andersons' three boys were all teenagers. They were tall, well-mannered, good-looking kids, busy with their own lives. Judd at eighteen was the oldest. After greeting Jordan, he grabbed a chicken leg off the platter in the kitchen, kissed his mother's cheek and left, claiming he needed to go to Angela's to study for an important test. Peter and Adam had eaten earlier, following football practice, and after shaking hands with Jordan, disappeared.

Jordan found it almost painful to watch Doug and Mary with their sons. This was what it would've been like for him and Molly had Jeffrey lived, he mused. He could picture his son as a teenager, interrupting Molly's scolding with a peck on the cheek and a promise to be home before ten. He could see himself handing his son the car keys so he could study for a test with a girl named Angela.

After dinner, Doug and Jordan had coffee in front of the fireplace. "I'm worried about Molly," Jordan admitted. "We haven't been on the best of terms lately." He hesitated, then added, "Mostly that's my fault. I've had a hard time with this pregnancy."

"It's difficult, I know."

Jordan was sure Doug had plenty of experience with couples who'd lost infants to SIDS, but only someone who'd lived through this agony could fully appreciate it.

From what Molly had told him, Doug was closely monitoring her pregnancy. He was pleased that his friend had taken special care with her, although he knew Doug would have done so with any patient who'd lost a child.

"I remember how I felt when we learned Mary was pregnant after we lost Joy."

Jordan's head snapped up. "Joy?"

"We lost a daughter to SIDS nearly twenty-three years ago. I thought you knew."

Jordan shook his head. Perhaps he did remember Doug and Mary saying something to him at Jeffrey's funeral, but he'd been in so much confusion and pain it hadn't registered.

"She was only three months old," Doug said. "It nearly destroyed Mary. Trust me, Jordan, I've walked in your shoes. In some ways I've been in Molly's, too. Because we're both in the medical profession, I know the torment of doubts she suffered. I felt there must've been something I should have done, should have known. All those years in medical school, and I couldn't save my own child."

"How long did it take to get over it?"

Doug sipped his coffee. "I can't really answer that— not in terms of months or years, at any rate. We both got on with our lives, but we waited nearly five years before we decided to have Judd. In many ways it took me longer to come to terms with Joy's death than it did Mary."

"Molly seems to have dealt with it better than me." This was the first time Jordan had openly discussed Jeffrey with anyone other than his wife.

"I think it takes a man longer to process grief," Doug said. "We aren't as likely to express our emotions. I envied Mary her ability to cry."

"How did you feel when you learned Mary was pregnant with Judd?" Jordan leaned forward in his chair, anxious to hear the answer.

"Terrified. I'm not going to tell you it was easy for either one of us, but it was time to move forward and we both knew it. Molly's going to do just fine with this child, and so are you."

Jordan wished he was as confident as his friend.

"By the way," Doug said casually, "we've done two ultrasounds of the baby. Molly's been adamant about not wanting me to let her know the baby's sex, but if you're curious I'll tell you."

Jordan felt the weight of indecision; he couldn't help wanting to know, but at the same time he wasn't sure. "All right," he found himself agreeing, "tell me."

"You're going to have a little girl."

A daughter.

For some reason, certainly not one he could explain or understand, Jordan had assumed their baby was a boy. Molly had always referred to their baby as "him," and he'd believed she'd said so knowingly.

"Congratulations," Doug said, sending him a wide grin.

"Thanks," Jordan mumbled. His hand was shaking as he set down the coffee mug.

A daughter.

One who resembled Molly, with bright blue eyes and pretty blond hair… He felt a powerful surge of emotion at the thought.

"Have you decided on names yet?" Mary asked, joining them.

Jordan looked at his friend's wife. "No," he whispered.

He stood and set the coffee aside.

"A daughter," he repeated. He kissed Mary on the cheek, shook hands with Doug and let himself out the front door.

Jordan walked out to his truck, still in a daze. He'd just made one of the most profound discoveries of his life.

He wanted this child.

He felt like the biggest fool who'd ever walked the face of the earth. He'd behaved like a jerk for months. It was a miracle Molly had put up with his stupidity this long. He didn't deserve her, but he vowed he'd find a way to make it up to her.

Jordan resisted the urge to drive directly over to Molly's apartment. He'd give her time to recover from the flu, and then they could sit down and talk about this.

When he walked into the house, he saw that he had a voice mail message. Praying that Molly had finally returned his calls, he listened to it immediately.

"Jordan, this is Michael Rife. Your office gave me your home number. I hope you don't mind me calling you there, but this is important.

"It's after six now, and I'll be leaving soon. I got a call from Molly. She asked me to petition the court for a date so the final divorce papers could be filed.

"I thought you'd decided to wait until after the baby

was born. I'm confused, but Molly was adamant that she wanted to go through with the divorce. Give me a call first thing in the morning. Thanks."

Twelve

Molly had endured a full week of the worst flu she'd ever had. The only time she'd been out of the house in five days was to see Dr. Anderson, who'd offered her sympathy and advice.

The flu wasn't the only thing affecting Molly's spirits. She'd cried frequently since her last confrontation with Jordan. Her frustration with him was stronger and more debilitating than any virus. Every time she thought about him, she suffered an emotional relapse.

Their marriage was over.

The time had come for Molly to stop kidding herself. For days she'd lain on the sofa and stared into space, reliving the past six months with its tumultuous ups and downs.

She'd almost believed it was possible for them. She now recognized that it wasn't, and the bitter disappointment was difficult to swallow. She knew they'd both wanted to salvage their relationship.

She'd forced herself to call Michael Rife, although she'd barely been able to speak. Her voice trembled when she told him the reason for her call. Several times she'd had to stop and compose herself before continuing.

Michael had tried to persuade her to wait, but she'd insisted. She wanted the divorce over with before she had the baby. That was important to her. Jordan had repeatedly told her he intended to distance himself emotionally from their baby. It would be better, she decided, to completely isolate their child from Jordan. She'd seen no evidence that his attitude would change. The baby deserved better. For that matter, so did she.

Having made the phone call, she was left to face the doubts and regrets. She refused to cry, though; she'd shed all the tears she cared to in the past few months.

Now was the time to heal. The time to rejoice in the birth of her son or daughter. The time to pick up the pieces of her life and move forward.

The phone rang and she tensed. Over the past week Jordan had called repeatedly, but she wasn't emotionally or physically ready for another confrontation with him. Voice mail had collected his messages. As they accumulated, she heard his anger and frustration, followed by his insistence that she return his calls. Then he'd stopped phoning.

Molly got up to check call display and saw that it was Michael Rife, the attorney.

She listened to what he'd said. "Molly, I wasn't able to get hold of Jordan, but I left him a message. I'll get back to you as soon as I've talked to him. I don't expect that to take long. If you have any questions, give me a call here at the office. And, Molly—" he paused "—if you want to change your mind, all you need to do is say so. I'll wait for your instructions."

So, according to Michael, Jordan knew that she intended to go through with the divorce. Or he would shortly. She wondered how he'd react....

Molly spent the night on her sofa. The effort of making her way down the hall to her bedroom was more than she could muster.

She woke around six and felt wretched, but she wasn't sure if her condition was physical or emotional. Probably both.

She showered, washed her hair and changed clothes. By the time she finished, she was so weak she needed to sit down. Her knees shook and she pushed the wet hair away from her face, hoping she could resume her everyday life soon.

Around eight, she managed to eat a piece of dry toast and drink a glass of water. She propped herself against the end of the sofa with a couple of pillows and picked up the remote control. She settled in to watch a morning talk show, something she virtually never did.

Just when she was comfortable, the doorbell chimed. A glance at the wall clock told her it was barely nine o'clock. Seconds later, the doorbell rang again. And again.

It had to be Jordan. No one else rang a doorbell quite like he did. He was always in a hurry, always impatient.

"I know you're in there," Jordan shouted. "Open up!"

"Go away," she called back. "I've got the flu."

"I'm not leaving until I've talked to you, so either let me in or call the police right now, because I'll bash in your door if that's what it takes."

Groaning, Molly threw aside the comforter and stumbled toward the door. Her back ached and she wasn't up to a showdown with Jordan, but she had few options. It was face him now or do it later. She preferred to have this scene over with as quickly as possible.

She unlocked the door. "It'd serve you right if I did call the police," she muttered.

He marched in and was halfway into the living room, when he whirled around. His teeth were clenched, his eyes as angry as she'd ever seen them.

"I assume you've talked to Michael," she said.

"Not yet. I decided to have this out with you first."

"I suggest you talk to him."

The anger left his eyes as if he were seeing her, really seeing her, for the first time. His fists relaxed and fell slack at his sides.

Molly knew she looked dreadful. It wasn't as if she'd spent the past week at a spa, receiving beauty treatments.

"How are you?" he asked quietly.

She closed the front door and leaned against it. "I've never felt better," she lied.

"Sit down," he urged. He moved to help her back to the sofa, but she pulled away from him, avoiding his touch.

"You wanted to say something," she pressed, willing him to get this over with.

He waited until she'd seated herself and pulled the comforter over her legs. For having threatened to break down her door, now he didn't seem to know what to say.

"I had a long talk with Doug Anderson last night," he finally told her.

Of all the things he might have said, this wasn't one she'd expected. She didn't respond, just waited for him to continue.

"They had me over for dinner," he elaborated. "I saw their three boys."

Molly looked up at him, wondering exactly where this conversation was going.

He thrust his hands inside his pockets. "I talked to your father, too."

"You certainly made the social rounds."

He smiled briefly at that.

"Doug and Mary lost a daughter to SIDS over twenty years ago," Jordan said next, his voice low. "I wasn't sure if you knew that or not."

"We've talked about it several times." She didn't dare look at him. She didn't want to be reminded how much the divorce was going to hurt. Even one glance was too risky.

"Michael's message was waiting for me when I got home."

Her gaze was level with his hands. She watched, mesmerized by their expressive movements. First he clenched them, then seemed to force himself to relax.

"I can't think of a single reason why you should delay the divorce," he surprised her by saying. "I've given you plenty of cause to wish you'd never met me."

Loving him the way she did, Molly couldn't make herself regret their years together. If for nothing more than Jeffrey and the life she carried within her now, Molly would always be grateful.

"Jordan, please, I don't have the strength to argue

with you. I've made up my mind. Nothing you say now is going to change it."

"I love you."

She closed her eyes. "Love isn't always enough. Please don't make this more difficult than it already is."

"You're sure this is what you want?"

Molly closed her eyes and nodded.

"Even though I don't have the right, I'm going to ask one small favor of you. Wait." She started to object, but he stopped her. "All I'm asking for is a few months."

"No," she said immediately, "I can't...."

"Until the baby's born."

For her own peace of mind, Molly didn't know if she could.

"Please," he added.

She'd expected his anger, but not this. He seemed almost humble. She couldn't remember Jordan asking anything of her before, certainly nothing like this.

The hands that had clenched and unclenched moments earlier flexed, then turned palms up as if to silently plead his case.

"On one condition," she said when she found her voice.

"Anything."

"I'll wait, as long as you don't make any attempt to see me again. It's over as of now, Jordan. I won't make it legal until after the baby's born, because that seems to be important to you, but that's all I'm willing to concede."

"But, Molly, I—"

"I'm serious, Jordan. Either you agree or I'll go through with the divorce as soon as Michael can arrange a court date. If you break your word, I'll contact him immediately."

Hours seemed to pass before Jordan responded. "If that's your one request, then I don't have any choice but to agree."

Molly was feeling nauseated. "I think it would be a good idea if you left now."

"Can I get you anything?"

"No." She wished he'd hurry. "Please just go."

He turned and walked toward the door, then turned back. "Do you have any names picked out for the baby?"

"Yes." But she didn't understand his sudden curiosity.

"Would you mind telling me?"

"I...I wanted Richard for a boy. I'd like to name him after Dr. Morton. He's back in Africa, by the way. He's the kindest, most gentle man I've ever known and he'd be thrilled to learn I'd named *my* baby after him." She made sure he heard the inflection.

As far as Molly was concerned, he'd relinquished all rights to their child. The baby was hers and hers alone.

"What about a girl's name?" Jordan asked.

"Bethany Marie." If Jeffrey had been a girl, they'd planned on the name Lori Jo. They'd studied baby name books for weeks before arriving at their final decisions.

Jordan smiled. "That has a nice sound to it. Are you naming her after anyone in particular?"

"Marie was my mother's middle name, and I've always liked the name Bethany."

"I do, too," he said and opened the door.

It seemed to take him a long time to leave. The

minute she could, Molly threw aside the covering and rushed into the bathroom. She didn't know if she'd taken a turn for the worse or if this bout of vomiting was the result of yet another nerve-wracking encounter with Jordan.

A month passed and Jordan didn't hear a word from Molly. Not that he'd thought he would. But he'd hoped.

Thanks to Ian and Doug, he received regular updates on Molly's condition and savored each report about Bethany Marie's progress. He drilled Doug with so many questions that his friend had eventually handed him a book on what to expect during the last trimester of pregnancy. Jordan read it twice.

Thanksgiving was lonely. He flew to Arizona and spent the holiday with his mother, who'd retired there several years earlier. She was pleased to have him there. He hadn't been to visit her since Jeffrey's birth. His father had died years earlier while he was in high school, and his sister lived in Oregon.

When he arrived at his mother's home, one of the first things Jordan saw was a framed photograph of Jeffrey on the foyer wall. It disconcerted him so badly that he had to ask her to put it away.

He felt bad about that later, when he returned to Chicago, to an empty house and an emptier life. Molly and Bethany had been constantly on his mind. He wondered how she'd spent the holiday and was tempted to call Ian and ask.

He rummaged around the house and resisted the urge to phone, knowing he'd made a regular pest of himself recently. He was tired from the weekend travel and the craziness that was involved in flying during a major holiday.

He listened to his messages and checked his email. Nothing important. No one he needed to get back to. No word from Molly.

Walking up the stairs, Jordan passed the room that had once been Jeffrey's nursery. He hadn't gone in there in more than four years. Not since the day he'd taken away everything that had been their son's. Not since he'd attempted to wipe out every piece of evidence that Jeffrey had ever lived.

The fight he'd had with Molly that terrible afternoon would forever stay with him. And with her, too, he guessed. He'd carried down the baby furniture and she'd come crying after him, begging him not to give Jeffrey's things away. She was rooting through the boxes, sobbing hysterically, when the truck driver arrived for the charity pickup.

The man had sat down on the steps with Molly and talked to her gently. Jordan had stood in the doorway demanding that the agency remove everything. It appalled him now that a stranger had been more sensitive to Molly's pain than he'd been.

Some force he couldn't name directed him to Jeffrey's room. He opened the door and walked inside. The floor was bare. As were the walls. The one thing that remained was Molly's rocking chair.

He'd forgotten about that. She used to nurse Jeffrey by the fireplace in their bedroom. After his death, she'd moved the chair into his room and sat in there alone for hours on end.

Often he'd come home from work and find her sitting in that chair, staring into space, tears streaking her face. He guessed she'd spent the entire day there.

Stepping into the bedroom, Jordan sat down in the chair. He placed his hands on the wide arms and rocked back and forth. He closed his eyes and recalled Molly holding Jeffrey, talking softly while she rocked. Sometimes she sang to him in a soft voice that vibrated with her love.

It was like a childhood remembrance—something that had happened years and years earlier. A dream from his youth.

Jordan thought again about Doug and Mary Anderson's sons, and how he'd pictured Jeffrey as a young man, had he lived.

"You're going to have a sister," he whispered.

The sound of his own voice shocked him, and he pressed his lips together. It was the loneliness, he decided, that had made him talk to a baby who was long dead.

"I have a younger sister, too," Jordan whispered, then surprised himself by laughing out loud. "She was a pest from the moment she was born. The very bane of my existence until I was a high school senior." He stopped rocking, remembering how fortunate he'd been to have a younger sister who was an "in" for him with the sophomore girls.

Caught up in the memories of his childhood years, Jordan glanced out the window to the manicured grounds of their yard. Perhaps he was simply tired from the trip, he didn't know, but he wanted something to blame for what happened next.

He could see his seven-year-old son running around,

flying a kite. Bethany, barely old enough to stand, was reaching toward the sky, laughing with glee. The vision left him as quickly as it had come.

Was he losing his mind?

He didn't know what was going on, but all at once his chest felt as if he were being shoved against a concrete wall. His heart thudded; he felt every beat as it pounded and pulsed.

Hot, blistering tears filled his eyes.

A man doesn't cry... A man doesn't cry...

Apparently whoever was supposed to listen didn't. Huge sobs racked his shoulders. He hung his head, then covered his face, embarrassed, although no one could see him.

The tears stopped abruptly, replaced by a savage rage. It threatened to consume him, and Jordan realized he'd carried it with him, inside him, for years.

Right or wrong, justified or not, he was furious. Jeffrey was gone and there was no one to blame, no one he could slam up against a wall, no one he could send to jail. So he'd allowed it to weigh down his own life.

He vented his anger now because he hadn't let himself to do it back then. Hadn't let himself grieve the way Molly had. He hadn't supported her desire to see a therapist, to talk about it with a professional.

He was a man. A man didn't reveal his pain. A man didn't cry. A man buried his son and then went on with his life. A man comforted his wife. A man held his family together. That was what Jordan believed a man should do.

Only he was weeping now.

Weeping alone.

SIDS had taken far more than his perfect, innocent son. SIDS had robbed him of his wife and his marriage. In many ways, SIDS had taken a part of his sanity.

Jordan was standing now, fists clenched at his sides, the chair rocking behind him. He didn't remember coming to his feet. Falling back into the rocker, he closed his eyes and waited for his pulse to return to normal. The room was silent, except for the heavy thud of his heart.

Jordan waited for a release, anything that would end his agony, his pain. But he knew that this catharsis had to run its course. He was walking through the valley, and he had to keep walking. It was the only hope he had of reaching the other side.

"I'm pregnant," Amanda squealed when Molly answered the phone a few days after Christmas.

"Congratulations!"

"Oh, Molly, I'm so excited I can hardly stand it."

Molly wasn't emotional these days, not like when she was first pregnant, but she wiped a tear of shared happiness from her eyes. "Does Tommy know?"

"Yes. I just called him at work and you know what he did? Oh, Molly, he's so sweet. He started to cry right there on the phone, with everyone watching. Then I started to cry, too. I can't remember when I've been so happy. Yes, I can…but this time, well, this time it's different."

"When are you due?" Molly asked. She was sitting on the sofa, her swollen feet propped up on the coffee table. She'd quit work the week before and had intended to put away her Christmas decorations, but she hadn't started yet. She'd been too busy with appointments and parties and get-togethers.

"The doctor seemed to think early August. I can't believe I'm going to have to spend the hottest part of the summer pregnant. You'd think we'd know how to plan better, wouldn't you?"

Molly wondered if there was ever an easy time to be pregnant. She had three weeks to go before her due date, and she felt enormous. Ian had been acting like a mother hen, calling her at all times of the day and night. Her father called, but not Jordan. She'd made it plain she didn't want to hear from him, and apparently he'd accepted her decision.

Fool that she was, Molly kept hoping he'd call. He'd sent her a Christmas gift via her father, and it had depressed her so much she'd wept for days afterward. Ian had wanted to call the doctor. He couldn't understand why a pair of black baby-doll pajamas would upset her like that.

She knew Jordan had company for Christmas. His friend, Zane Halquist, the mercenary he'd hired to get her safely out of east Africa, had flown into Chicago, and the two men had spent the holidays together. Molly would've thanked Zane herself, had she known he was in town.

She'd received a long letter from Jordan's mother shortly before Christmas and was surprised to learn he'd spent Thanksgiving in Arizona. Martha Larabee told that Jordan had asked her to put Jeffrey's picture away. Her mother-in-law told her how sorry she was that she and Jordan hadn't been able to work things out. She asked Molly to let her know when the baby was born and had mailed a beautiful hand-knit blanket as a gift.

"I'll save my baby things for you," Molly promised Amanda.

"Thanks. We have plenty of things from Christi, too."

Molly noted how much easier it was for Amanda to talk about the daughter she'd lost to SIDS. It was easier for her to discuss Jeffrey, too. Together they'd found a support group for parents whose children had died, and it had helped them both tremendously. Each time she attended a meeting, she thought of Jordan. The process of openly acknowledging her son's death was painful, but she came away stronger and more confident.

"I haven't told my dad yet, so I'd better get off the phone," Amanda said. "I need to call him."

"Of course. Give him my best."

"I will. And thank you, Molly."

"Me? I didn't do anything."

"You've been the best friend I ever had."

"You've been a good friend to me, too."

"Call me when you go into labor," Amanda said.

"It won't be for several weeks."

"But you'll phone me right away?"

"You're second on my list. My sweetheart of a dad insists on being first."

"Are you going to contact Jordan?"

Molly's gaze fell on the baby blanket his mother had sent. Jordan couldn't even look at a framed photograph of Jeffrey. He wouldn't be able to deal with the birth of this child.

"No," she said sadly. "He doesn't want to know."

"You're sure about that?"

"Positive. Now call your father, and give him my love."

Pleased at her friend's news, Molly hung up the phone and walked into the kitchen. She felt good. Although she seemed to require a nap every afternoon, she was full of energy now. After putting away the Christmas decorations, she phoned her father and invited him over for dinner.

Ian arrived promptly at six with a bouquet of flowers and a carton of milk. Molly kissed him on the cheek and led him into the kitchen.

"How are you feeling?" he asked, studying her closely.

"I've never felt better," she said with a smile, taking the casserole out of the oven and carrying it to the table.

"I talked to Jordan today," her father said nonchalantly, smoothing the napkin across his lap.

"Dad, I told you I don't want to discuss Jordan." Molly had given up counting the ways Ian had of introducing her husband into their conversations.

"He's worried about you."

"Mild winter we're having, isn't it?" she said, setting the serving spoon on the steaming ceramic dish. She waddled over to the refrigerator and brought out the salad she'd prepared earlier.

"He calls at least once a day to ask about you."

She noticed that Jordan didn't inquire about the baby. Molly ignored her father and served herself some salad, then passed him the bowl. She set the dressing down with a thud. "I was thinking of planting roses this spring. The same variety Mom loved."

"I was talking about Jordan," Ian returned stubbornly.

"I was talking about roses," Molly said with equal stubbornness.

"He loves you."

"I love that rich deep red you get with some roses."

Ian slammed his fork down. "I don't know what I'm going to do with the pair of you. Jordan's just as bad as you are. Worse. I've told him a dozen times that I refuse to answer his questions. If he wants to find out how you're doing, he can ask you himself."

Molly shrugged, unwilling to comment.

"You know what he does, don't you?" Ian went on. "He phones Doug Anderson right from my home. When he hangs up, he repeats everything to me—as if I need a physician to tell me about my own daughter."

"Dad," Molly said gently, placing her hand on his. "It's over between Jordan and me."

"Fools," he muttered. "The pair of you."

Molly didn't argue. Personally she agreed with him.

It had started out as a perfectly normal January day. Jordan was on the job site talking over a supply problem with Paul Phelps when his pager went off. Absently he reached for it, removing it from his belt, and glanced at the phone number on the miniature screen. His heart froze solid when he recognized the caller's number.

"Jordan." Paul's voice broke into his confusion. "What is it?"

"That's Ian. There's only one reason he'd contact me this time of day."

"Molly's having the baby?"

"That would be my guess." Jordan took off for the construction trailer at a dead run. A hundred times, possibly a thousand, he'd warned his crews to put safety first. At the moment, Jordan didn't care what he tripped over as long as he found out what he needed to know.

He punched in Ian's home number—then he waited. The phone rang five times before his father-in-law deigned to answer.

"Jordan, my boy," he said jovially, "it didn't take you long to get back to me."

"Where's Molly?" he demanded breathlessly.

"Molly? What makes you think this has anything to do with my daughter?" He gave a rather forced laugh.

"Ian, if this is some sort of prank, I don't find it the least bit funny."

Ian's laughter died. "As it happens, you're right. Molly's on her way to the hospital as we speak. She was adamant that you not know, but I decided otherwise. The problem with my daughter is that I've spoiled her. She seems to think I should do everything she asks."

"Ian, is she okay?"

"I assume so. She sounded fine when she called me. A little excited. A little afraid. I'm leaving now, and I've even got cigars to celebrate. You are coming, aren't you?"

Now it was Jordan's turn to laugh. "I wouldn't miss this for the world."

Thirteen

Everything seemed to move in slow motion once Molly arrived at the hospital. The labor room nurse, Barbara, middle-aged and motherly, was gentle and encouraging as she prepared Molly for the baby's birth.

By the time Molly was situated in bed, connected to the fetal heart monitor, she heard some type of commotion at the nurses' station. Her father was there and wanted to see her.

"That's quite the father you have," Barbara reported when she came to check on Molly. "He's demanding to know what's taking so long. He expected his grandchild to be here by now. He's convinced something's gone wrong."

Ian had been away on a business trip when Jeffrey was born and seemed to forget that these things took their own time.

"You'd better talk to him," the nurse suggested.

"By all means," she said, "send him in before he makes a *real* pest of himself." Molly couldn't help smiling. She was sure the last time her father had been anywhere close to a maternity floor was when she herself was born.

At the approach of a contraction, Molly laid her head against the pillow and breathed in deeply. The labor pains were gaining in intensity now, coming every three or four minutes.

Her concentration must have been even more focused on the contraction than she'd realized, because when she opened her eyes she found Jordan standing at her bedside, his face pale with concern.

Molly stared speechlessly up at him. It'd been nearly three months since she'd seen him, and she needed a moment to recover. "How—how'd you get here?"

"I drove," he answered with a smile. "How are you?"

"I'm having a baby."

"So I see."

Self-conscious, she tugged the sheet up to her chin. "How'd you know I was here?"

"Your father called me."

Furious, Molly pinched her lips together, suppressing a tirade. Later she'd talk to Ian and tell him, in no uncertain terms, how displeased she was with his treachery. Her father knew she didn't want to see Jordan again. She couldn't have made her feelings any clearer.

"Where's my father?" she asked, looking away from him.

Jordan chuckled. "Believe it or not, he lit up a cigar and was escorted from the hospital by two orderlies."

"Dad knows better than that."

"He's nervous."

"That's no excuse," she returned primly.

"I agree, and it's not like there aren't No Smoking signs posted all over the place."

Doug Anderson stopped in regularly to see her, telling her she was doing fine and chatting with Jordan in a friendly, relaxed manner.

Another pain came, and Molly closed her eyes at the sudden sharpness.

"What can I do?" Jordan asked, instantly sensing her distress. She shook her head, not wanting to be distracted. Silently she sent loving thoughts to her baby, encouraging him or her through the contraction.

When the pain passed, Molly opened her eyes and discovered that Jordan was holding her hand between both of his. His eyes were warm and loving.

She was tempted to ask him to stay with her, to help her through this birth the way he'd helped her when Jeffrey was born.

"I don't know if you should be here," she said finally, wishing with all her heart that he'd leave now before she broke down and begged him to stay.

"Why not? I was there at the beginning, wasn't I? It only seems fair that I should get to see the result. Besides, there's no place else I'd rather be," he told her. "I love you, Molly, and I love our baby."

Uncertain if she should believe him or not, Molly glanced away. She was about to ask him to leave when another contraction struck. Tensing with the pain, she gritted her teeth.

Jordan spoke softly, encouraging her through the worst of it. When she opened her eyes, she saw that he'd taken a chair and planted himself at her side. The look on his face challenged her to send him away, making very clear that he wouldn't go without a fight.

"I'm staying," he said, as if he needed to emphasize his determination. "It's my right."

"Why are you demanding parental privileges *now?* They certainly didn't interest you before."

"I've learned some hard lessons these past few weeks. First and foremost, you're right, Molly, I'm going to love our daughter…or son. I won't be able to help myself."

"You're saying that because you know it's what I want to hear." Molly was afraid to believe him, afraid to put her trust in what he'd said for fear he'd break her heart one more time.

"No, Molly, I've given a lot of thought to this. I already love Bethany…or Richard."

Molly bit her lower lip. She wasn't capable of making sound decisions at the moment. Jordan must have sensed her confusion because he brushed the hair from her damp forehead, bent forward and kissed her lips.

"Let me stay with you. Please?"

Molly hadn't the strength to refuse him. "All right."

As the hours and her labor progressed, Molly felt grateful that Jordan was at her side. He was a tremendous support. He encouraged her and rubbed her back to soothe away the pain she experienced there. He cooled her face with a wet cloth and gripped her hand when the contractions were at their fiercest.

The pains were growing in intensity now. Jordan charted the seconds for her in a calm, reassuring voice as they gripped her body.

"You're smiling," he murmured as he wiped the perspiration from her face. "Care to let me in on the joke?"

"You want a little girl, don't you?"

"What makes you think that?"

"Oh, come on, Jordan, you couldn't be more obvious. You've referred to the baby as Bethany several times. You've only called him Richard once."

"Would you mind a daughter?" he asked.

Molly hadn't given the subject much consideration. She had no preference, she'd believed, but now she wasn't so sure. Was she looking for a son to replace the one she'd lost? A son to ease the ache of her loss?

As soon as the thought went through her mind, Molly knew that wasn't true. No child could ever replace Jeffrey. He held his own distinct place in her heart.

"All I want is a healthy baby," she answered.

"That's what I want, too," Jordan assured her.

Molly turned her head to one side so she could look up at him. "Do you want this child?"

"Yes, Molly, I want this baby as much or possibly even more than I wanted Jeffrey."

His words confused her and she wondered if she could trust him. "I want to believe you so badly," she whispered, "but I don't know if I dare."

"Dare," he whispered, kissing her temple.

When it came time for Molly to be moved into the delivery room, Jordan left her. She tried to hide how disappointed she was that he'd decided to stay away for the final stage of their child's birth, but couldn't.

"Don't look so depressed," Barbara said, patting her

hand. "Your husband will be right back as soon as he's changed his clothes."

Molly all but wept when Jordan reappeared a few minutes later, wearing a green surgical top and pants. She didn't realize she was crying until he wiped the tears from her cheeks.

"It won't be long now," Doug Anderson said.

Once everyone was in place, Molly heard Jordan and Doug chatting again. She hadn't realized they were such good friends. Leave it to Jordan to talk golf scores with her physician. Both men were so involved in their conversation they seemed to have forgotten all about her and the baby.

"Push," Doug urged Molly.

"What do you think I'm doing?" she snapped, then gritted her teeth and strained for all she was worth.

"I wouldn't advise you to cross her just now," Jordan said to his friend, and Doug laughed.

"You're doing great," he told her, and Jordan squeezed her hand.

This was hard, so much more difficult than she remembered.

"Molly, look, you can see the top of her head." Jordan sounded as excited as if he'd won the lottery.

"It could be a boy," she reminded him.

"No way," Jordan said confidently, "that's the hair of a beautiful baby girl. No boy would be caught with soft blond curls."

"You don't know that she's going to be blonde."

"Ah, but I do," he said, bending forward and whispering close to her ear. "Just like her mommy."

"Not long now," Doug told them both.

"You said that an hour ago," Molly reminded him waspishly.

"It just seems like an hour."

Molly glared up at her husband. "Do you want to trade places?"

Jordan's smile was wide. "Not on your life. I'm quite happy with my contribution to this effort."

"This isn't the time to joke." No sooner had the words escaped Molly's lips than she felt a tremendous release, followed by the husky cry of her newborn baby.

"Welcome to our world, Bethany Marie," Doug said.

"A girl. We have a girl," Molly whispered. She felt overwhelmed by joy. Her breathing went shallow and unrestrained tears flooded her eyes, running down her face.

"Come here, daddy, and meet your little girl," Doug told Jordan.

Molly watched as her husband left her side. Bethany, who didn't appear to be the least bit delighted with her new surroundings, squalled lustily while being weighed and measured. Her tiny face was a bright red as she kicked her arms and legs.

The nurse wrapped Bethany in a warm blanket and handed her to Jordan, who was sitting down. Molly watched her husband's face as his daughter was positioned in his arms. Jordan looked down on Bethany for several seconds and then, as if he was aware of Molly's scrutiny, looked up.

It was at that moment that Molly saw the tears rolling down Jordan's cheeks.

Jordan crying. It must be an illusion, Molly decided.

She'd never seen Jordan weep. Not even when they'd buried Jeffrey.

The tears seemed to embarrass him as the nurse lifted Bethany from his arms and carried her over to Molly. Apparently worn out by the ordeal, Bethany nestled comfortably into Molly's embrace.

"She's perfect," Molly whispered when Jordan came over to stand by her bedside.

"So's her mother." Jordan bent to kiss her on the forehead.

Molly didn't feel perfect. She felt exhausted. Time had lost meaning and she had no idea whether it was afternoon or evening. For all she knew, Monday could have turned into Tuesday. It was Monday when her water broke, wasn't it?

"You were so confident we'd have a girl," Molly said to Jordan.

He raised the back of her hand to his mouth and kissed it. "I have a confession to make." He paused. "I've known for weeks we were having a daughter."

"How?" she demanded.

Jordan grinned. "Doug told me. You said you didn't want to know, but I felt no such restraint." He paused. "Do you mind?"

"No." She yawned, barely able to stay awake.

"I love you, Molly. I love you more at this moment than I believed it was possible to love anyone."

"I love you, too."

He stroked her hair. "Go ahead and sleep—you're exhausted. We'll have plenty of time to talk later."

Molly nodded. Then she sighed, completely and utterly content.

* * *

Molly might be exhausted, but Jordan had never been more wide-eyed and excited in his life. Ian was pacing the waiting-room floor when Jordan dashed through the swinging doors, still in his surgical greens.

"Well, don't keep me in suspense!" Ian said impatiently. "I haven't been this nervous since Molly's mother went into labor."

"Mother and child are doing fine." It was payback time. For once, Jordan had the information Ian wanted—but it wasn't in him to keep the older man guessing for long. Not when it was all Jordan could do not to shout out the wonderful news.

"Boy or girl?" Ian barked.

"You have a beautiful granddaughter."

"A little girl." Ian slumped down into a chair as if his legs had suddenly turned to rubber. "By heaven, a girl.

"Molly's fine?" he asked, looking up at Jordan.

"Sleeping. You can see her for a moment, if you want."

Recovering quickly, Ian stood and rubbed his face. "I don't know about you, young man, but I can't remember a more wretched night."

Jordan disagreed. This had to be one of the most fantastic nights of his life.

"I'm headed home, and the minute I get there I'm pouring myself a stiff Scotch." He threw his arm companionably over Jordan's shoulders. "Care to join me?"

Jordan was sorely tempted. "Give me a rain check. I think I'll stick around here for a while. I want to watch

Bethany have her first bath. The nurse said she'd let me hold her again when they're finished."

Ian slapped his back affectionately. "What about you and Molly? Are you going to be all right?"

"I think so."

"Good." With a farewell nod, Ian left the hospital.

Jordan spent the next hour with his newborn daughter, then slipped into Molly's room. As he suspected, his wife was still asleep. He'd intended only to stay long enough to be sure she was resting comfortably. They could talk in the morning. But he soon discovered he couldn't make himself leave.

He felt extraordinarily happy. Tired, too, but unlike any other tiredness he'd ever experienced. Sitting beside her, he studied the face of the woman he loved, his heart full of wonder.

He must have fallen asleep because the next thing he knew Molly's hand was on his head.

"Jordan," she whispered, sounding dreamy and vague, "what are you doing here?"

He'd closed his eyes, he recalled, crossed his arms against the side of the bed and leaned forward, but he hadn't intended to rest more than five minutes.

"It seems to me," he said, yawning, "this was where the conversation got started sometime yesterday afternoon. You asked me what I was doing here then, too."

Her smile was the most beautiful sight he'd ever seen, with only one exception—when she'd held Bethany immediately following her birth.

"How are you feeling?" he asked.

She didn't answer him. "You were crying."

The display of tears embarrassed him, but he didn't

regret them. They'd come of their own accord; he hadn't even realized what was happening. His emotions had taken control more than once in the past few weeks.

"I've never seen you cry before," she continued.

His male image had been too important for that. "I've done my fair share of weeping lately," he confessed, "sitting in Jeffrey's nursery...."

Molly looked about to break into tears herself. They should be celebrating instead of crying, he thought, but this acknowledgment, these tears, were a necessary thing.

"I'm sorry, Molly, for being such a jerk," he said in a low voice. "Can you forgive me?"

"Yes," she said. "It's past and forgotten."

"I'll find a way of making it all up to you. I have a lot of ground to cover, starting from the moment you found Jeffrey's body until a few months ago."

She smiled through her tears. "I hope you're aware that could take some doing."

"You could sentence me to a life term—with you."

"Consider yourself sentenced." She raised her arms and Jordan wrapped her in his embrace.

"You never tried to call me," she whispered, "not even once."

"When?"

"These past few months. I needed you the most then."

"But you said you didn't *want* to see me!" Staying away had been torment, but he'd felt he had no choice other than to abide by her wishes. Now she was telling him she'd wanted him.

Before she could explain, he reassured her. "You won't have to worry about that happening again," he said. "I've got a life sentence—of the best kind—and I'm not about to be cheated out of a single day."

Molly smiled softly and directed his mouth to hers. "The penalty should begin soon, don't you think?"

Jordan laughed and then his lips met hers. Being with this woman for the rest of his life wasn't a penalty, it was a gift. The greatest gift of all.

* * * * *

YESTERDAY ONCE MORE

One

Julie Houser pushed the elevator button and stepped back to wait. An older woman whose office was on the same floor joined her and they exchanged smiles.

Absently Julie glanced at her watch; she'd have plenty of time to finish unpacking tonight. Not wanting to prepare a meal, she considered picking up something from the local deli.

The elevator doors swooshed open, and the two women entered, then moved to the back, anticipating the five-thirty rush. By the time the car arrived at the ground floor it would be filled to capacity.

The next floor down it stopped, and three men boarded. Julie was concentrating on the lighted numbers above the door when the elevator came to a halt again. Another man got in and Julie squeezed herself into the far corner to make room.

The strap of her purse slid off her shoulder and as she eased it back up she felt someone's eyes on her. Accustomed to the appreciative gaze of men, Julie ignored the look and the man. The close scrutiny continued and she could practically feel his stare. Abruptly Julie turned her head, wondering who he was.

But when she finally saw her admirer, she nearly choked. She felt chilled and on fire at the same moment. Her heart hammered wildly, and her hand tightened around the purse strap as if that would hold her upright.

"Daniel." The name fell from her lips as her eyes met those of the man standing closest to her. His dark eyes narrowed and an impassive expression masked his strikingly handsome face.

Unable to bear his gaze any longer, Julie glanced away.

The elevator stopped and everyone filed out until she stood there alone, her breath coming in uneven gasps. So soon? She'd only been back in Wichita for six days. Never had she dreamed she'd see Daniel so quickly. And in her own building. Was his office here? *Oh, please,* she begged, *not yet. I'm not ready.*

"You coming or going?" An irritated voice from the foyer broke into her thoughts and Julie moved out of the elevator on unsteady legs.

Her heels clicked noisily as she hurried across the marble floor and outside. The downtown sidewalks were filled with people rushing and Julie made her way through the crowds, uncertain where she'd parked her car that morning. Pausing at a red light, she realized she was walking in the wrong direction and turned around. Ten minutes later she'd found her car. Her hand trembled uncontrollably as she opened the door.

She felt as if she'd been running a marathon as she slipped into the driver's seat and pressed her forehead against the steering wheel. Nothing could have prepared her for this meeting. Three years had passed since she'd last seen Daniel. Years of change. She'd only been twenty-one when she'd fled in panic. He had cause to be bitter and she was sorry for what she'd done. The regret she felt at hurting the man she loved was almost more than she could bear.

And she *had* loved Daniel. The evening he'd placed the diamond engagement ring on her finger had been the happiest of her life.

Julie's thoughts drifted back to that night as she started her car and headed toward her apartment. Daniel had taken her to an elegant French restaurant. The lights were dim, and flickering candlelight sent shadows dancing over the white linen tablecloth. Julie tried not to reveal how ill-at-ease she was in such a fancy place. She'd been so worried that she'd pick up the wrong fork, or worse, dump her soup in her lap. She was so much in love with Daniel and desperately wanted to please him. Julie let herself remember....

"Happy?" he asked.

She glanced over the top of the gold-tasseled menu and nodded shyly. Everything on the menu was in French with an English translation below. Even with that she didn't recognize half of what was offered. "What would you suggest?"

Daniel set his menu aside, his expression preoccupied. Julie noticed that from the moment he'd picked her up that evening he'd been unnaturally quiet. Nerves tightened her stomach.

"Daniel, is something the matter?" she ventured.

He stared at her blankly.

"I'm not wearing the right kind of dress, am I?" She'd changed clothes three times before he'd arrived, parading each outfit in front of her mother until Margaret Houser had demanded that Julie stop being so particular. Any one of the outfits was perfectly fine.

"You're beautiful," Daniel whispered and the look in his eyes confirmed the softly murmured words.

Julie lowered her gaze. Her hand smoothed an imaginary crease from her crisp skirt. "I wanted everything to be perfect tonight."

"Why?"

Julie answered him with a delicate shrug of one shoulder. She wanted everything to be perfect for Daniel *all* the time. "You've been very quiet," she said. "Have I done something to upset you?"

He chuckled, shaking his head. "Oh, my adorable Julie, is it any wonder I love you?" His hand reached for hers. "I've been trying to find a way to ask you a question."

"But, Daniel, all you need to do is ask."

He sighed expressively. "It's not that simple."

Julie couldn't imagine what was troubling him. Daniel was always so thoughtful; he did everything possible to make her comfortable. When they met his friends, he kept her beside him because he knew how reserved she was. A thousand times over the past six months, he'd been so loving and caring that it hadn't taken Julie long to lose her heart to him. Slowly he'd brought her into his world. He often took her to the Country Club and had taught her how to play golf and tennis. Gradually his friends had become hers until, reticent though she was, Julie had flowered under his love.

But she knew that a blossom had its season and would soon wilt and droop. Maybe Daniel was trying to think of a way to let her down gently. Maybe he was tired of her. Maybe he didn't want to see her again. Panic filled her and she clutched the linen napkin in her lap, praying that she wouldn't make a fool of herself and burst into tears when he told her.

"I've been accepted into the law practice of McFife, Lawson and Garrison."

Julie jerked her head up. "That's wonderful news! Congratulations."

He smiled. "It's only a junior partnership."

"That's the firm you were hoping you'd get into."

"Yes, it is, for more reasons than you know."

Now she understood why he'd chosen such an expensive restaurant. "We're here to celebrate then."

"Not quite yet." He leaned forward and clasped her hand in both of his. "These last few months have been the happiest of my life."

"Mine, too," she whispered.

"I know you're only twenty-one and I should probably wait a couple of years." He paused. "Julie…"

Her heart was pounding so loudly she was afraid he could hear it. Her eyes met his. "Yes, Daniel?"

"What I'm trying to say is…I love you, Julie. I've never kept that a secret. Now that I've been accepted by a good law firm and can offer you a future—will you marry me?"

Julie closed her eyes, savoring the warmth of his words.

"For heaven's sake," Daniel said. "Say something."

Julie bit her bottom lip, convinced she'd start to cry if she tried to speak.

"Julie," he pleaded.

She nodded wildly.

"Does that mean yes?"

Her voice trembled. "Yes, Daniel, yes! I love you so much. Nothing would make me happier than to spend the rest of my life with you."

The look in Daniel's eyes was enough to melt her bones. "I didn't think anything this delicate could be so heavy," he said, pulling a jeweler's box from his jacket pocket. He lifted the lid, revealing a diamond so large, Julie gasped.

Tears blurred her gaze. "Oh, Daniel."

"Do you like it? The jeweler said we can exchange it if you'd prefer something different."

"It's the most beautiful ring I've ever seen."

"Here." He took her hand again and slipped the diamond onto her finger....

Julie fought to suppress the memory of that night. She pulled into the apartment parking lot and turned off the engine. Her fingers toyed with the gold chain that hung around her neck, seeking the diamond ring she'd kept there these past three years. She'd continue to wear it this way until it was back on her finger where it belonged. But after seeing Daniel today, Julie realized how difficult that would be. Daniel wouldn't forgive her easily.

Determined, she climbed out of her car and walked to her uninspired furnished apartment.

The bright, sunny place she'd left in California had been shared with good friends, people who cared about her.

The most difficult decision she'd ever made was to flee Wichita three years ago. The second hardest was to come back. But she had no choice. She loved Daniel, and if at all possible, she needed to set things right with him.

Julie hung her coat in the closet. She entered the living room to find several stacks of boxes, but felt too exhausted to unpack.

Until today, everything had happened exactly as she'd hoped. Her job had been lined up before the move, and she'd managed to locate an apartment with no lease that was within her budget, and in a relatively good area. The transition had been smooth. But running into Daniel after only six days was something she hadn't counted on. She sat on the couch and rested her head against the back cushion for a few minutes.

Julie moved onto the floor, then crawled along the carpet until she got to the box containing their engagement portrait. She stared at the two smiling faces. They'd been so much in love. As tears filled her eyes, the happy faces swam in and out of her vision.

She traced her fingers across the image of Daniel's face and recalled their encounter that afternoon. His carefree smile had disappeared. The years had added a harshness to him, an arrogant aloofness. Even his sandy-colored hair was no longer casual but styled.

Julie's finger idly moved over the lean, proud jaw, pausing at the tiny cleft in his chin. She smiled sadly as she recalled how she'd loved to kiss him there. To tease him with her lips. And he'd been so wonderful, so understanding of her need to take things slow. Julie wondered if he regretted that now. There'd been many opportunities to consummate their love, but Daniel had always been the one to put a stop to it. She'd respected and loved him for that. He'd refused the ring when she'd tried to return it, which was how she'd come to wear it around her neck, keeping it close to her heart, no matter how many miles stood between them. Or how much pain.

Early the next morning Julie arrived at work intent on checking the list of occupants in her office complex. The Inland Empire Building housed fifteen floors of offices. As she studied the directory in the foyer, the listing for Daniel Van Deen, Attorney, seemed to leap off the board. Only one floor separated her from Daniel. For five of the six days she'd been in Wichita, they'd been this close without even knowing it.

A shiver ran down her spine and she slowly turned to see Daniel approaching the elevator, a newspaper wedged under his arm. He pushed the button and the wide doors opened. He stepped inside and turned around, his eyes locking with hers from across the foyer.

She watched as frustration swept over his features. His dark eyes narrowed as he stared back at her—and then the elevator doors glided shut.

Julie released a deep breath. Daniel hadn't forgiven her. The seething look he'd just sent her confirmed that.

Her legs felt unsteady as she took the next elevator up to the office of Cheney Trust and Mortgage Company. Grateful that she was the first one in that morning, she sat at her desk, trying to calm her nerves. Her hand trembled as she opened the bottom drawer of her desk and set her purse inside.

Sherry Adams, Julie's pretty blonde coworker, strolled in about fifteen minutes late. Their employer, Jack Barrett, had arrived before Sherry and had pointedly frowned at the empty desk, silently noting her absence. Julie had only been working at the office a few days and she didn't know Sherry well, but she could see that, despite her faults, the young divorcee was a valuable asset to the company.

"Morning," Julie said. "You seem to be in a good mood."

"I am." Sherry gave a brilliant imitation of a fashion model, her skirt flaring as she whirled around.

"I take it you want me to guess?" Julie asked.

Sherry shrugged playfully. "Not really. I just thought you'd be interested to know that I was asked out by the most eligible man in town."

"Congratulations."

"Thank you." Sherry smiled. "Actually, this is the culmination of five weeks of plotting and fine-tuning my womanly charms. I must admit, this guy's been one tough fish to catch."

"Well, double congratulations then," Julie said with a laugh.

Sherry sat and rolled her chair over to Julie's desk. "I don't suppose...you-know-who...is in yet?" Sherry inclined her head toward the closed door of Jack Barrett's office.

"'Fraid so," Julie said. "About fifteen minutes ago."

"Did he say anything about me being late?" Sherry asked, not looking the least bit concerned.

"Not to me he didn't."

"One of these days, old Barrett's going to fire me—and with good reason."

"I doubt that," Julie assured her. "Now tell me about your hot date."

"It's with Danny Van Deen."

Julie bit back a gasp and lowered her gaze, hoping to hide her surprise.

"He's a lawyer in the building," Sherry continued. "I've had my eye on him for a while. He's only taken a nibble so far, but it won't be long before I reel him in."

Julie forced her voice to maintain the same level of cheerfulness. "Good luck."

"Of course, I can't let him know how interested I am. That would be the kiss of death with a guy like Danny. But keeping my cool shouldn't be too difficult. By the time we're standing at the altar, he'll think it was his idea."

"I thought you didn't believe in wedded bliss anymore."

"Sure I do. It just didn't work out with Andy. I feel bad about that, but we fell out of love with each other. Not much either of us could do about it, really."

"And...this Van Deen...has he ever been married?"

"Nope. I can't understand it. He's perfect husband material—handsome, intelligent and sensitive under that cool exterior of his. He dates often enough, but nothing ever comes of it. Until now." She laughed softly. "I'll have him at the altar before he knows what hit him."

"Good luck," Julie murmured.

"I'm going to need all the luck I can get," Sherry added, straightening her desk. "Are you taking the first lunch today?"

"If you'd like," Julie replied absently as she flipped through the pages of a report on her desk.

"Would you mind cutting it short so I can get out of here by twelve-thirty? I'll make it up to you later, I promise." Sherry's brilliant blue eyes held a pleading look. "There's a dress I saw this morning and I want to try it on. That's actually the reason I was late. Wait until Danny Van Deen sees me in that."

"Sure," Julie agreed. "I can be back early."

The remainder of the morning was quiet. The two women took turns answering the phone. Because she wasn't fully accustomed to the office, Julie relied on Sherry for help, which she willingly supplied. Sherry was a generous person, who seemed to harbor no ill against anyone. That was what made her divorce so hard to understand. Julie couldn't imagine a woman like Sherry giving up on something as important as a marriage.

Shortly after noon, Sherry reminded Julie of their agreement. Julie removed her purse from the desk drawer and stood, ready to leave for her lunch break when Jack Barrett strolled out of his office.

"Are you going for lunch?" the balding man asked.

"Yes," Julie replied. "Would you like me to get you something?"

"Not today, thanks." He handed her a large manila envelope. "But would you mind dropping this off at Daniel Van Deen's office?"

Two

Panic filled Julie's eyes as she cast a pleading glance at Sherry.

"Go on. You might catch a glimpse of him and then you'll know what I mean!" Sherry seemed oblivious to the real reason behind Julie's reluctance.

Jack Barrett looked suspiciously from one to the other. "Is there a problem?"

"No problem," Sherry said.

Julie nodded her agreement, hoping to bow gracefully out of the situation.

"His office is one floor down. Number 919, I think." Sherry wrinkled her nose. "His name should be on the door."

Julie managed a smile and walked out of the office. By the time she reached Daniel's floor, the envelope felt as if it weighed fifty pounds.

Her hand was clammy as she turned the knob and entered the office.

A round-faced secretary glanced up and smiled. "Can I help you?"

The first thing Julie noticed was the woman's ring.

She was married. But why should it matter that Daniel's secretary was married?

"I...have a package," she stammered. "For Mr. Van Deen. From Jack Barrett."

"Agnes, did you find—" Abruptly, Daniel had appeared, his words cut short as he caught sight of Julie. For a moment there was a hard look in his eyes, but then they softened and an expression Julie couldn't define came over his features.

"Mr. Barrett's sent the papers you asked about this morning," Agnes said, and although Julie heard her speak, it somehow felt as if she and Daniel were alone in the room.

"You did ask about the Macmillan papers?" The woman's words sounded distant.

"Yes," said Daniel, his words breaking the spell as he continued to stare at Julie.

The secretary took the envelope from Julie's limp hand, her sharp gaze shifting from one to the other. "Was that all?"

Julie snapped to attention. "Pardon?"

"Was there something else?"

"No," she mumbled. "Thank you."

A puzzled look appeared on the woman's face. "Thank you for dropping this off."

Julie smiled and turned, walking out of the office with her head held high.

The rest of the day passed in a blur and by the time she got home that night, Julie felt physically and mentally drained.

As she entered her apartment, Julie discovered her new phone had been installed. She decided to call her mother.

"Hi, Mom," she said, trying to sound cheerful.

"Julie. How are you?" Her mother sounded concerned. Margaret Houser lived in San Diego, where she'd moved when she was widowed. With Julie's older brother, Joe, in Montana, none of her family lived in Wichita anymore.

"Fine, Mom. Everything's fine."

"I'm so glad you called. I've been worried."

"Have you looked up any of your old high school friends?"

"Not yet," said Julie, though truthfully, she doubted she would. The only real friends she'd had in Wichita had gone elsewhere. "Mom." She took in a deep breath. "I've seen Daniel."

The concern in her mother's voice returned. "How is he?"

"We...we haven't talked. But I can tell he's changed. I feel like I hardly know him. He never understood why I left. He's not likely to understand why I came back."

"Don't be so sure, sweetheart." Her mother's voice was reassuring. "He's been hurt, and it makes sense that he's changed over the years."

"Mom, I don't think he'll talk to me."

"I've never known you to be a defeatist," her mother said in a supportive tone. "But I do worry about Daniel's mother. Be careful if you have to deal with her."

"I will." Julie's fingers flipped through the white pages of the telephone directory. Clara Van Deen's number was unlisted, but Daniel's was there. As her mother continued, Julie ran her finger back and forth over his name. The movement had a strange, calming effect on her, as if she were reaching out to him.

"Did you hear me, Julie?"

The question pulled Julie back into the conversation. "I'll be careful around Mrs. Van Deen, I promise."

"That woman can be completely unreasonable," her mother went on. "Don't forget, I was the one who had to deal with her after you left."

"I know and I'm sorry about that."

"I still think you did the right thing, honey."

Even after three years, Julie wasn't certain. She'd been so naive. There'd been many times she should have objected more strongly, should have forced a stop to the outrageous wedding plans. But like Daniel, she'd been overwhelmed by his mother's dominant personality. Even when Julie had tried to tell Mrs. Van Deen how she felt, her wishes were quickly pushed aside.

"Julie, are you still there?" her mother asked.

"Yes, I'm here. Sorry, Mom, it's been a long day. I'll talk to you next week."

"I'll be thinking about you."

"Thanks, Mom." Her mother's support had gotten her through some difficult times in the past and she was grateful to have it now.

Julie replaced the receiver, then slumped forward on the couch, burying her face in her hands. A tightness was building in her throat. It felt as though no time had passed. Her anxiety was as keen now as it had been three years ago.

Julie had been aware right from the start that Daniel's mother wanted her son to marry a more socially prominent girl. To her credit, Clara Van Deen had accepted Julie as Daniel's choice, but then she immediately set to work making Julie into something she'd never be. First came the makeover. Julie's hair was cut and styled to meet Clara's standards. Clara then purchased an entire wardrobe of what she claimed were outfits better suited for her new role as Daniel's wife.

Julie had found herself swallowing her pride a hundred times over. She tried to do exactly as Mrs. Van Deen asked. She wanted to make Daniel proud. He was climbing the corporate ladder and Julie didn't want to do anything that might jeopardize his success.

The out-of-control wedding plans were what had finally caused Julie to run. All she'd wanted was a simple ceremony with only their immediate families, but before she knew it, Daniel's mother had issued invitations to four hundred supposedly close and intimate friends she couldn't possibly insult by not including.

"But, Daniel," Julie had protested, "I don't know any of these people."

"Don't worry about it," Daniel had said, kissing the tip of her nose. He'd never fully understood the depth of her anxiety. "They'll love you as much as I do."

Daniel had negated any further protests with a kiss that left Julie unable to argue.

As the date drew closer, Julie's marriage to Daniel became the talk of the town, making Julie herself the reluctant focus of many a social gathering.

After each event, Mrs. Van Deen would run through a list of things that Julie had done wrong. No matter how hard Julie tried, there was always something worth criticizing.

"I can't take it anymore," Julie cried to her mother one night.

"You need to speak up," her mother advised. "Tell her how you feel."

"Don't you think I've tried?" Julie hid her face in her

hands. "This isn't a wedding anymore, it's a Hollywood production."

Every day the pressure mounted. The wedding plans grew until what had started out as a simple ceremony was now a monster that threatened to devour Julie whole. Everything was beyond her control—the caterers, musicians, flower girl, bridesmaids and dresses. Even their honeymoon had been arranged by Mrs. Van Deen.

"Daniel, please listen to me," Julie had begged a week before the wedding. "I don't want any of this."

"Honey, I know you're nervous," he'd said soothingly. "But it's only one day and then we can go ahead with the rest of our lives."

But Julie had doubted they could. Every incident with his mother just reinforced her belief that the wedding was only the beginning. Eventually, Mrs. Van Deen would take over every aspect of their marriage, and when Daniel's mother made a large down payment on a house for them, Julie's suspicions were confirmed.

"It's her wedding gift to us," Daniel had explained. But the house was just a short distance from his mother's and the writing on the freshly painted walls was clear. His mother had insisted on helping Julie decorate. Such important details couldn't be left in the hands of an immature twenty-one-year-old, she'd implied.

"Doesn't it bother you that she's taken over our lives?" Julie had asked plaintively.

She could see that Daniel did care, but would do nothing.

"For the first time since Dad died, my mother has a purpose. Can't you see how much happier she is now?"

But Julie couldn't see anything other than a growing case of claustrophobia.

That night she couldn't sleep, and by the time the sun rose the next morning, Julie had packed her bags.

"You can't do this," her mother protested when she realized her daughter's plans.

"I've got to," Julie said, her eyes red from crying. "I wouldn't be marrying Daniel. I'd be marrying his mother."

"But the wedding's in five days!"

"There isn't going to be a wedding," Julie said adamantly. "What should have been a simple and beautiful ceremony has turned into a three-ring circus and I won't be part of it."

"But Julie—"

"I know what you're going to say," she interrupted. "But this isn't just pre-wedding jitters. Daniel and I are never alone anymore. His mother's taken over every aspect of our relationship."

"Talk to him, sweetheart. Explain how you feel," Margaret advised. "At least do that much. This is a serious step you're considering."

Julie took her mother's advice and went to Daniel's office. They met as he was on his way out the door.

"Julie." He seemed surprised to see her.

"I need to talk to you," said Julie, her hands tightly clenched.

Daniel glanced at his watch. "Can it wait? I'm short on time."

She shook her head forcefully. "No. It can't wait."

Daniel seemed to notice her agitated manner. He pressed a hand to the small of her back and led her into his office. "Honey, I know things have been hectic lately, but it's bound to improve once we're married. We'll have lots of time together then, I promise."

"That's just it, Daniel," Julie said. "We aren't going to be married."

Daniel inhaled sharply. "What do you mean? What's this all about?"

With a trembling finger, she removed the diamond ring and held it out to him. "I can't marry you, Daniel."

"Julie!" He was completely stunned. "Put that ring back where it belongs!"

"I can't."

He slumped onto the arm of his office chair. "I don't understand."

"I didn't expect you would." Julie bowed her head. "Do you remember last week when I suggested we drive across the border and elope? You laughed." Her voice wavered. "But I was serious, Daniel. Dead serious."

"My mother would never forgive us if we did something like that."

Julie sighed. "That's the problem, Daniel. You wouldn't dream of crossing your mother, but you don't seem to care what all of this is doing to me."

"My mother loves you."

"She loves the woman she's created. Haven't you noticed? Look at me, Daniel. Am I the same woman you proposed to three months ago?"

Daniel averted his eyes. "I don't know what you're talking about."

"Look at me," she repeated. "My hair is different, my nails are manicured, and my...my clothes..." Tears welled up in her eyes as her voice broke. "Do you realize she expects me to call her every morning to ask what I should wear? I haven't worn a pair of jeans in weeks," she exclaimed. "I'm slowly being molded into what she thinks your ideal woman should be. I can't take it anymore."

Daniel stood, threading his fingers through his hair. "Why didn't you refuse?"

"Don't you think I've tried? No one listens to me— not even you, Daniel. What I think or feel doesn't seem to matter anymore. I'm…not sure how I feel about you anymore."

"Is that so?" he demanded.

"It is," Julie said defensively. "I want out. Here." Again, she tried to return the ring.

Daniel stared at her for a long moment before dropping his gaze to the diamond in her hand. He turned and stalked to the window on the far side of the room, his back to her. "Keep it."

"But, Daniel," she began. "I'm—"

"I said keep it," he broke in. He turned to face her, his mouth a rigid line. His dark eyes were clouded with hurt and pain. "Now get out of my life and stay out."

Tears ran down her face as she drove straight to her mother's. The clothes, the wedding dress—she left everything Mrs. Van Deen had purchased strewn across her bed. Julie then loaded her suitcases into the back of her car and drove to her aunt's in California.

That had been three years ago and every night since she'd wondered if she'd done the right thing. She straightened on the sofa. The guilt had been weighing on her, but her love for Daniel had never died. She'd hurt him and his mother. Right or wrong, there were better ways to handle the situation.

Now, she'd come back to ask for Daniel's and Mrs. Van Deen's forgiveness.

Three

The next morning, Julie waited in the Inland Empire foyer for Daniel to enter the building. She needed to talk to him. She'd dreamed of it for months, praying that a heartfelt apology would wipe out the pain she'd caused him. Then—and only then—could they start to rebuild their relationship.

She spotted him the moment he pushed past the double glass doors.

Julie watched him approach the elevator. Without a sound, she moved closer so that when the doors opened, she could enter behind him.

Frustration knotted her stomach as two other people boarded the elevator.

If Daniel was aware of her, he didn't let on. But Julie had never been more aware of anyone or anything in her life. She felt his presence beside her. The years had been good to him. He'd been boyishly attractive three years ago; even though he'd lost the relaxed, carefree quality he'd had then, he was still devastatingly handsome. No wonder Sherry had set her sights on him.

A long moment passed and Julie yearned to reach

out and touch him, anything to force him to acknowledge that she was there. He couldn't ignore her forever. Sooner or later, they'd have to talk.

He stared straight ahead as the creases around his mouth hardened. Julie's stomach tightened. She couldn't take her eyes off him. His features were so achingly familiar, but on closer inspection, the changes in his appearance were even more prominent. Streaks of gray mingled with the sandy-colored hair at the side of his head and Julie had to restrain herself from brushing her hand across his temple. She leaned against the back wall for support.

The two strangers exited on the fifth floor, leaving Julie alone with Daniel. This was exactly what she'd hoped for, and yet her tongue was suddenly uncooperative. There was so much she wanted to say, and she'd practiced exactly how to begin so many times. But now that the opportunity was there, she found herself incapable of uttering a single word.

"Hello, Daniel," she managed after an awkward silence. The air between them felt charged, adding to Julie's discomfort.

Daniel ignored her, staring straight ahead.

"We need to talk," she continued, her voice barely above a whisper.

Silence.

"Daniel, please."

The thin line of his lips tightened as he directed his attention away from her.

She laid her hand gently on his forearm and sighed. The hopelessness of the situation overwhelmed her. The man who stood beside her became a watery blur as tears filled her eyes. Julie dropped her hand. The elevator stopped and she watched him leave.

Julie was grateful to be the first one in the office again. She collapsed into her chair, fighting off waves of nausea. Pain pounded at her temples. It was too soon. She'd been expecting too much. Daniel needed more time; she had to be patient. When he was ready, she'd be waiting.

Sherry strolled into the office five minutes early, a wide grin on her face. "Morning," she said.

Julie pretended to be absorbed in reading a paper on her desk.

"Aren't you going to ask how my hot date went?"

Julie didn't want to hear it, but knew she should play along. "Sure." She swallowed hard and banished the mental image of Daniel holding Sherry in his arms.

"Awful," Sherry admitted with a wry grin. "Talk about disappointing! I could've had two heads for all the attention he paid to me and my new dress."

"Maybe he was worried about a case or something." Julie couldn't repress her delight. If Sherry became involved with Daniel, things would become unpleasant.

"*Or something* is right," Sherry shot back.

"If last night was such a disaster, how come you're so cheerful this morning?"

"Because Danny apologized and asked me out again this weekend," Sherry said. "And when he takes a woman out, he spares no expense. We went to the best restaurant in town—what a waste. Danny barely touched his dinner."

Danny! Julie shuddered at the casual use of his name. Daniel used to hate it. No one called him Danny.

Julie smiled stiffly. "I hope everything works out better next time."

"It will," Sherry said confidently. "Next time, he won't be able to take his eyes off me." She laughed lightly. "I won't let him." She smiled and hung her jacket in the closet.

"Are you doing anything special this weekend?" Sherry asked a while later.

"Painting my living room," Julia said. Such distractions were vital at the moment. Anything to keep her mind from the thought of Sherry and Daniel falling in love. Throughout the morning, Julie debated whether or not she should say something to Sherry. But what? She had no claim to Daniel now.

When Julie woke on Saturday morning, the sun was shining. It was far too beautiful a day to spend indoors. She recalled how Daniel's mother loved to garden; Clara Van Deen grew the most gorgeous irises.

When Julie climbed into her car, her destination had been the paint store, but as she drove, she found herself on the street that led to Clara's house instead.

She pulled to a stop across from the lovely two-story home with the meticulously landscaped front yard. A fancy sports car was parked in the driveway. Julie doubted that Mrs. Van Deen would ever drive something like that.

The long circular driveway was bordered on both sides by flowering red azaleas. Julie stared at the house for a long time, undecided about whether or not she should approach Daniel's mother, having had no luck with Daniel himself. She wondered what had become of Clara Van Deen, realizing that she could be a greater challenge than her son.

No. Julie shook her head. Now wasn't the time. Not when she was dressed in jeans and a sweatshirt. She'd need to look and feel her best when she faced Mrs. Van Deen. Her desire to get the confrontation over with as quickly as possible would benefit neither of them. Before she could change her mind, she pulled away from the curb and headed toward the closest shopping center.

The paint she chose for the living room was an antique white that would brighten the place up. Her spirits lifted as she returned to the apartment. She was actually looking forward to a quiet afternoon painting.

She unhooked the drapes and carefully laid them across the back of the sofa. As she began to spread out newspapers, a knock at the door caught her off guard. She rushed to answer, stumbling over the ottoman on her way.

Stooping to rub her injured shin, she opened the door.

Daniel stood there, and he did not look amused.

"Leave my mother alone," he said.

Julie stared back at him, completely speechless.

"Did you hear what I said?" he demanded, his expression cold.

She nodded.

"I saw you parked in front of her house this morning. Stay away from her, Julie. I'm warning you."

Julie jutted her chin out defiantly. "The time will come when I'll have to talk to her." She retreated into the living room.

Daniel entered and followed, closing the door behind him. "Not if I can help it."

Julie turned to face him. "You can't."

"Don't bet on it," he snarled.

"Daniel, I've come a thousand miles to talk to you and your mother."

"Then you wasted your time because neither of us cares to see you."

Julie met his gaze. "I didn't come back to hurt either of you. I've come to make amends."

"Amends?" He threw the word back at her as he paced the carpet, his hands buried deep in his pockets. "Do you really think you could ever undo the humiliation I suffered when you walked out?"

"I'm sure I can't, but I'd like to try. I was young and stupid. Don't you understand? A thousand times I've regretted what I did—"

"Regretted," he repeated sarcastically. "I used to dream you'd say that to me. Now that you have, it means nothing. Nothing," he muttered. "I look at you and I don't feel a thing. You came back to apologize? Fine. You've made your peace. But don't go to my mother, bringing up the past. She has no desire to see you. Whatever you and I shared is over and done with."

Julie closed her eyes, warding off the sting in his voice. She wouldn't be so easily swayed from her goal. "You don't mean that," she whispered.

"I've blocked you from my mind," he continued. "But unfortunately, my mother has never been the same. I can't forgive you for what you've done to her."

"But that's the reason I've come back," Julie said, trying to stay calm although her stomach churned uncomfortably. "I want to make it up to you both. Can't you see how sorry I am? I never stopped thinking about you. Not for a day. Not for a minute. You've haunted me all this time."

"Do you expect me to pat you on the head and tell you everything's just fine? That we can pick up where we left off?" His eyes narrowed. "It's not that easy."

Julie struggled to keep her composure. "You've changed so much." She raised her hand to his mouth, her touch light against his lips. Daniel abruptly jerked his head away and took a step back.

"I don't want to hurt you or your mother," she said again.

"Then leave before you do."

"I can't. This is too important to me. I've got to make things right."

"You'll never be able to do that. Sometimes it's best for the past to remain buried."

"Believe me, I've tried to put this behind me. I can't."

Daniel looked exhausted. "Leave, Julie. You'll only make everything worse."

"I won't go," she insisted. "Not until I've talked to your mother. Not until I pay her back every penny."

"Why now?" He sank onto the sofa and leaned forward until his elbows rested on his knees.

"You're not the only one who's changed, Daniel. I'm not a naive twenty-one-year-old anymore. I'm an adult willing to admit I made a terrible mistake. I was wrong to have run away instead of confronting the problems we faced. I regret what I did, but more than that, I've realized there isn't anyone I could ever feel as strongly about as you. Whenever another man held me, I found myself wishing he was you. It's you I came back for, Daniel."

He stared at her disbelievingly. "You mean to tell me what? That your conscience hasn't quit bothering you?"

"Yes, but it's so much more than that. I want to make everything up to you."

"Well, that's fine and dandy, Julie. You've come here, we've talked and now you can go. I absolve you of everything. Just stay out of my life—understand?"

Pain flashed across his face, and for a fleeting moment, Julie saw a glimmer of the old Daniel. Something was troubling him, something deep beneath the surface.

"Daniel." She moved to sit beside him, wishing she could comfort the man she loved. She weighed her words carefully. "Something's wrong. Won't you tell me what it is?"

He looked right through her and Julie knew his thoughts were elsewhere.

He stood, impatiently shaking off his mood. "Leave my mother alone," he said again. "Do you understand?"

"I'm so sorry." Julie hung her head in defeat. Everything she'd tried to explain had meant nothing.

As he started to go, she stood and faced him. "I promise not to do anything to hurt her. Will you trust me?"

"I shouldn't." A nerve moved in his jaw and again Julie was aware of some internal struggle. Without another word, he walked out of the apartment.

Julie remained exactly where he'd left her, numb and completely unaware of how much time passed. Finally forcing herself into action, she finished covering the floor with newspapers and opened the first gallon of paint.

She worked until well past midnight. By the time she finished, the room was barely recognizable. The sense of accomplishment helped lift her spirits.

Her hand skimmed the ring dangling from her neck. Her body ached as she cleaned the paintbrushes under the kitchen faucet, but her mind raced.

Maybe Daniel was right. Maybe contacting Clara Van Deen would do more harm than good.

Later that night, as she lay in bed, staring at the darkened ceiling, Julie couldn't let the thought go. She'd come this far. The clock dial illuminated the time— 2:00 A.M. Although she was exhausted, she hadn't been able to sleep. Julie pounded her pillow and rolled over to face the wall.

Write to her.

The idea suddenly flashed through her mind. She threw back the covers and sat up, eager to search for a pen and pad.

Sitting on the bed, Julie drafted the letter:

Dear Mrs. Van Deen:
I know this letter will come as a shock to you. My hope is that you're willing to hear what I have to say.

I wonder if you've ever done anything in your life that you've regretted. Something that's haunted you over the years. Something you'd give anything to do over again. I have. For three years I've carried the guilt of what I did to you and Daniel. I know there's nothing I can say that would ever undo the embarrassment or hurt I caused, but I do beg your forgiveness, and ask that you allow me to make this up to you in some way. I'd do anything for that opportunity.

You'll find my address above, along with my phone number. Please contact me if you're willing to talk.

Julie read the letter again the following morning and typed it into her computer, printed it and mailed it off. The next move would be Mrs. Van Deen's.

A week passed before Julie received a response, but she saw Daniel almost every day in between. Not once did he speak to her, but his eyes held an unspoken warning that made Julie wonder if his mother had told him about the letter.

The scented envelope addressed in delicate handwriting caught her attention the minute she picked up her mail on Saturday afternoon. Julie's heart soared.

She'd hardly got inside her apartment before she ripped open the envelope. Her fingers shook as she removed the single sheet of stationery.

It read simply: *Saturday at four.*

"That's today," Julie said aloud. Frantically, she glanced at the kitchen clock. It was just after one— only three hours to prepare. Surely, Mrs. Van Deen had done that deliberately, hoping to catch her off guard. But she'd be disappointed. Julie was ready. She knew what she had to say and she was eager to finally say it.

After carefully surveying her wardrobe, Julie decided on a simple blue business suit. It was the same one she'd worn to her job interview with Mr. Barrett six weeks earlier. She wanted to show Mrs. Van Deen that she wasn't an awkward young girl anymore.

At precisely four o'clock, Julie pulled into the curved driveway. Mrs. Batten, the elderly cook who'd been with the family for years, answered the door. She didn't appear to recognize Julie.

"Yes?" The woman's tone wasn't particularly civil.

"Good afternoon. I'm here to see Mrs. Van Deen."

Mrs. Batten hesitated.

"We have an appointment today at four," Julie added.

Again the woman paused, but then stepped aside, allowing Julie to enter the foyer.

The interior of the house was exactly as she remembered it. The same mahogany table and vase sat beside the carpeted stairway that led to the second floor. To her left was the salon, as Mrs. Van Deen called it; at one time Julie had regarded it as a torture chamber. To her right was the massive dining room.

"This way," Mrs. Batten instructed, her voice only slightly less frosty.

Like an errant student being led to the principal's office, Julie followed two steps behind the elderly woman. She was escorted through the house to the back garden Mrs. Van Deen prized so highly.

"You may wait here." Mrs. Batten pointed to a pair of cast-iron chairs separated by a small table.

Julie did as she was told.

"Would you like something to drink while you wait?" the woman asked, refusing to look at Julie.

"No. Thank you," she mumbled, clasping her hands in her lap.

Fifteen minutes passed and still Julie waited. Daniel's mother was doing this deliberately. Testing her. But Julie was determined to sit there until midnight if necessary.

She tensed at the sound of footsteps behind her.

"Hello, Julie." The words were said in a low and trembling voice.

Julie stood and turned to see Daniel's mother—frail and obviously weak. She leaned heavily on a cane, her back hunched, and yet she was elegant as ever. Her hair was completely white now and she was thin, far thinner than Julie remembered.

"Sit down." Mrs. Van Deen motioned with her hand and Julie perched on the hard metal chair, grateful for its support.

Daniel's mother took the seat beside her, both hands resting on her wooden cane. "To say I was surprised to receive your letter would be an understatement."

Julie's grip on her purse tightened. "I'd imagine so."

"Does Daniel know you're back?"

Julie nodded. "We work in the same building."

Mrs. Van Deen didn't comment, but smiled weakly. The changes Julie had noticed in Daniel were nothing compared to those she saw in his mother.

"You have a Wichita address?"

"Yes." Julie's voice quavered slightly. "I moved back here."

"Why?"

"Because—" Julie swallowed "—because I hope to make amends and I didn't think I could do that if I flew in for a weekend."

Mrs. Van Deen smiled knowingly. "That was wise, dear."

"I came because I deeply regret my actions—"

"Do you still love my son?"

Julie focused on her hands, which were tightly coiled around the small leather purse. The question was one she'd avoided since her return, afraid of the answer. "Yes," she admitted. "Yes, I do, but I..."

"But you hate me?"

"Oh, no." Julie met her gaze. "The only person I've hated over the years was myself."

The old woman's smile was thin. "There comes a time in a woman's life when she can look at things more clearly. In my life, it comes as I face death. As you've probably guessed, I'm not well."

Julie's vision blurred with sudden tears. She hadn't expected Daniel's mother to be so kind or understanding.

"There's no need to cry. I've lived a full life, but my heart is weak and I can't do much of anything these days. Ill health gives one an opportunity to gain perspective."

"Then you forgive me?" Julie whispered, her voice close to cracking.

The frail hand tightened around the cane. "No."

Julie closed her eyes. An apology would have been too easy; she should have realized that. Daniel's mother would want so much more. "What can I do?" Julie asked softly.

"I want you to forgive *me*." Mrs. Van Deen's voice was gentle. She reached across the space that separated them and patted Julie's hand. "I was the reason you did what you did. I've buried that guilt deep in my heart. I behaved like an interfering old woman."

Julie noticed several tears sliding down Mrs. Van Deen's weathered cheek, and knew that her own face was wet, too.

"We've both been fools," Julie said.

"But there's no fool like an old one." Mrs. Van Deen

wiped her tears with the back of her hand. She looked pale and tired, but her eyes held an unmistakable radiance.

As if on cue, Mrs. Batten carried in a silver tray with a coffeepot and two china cups. Mrs. Van Deen waited until the woman left before asking Julie to do the honors.

Julie poured the coffee with a smile, stirring sugar into Mrs. Van Deen's before presenting it to her.

Mrs. Van Deen nodded approvingly. "Very good."

Julie laughed, perhaps her first real laugh in three years. "I had a marvelous teacher." She sat back and crossed her legs, her own cup and saucer in one hand.

"Tell me what you've done with yourself all this time." Mrs. Van Deen looked genuinely interested.

"I went to school in California for a while and lived with my aunt. My mother joined me later on and I got a job as a bank teller before working my way into the loan department. From there, I got a job in a trust company. Nothing too exciting."

"What about men?"

The abrupt question flustered Julie. "I...dated some."

"Anyone serious?"

Julie shook her head. "No one— Did Daniel find anyone...serious?"

The former radiance dimmed. "He never tells me."

"He's changed."

"Yes, he has," his mother admitted. "And not for the better, I fear. He's an intense young man. Some days he reminds me of..." She paused.

"Mrs. Van Deen, are you okay?"

"I'm fine, Julie. You sound like Daniel. He's always

worried about me. And please, I'd prefer it if you called me Clara."

Even when she was engaged to Daniel, Julie had never been granted the privilege of using Mrs. Van Deen's first name. Permission to do so now confirmed their new understanding.

"All right then. Clara." The name felt awkward on Julie's tongue.

"I do have regrets." The older woman looked as if she were someplace far away. "I would so have liked to hold a grandchild."

Julie took a sip of her coffee, hoping the warm liquid would ease the tightness in her throat.

"I know what it's cost you to come here," Mrs. Van Deen continued. "You have far more character than I gave you credit—" The woman paused to take several deep, labored breaths. "I'm sorry, Julie, but I'm suddenly not feeling very well." Mrs. Van Deen raised her hand to cover her heart.

A wave of panic swept through Julie. Daniel's mother wasn't just weak, she was on the verge of collapse. "I'm calling for help," Julie said.

She retrieved her cell phone from her purse and dialed 911, trying to remain calm as she relayed the address to the operator.

After being told that an ambulance was on its way, Julie struggled to recall the lessons she'd taken in CPR. She moved to kneel next to Daniel's mother, taking one weathered hand in hers.

"Don't worry, child," Clara assured her. Her voice was weak.

Julie began loosening the older woman's clothes, words of reassurance tumbling from her lips. Clara was slowly losing consciousness. How soon would help arrive? Julie eased her onto the ground. Sirens could be heard in the distance and Julie breathed a little easier.

The ambulance pulled up and Julie stumbled aside as two men approached and set to work on the now-unconscious woman. They lifted her onto a stretcher, then transported her to the waiting vehicle.

Julie's heart pounded wildly as she followed close behind. Mrs. Batten joined her on the front lawn and the pair watched as the EMTs loaded Daniel's mother into the ambulance.

"What happened?" Mrs. Batten asked. Her face was pale.

"We were just talking," Julie explained. "And then she suddenly had trouble breathing. She just…collapsed."

Mrs. Batten raised her hand to her chest in silent prayer.

"I'm going to the hospital," Julie said. She knew she'd go crazy waiting around here.

The hospital was a whirlwind of activity when she got there. She almost collided with Daniel as she hurried down the wide corridor. He stopped and glared at her accusingly, as though he blamed her for his mother's poor health. He entered the waiting room, leaving Julie alone in the hall.

Daniel didn't want her there, but she couldn't leave without knowing how Clara was.

The hospital's chapel offered her the solitude she sought. She sat in the back pew and covered her face with her hands. An eternity seemed to pass before she felt strong enough to stand.

Daniel was pacing the small waiting area when she

returned. He swiveled to face her as she walked into the room.

"Don't ask me to leave," she said.

He ran his fingers through his already rumpled hair. "The EMT told me you're the one who called in time to save her life."

Julie didn't answer. Her arms cradled her stomach as she paced alongside him. They didn't speak. They didn't touch. But Julie couldn't remember a closer communication with anyone. It was as if they were emotionally connected, offering each other hope.

The universe seemed to come to a stop as soon as the doctor stepped into the room. "She's resting comfortably," he announced.

"Thank God," Daniel said. He released a shuddering breath.

"Your mother's a stubborn woman. She insists on seeing both of you. But, please, take only a minute. Is that clear?"

Julie glanced at Daniel. "You go."

"She asked for both," the doctor repeated. "She was very specific about that."

Clara Van Deen looked as pale as the sheets she was lying against when Julie and Daniel entered her room in the intensive care unit.

She opened her eyes and attempted to smile when she saw them. "My dears," she said, "I'm so sorry to cause you all this trouble."

"Don't worry about that," Daniel whispered. "You need to rest."

"Not yet," she murmured. "Julie, you said you'd do anything to gain my forgiveness?"

"Yes," Julie said, her voice hardly sounding like her own.

"And Daniel, will you do one last thing for me?"

"Anything. You know that."

Clara Van Deen's tired eyes closed and opened again as if she was on the brink of slipping away. "I would like the two of you to marry—for my sake."

Four

Julie woke in the gray light of early morning. She hadn't slept well and imagined Daniel hadn't either. They'd hardly spoken as they left the hospital; they'd scarcely even looked at each other. The tight clenching of Daniel's jaw said plenty about his feelings on the matter of any marriage between them.

When she'd arrived home Julie changed into something comfortable and made herself a cup of strong coffee. She sat in the living room, bracing her feet against the coffee table as she slouched on the sofa. Daniel's mother was so different from what Julie had been expecting. She'd been so sure that Clara would lash out at her, but instead she'd discovered a sick, gentle woman who suffered many regrets. Julie longed to ease Clara's mind, knowing that as she lay weak in a hospital bed, facing death, she needed the assurance that her son would be happy.

But, Julie also knew that she and Daniel could never grant her request, not when Daniel resented Julie so much.

Later that evening, as she lay awake in bed, a calm

came over her. She loved Daniel, had never stopped—
and, if possible, found she loved him even more now.
Every time she looked at him, she felt it. As she closed
her eyes, Julie reminded herself of the reasons she'd
returned to Wichita.

When she got to the hospital the next morning, the
parking lot was full. Although she hadn't reached a decision, Julie felt a sense of peace. She'd talk to Daniel—
really talk—and together they'd decide what to do.

A faint antiseptic odor greeted her as she pushed
through the glass doors that led to the hospital foyer.

Daniel was in the waiting area outside the intensive
care unit. He glanced up as Julie approached, his eyes
heavy from lack of sleep.

"Good morning," she said. "How's Clara?"

"My mother," he returned stiffly, "is resting comfortably."

Julie took the seat across from him. "Can we talk?"
Sitting on the edge of the cushion, she leaned toward
him, clasping her hands together.

Daniel shrugged.

"Did you sleep at all?" she asked.

A quick shake of his head confirmed her suspicions.
"I couldn't. What about you?"

"Some." She noticed that Daniel wouldn't look at her,
not directly. Even when she'd entered the room his gaze
had met hers only briefly before shifting to something
behind her.

"The doctor's with her now," he said.

"Daniel." Julie found it difficult to speak. "What are
we going to do?"

His laughter was mirthless, chilling. "What do you

mean, *do?* My mother didn't know what she was saying. They gave her so many drugs yesterday she wasn't thinking straight. Today she won't remember a word."

Julie didn't believe that any more than she thought Daniel did, but if he wished to avoid the issue there was little she could say.

They sat in silence, his eyes still refusing to meet hers, which allowed Julie the opportunity to study him. The lines on his face were more pronounced now, deeply etched with his concern. His brow was furrowed. Julie knew that Clara was all the family he had.

The coffee machine across the hall caught her attention and Julie walked over to it, retrieving enough change from her purse for two cups. She added sugar to each and cream to Daniel's. He glanced up briefly as he accepted the paper cup. He looked surprised that she remembered how he liked his coffee.

They both set their cups aside and stood when the doctor came into the room.

"How is she?" Daniel asked.

"She's very weak, but better than we'd expected. The fact that she survived the night is nothing short of a miracle." The doctor paused to study them both. "Your mother seems to be a fighter. And since she's come this far, the chances of her making a complete recovery are good."

Julie felt as though a weight had been lifted from her shoulders.

"She's resting now, and both of you should do the same."

Daniel nodded. "I didn't want to leave until I was sure she'd be all right."

The doctor shook his head. "I don't know what you talked about last night, but it's certainly made a world of difference in her attitude. She's been improving ever since."

Julie's eyes met Daniel's. All the color had drained from his face.

"Go home and get some rest. There's nothing you can do here. I'll call you the minute there's any change."

"Thank you, Doctor," Daniel said.

They remained standing even after the doctor left. Daniel closed his eyes and released a long sigh.

"Can I give you a lift?" Julie asked quietly. Daniel didn't look as if he was in any condition to drive.

He shook his head. "No."

"You'll call me if you hear anything?"

Daniel nodded that he would.

"Everything's going to work out for the best," Julie whispered. She turned and walked away, ready to head home to her apartment.

Julie didn't mean to fall asleep, but after calling her mother to tell her about Clara Van Deen's attack, she decided to stretch out on the sofa and rest her eyes for a few minutes. The next thing she knew, someone was knocking on the door.

Julie glanced at her wristwatch and was shocked to see that it was after two.

"Just a minute," she called and hurriedly slid her feet back into her shoes as she ran her fingers through her tangled hair. "Who is it?" she asked before releasing the lock.

"It's Daniel."

Julie immediately threw open the door. "Is she all right? I mean, she's not worse, is she?"

"No, she's doing remarkably well."

"Thank God," Julie whispered as she stepped aside to let Daniel in.

"Did I wake you?" he asked.

With a wry smile, Julie nodded. "It's a good thing you did or I wouldn't be able to sleep tonight."

"They let me see her for a few minutes," Daniel said. He stood uneasily in the center of the living room.

"And?"

"And—" he paused and ran a hand through his hair "—she asked when we were planning to have the wedding."

Julie sat down on the sofa. "I was afraid of that."

Daniel remained standing. "Apparently she's been talking to the nurses about us. The head nurse told me she firmly believes that the fact you and I are going to be married was what kept my mother alive last night."

"And," Julie finished for him, "you're afraid that telling her otherwise could kill her."

Daniel moved to the far side of the room and spoke with his back to Julie. "I talked to the doctor again. He explained that if my mother can grow strong enough in the next few months, there's a possibility that heart surgery could correct her condition."

"That's wonderful news!"

He turned to her with a hard look in his eyes. "Yes, in some ways it's given me reason to hope. But in others…" He shook his head and let the rest of his words fade away. "Why did you come back, Julie? Why couldn't you have left well enough alone?"

"I already explained," she answered. "I want— No," she amended, "I *need* your forgiveness."

"My forgiveness," he repeated and lifted his head so

she could read the conflict in his eyes. "I wish to God I'd never seen you again."

The pain of his words slammed into her and she struggled to remain composed. "But I *am* here and I won't leave until I've accomplished what I came to do."

He muttered a curse under his breath. "I don't know what to do. I can't see us getting married. Not with the way I feel about you now."

"No," she agreed. "I can't see adding that complication to our relationship."

"We don't have a relationship," he reminded her. Then he left the apartment, slamming the door behind him.

On her way home from work on Monday, Julie dropped by the hospital with a flower arrangement. Mrs. Van Deen remained in intensive care. Julie doubted she'd be able to see her, but when she reached the nurses' station, she was informed that special permission had been granted for her to visit. The same five-minute limitation applied.

Clara Van Deen opened her eyes and gave Julie a feeble smile as she entered the room.

"I'm so pleased you came," Clara whispered, reaching out to squeeze Julie's hand.

"I can only stay a few minutes," Julie told her in a soft voice.

"I know."

"How are you feeling?"

"Much better now that I know Daniel will be happy."

A strangling sensation gripped Julie's throat. She couldn't think of any way to tell Clara that she and Daniel weren't going to be married.

"It was all my fault," Clara said. "With you and Daniel married, I can undo some of the harm I did."

"But…" Julie groaned inwardly. "Marriage isn't something to rush into. I'm still very much in love with Daniel, but he's been badly hurt and needs time to forget the past."

Clara closed her eyes. "Daniel loves you. He always has. His pride's been hurt, but he'll come around. I know he will."

So much for that argument, Julie mused, recalling her conversation with him the day before.

"Trust me, Julie," Clara said, opening her eyes once more. "The reason he's hurting so much is because he loves you."

The nurse came into the room. "I'm sorry, but I'm going to have to ask you to leave now."

Julie leaned down and gently kissed Clara on the cheek. "You rest now. I'll stop in tomorrow afternoon."

"Tell Daniel you love him," she whispered, her voice barely audible. "He needs to know that."

Julie didn't answer one way or the other. How could she admit that to a man who fought her every chance he got? Julie couldn't set herself up for that kind of pain.

Daniel was in the waiting room when she entered. He stood and looked at her expectantly.

"She seems much better today," Julie said.

He nodded. "Can we go someplace to talk?" he asked.

The hospital cafeteria was almost empty, with only a few people sitting at tables near the window.

"Go ahead and sit. I'll bring us something. Iced tea?" he suggested, arching a questioning brow.

The day had been warm for early spring and Julie smiled her thanks.

He carried the two glasses on an orange tray, setting them down before taking a seat himself.

"I talked to Dr. Givens," he said, staring into his tea.

Julie's hand curled around the icy glass, the cold seeping up her arm.

"He seems to feel that if we…if I…were to disappoint my mother over this marriage it could be detrimental to her recovery."

The cool sensation stopped at Julie's heart. "Does this mean you want to go ahead with the wedding?" she asked softly.

"No." He sighed. "A marriage between us would never work. Any possibility of finding happiness together ended when you left. But my mother's health—"

"Daniel," she said, her voice gaining strength, "I know you may find this hard to believe, but I never stopped loving you."

His gaze hardened. "If you'd loved me, you'd never have walked out. I don't think you know what it is to love, Julie."

Her mouth trembled with the effort to restrain an angry retort. She'd done what Daniel's mother suggested; she'd humbled herself. Daniel had to know how difficult it was for her to say those words and yet he threw her declaration of love back in her face. "If you honestly believe that, there's no point in having this discussion." She stood and hurried from the room. Tears blurred her vision as she made her way to the parking lot.

Before she could reach her vehicle, a hand gripped her upper arm, spinning her around.

"Running away again?" he said coldly. "Not this time. I need you to marry me, Julie. As soon as I can make the arrangements."

"I'd have to be crazy to marry a man like you!"

"Do you want to carry the guilt of my mother's death on your shoulders? If you leave now, that's what'll happen. It'll kill her. Are you ready to face that, Julie? Or don't you care?"

Julie pulled herself free of his grip. "Daniel," she said, "marriage is sacred."

"Not always," he insisted. "This'll be one of convenience."

"Will it stay that way?" Her questioning eyes sought his.

"Yes." His gaze was steady. "I couldn't touch you."

Biting her inner cheek, Julie refused to reveal the hurt he'd inflicted. It shouldn't matter. Considering how he felt, Julie didn't want Daniel to make love to her. "And after your mother…" She couldn't bring herself to mention the possibility of Clara Van Deen's death.

"You'll be free to go—no strings attached. An annulment should be fairly simple."

"I don't know." Julie smoothed a hand across her forehead. "I need time to think."

"No," Daniel shot back. "I need to know now. "

What choice did she have? Slowly, deliberately, Julie nodded. "All right, Daniel, I'll marry you. But only for your mother's sake."

His lip curled sardonically. "Do you think I'd marry you otherwise?"

"No, I don't suppose you would." Unfastening the chain from around her neck, Julie handed him her original engagement ring.

"You kept it?" Shock rang through his voice.

Julie stared into his dark eyes. "I couldn't bear to part with it. I wore it all these years. Close to my heart. That must tell you something."

He laughed shortly. "It must have given you a sense of triumph to have kept that all this time. To be honest, I'm surprised there's only one. In three years I would have expected you to add at least that many more."

"No," Julie answered, lowering her gaze, "there was never anyone but you."

"You don't honestly expect me to believe that, do you?"

"It doesn't matter what you believe."

"Keep it around your neck. That ring represented feelings I don't have anymore. I'll buy another one later."

"If that's what you want," Julie whispered.

"I'll make the arrangements and get back to you."

Julie didn't have to wait long. Daniel called the following afternoon with more information. The wedding would be in one week. Daniel picked her up after work Tuesday night so they could apply for the marriage license. After the required three-day wait, they'd have a wedding—of sorts. Everything was cut-and-dried. Even as he relayed the details, Daniel had remained emotionless.

Julie's mother was shocked but pleased, and planned to fly in for the wedding. Unfortunately she'd have to get back to her volunteer job the next day and Julie was relieved that her mother's stay would be cut short. She wasn't sure how long she could act the role of a happy bride.

The night before the wedding, with her mother sleeping in her bed, Julie tossed restlessly on the sofa. Just before six, she decided to give up and moved from the couch. She doubted she'd slept more than a couple of hours.

Standing at the window, she stared into the night, watching the dawn begin to overtake the darkness.

She bit her lip nervously. Today was her wedding day and in these last hours before the ceremony, she felt her freedom slipping through her fingers. Even now, Julie wasn't sure she was doing the right thing. Of one thing she was sure; right or wrong, she wouldn't walk out on Daniel a second time.

Several hours later, long after the last stars had faded with the morning sun, a car came to take Julie and her mother to the church. Clara Van Deen had insisted that her minister marry them. Neither Julie nor Daniel had any objections.

Daniel met them at the church. His eyes roamed over the long white dress Julie had chosen and something unreadable flickered across his face.

"Are you ready?" he asked casually, stirring her fear that she was making a terrible mistake. Julie swallowed hard and decided to ignore it.

The ceremony was short. Daniel responded methodically to the minister's instructions as if the words held no meaning for him. In contrast, Julie's voice wavered as she recited her vows.

Daniel glanced at her when she pledged her love, a glint of challenge in his gaze.

Julie's fingers trembled as he slipped a plain gold band on her finger. The simplicity of the ring suited her, but she was sure Daniel had chosen it in contrast to the beautiful diamond he'd given her the first time. Julie was confident the difference didn't stop there.

After the ceremony, Julie's mother hugged them both, her eyes shining with happiness. They rode to the hospital together and were allowed a short visit with Daniel's mother.

Clara Van Deen smiled as a joyful tear escaped from the corner of her eye.

"Trust me, Julie," she whispered. "Things will work out."

Julie nodded, smiling feebly as she kissed Clara's wrinkled brow.

From the hospital, Daniel and Julie drove her mother to the airport. Margaret Houser insisted on paying for everyone's lunch. If she noticed the stilted silence between the bride and groom, she said nothing.

Julie suddenly wished for a longer visit with her mother, but Daniel was obviously in a hurry and after an abrupt goodbye, he ushered her back to the car.

Watching him as he drove, Julie clutched the small bouquet of flowers her mother had given her. The unfamiliar gold band felt strange against her finger and she found herself toying with it.

At a red light, Daniel caught her staring at her hand. "Don't be so anxious to remove that wedding ring. It's not going anywhere anytime soon."

Julie glared at him. "Of course. You've made your feelings perfectly clear."

Neither spoke again until Daniel had parked at his condominium in Wichita's most prestigious downtown area. The doorman smiled as he held the door open for Julie.

"Good afternoon, Mr. Van Deen," he said, eyeing Julie and the two suitcases Daniel carried.

Daniel nodded and placed his hand under Julie's elbow, hurrying her toward the elevator. The doors parted at the press of the button and Julie was ushered inside. The strained silence continued as he unlocked the door of the condo, swinging it wide to allow Julie to enter first.

Julie hesitated, wondering what lay before her.

"You don't expect me to carry you over the threshold, do you?"

"Of course not," she replied shortly. She took a deep breath and entered her new home.

The condo was surprisingly spacious. The tiled entry led to a sunken living room carpeted in plush brown pile. Two picture windows overlooked the downtown area and Julie paused to admire the view from fifteen floors up.

Daniel moved around her and carried her suitcases to one of the bedrooms. He stopped outside the door. "This is your room," he said, interrupting her search for city landmarks.

Julie moved away from the window and followed the sound of his voice.

A glance inside the room confirmed her belief that this had been a guest room. Fitting, Julie thought, since she was little more than an unwelcome guest in Daniel's life.

"The rest of your things will be delivered sometime this afternoon," he informed her. "I have to get back to the office for a couple of hours."

Back to the office! Julie couldn't believe it. They'd

barely been married three hours. She'd taken the day off work. He could've done the same.

"What am I supposed to do?" she asked. "Make myself at home in a strange house—alone?"

"Unpack," he replied flippantly.

"That'll take all of five minutes. Then what?"

"Don't tell me I have to stay home and babysit you for the next twenty years."

"Go ahead and leave," Julie said. "No need to hurry back on my account."

Daniel laughed mirthlessly as he headed out the door. "Don't worry, I won't."

As she'd told him, five minutes later, both suitcases were empty. After a quick tour of the condo, Julie returned to her room. She yawned, and her neck hurt from a sleepless night on the sofa, so she decided to take a nap. The bed was soft and welcoming; within minutes she fell into a deep, comfortable slumber.

She woke around four, feeling refreshed. Daniel had been gone for several hours. After leafing through a magazine, she considered going out for dinner, letting him come home to an empty apartment. It would serve him right. But no, being antagonistic wouldn't help their situation. She'd prepare dinner and try to make the best of things.

The kitchen was beautifully organized and well stocked—either Daniel enjoyed cooking or he had someone come in to cook for him. Julie's hand tightened against the counter. She couldn't deny that the thought of Daniel bringing another woman into this kitchen made her feel jealous.

She quickly prepared a fresh salad and dessert, and

then thawed two large steaks in the microwave until they were ready to grill.

After a moment's deliberation, she chose to set the dining room table rather than the small one in the kitchen. This was, after all, their wedding day—although Daniel seemed to be doing his best to forget that.

Another suitcase and several boxes from her apartment were delivered shortly after five and Julie spent the next hour unpacking and arranging her things among Daniel's. She wasn't surprised to find that they shared similar tastes in literature and art. As she placed each book on the shelf, she frequently discovered that Daniel already owned a copy.

Julie didn't know why this astonished her. They'd discovered a number of similarities since their first meeting. Julie wondered if Daniel still played tennis. That was how they'd first met. The attraction had been immediate and intense. They'd fallen so deeply in love.

As dusk fell over the city, Julie lit the candles, creating a warm, romantic mood. She regretted the harsh parting words she'd exchanged with Daniel that afternoon. Maybe this dinner would show him that she was willing to work things out. She'd taken the first step. But the next one had to come from Daniel.

Minutes ticked into hours and at eleven Julie finally accepted that Daniel wouldn't be coming home for dinner. She wasn't sure if he'd be home at all.

After blowing out the candles and turning on the lights, she began to clear the table piece by piece, returning the china place settings to the rosewood cabinet.

When half the dishes were cleared, the door opened.

Julie paused, clutching the expensive plate tightly to her stomach, her heart pounding wildly.

From across the room, Daniel's eyes met hers.

Julie smiled nervously and resumed her task, praying he wouldn't comment. She should have known better.

"A romantic dinner complete with candlelight? What's this, Julie? An invitation to your bed?"

Five

"No," she said, hoping her voice sounded light and carefree. "It wasn't that at all."

"Pity," he mumbled under his breath.

Julie had to bite her tongue to keep from asking where he'd been. That was exactly what he wanted her to do, but she refused to play his games.

"If you'll excuse me, I think I'll go to bed."

Daniel continued to stare at her from the tiled entryway. "I didn't know if you'd eaten or not."

Julie shook her head. "No, I thought I'd wait for you."

"I'm surprised you did."

She moved past him and down the hall to her room. Daniel had made it clear they'd make no pretense of a honeymoon and Julie was going back to work in the morning. As she undressed, she could hear Daniel's movements in the kitchen.

Tying the belt on her housecoat, Julie moved across the hall to the bathroom to brush her teeth. The appealing aroma of broiling steak reminded her that she hadn't eaten since lunch. She tried to focus on brushing. Not for anything would she go back into that kitchen.

In her room, she sat on the bed and opened the novel she'd been reading. The light tap at the door startled her.

"Your steak is ready." Daniel stuck his head in and smiled. "Medium rare, as I recall."

Julie opened her mouth to tell him exactly what he could do with the steak, then stopped herself. It had been a tiring day for both of them and the last thing they needed was an argument.

"I'll be there in a minute." Strangely pleased with this turn of events, Julie put on her slippers and joined him in the kitchen.

The table was set for two. Their steaks were served with grilled tomatoes and melted cheddar.

Julie opened the refrigerator and brought out the salad she'd made.

As she set the bowl on the table, Daniel said, "There were some briefs I needed to review for a court case in the morning."

Julie paused as she sat at the table, fork in hand. Daniel was telling her why he was late. She hadn't expected it, sure he'd wanted her to fret.

"Perhaps it would be best to let the other person know if one of us is going to be late," she said as her knife cut into the steak.

"Sounds fair," Daniel commented.

Julie smiled. The evening had gotten off to an uneasy start, but they were working things out.

"We should probably decide on some house rules," she suggested casually.

"Such as?"

"Since you did the cooking, I'll do the dishes."

"That seems reasonable." Daniel grinned approvingly. He hadn't smiled at her—really smiled—since she'd returned. She'd almost forgotten how wonderful it felt.

Julie laid her knife on the plate and looked up. "That was wonderful. I don't remember you being such an excellent cook."

"I've managed to pick up a few skills," he said dryly.

Julie stood and carried their plates to the sink while Daniel poured them each a cup of coffee.

"Shall we drink this in the living room?" he asked.

"I'll be there in a minute. I want to get these in the dishwasher."

When Julie joined him, Daniel was standing at the window looking out at the sparkling lights of the city.

"My mother seemed better today, didn't she?"

Julie took her coffee cup from the end table and sat down. "Yes, she did. There was some color in her cheeks for the first time since she collapsed."

"It's going to be an uphill battle for her in the coming months."

"I know. I'll do anything I can to help her," Julie said, taking a sip of her coffee. Daniel remained at the window with his back to her.

"I think we should agree that no matter what happens between us, we won't take our squabbles to my mother."

"Of course not." Julie blinked. She was surprised that Daniel would think otherwise. "If we need to talk something over, the person I'll come to is you."

"Good." He moved to sit in the wing-back chair

beside her. "Don't worry about the housework. The cleaning lady comes twice a week."

"What about the cooking?" She focused on the mug in her hands. "I hate to admit it, but I'm not much good in the kitchen. You're probably more adept—do you want to take turns?"

"If you'd like."

"It might be the easiest thing." She shrugged. How could they sit beside each another—husband and wife—and talk of trivialities? Julie didn't want her marriage to begin this way. Twice before the wedding, she'd tried to discuss their past and both times Daniel had cut her off. He obviously wanted to leave that period in their relationship behind them. Julie realized they'd have no future until they faced the hurts and misunderstandings of the past. But tonight wasn't the time.

"You look tired," Daniel commented.

"Sorry." Julie shook her head to clear her thoughts. "I guess I am."

"Let's turn in."

Together they carried their cups into the kitchen. Julie put them in the dishwasher and Daniel showed her how to start it. The soft hum of running water followed them into the hallway.

Daniel flipped off the light switch and the condo went dark. Julie's eyes adjusted to the moonlit room.

"Can you find your way?" Daniel asked.

"Sure," Julie said. Their eyes met in the darkness and everything went still. She couldn't see his expression well enough to know what he was thinking, but time seemed to slow.

When his hand reached out to caress her cheek, a

warm sensation spread down her neck. She sighed, closed her eyes and placed her hand over his.

"Good night, Julie," he said tenderly, removing his hand. He walked her to her room, but then hesitated in the open doorway.

For a fleeting moment, the hurt that had driven them apart faded. Julie took a wishful step in his direction. This man was her *husband*. They were meant to be together.

"If you'd like, I'll cook breakfast in the morning," she offered, wanting an excuse to linger with him in the darkness.

He didn't answer, and Julie wondered if he'd heard her. "I thought you said you weren't much of a cook," he finally said.

"I can manage breakfast."

"Did you eat out often? Is the reason you can't cook because you dated so much?"

"No," she answered simply. "Not much at all."

Silvery moonlight filled the narrow hallway as Julie studied her husband, waiting for a reaction.

"I wish I could believe that," he said with a sigh, "but you're much too beautiful not to have men fawning over you." And with that, he abruptly walked away.

Julie's clock radio went off at six, filling the silent room with music. She lay in bed for several minutes, listening to a couple of songs before throwing back the covers and climbing out of bed.

Slipping into her housecoat, she hurried into the kitchen to put on a pot of coffee. The morning was glorious. The sun was shining and Julie stood at the window looking down on the city as it stirred to life.

When she turned around, she found Daniel waiting by the coffeepot, clutching a large mug.

"Good morning," she greeted him with a warm smile.

Daniel mumbled something unintelligible under his breath.

"What did you say?" she asked as she took his empty mug out of his hand, and poured in what little coffee had drained through.

"Nothing," he said.

"No one told me you were such a grouch in the mornings," she teased. "I'll go get dressed and stay out of your way until you've had your coffee."

"That's probably a good idea."

Julie returned to her bedroom and dressed, choosing a new outfit—a gray-and-blue striped dress with a wide vee neckline. Putting on a pair of pumps, she did her makeup and brushed her hair before re-entering the kitchen.

The bacon was sizzling in the pan when Daniel came in to pour himself a second cup of coffee.

"How do you want your eggs? Over easy?" She was surprised to see the scowl on his face. "Is something wrong?"

"That dress."

"It's new. Don't you like it?" She swallowed uncomfortably.

"It's a little revealing, don't you think?"

"Revealing?" Julie gasped. "In what way?"

Daniel grabbed the paper and sat down to read it. "The neckline."

"The neckline?" Julie's hand flew to the V-shaped

front. She hadn't found it to be too low. "There's nothing wrong with this dress," she insisted.

"That's a matter of opinion," he said from behind the paper.

"How do you want your eggs?" Julie repeated, choosing to ignore his reaction to her dress.

The newspaper was a barrier between them. "I've lost my appetite," he muttered.

"So have I," she whispered, turning off the burner.

The office was only a few minutes away. Neither spoke on the drive over. Julie kept her hands folded in her lap, her head rigid as she focused straight ahead. She hadn't changed her outfit, nor would she. Daniel was being unreasonable. A wry smile touched her mouth. And she'd expected him to *like* the new dress.

He pulled into the parking garage across the street and into his allotted space.

"I may be late tonight," he said.

Julie nodded without looking at him. "I thought I'd go to the hospital after work."

"Then I'll meet you there."

They sounded like robots, their voices clipped and emotionless.

Julie did a double take when she entered the office— Sherry was already at her desk.

"Are my eyes deceiving me?" Julie teased. "Sherry early? That's impossible."

Sherry's smile was weak. "Morning." She lowered her head and blew her nose in a tissue. "I guess it's a bit of a shock, isn't it?"

"What's wrong?" Julie asked.

"Wrong?" Sherry laughed. "What makes you think something's wrong?"

"Maybe it's the mountain of wet tissues, or perhaps the red eyes. But then I've always had a reputation for being a good sleuth."

Sherry made a gallant effort to smile.

"I guess I should've said something the first time you mentioned Daniel," Julie explained, realizing what this was probably about. "I didn't want to hurt you, Sherry. Not for anything. Daniel and I have known each other for several years."

Sherry glanced up tearfully. "It's not that. I *was* surprised to hear about you two, but that's not the problem."

Julie was confused. "Then why are you crying?"

"It's Andy." Sherry said, her voice wavering.

"Your ex-husband?"

Sherry tugged another tissue from the brightly colored box and nodded. "The divorce isn't final until the end of the month."

"And you're having second thoughts?" Julie's knowledge of Sherry's marriage was limited to the bits of information her friend had shared. As far as Julie could tell, they didn't have any one specific reason to separate. Both had been too involved in their jobs and they'd grown apart. The trial separation had led to the decision to file for the divorce. In the short time Julie had known Sherry, it had been obvious that Sherry wanted to prove how much fun she could have without her husband.

"I...I saw Andy last night."

"Did you two talk?" Julie asked. She didn't want to pry, but figured Sherry would feel better if she confided in someone.

"Talk!" Sherry hiccuped loudly. "There was a voluptuous blonde draped all over him."

"But Sherry, that shouldn't bother you. For heaven's sake, you've been out with a dozen different men just since I've known you."

"Yes, but that was different," Sherry said.

"How?"

"Andy didn't care if I saw someone else."

"How can you be so sure?" Julie asked. "Maybe he did care. But maybe he's decided the time has come for him to start dating again, too."

"Not Andy. He's always hated blondes."

"You're blonde," Julie pointed out.

"I know, but the woman he was with last night isn't like his usual type."

Julie couldn't question her further because Mr. Barrett entered the room just then, nodding a brief greeting as he hung his coat in the closet. He seemed about to say something when he noticed Sherry's red face. Swiftly, he retreated into his office, closing the door.

"Why don't we see if we can take our lunch hour together and talk some more," Julie suggested.

"I'd like that," Sherry said, dabbing at the last of her tears. "I meant to tell you earlier how nice you look today. Is that a new outfit?"

"Yes." Julie smiled. "Do you like it?"

"It's perfect on you."

"What about the neckline?" Julie tilted her head back and arched her shoulders.

"What about it?" Sherry asked.

"It's not too revealing?"

"Revealing?" Sherry echoed. "No way."

"That's what I thought."

* * *

Clara Van Deen was looking much improved when Julie arrived at the intensive care unit that afternoon. She took Julie's hand in hers as Julie approached the bed.

"How's my new daughter?"

"How's my new mother?"

Clara closed her eyes and when she opened them again, they were glistening with tears. "Better now that I've made up for some of the pain I caused you and Daniel."

"I'm glad to hear that," Julie said. "I love him, Clara."

"And Daniel loves you. Don't ever doubt that, Julie. I don't know much about his life anymore—I understand he saw lots of women—but, Julie, there was never anyone he truly loved. No one but you."

Julie squeezed the old woman's hand gently. "I'll be a good wife to him."

"I don't doubt that for a minute." Clara's smile was weak, but infinitely happy.

When Daniel got there thirty minutes later, Julie was in the waiting room leafing through a dog-eared magazine she'd already read twice. She glanced up to see that his gaze had fallen on her neckline and the fullness of her breasts, but his expression was unreadable.

"Your mother seems better," Julie said.

Daniel nodded. "I'm looking forward to visiting with her."

Julie's eyes were drawn to her husband. His rugged appeal gave the impression that he worked outside. His face was quite tanned for early spring and Julie suspected he was exercising regularly. She wondered if he still played tennis.

"I talked to the doctor this afternoon," Daniel said as he rubbed his hand along the back of his neck.

"And?" Julie uncrossed her legs, setting the magazine aside.

"He said she's improved enough for him to consider open-heart surgery."

"When?" Julie breathed.

"A month from now."

"That's wonderful!" If the surgery was a success, the possibility of Daniel's mother returning to a normal life would be greatly increased.

"Is it?" Daniel responded almost flippantly. "Even if she gains enough strength for the surgery, her chances of survival are only fifty-fifty."

"But what would they be without it?"

Daniel wandered to the far side of the room, then pivoted sharply. "Far less than that."

Julie understood and shared his concern, but she felt that the chance of a longer, healthier life for his mother was worth the risk. "Everything's going to be fine," she assured him.

"How do you know that?"

"I don't," Julie admitted. "But your mother's content. Her spirits are high and she has the will to live. A positive attitude is bound to help." It was on the tip of her tongue to reveal that on the day Clara had collapsed, she'd mentioned how much she longed for grandchildren. Julie believed sheer willpower would see her mother-in-law through this surgery.

Daniel's expression tightened as he studied her.

The nurse arrived and told Daniel he could go in to see his mother.

Later, when they'd driven home, Julie noticed a spark of amusement in Daniel's eyes, an expression that was still there as she set the table for dinner.

"What's so funny?" she finally asked.

"What makes you think anything's funny?"

Julie pretended an interest in the green salad she was tossing. "Every time I look up, you're trying to keep from laughing."

"Something my mother said, that's all," Daniel told her.

"About me?" Julie asked stiffly, hoping she wasn't the brunt of some joke.

"Indirectly."

They ate in near silence. Not an intentional silence, at least not on Julie's part, but there was very little to talk about, since Daniel hadn't allowed her into his life. Julie was confident that he'd open up in time, but the one thing they desperately needed to talk about, Daniel refused to discuss.

"Are you still playing tennis?" Julie asked as she cleared the table.

"Often enough."

Julie noted that he didn't ask if *she* still played. They'd met on the courts and had regularly played as a doubles team. Julie still enjoyed the game, but didn't know how to volunteer that fact without making it look as if she was seeking an invitation—which, of course, she was.

"I'll do the dishes later." Daniel broke into her unhappy thoughts. "There are a few papers I want to go over tonight."

"Do you bring work home a lot?" Julie hadn't meant to sound so accusatory.

"Hardly at all," Daniel replied defensively.

She offered to do the dishes for him so he could work, but Daniel turned her down. "When I say I'm going to do something, I do it," he said pointedly.

Julie gripped the edge of the oak table. "In other words, you don't walk out five days before a wedding. That's what you're saying—isn't it, Daniel?"

"That's exactly what I'm saying," he snapped.

Julie stood and pushed her chair back from the table. Without a word, she left the kitchen, reached for her jacket and headed for the door.

"Where are you going?" Daniel demanded.

"Out," she replied and closed the door behind her. Half hoping Daniel would come after her, Julie lingered in the hall, but he didn't follow. She should have known.

Without her purse and nowhere to go, Julie was back in an hour after taking a brisk walk.

When she returned, Daniel was in his office, or so she assumed. The two pans from their meal were washed and stacked on the kitchen counter. Julie dried them and put them away. When she'd finished she glanced up to see that Daniel was standing in the doorway of the office, watching her.

"You came back."

"What's the matter?" she asked. "Were you hoping I wouldn't?"

A muscle twitched in his jaw as he broke the pencil he was holding. He pivoted and returned to his office.

Julie closed her eyes and took several calming breaths. This tension between them was taking its toll. She couldn't live like this. When she was younger, she'd avoided confrontation and had paid dearly for it, but she wasn't the same Julie now as she'd been then. She didn't avoid conflict these days, but she didn't instigate it either.

Daniel remained in his office with the door shut, while Julie sat alone in the living room reading. She felt drowsy, but shook herself awake, determined to be up when Daniel came out. She wasn't going to run away, not anymore. It was important that he recognize that.

But as her eyelids became heavier, she was afraid she couldn't fight off sleep anymore. She closed her book, switched the light to its lowest setting and leaned her head against the back of the chair, finally surrendering.

"Julie." Daniel's whisper woke her. "You'll get a crick in your neck."

She opened her eyes and stretched. The soft glow from the lamp was the only light in the house. Daniel stood above her, his shirt open. He studied her carefully and Julie yearned to reach out to him, slide her arms around his neck and gently place her mouth on his. He hadn't kissed her, had avoided touching her, but Julie felt that if he walked away from her now, she couldn't bear it.

"Julie," he whispered.

Surely he could see the hunger she was feeling for his touch, her need to be loved, forgiven and trusted by him again.

He helped her to her feet, his manner impersonal.

"Daniel," she pleaded softly.

Without a word, he wrapped his arms around her,

his gaze drawn to her lips as he slowly closed the distance between them.

Julie sighed as she slid her hands over his shoulders and linked her fingers at the base of his neck. "Oh, Daniel," she whispered, "it's been so long."

He held her against him, his mouth moving sweetly over hers as he brought her closer.

Julie thrilled to the urgency of his mouth as he kissed her. He buried his face in the curve of her neck as Julie drove her hands through his thick hair.

Daniel pulled away and looked into her eyes. Julie smiled and brushed her mouth over his, kissing the tiny cleft in his chin. That was something he'd always loved and she wanted him to know she hadn't forgotten.

His body stiffened against hers as he tugged his arms free. "Good night, Julie," he murmured before turning and walking away. He hadn't forgotten anything, either.

How many times would he walk away from her before they were even, before she'd been punished enough for the way she'd left him? Standing alone in the darkened room, Julie had no answer. Defeated, she retired to her room, hoping to find some peace in sleep.

The next day, they continued their new routine. They rode to work together in silence, and from there they went to the hospital, taking turns visiting his mother. Daniel cooked dinner while Julie changed out of her work clothes.

"I'm going to the library," she announced as she set their plates in the dishwasher.

"How long will you be?" Daniel asked without looking up from the mail he was sorting through.

"About an hour." Anything was better than sitting

in a silent house again while Daniel closed himself off in his office.

He shrugged, but said nothing.

"Would..." Julie hesitated. "Would you like to come?"

"I've got things to do around here," he replied.

Julie let herself out the front door, her heart aching. The first night, she'd accused Daniel of playing games. Now she was the one escaping, hoping that he'd somehow show that he wanted her to stay. He didn't.

Six

Saturday morning, Daniel left the condo before Julie climbed out of bed. Lying awake with her bedroom door partially open, Julie listened to his movements as he walked down the hall. She expected him to go into the kitchen but was surprised to hear the front door click a few moments later.

Julie slipped out of bed and found a pot of coffee on the kitchen counter along with a note. The message read: *Playing tennis all day.*

All day, Julie mused resentfully. They'd talked about tennis earlier in the week. There'd been ample opportunity for him to include her in today's outing had he wished to.

After brewing a fresh pot of coffee, Julie sat at the round oak table, mug in hand. She'd known when she agreed to marry Daniel that there were several factors working against them. Some days, Julie was convinced that he'd never forgive her for leaving. But at other times, she could feel him studying her, apparently still interested. He hadn't touched her since the other night. Julie could tell he regretted that one slip and was taking measures to ensure that it wouldn't happen again.

She cooked a light breakfast, then dressed in jeans and a sweatshirt. The last of her things had arrived from the apartment. Only a few of her everyday items were necessary, since Daniel's condo was fully furnished.

Stacking the cardboard boxes in the bottom of her closet, Julie located the one full of mementos from her relationship with Daniel. Now that they were married, she could set them out freely. If she left their engagement photo out in the open, it might prompt him to discuss the things he chose to ignore.

Encouraged by the thought, she set the gold-framed picture on top of the television and stepped back to examine it. As always, she was struck by how happy they looked and vowed that one day they'd be that happy again.

She placed a few other things around the room and then stood back to admire her efforts. The condo now reflected who they'd been as a loving, happy couple. Daniel couldn't help being affected by it. Undoubtedly he'd be surprised that she'd kept all these things, but she wanted him to understand that although she'd left, she'd never stopped loving him.

After a shower, Julie had lunch and decided to drop in at the hospital to visit Clara.

"Good afternoon," Julie said, leaning over to lightly kiss Clara's cheek. "How are you feeling today?"

"Much better."

She looked well, and Julie felt encouraged.

"Where's Daniel?" Clara asked.

"He's playing tennis." Julie hoped that her mother-in-law wouldn't ask for details because Julie wouldn't know what to say. She hoped to paint an optimistic picture of their marriage, but she wasn't willing to lie.

"That's right," Clara said. "Daniel mentioned something about playing in a tournament this weekend. I'm surprised you aren't at the club with him. As I recall, you two made an excellent team."

So he'd told his mother but hadn't bothered to say anything to her. Maybe he had another partner and didn't want Julie interfering with his plans. The thought made her jealous, but she squashed the feeling before her mother-in-law could read her expression.

"You still play, don't you?" Clara asked.

"I'm a bit rusty," Julie admitted. The Country Club— Julie could vividly recall how uncomfortable she'd been around those people. Daniel had taken her there several times for dinner or tennis, but Julie hadn't been able to overcome her insecurity.

"I thought you'd want to be with him," Clara continued, studying Julie carefully.

"I'm meeting him later," Julie said. It wasn't exactly a lie. She *would* show up at the Country Club. The time had come for her to face some of the other ghosts of her past.

"There was no need to disrupt your day to come and visit me," Clara said. "I already know how much you care. Whether I live or die is of no consequence to me. All I want before I go is the assurance that the two of you are happy." The white-haired woman regarded Julie seriously. "I wouldn't, however, mind a grandchild or two." She smiled. "Daniel seemed quite amused when I mentioned how much I was looking forward to grandchildren."

So that was what he'd been so smug about the other night. "I think he feels we should wait," Julie improvised.

"His words exactly. But try to convince him, Julie. I don't have all the time in the world. And he's at the age when he should be thinking of starting a family."

"I'll bring it up," Julie promised. "But remember we've only been married a little while."

Clara closed her eyes. "It seems so much longer. In my muddled mind, it's difficult to remember you were gone all those years."

"My heart was here," Julie said softly.

"Would you read to me, dear?" Clara asked, handing over a book from her nightstand.

"I'd be happy to."

Julie read until she was certain Clara was asleep, then she slipped quietly from the room. She was set on facing Daniel at the Country Club, but her determination began to waver. Her unexpected arrival could be uncomfortable for everyone involved. No, she reasoned. As his wife she had a right to see her husband. Resolutely, she left the hospital, got into her car and headed for the outskirts of town.

Julie was lucky to find a parking space in the crowded lot. The tennis courts and surrounding areas were jammed with spectators. Julie signed in as Daniel's wife and was grateful no one questioned her.

It only took her a few minutes to find him. He was on the courts in what she learned was the men's singles semifinal. She sat in the bleachers, silently engrossed in the competition, proud when Daniel won. The championship game followed fifteen minutes later. It was a tense match and Daniel's composure astonished her. He lost the title, but shook hands with his opponent, smiling as he exited the court.

The crowd gathered around the winner as the stands emptied. Julie made her way to her husband.

Daniel was wiping his face with a hand towel.

"Nice game," she said from behind him.

He didn't pause or give any indication that he was surprised as he turned toward her. "How'd you know where to find me?"

"Well, your note. And then your mother mentioned the tournament, so I thought I'd stop by to cheer you on."

"I saw you in the stands," he said.

She noticed that he didn't indicate one way or the other how he felt about her being there. "You were good. Your game's improved."

"I've played better," he said, packing away his racket.

"Good game, Van Deen," a deep baritone voice said from behind them.

Daniel's posture stiffened. "Thanks." He slung the towel around his neck.

Julie didn't recognize the tall, athletic man who'd joined them.

"I see you brought your own cheering section," the man said.

Daniel wrapped an arm around Julie's waist, bringing her to his side. "Patterson, meet my wife, Julie. Julie, this is my friend and associate, Jim Patterson."

"Your wife!" Jim exclaimed. "When did that happen?"

"Recently," Daniel said.

Jim chuckled and rubbed the side of his jaw, bemused. "It must've been recent. Does Kali know?"

At the mention of another woman's name, Julie eyed her husband speculatively. She'd briefly wondered if there was anyone Daniel was seeing seriously, but figured Sherry would have known if he'd been involved with someone else. Clearly, Jim knew more than her coworker.

"I haven't talked to Kali yet," Daniel replied.

"This calls for a celebration," Jim said, obviously trying to cover the awkward moment. "Let me buy you two a drink."

"Not today," Daniel answered. "Unfortunately, Julie has an appointment she needs to get to." His arm slid from around her waist to her lower back. "I'll see you to your car, honcy." He steered her toward the parking area.

Julie looked back over her shoulder. "It's a pleasure to have met you...Mr. Patterson."

"We'll have that drink another time," Jim promised with a brief salute.

Once they were alone, Julie shook Daniel's hand loose. "What was that all about? And who's Kali?"

He clenched his jaw. "No one you need to concern yourself with."

"And why couldn't we stay for a drink?" she sputtered. "It's time I met your friends. I'm your *wife*."

"Don't remind me."

She looked away, refusing to let him see how badly his words had hurt her.

Daniel jammed his hands into his pockets. He looked as if he was about to say something more, but Julie didn't wait to find out. She turned and walked briskly to her car. She couldn't get out of that parking lot fast enough.

Unwilling to return to the empty condo, she drove around until the hurt and anger had faded. So there'd been another woman. She could accept that as long as this Kali remained in the past. She'd need to be told, of course, that Daniel had married or there'd be trouble down the road.

Julie wasn't so naive as to think that Daniel had lived like a monk during the time she was gone. But it still hurt more than she thought possible. What worried her most was his reluctance to tell her anything about Kali.

When she got home two hours later, Daniel was sitting the living room.

"Julie." He jumped up and approached her, running a hand through his hair. "Where were you?"

"I went for a drive. I needed time to think."

He scowled and nodded.

She glanced at her watch. "I didn't realize it was so late. It's my turn to cook, isn't it? I'll start something right away. You must be starving."

The sound of his voice followed her as she headed for the kitchen. "I thought I'd take you out tonight."

Julie froze. "Take me out?"

"As you said earlier, it's time you and I were seen together."

Julie breathed a sigh of relief. This dinner invitation was his way of telling her he was sorry for what had happened that afternoon. It wasn't an eloquent apology, but it was encouraging.

"Well?" Hands deep in his pockets, he studied her.

She replied with a slow, sensual smile. "I'd like that."

"Wear something elegant."

Her smile faltered. "I'm afraid I may not have anything appropriate. Would you mind if we went somewhere less formal?"

"As I recall, you liked fancy places."

"I was twenty-one," she explained. "I never really liked it, but I couldn't tell you that. I was afraid if you knew how shy I really was…"

A flicker of surprise touched Daniel's features. "Our relationship was riddled with misunderstandings, wasn't it? Why didn't you tell me how you felt?"

"I was so crazy about you, I was ready to be anything you wanted."

"Everything but my wife," he said, his expression impassive.

"I couldn't," she said. "Not then." She left the kitchen and moved into her bedroom. Leaning against the door, she closed her eyes. Surely Daniel must realize that if they'd gone through with the wedding three years ago their marriage would have been doomed. Julie knew that it wasn't any more secure now and the thought saddened her.

She changed into a pale blue dress and a white jacket. A glance in the mirror confirmed that even the most critical eye would find no fault with the neckline. She completed the outfit with white high-heeled sandals and a single strand of pearls which Daniel had given her. She doubted he'd remember, though. He'd given her so many beautiful things.

She went into the living room, where Daniel was waiting. He wore dark slacks with a blue shirt under a sports coat.

"I made a phone call and was able to get last-minute

tickets for the dinner theater," he said as he pulled out of the parking garage.

Julie nodded. "That sounds wonderful. Thank you. What's playing?"

"Never Too Late," he said, casting an amused glance at Julie.

"Seems appropriate," she said, returning his smile. She prayed it wasn't too late for them.

When his hand reached for hers, Julie felt a warm sensation radiate up her arm from his touch. It had always been like that. Daniel was capable of stirring emotions in her that she'd only dreamed existed.

Dinner was delicious and the comedy had both of them laughing. For those few hours, they managed to set aside their difficulties and were husband and wife without the past intruding.

"Would you like to go someplace for a drink?" Daniel asked on their way out of the dinner theater.

"We could if you like," she said. "But I think I'd prefer a cup of coffee in our own kitchen so I can prop up my feet. I shouldn't have worn these shoes."

"If you promise to wear a more sensible pair the next time I take you to dinner, then I'll give you a foot rub," Daniel admonished with a lazy smile.

"You're on." It felt good to joke with him. Tonight it had been so easy to pretend they were a loving husband and wife enjoying an evening out together.

Back at the condo, Julie made them cappuccinos, while Daniel put on a CD. Mellow music filled the space, a beautiful love ballad.

She carried the cups into the living room and sat on the opposite end of the sofa from Daniel. "Here." She swung her feet onto his lap. "Work your magic."

While she sipped from the cup of creamy coffee, Daniel gently massaged her feet.

"Why do you wear those silly things?" he asked. "You've got a blister on your heel."

"I know," Julie said, "but they're the only decent pair of dress shoes I have."

"Is that a hint for me to hand over my credit card?"

Julie swung her feet onto the floor. "No," she answered evenly. It was difficult to tell if he was teasing or not. She studied his face, but he hid his emotions well.

"A husband enjoys buying his wife gifts. You certainly had no difficulty accepting things from me in the past. You kept them, too, if the pearls are any indication."

"I kept every reminder of you I could," she whispered. She looked at the television and stiffened when she saw that the framed engagement photograph was missing.

"What happened to the picture?" She got to her feet. "I put it here this morning and now it's gone."

"I put it away," Daniel said.

"Away?" she echoed in disbelief. "What do you mean, *away?*"

Daniel stood up and moved to the opposite side of the living room. "It's in your bedroom."

"But why?" she asked, watching his reaction.

"Because I was angry and I took it out on the photo."

Julie went pale. "You...didn't destroy it, did you?"

"No, but I was tempted. I don't want reminders of that time in my life."

"I see," Julie said, trying to remain calm. She refused to give in to the tears. For a minute she thought he would explain further, but he just walked into his office and closed the door.

Julie was shaking so badly the cappuccino sloshed over the rim of her cup and into the saucer as she carried it to the kitchen. After rinsing everything in the sink, she returned to the living room and removed the other mementos she'd placed there. Those items, however small, meant a great deal to her. She couldn't bear to have Daniel reject them as he had the photograph.

That night, she woke from a fitful slumber around three. Just when it looked like she was making progress with Daniel, something would happen and she'd realize how far they still had to go.

She got out of bed and wandered to the kitchen for a glass of milk. She stood at the picture window, looking down on the silent, sleeping city below. She sensed more than heard Daniel coming up behind her. Julie remained where she was.

"You couldn't sleep?"

"No." The word tumbled from her mouth as tears filled her eyes.

His hand clasped her shoulder and he pressed his face into her hair. "Julie, I'm sorry about the picture. The minute I saw how much it meant to you, I regretted taking it down. To be honest, I wasn't sure why'd you put it out. I thought you wanted to torment me."

"Torment you?" She turned, her gaze seeking his in the moonlight.

He took the glass of milk from her, set it aside and brought her into the warm circle of his arms. His chin rested on her head as his hands roamed soothingly up and down her back.

It felt so right to be in his arms again, almost as if she'd never left.

With one finger under her chin, he lifted her mouth to his. Julie stood on tiptoe and fit her body to his, feeling Daniel resist momentarily as she melted against him.

"I'm sorry, Julie," he whispered against her lips.

"I know," she said, kissing him once more. Daniel moaned and hungrily kissed her back, holding her so close it was difficult to breathe.

"I won't make you cry again," he promised.

Julie sighed longingly and pressed her face to his shoulder. Nestled in the comfort of his embrace, she tried to stifle a yawn.

"Come on, sleepyhead," he whispered and kissed her temple. "I'll tuck you in."

Daniel led her back to the bedroom, his arm around her waist. Julie's heart was pounding as he helped her into the bed. He wanted her, Julie was sure of it. She was his wife and he longed to take her in his arms and love her as a husband should. Yet he kept his distance, his face revealing the conflict he felt.

"Good night," he whispered, finally turning away.

"Good night," she repeated, suppressing her own frustration.

Daniel lingered in the doorway and Julie leaned up on her elbows. "Daniel?"

"Yes?" He turned back eagerly.

"Thank you for tonight. I enjoyed the show."

"I did, too," he said softly. "We'll do it again soon. Next time I'll take you to Gatsby's."

"Really?"

"If you'd like, we could take up tennis again," he suggested.

"I would like that," she responded happily. "Very much."

"Tomorrow?"

"That would be lovely."

To his credit, Daniel did play a set of tennis with her the following morning. But he glanced repeatedly at his watch, distracted from their game. He beat her easily, but then it'd been a long time since Julie had played anyone who challenged her the way Daniel did. He seemed out of sorts by the time they finished. Julie couldn't understand his attitude. And she'd been hoping to meet more of his friends, but Daniel introduced her to no one.

"Half the morning's gone," he commented as they left the court. Again, he glanced at his watch impatiently. "I've got several things I need to do this afternoon."

Julie remained tight-lipped as they returned to the condo. Daniel had been the one to suggest the game, not her. Almost immediately, he closed himself in his office. When lunch was ready half an hour later, Julie entered to find him poring over papers and checking the internet. He barely noticed she was there.

"Would you prefer to eat in here or the kitchen?"

Daniel looked up. "Here," he said.

Julie brought in a tray with tomato soup and two grilled cheese sandwiches.

"Thanks," he muttered.

Julie ate silently while leafing through the Sunday paper. Later in the afternoon, she did the weekly shopping and ran a few other errands. On her way back home, she dropped by the hospital. Clara was being transferred out of intensive care the next morning and Julie promised to stop in for a visit the following evening on her way home from work.

After leaving the hospital, Julie picked up some hamburgers at a drive-thru for dinner. To her surprise, Daniel was still in his office when she returned. "You're still at it?" she asked as she entered the room.

He looked up and nodded. "This case is more involved than I thought."

"I brought you some dinner."

"Thanks," he said. "I could use a break. What've you made?"

Julie glanced at him guiltily. "Well, I didn't exactly cook..." She held up the paper take-out bag.

"Julie," Daniel groaned. "Sometime in the next twenty years, you're going to have to learn to cook."

That meant they'd still be together in twenty years, she mused contentedly.

Seven

"Married life doesn't seem to agree with you," Sherry commented as she watched Julie work.

"What do you mean?" Julie asked. Another week had passed and just when she thought the tension was lessening between her and Daniel, something would happen to set them back. They hardly spoke in the mornings—not even on their drive to work. In the evenings they visited his mother, came home and ate dinner. Immediately afterward, he'd hole himself up in his office, and sometimes Julie wondered if he forgot she was there. He treated her more like a roommate than a wife.

"Maybe I should keep my mouth shut," Sherry continued, "but you don't have the look of a happy bride."

Julie bit her lip as she opened a file and stared blankly at the pages inside. "I don't feel much like a bride."

"Why not?"

A tear traced its way down Julie's cheek. "Daniel's so busy right now. I hardly ever see him."

Sherry rolled her chair close to Julie's desk and

handed her a tissue. "Believe me," she said sympathetically, "I know the feeling. That's how all of my problems with Andy started. He worked such long hours that we didn't have time to be a couple anymore. He was so involved with his job that eventually we drifted apart. It reached the point where I'd be gone a week before he even knew I was missing."

Julie felt comforted to know she wasn't alone.

Ten minutes later, Mr. Barrett came out of his office. "I was wondering…" he started. "Would you two like to take an extra half hour for lunch today? It's been a hectic week."

Julie and Sherry exchanged surprised glances. "Thank you," Sherry said. "We'd love to."

The long lunch with Sherry proved to be just what Julie needed to raise her spirits.

"You know," Sherry said between bites of her chicken and cashew salad, "if I had it to do all over, I'd make it so Andy never wanted to leave the house again."

Julie stirred her clam chowder without much interest. Her appetite had been nonexistent lately. "What do you mean?"

"Think about it." Sherry leaned against the table, her eyes shining mischievously. "There are ways for a woman to keep her husband home at night."

Julie simply nodded, her thoughts spinning.

As the day progressed, Julie gave more thought to Daniel's actions. In the beginning he'd been bitter, but as the weeks progressed, his hostility was fading. He'd promised after taking down their engagement photo that he wouldn't hurt her again. And he hadn't. If anything, he was all the more gentle—and the other night, she'd found him holding the photo, studying their young, happy faces. Julie had held her breath, worried he'd look at the picture and remember the pain and embarrassment she'd caused. Instead his gaze had held an odd tenderness. She'd been puzzled when he then retreated into his office. If he'd forgiven her, if he loved her and wanted her, wouldn't he come to her? Julie was beginning to hate that guest bedroom. She didn't belong there; she was his wife, and she longed to fill that role completely.

In the weeks since their wedding, physical contact between them had been brief, but she'd seen the desire in his eyes. He wanted her. He spent the evenings avoiding her for fear of what would happen otherwise. His pride was punishing them both.

A smile touched Julie's lips as she recalled a pearly-white satin nightgown she'd recently admired in a department store window. Perhaps she should do as Sherry suggested and lure her husband to bed without involving pride or egos. The more she thought about it, the more confident she became.

That evening, Julie and Daniel drove to visit Mrs. Van Deen in the hospital.

"It's so good to see you," she murmured in a cheerful tone.

"Hi, Mom." Daniel kissed her cheek and held Julie close by his side.

"Julie, you're looking lovely. That color agrees with you."

Daniel looked at his wife as if seeing her for the first time that day. His eyes softened as he noted the way the pink dress accented her figure. "It certainly does," he agreed.

"How are you feeling?" Julie asked, still blushing from Daniel playing the role of the loving husband.

"Better," Clara said with a sigh. "The doctor said he'd never seen anyone make a swifter recovery. I told him I have something to live for now. My son has the wife he's always wanted and I'll soon have the grandchildren I've dreamed of."

Daniel's grip tightened around Julie's middle and she had to suck in a breath to keep from crying out. Her hand moved over his to silently let him know he was hurting her. Immediately, his grip slackened.

"My grandchild will have the bluest eyes," Clara continued, oblivious to the tension in the room. "My husband's eyes were blue. Deeper than the sea. I wish you'd known him, Julie. He would have loved you just as I do. He was a good man."

"I'm sure he was," Julie said.

"A lot like Daniel." Clara gestured toward her son.

Julie glanced up at him as Daniel's mother continued reminiscing about the late August Van Deen.

When Julie and Daniel returned home that evening, Julie breathed a long sigh.

"What was that about?" Daniel asked.

"It's nothing," Julie said. "I was just hoping that our lives will be as rich and rewarding as your parents' were."

Daniel smiled. "They did have a wonderful life together."

Daniel went to drop his briefcase in his office. It was nearly seven and they hadn't eaten dinner.

Julie put some noodles on to cook then headed for her room to change clothes, donning a pair of navy-blue cords and a thin sweater that clung to her curves. She refreshed her makeup and dabbed on Daniel's favorite perfume for good measure, then returned to finish preparing dinner.

Daniel looked surprised as he joined her in the kitchen. He studied her for a moment, noting the change in outfit.

"I didn't want to spill anything on my dress," Julie told him, hiding a smile.

He answered with a short nod, but couldn't seem to keep his eyes off her as she deftly moved around the tiny kitchen.

He didn't talk much during dinner, but that wasn't unusual. Perhaps Julie was reading too much into his actions. After so many years of living alone, he was probably used to keeping his thoughts to himself.

With seduction plots brewing in her head, every bite of her meal seemed to stick in her throat. After a few minutes, she stood and scraped half her dinner down the garbage disposal before placing her plate in the dishwasher.

"I thought I was doing dishes," Daniel said, looking up from the table.

"There aren't many," Julie said dismissively.

"Hey, we made a deal. When you cook, I wash the dishes," he said. "Now scoot."

Having been ousted from the kitchen, Julie sat to watch some TV, but her mind wasn't focused.

Daniel worked away in the kitchen, but Julie felt his eyes occasionally rest on her. A few times she'd glanced up and smiled at him.

"A penny for your thoughts," he said, handing her a hot cup of coffee.

Julie swallowed a laugh. "You wouldn't want to

know," she teased. "You'd run in the opposite direction."

"That sounds interesting."

"I promise you it is."

Daniel surprised her by sitting in the wing-backed chair beside her. "Julie." He took the remote control and muted the television. "Can we talk a minute?"

"Sure." She turned toward him expectantly.

"I haven't been the best of company lately," he started.

"There's no need to apologize," Julie told him. "I understand."

"You do?"

"You must be exhausted. Heaven only knows when you sleep. You've been working yourself half to death this last month." Crossing her legs, Julie leaned back into the couch. "And then this evening your mother started talking about grandchildren and neither one of us has the courage to tell her we aren't sharing a bed." Nervously, she glanced down at the steaming coffee. It was on the tip of her tongue to admit how much she wanted that to change, how much she longed to be with him and start a family together.

"Julie, listen."

Just then, the phone rang, distracting them both.

"Hold that thought," Julie said, reaching for the receiver. Whoever it was, she'd get rid of him in a hurry. For the first time, Julie felt like they were making strides in their marriage. "Hello," she answered.

There was silence on the other end.

"Hello?" Julie repeated.

"Who's this?" a husky female voice replied.

"Julie Van Deen," she answered. "Who's this?"

"So it's true," the woman said, clearly shocked.

"Who am I speaking to?" Julie asked, already certain it had to be the woman Jim Patterson had mentioned at the club the other day. Julie had bitten back many questions about her, but now they were resurfacing.

"Kali Morgan," the woman answered.

A chill raced up Julie's spine. "Would you like to talk to Daniel?"

Kali paused. "No. Just...just give him my best...to you both."

"Thank you," Julie murmured. Confused, she hung up the phone.

Daniel was looking at her expectantly. "Who was it?"

"An old friend of yours," she said weakly.

"Who?"

"Someone who clearly didn't know you had a wife."

"Kali." The word was a statement, not a question.

"You didn't tell her about us, did you?"

Daniel stood, putting some distance between them. His voice was unsure, worried. "What did Kali say?"

Julie searched his expression. The man who stared back had become a stranger. Daniel didn't seem to find it necessary to tell Kali that he got married. Maybe he believed that he'd go back to his old life eventually, keep his options open in case his mother didn't survive. He could quickly annul their marriage. Or maybe he was just looking for ways to hurt her as she'd hurt him. If so, he'd succeeded.

Daniel took a slow step toward her. "Julie, please don't look at me like that."

She felt her chest tighten as she got up and moved

down the hall to her room. The bag containing the nightgown she'd bought rested on her bed. She stared at it in disbelief. Only minutes before she'd intended to seduce her husband.

Daniel appeared in the doorway. "Julie, be reasonable. Surely you didn't think I've lived the last few years like a priest."

Everything went incredibly still. "For three years, my heart grieved for you until I couldn't take it anymore...and I came back because...because facing your bitterness was easier than trying to forget you."

"Julie." His voice took on a soft, pleading quality. He paused as if desperately searching for the right words. "Kali and I had been dating for several months," he explained. "But that's in the past. I haven't touched her since the day I saw you in the elevator."

"Touched her," Julie repeated shakily. "Is that supposed to reassure me? You haven't touched me either!" She felt her stomach heave and she rushed into the bathroom.

Daniel followed her. Julie stood in front of the sink and pressed a cool rag to her face.

"What did you expect me to do?" he shouted. "You walked out on me!"

Julie turned sharply to face him. "You didn't tell her we were married!" She hiccuped on a sob. "And...and all these years I've loved you."

"Don't tell me there hasn't been anyone in—"

"No," she shouted. "I seldom dated. You were the only man I ever loved. The only man I ever could love." She wept into the washcloth.

"Julie." He moved to stand behind her, a hand on each shoulder.

"Don't touch me," she commanded and shrugged her upper torso to shake him off. "Your tastes have changed, haven't they, Daniel? You must find me incredibly stupid to think you still care."

She started to leave but he pulled her into his arms. "You're going to listen to me, Julie. Perhaps for the first time since we met, we're going to have an honest discussion."

Julie was in no mood to be reasonable. "No," she cried, pushing past him to get back to her room. Grabbing the package from her bed, she shoved it in his arms. "Here. Once I'm gone, you can give this to one of your other women." With that she slammed the bedroom door.

Sherry was at her desk when Julie got to work the following day.

"Morning," Julie greeted her, doing her best to disguise her misery. She knew she looked terrible. Makeup had been unable to camouflage the effects of her sleepless night. For the first time since getting married, Daniel had left for work without Julie.

"Morning," Sherry replied without looking up. It was obvious she'd been crying again.

"Did something happen?" Julie pried.

Wiping her face with the back of her hand, Sherry sat up and sniffled. "After our talk yesterday, I got to thinking about how much I miss Andy...so I saw him last night."

"Was he with another woman again?"

"No, this time he was with me," Sherry said. "I...I told him I wasn't positive I wanted the divorce and that

I thought we should talk things over more thoroughly before we take such a serious step."

"I think that's wise." Julie recognized how difficult it must have been for Sherry to contact her husband and suggest that they meet. She and Daniel weren't the only ones with an overabundance of pride.

"We sat and talked for ages and, well, Andy ended up spending the night." Sherry continued, her fingers nervously toying with a tissue. "Then this morning when I woke up, Andy was gone. No note. Nothing. He regrets everything—I know he does. I feel so cheap and used and…" She paused and blew into the tissue.

"Sherry." Julie moved to gently pat her on the back. Julie definitely felt her friend's pain. Like a pair of idealistic fools, they'd hoped everything would work out because they loved their husbands. "I'm sure there's a perfectly logical explanation for why Andy left." Julie tried to sound optimistic.

"I feel like a one-night stand."

"But you are married," Julie said.

"Yes, but not for very much longer."

"Things have a way of working out for the best," Julie assured her, hoping it was true.

Sherry attempted a smile. "How did everything go for you?"

"Fine," Julie lied but, at Sherry's narrowed look, amended, "Terrible."

The office door opened and Julie and Sherry lowered their heads, pretending to be absorbed in their work. Mr. Barrett passed through the room with his usual morning greeting.

"He must think we've gone off the deep end," Sherry

whispered once he was in his office with the door closed.

"Maybe we have."

They worked companionably, taking turns answering the phone. When she had a free moment, Sherry placed her purse on the desk and took out her make-up case. "Count your blessings, Julie. You're much too levelheaded to do some of the dumb things I've done."

"Maybe you should reach out to him?" Julie suggested.

"I couldn't...not after what happened."

"I'm sure he'd be willing to talk, especially after last night," Julie insisted.

"I wish that was true," Sherry said. "But somehow, I doubt it."

Daniel was already in his office when Julie got home that evening. At their usual visit, Clara had mentioned that her son had been by earlier. Her mother-in-law had noticeably studied the dark shadows under Julie's eyes, but didn't comment. Julie was grateful. Answering Clara's questions would have been her undoing.

Hanging up her jacket in the closet, Julie headed for the kitchen. A package of veal cutlets rested on the countertop. Julie sighed as she reached for the frying pan.

"I thought it was my turn to cook," Daniel said from behind her.

"All right," she muttered. "But I'm not very hungry. In fact, I think I'll lie down for a while."

He took so long to answer that Julie feared another confrontation.

"Okay," he said at last. "I'll call you when dinner's ready."

"Fine." They were treating each other like strangers.

Julie moved into the room and sat dejectedly on the side of her mattress. A month into their marriage and she was little more than an unwelcome guest in Daniel's life. She leaned back and closed her eyes.

It seemed only minutes later when Daniel knocked lightly against the open door. "Dinner's ready."

Julie toyed with the idea of telling him she wasn't feeling well. But Daniel would easily see through that excuse. It was better to face him. Things couldn't possibly get much worse.

The table was already set when Julie pulled out a chair to join Daniel.

"Your mother looked better tonight," she said.

Daniel deposited a spoonful of wild rice on his plate before answering. "She asked about you. I didn't know if you'd be stopping in to see her or not."

"I did," she told him.

"So I surmised."

Five minutes passed and neither spoke. Julie looked out the window and noted the thick gray clouds rolling in.

Daniel noticed them, too. "It looks like rain."

Julie nodded. Another awkward silence filled the kitchen until Julie stood and started to load the dishwasher.

"I'll do that," Daniel volunteered.

"It's my turn."

"You're beat."

"No more than you," Julie countered, stubbornly filling the sink with hot tap water.

The dishes took all of ten minutes. The hum of the dishwasher followed her into the hallway. The thought of spending another night in front of the television was intolerable. But going out was equally unappealing. Daniel had disappeared inside his office and Julie doubted she'd be seeing him again that evening, which was just as well.

Deciding to read, she returned to her room. Once she was settled on her bed, a flash of satin caught her attention. Setting her book aside, she discovered that the nightgown she'd shoved at Daniel was hanging in her closet. She ran her fingers over the silky smoothness, suddenly feeling emotional. She'd so wanted things to be different.

"Julie," Daniel called through the closed door. "Are you all right?"

"I'm wonderful," she said sarcastically. "Just leave me alone."

For a moment, nothing happened. Then the door was shoved open.

Julie gasped as Daniel marched into her room and hoisted her in his arms.

"Put me down," she cried.

"You're my wife, Julie Van Deen. And I'm tired of these games." He marched down the hallway to his bedroom and slammed the door closed with his foot.

Eight

"You didn't even tell Kali you were married!" she shouted.

"I couldn't," he shouted right back. "She was in England on a business trip."

Julie's anger died a swift and sudden death. She went completely still.

"I don't know what's going on in that head of yours," Daniel continued. "For heaven's sake—we're married. What's Kali got to do with us now?"

"Nothing," Julie whispered, laughing softly. "Nothing at all."

"What's so amusing?" he barked. He sank onto the edge of his bed, his hold on her loosening as she rested in his lap.

"You wouldn't understand," she murmured, linking her arms around his neck. "I thought you were planning... Never mind." Gently, she kissed him.

"Julie," he breathed, his arms tightening around her.

"Are you really tired of playing games?" she asked, teasing him with a series of short, playful kisses along his jaw.

"Yes," he said, gripping the back of her head and directing her lips to his. "Oh, yes."

His hands began undoing the tiny buttons of her blouse. Frustrated with the small pearl-shaped fastenings, he abandoned the effort and broke the kiss long enough to try to pull the blouse over her head.

Winded, Julie stopped him. "We've waited a whole month. Another thirty seconds shouldn't matter."

As she freed her blouse, Daniel softly cupped her breasts and buried his face in the hollow of her throat. "I couldn't live another month like that," he told her. "I couldn't sleep knowing you were just down the hall. Every time I closed my eyes, all I could see was you."

"I've wanted you so badly," she said, sliding her hands up and down his shoulders.

Hungrily, he kissed her again. "You're my wife, Julie, the way you were always meant to be."

"Wake up, sleepyhead," Daniel whispered lovingly in her ear. "It's morning."

"Already?" Julie groaned, resting her head in the crook of his arm. Her eyes refused to open.

"How are you this morning?" Daniel asked, kissing the crown of her head.

"Very happy." Julie smiled.

"Me, too. I never stopped loving you, Julie. I tried. Believe me, I tried every way I could to forget you. For a time I convinced myself I hated you. But the day I saw you in the elevator, I knew I'd been fooling myself. One look and I realized I'd never love another woman the way I love you."

Raising her head, Julie rolled onto her stomach and kissed him.

The hunger of his response surprised her. Quickly he spun them sideways so that Julie was on her back, looking up at him.

"Daniel," she protested lightly. "We'll be late for work."

"Yes, we will," he agreed. "Very late."

An hour later, while Julie dressed, Daniel cooked breakfast, humming as he worked.

"You're in a good mood this morning," she teased, sliding her arms around his middle.

Daniel chuckled. "And with good reason." He pulled her into his arms, kissing her soundly. "I love you."

She smiled. "I know."

"I think it's time we took that diamond ring hanging around your neck and put it on your finger, where it belongs," he said. He helped her remove the chain and slid the solitaire diamond onto her finger with a solemnness that told her how seriously he took his vows. "I wanted you the minute the minister pronounced us husband and wife," he admitted sheepishly. "I had to get out of the house that day because I knew what would happen if I stayed."

"And I thought—"

"I know what you thought," he said. "It was exactly what I needed you to believe. My ego had suffered enough for one day. I couldn't tolerate it if you knew how badly I wanted you."

The workdays flew by and after a wonderful weekend together, Julie and Daniel spent a quiet Sunday with his mother at the hospital. Clara Van Deen's heart surgery was scheduled for the following Tuesday and both

Julie and Daniel wanted to spend as much time with her as possible.

"Have you told Julie about her surprise yet?" Clara asked as Daniel wheeled his mother into the sunny hospital courtyard.

"Surprise?" Julie's face lit up. "What surprise?"

"Oh, dear." Mrs. Van Deen glanced over her shoulder at her son. "I didn't let the cat out of the bag, did I?"

Leaning forward, Daniel kissed his mother's cheek. "Only a little," he whispered reassuringly. "I was waiting until later."

"Later?" Julie spoke again. "What's happening later? Daniel, you know how much I hate secrets."

"This one you'll enjoy," he promised. He laughed at her puzzled expression and slid a hand around her waist. "I won't make you wait any longer than this afternoon," he said. The mischievous look in his eyes was enough to make her feel light-headed.

After an hour in the fresh air, Clara Van Deen announced that it was time for her to go back inside.

Daniel stood and started to wheel her inside. "We shouldn't have kept you out so long."

"Nonsense," Clara protested. "I've been wanting to feel the sun for days."

Within half an hour Clara was fast asleep. Standing on opposite sides of the hospital bed with the railing raised, Daniel whispered, "Are you ready for your surprise now?"

Julie nodded eagerly. Now that she thought about it, he *had* been acting suspicious. Several times he'd looked as if he wanted to tell her something, but then stopped himself.

Holding hands, they strolled out to the parking lot.

Daniel opened the car door for her and stole a lingering kiss when no one was looking.

"Are you going to give me any hints?" Julie asked excitedly.

"Not a one," he teased. "You'll just have to be patient."

Daniel took the freeway that led past the densely populated suburbs and out of town. Finally, he exited, turning down a winding road in the countryside.

"For heaven's sake, Daniel, where are you taking me? Timbuktu?"

He chuckled. "Wait and see."

Julie felt so lucky to be with him. Finally. Everything was so perfect. So right.

When he pulled the car into the long driveway of a newly built two-story house, Julie was awestruck.

"What do you think?" he asked, one brow raised inquisitively.

"What do I think?" she repeated. "You mean this... house...is my surprise?"

"We're signing the final papers on Monday morning. There are several things you'll have to decide. The builder needs to know what color you want for the kitchen counters, and you need to pick the design of the tile for the bathrooms. From what I understand, there are several swatches of carpet for you to look at while we're here."

Julie nodded, not knowing what to say. She couldn't understand why Daniel wanted a place so far from the city. It would mean a long daily drive both ways in heavy traffic. Julie loved the city. Daniel knew that.

"Come inside and I'll give you the grand tour." He

climbed out of the car, walked around to her side and extended his hand. "You're going to love this place."

Julie wasn't convinced. Why would he pick out something as important as a house without consulting her? Daniel took out the key and opened the front door, pushing it aside so she could enter before him. At first, she was overwhelmed by the magnificence of the home. The sunken living room contained a massive floor-to-ceiling brick fireplace. The crystal chandelier in the formal dining room looked like something out of a Hollywood movie. No expense had been spared. But the kitchen was compact and the only real eating space was in the formal dining room. It also didn't appear to have a family room.

"What do you think?" Daniel asked eagerly.

"Nice." Julie couldn't think of anything else to say. It was a beautiful home, that she couldn't deny, but it wasn't something she would have chosen. In many ways, it was exactly what she wouldn't want.

"The swimming pool is this way." He led her through the sliding glass doors off the kitchen to a deck. A kidney-shaped pool was just beyond. Although the cement structure was empty, Julie could picture aqua-blue water gently lapping against the tiled side.

"Nice," she repeated when he glanced expectantly toward her.

"If you think this is impressive, wait until you see the master bedroom." Daniel took her hand and pulled her through the hallway.

The room was so large that Julie blinked twice. Fireplace, walk-in closets, soaker tub in the private bath. It was perfect. Just not for Julie.

"What about the other bedrooms?" she asked.

"Upstairs."

Like a robot Julie followed him up the open stairway. The first bedroom they came to was a decent size and had a bath. The second room was smaller. Julie assumed it would be Daniel's office. The third room looked as if it could be an art room with huge glass windows that overlooked the front of the house.

Julie made the appropriate comments, but felt as if she was being suffocated. She didn't know how much more of this she could take. Abruptly, she turned and walked down the stairs.

"Julie." Daniel followed her out the front door. "What's the matter?"

Shaking her head, Julie tried to control what she was feeling. That Daniel would look for and buy a house without consulting her felt all too familiar—and not in a good way. She wasn't a naive young girl anymore. His mother had picked out their first home as a wedding present without consulting Julie. And now Daniel was doing the same.

"You don't like it, do you?" A hint of challenge was evident in his voice.

"That's not it," she admitted. She was angry with Daniel, but equally upset with herself. Most women would love a home like this. Unfortunately, she wasn't one of them.

"All right," Daniel breathed, scrutinizing her. "What don't you like? I'm sure whatever it is can be changed."

"Changed?" she flared back. "Can you change the location? I love Wichita. I want to live in the city. I thought you did, too. What suddenly made the country so appealing?"

"Peace, solitude—"

"What about the hour's commute in traffic every day?"

"I'll get used to it," he said, attempting to reason.

She crossed her arms. "Sure you will."

Frustrated, he mirrored her closed off pose. "Is there anything else?"

Julie swallowed hard. "Three years ago I didn't say anything when your mother bought us a house. I let everything build up inside until it exploded and I fled. I can't do that anymore. This is a beautiful house, but it's not for us. Someday I'd like to have children. This isn't a family home. It's for a retired couple, or a family with teenagers."

Daniel frowned; his forehead was lined with disappointment.

"I...I appreciate what you're trying to do, but—"

"Be honest, Julie. You don't appreciate anything about this." He held the car door open for her and shut it once she was inside.

She waited until he was in the driver's seat. "Daniel." His name rushed out in a low breath. "I'm sorry I seem so ungrateful. But something as important as a home should be chosen by both of us. I realize you were saving this as a surprise and I'm sorry if I ruined that."

Either he didn't hear her or he chose to ignore her. The tires squealed as he pulled out of the driveway and onto the road.

On the drive home, Julie sat in miserable silence. Moving into that house feeling the way she did wouldn't have been right. She'd come too far to allow something like this to happen a second time.

When they arrived back at the condo, Daniel went directly into his office to make a series of phone calls while Julie tried to understand what had motivated him. Only that afternoon, Julie had doubted that anything could destroy their utopia. Now she saw how fleeting their happiness was.

Julie was cooking dinner when Daniel joined her. She kept her back to him, needlessly turning the slices of beef every few seconds. "I wish you hadn't closed yourself off in your office," she began. "I thought we wcrc beyond that. It's important that we talk this out."

He didn't answer.

She turned to find him sitting at the table, reading the newspaper. "Are you giving me the silent treatment?"

He lowered the page. "No."

"Then let's talk," she continued, but his attention had returned to the paper. "If…if that house means so much to you then I'll adjust." Making a concession like this was one of the most difficult things Julie had ever done. But her marriage was worth more than her pride.

Apparently engrossed in his paper, Daniel didn't speak for several long minutes. "You're right. I should have consulted you first."

"Then why are you so angry?" she asked.

He set the paper aside. "I don't know," he admitted honestly. "When you left, my mother claimed you were ungrateful for everything we'd done for you. I'm beginning to understand what she meant. I bought that house for you, Julie, and for our life together."

"What a horrible thing to drag up now. You're being completely unfair."

"Was it fair when you walked out on me three years ago? Don't talk to me about fair."

Julie couldn't believe what she was hearing. Clearly

unconcerned about the damage he was causing, Daniel raised the newspaper and continued reading.

A full minute passed before Julie could move. She turned off the stove and walked out of the kitchen.

Daniel claimed to have forgiven her, but he hadn't. Not in his heart.

"Julie." He followed her into the living room. "I didn't mean that."

"I doubt that," she said. "I believe you meant every word."

"Maybe I did," he said.

The next thing Julie heard was the front door closing softly.

Julie left early the following morning, not waiting for Daniel. She was already at her desk when Sherry arrived.

"You're so punctual," Sherry commented as she sat in her rollback chair and stowed her purse in the bottom drawer.

"I try to be," Julie said, not looking up from her paperwork.

"I'm going to run down and grab a maple bar for breakfast. Do you want one?"

"Sure," Julie agreed rather than explain why she wasn't hungry. She was handing over enough money to cover it when the office door opened.

Standing on the other side was Daniel. A muscle twitched in his jaw as he glared at Julie. She could see his anger and the effort he made to control it.

Sherry looked from one to the other. "If you'll excuse me, I'll run downstairs."

Julie smiled a silent thank-you. Sherry winked and edged her way past Daniel.

"Don't do that to me again," he commanded.

"I needed some time alone," Julie explained. "I thought you'd understand.... You felt the same way yesterday."

"That was different," he snapped.

"If you can disappear until the wee hours of the morning then I have a right to leave for work unannounced."

The phone rang and she swiveled around to answer it, presenting Daniel with a clear view of her back. Halfway through the call, she sensed he'd left and the tension in her shoulders relaxed.

Sherry returned by the time Julie was off the phone. Julie could tell she was full of questions, but Julie didn't feel up to explaining and thankfully, Sherry seemed to pick up on that fact.

"You have tomorrow off, don't you?" Sherry asked, changing the subject.

Julie had nearly forgotten. "Yes. Daniel's mother is going in for heart surgery."

With Daniel under so much stress, he didn't need a war between them. Tonight, she'd insist they put an end to this.

The day dragged by but her visit with Clara that evening went well. Although Julie stopped by immediately after work, she learned that Daniel had already come and gone and they'd only missed each other by a matter of minutes.

Julie stayed for a longer visit than usual. They chatted together, and talked about gardening, which Clara enjoyed. The nurse arrived and gave the older woman a shot to help her relax. Julie waited until she was confident Clara was sleeping comfortably.

Daniel wasn't home when she came through the front door. Julie felt as if she were carrying the weight of the world on her shoulders. Briefly she wondered if he'd gone to Kali. No. He wouldn't. She couldn't believe he'd do something like that.

She forced herself to cook dinner, but had no appetite and only picked at the cutlet and salad. After washing her dishes, she turned on the television. Every five minutes, her eyes drifted to the wall clock. Where was Daniel? His mother was having major heart surgery in the morning. This was a time when they needed each other more than ever. Julie turned off the television and went to bed.

Shadows flickered against the dark bedroom walls as Julie lay staring at the ceiling. The front door clicked softly and Julie sat upright. A quick look at the clock confirmed it was after midnight.

Daniel paused in the open doorway of their room. He loosened his tie as his eyes locked with hers. He took off his coat and carelessly tossed it over the back of a chair. The space between them seemed impossibly wide.

Frantically, her mind searched for the right words. She should have been rehearsing what to say.

She reached out to him and for one heart-stopping moment, thought he might reject her. She watched as he stiffened, hesitant. With a low groan he crossed the room and fell into her arms.

"I'm sorry," she whispered. "Oh, Daniel, I'm so sorry. We need each other now more than ever. Let's forget the house." She hugged him tightly, wanting to laugh away the hurt they'd each foolishly inflicted.

"Julie," he said in a husky voice. The anger was gone. He buried his face in her neck and inhaled deeply. "I need you."

"Yes," she breathed, weaving her hands through his hair. "I love you." She drew his mouth to hers.

An hour later, her head lay nestled against the cushion of his chest, and Julie lovingly ran her fingers over his bare skin. "We can't settle all our arguments this way."

Daniel chuckled and ran his hand down the length of her spine. "I think it has its advantages."

"I feel terrible about our fight. The way I handled everything was wrong. You wanted to surprise me and—"

"No." He gave her a squeeze. "You were right. Anything as important as a house should be a mutual decision. When I got over being angry, I saw how unreasonable I'd been."

"It reminded me too much of what had happened before." She shrugged, unsure of dragging the past into this moment. "Do you really want to live in the country?"

The pause was long enough that she raised her head.

"Not if you don't," he answered.

"My home is with you." She snuggled closer to his warm body. She could still sense that something was troubling Daniel, something more than his mother's pending surgery. Whatever it was had to do with their marriage. Julie didn't know what, but she had a feeling she would soon.

Nine

Daniel paced the waiting room as Julie sat in a vinyl-cushioned chair, attempting to read. Repeatedly, her concentration wandered from the magazine to her wristwatch.

"What time is it?" Daniel inquired with a worried frown.

What he was really asking, Julie knew, was how much longer it would be. The doctor had informed them the surgery would take at least five hours—possibly longer.

"I'm sure it'll be anytime now," Julie said. They'd been in the waiting room most of the day. A nurse came at noon and suggested they break for lunch, but Julie couldn't have forced anything down and apparently Daniel felt the same way.

Her husband took the seat beside her and reached for her hand. "Have I told you how much I love you?"

Before Julie could answer, the doctor, clad in a green surgical gown, walked into the room. His brow was moist and he looked as exhausted as she felt.

Julie and Daniel stood, Daniel holding on to her hand with such force that her diamond cut into her fingers.

"Your mother did amazingly well," the doctor announced. "Her chances at a full recovery are excellent."

Julie smiled brightly at her husband as relief washed over her.

"Can we see her?" Daniel asked.

Julie knew him well enough to know that he wanted visual confirmation of his mother's condition.

"Yes, but only for a few minutes. You can both go in. She'll be in intensive care for a few days, then, if everything goes well, she'll be moved to a room on the surgical floor."

Julie appreciated the support the doctors and staff had given throughout this whole ordeal.

"Thank you, Doctor." Julie stepped forward to shake his hand. "Thank you very much."

Julie and Daniel were led into the intensive care area. When Julie saw Clara, her appearance came as a shock. She was deathly pale and surrounded by tubes and machines.

"How are you feeling?" Daniel leaned forward to hug her.

"I'm fine," she assured him. She tried to lift one hand, but it was taped to a board to hold the IV in place.

Daniel laid his hand over his mother's and gave it a squeeze.

"I'm afraid I'm going to have to ask you to leave," a nurse requested a few minutes later. "You're welcome to come back tomorrow, but for now, Mrs. Van Deen needs to rest."

Julie thanked the nurse and they said their goodbyes, promising to return the next day.

The air outside the hospital smelled fresh and clean. Julie paused to take several deep breaths before getting in the car. She was exhausted. With her head resting against the back of the seat, she closed her eyes as Daniel drove them home.

"Julie." A voice spoke softly in her ear. "Wake up."

She yawned and opened her eyes. "I didn't realize I was so tired."

"We didn't get much sleep last night," he reminded her. "And the way I feel right now, we may not tonight, either."

Daniel led her directly into the bedroom and pulled back the covers. "I want you to take a nice long nap and when you're rested, my mother has ordered us to have a night on the town."

"A night on the town?" She didn't think she'd have the energy.

"Mom and I had a long talk yesterday and she feels that we deserve a night out."

Julie opened her mouth to protest.

"No arguing," Daniel said sternly. "She insisted."

Daniel tucked her in and kissed her lightly on the forehead.

"Aren't you going to rest?" Julie asked.

"Honey, if I crawl in that bed with you, it won't be to sleep." He laughed and brushed the hair from her temple. "Actually I've got some work to do. That should take an hour or two. Just enough time for you to catch up on some sleep."

Julie relaxed against the fluffy pillow and pulled the blanket over her shoulder. Her mind drifted easily into happy, serene thoughts as sleep overcame her.

The next thing Julie knew, Daniel was beside her, holding her close.

"Is it time to get ready for dinner?" she muttered, reveling in the warmth of the bed.

"I think breakfast is more in order."

"Breakfast?" She sat up. "I couldn't have slept through the night." She looked around, confused.

"I could have paraded a marching band through here yesterday evening and you wouldn't have budged."

Julie leaned back against the oak headboard. "I can't believe I slept like that. I was dead to the world for fifteen hours or more."

"I imagine you're starved."

Strangely she didn't feel hungry, but once she ate some breakfast, she realized how famished she'd actually been.

"I'm sorry I ruined your night," she said, swallowing the last of her toast.

Daniel looked up from his plate and smiled. He reached over to trace the delicate line of her jaw. "You didn't ruin anything," he said. "Do you know how incredibly beautiful you are when you're sleeping? I could have watched you for hours. In fact I kinda did."

Somewhat embarrassed, Julie shook her head.

"I lay awake last night, and I realized I'm the luckiest man in the world."

"Yesterday was a good day to think that. Your mother survived the surgery, and we've been given a second chance."

"Yes, we have," Daniel agreed, his mouth seeking hers.

"What did you and Daniel decide on regarding this house business?" Sherry asked later that week over lunch.

Julie shrugged, setting aside her turkey sandwich. "It's on hold. We've more or less decided to wait until we have a reason to move."

"Do you want to start a family right away?"

"Yes." And no. Things weren't perfect. The incident with the house had proven that. Daniel loved her, but Julie was convinced he didn't completely trust her. It was almost as if he was waiting for her to pack her bags and walk out on him again. Julie realized that only time would persuade him otherwise. She wanted a secure marriage before they had children.

After lunch, the two women returned to work. The phone was ringing when they entered the office.

"I'll get it," Sherry volunteered, reaching for the receiver.

Julie didn't pay much attention to the ensuing conversation until Sherry laughed and handed the phone to her. "It's for you. Personal."

"Daniel?"

"Nope. Jim Patterson."

Julie hadn't encountered Jim since the day of the tennis match. "Hello, Jim," she greeted him, curious as to why he'd be contacting her.

"Julie. Sorry to call you at the office, but I didn't want Daniel to answer and I didn't have your cell number."

"It's no problem. What can I do for you?"

"The Country Club has voted Daniel Man of the Year. We'd like to keep it a secret until the big night so don't let on that you know."

"I won't breathe a word," she promised. "Daniel will be so pleased."

"Each year we do a skit that tells the life story of the

recipient. You know, *This Is Your Life* type of thing. Of course we tend to ham it up a bit."

Julie giggled, imagining the types of jokes they must come up with.

"I was wondering if you and I could get together and go over some of the details of Daniel's life. I'd ask his mother, but apparently she's in the hospital."

"I'd be happy to do that," Julie said.

They agreed on a time and Julie was beaming with pride when she hung up the phone.

Daniel turned up at her office at quitting time. Usually, she walked down the one flight of stairs to his suite and waited for him. But she was running behind, having stayed late to sign final escrow papers with a young couple. Julie was still with the Daleys when Daniel walked through the door.

Julie smiled at her husband and gestured for him to take a seat. "I'll be done in a minute," she told him.

"I didn't realize it was so late," Mrs. Daley said, glancing up from her wristwatch. "We've got to pick up our son from day care. Is there much else to sign?"

Julie scanned the documents. "No, you're both free to go as soon as you hand over the certified check."

"I've got that here." Mr. Daley reached into his jacket pocket.

Once everything was settled, Mr. Daley shook Julie's hand and thanked her again for her help. This was the best part of her job. The Daleys were buying their first home—a dream they'd saved toward for years.

After they were gone, Julie quickly sorted through the remaining paperwork.

"Why couldn't Sherry have stayed?" Daniel asked stiffly.

"Because I volunteered," she answered on the tail end of a yawn. She lightly shook her head from side to side. "I don't know what's the matter with me lately. I've been so tired."

Daniel set his briefcase down and claimed the chair recently vacated by Mr. Daley. "I don't understand why you continue to work. There's no need. I make a decent living."

"I'd be bored if I didn't work." Julie immediately shelved the idea, surprised he'd even suggest it.

"You might have time to learn how to cook."

"Are you complaining about my meals?" she joked, knowing he had every right to. As long as she stuck to the basics, she was fine, but their menu was limited to only a handful of dishes and Daniel wasn't too fond of the lack of variety.

"I'm not actually complaining," he began, treading carefully. "But I want you to give some serious thought to quitting your job. I don't like you having to work so hard."

"It's not hard," she protested. "Besides, I enjoy it. Sherry and I make a great team."

"Whatever you want." Daniel clearly wasn't pleased and Julie couldn't understand why.

Only a week after surgery, Clara Van Deen was sitting up in bed looking healthier than Julie could remember since returning to Wichita.

"I can't tell you how grateful I'll be to go home," she said. "Everyone's been wonderful here. I can't complain, but I do so miss my garden."

"And your garden misses you," Julie said with a wink to her husband.

"That's right." Daniel shook his head. "Weeds up to my knees."

Clara grimaced. "I can't bear to think what weeks of neglect have done to my precious yard."

Unable to continue the game any longer, Julie patted her mother-in-law's hand reassuringly. "Your garden looks lovely. Now, don't you fret."

"Thanks to Julie," Daniel inserted. "She spent a good portion of the weekend in that garden on her hands and knees."

"I should have been thinking of ways to keep my husband's mouth shut," Julie said with a sigh. "It was supposed to be a surprise."

Clara looked touched. "Did you really?"

"She has the blisters to prove it," Daniel said.

Clara smiled her thanks. "Say, Julie, isn't today the day you were meeting with—"

"No," Julie interjected before her mother-in-law could say anything more. After Jim had contacted her about Daniel's award, Julie had shared the good news with Clara. Apparently she'd forgotten it was supposed to be a surprise.

"What's this about Julie meeting someone?" Daniel asked.

"Nothing," Julie replied.

"It's a surprise," Clara explained. "I nearly let the cat out of the bag the second time. Forgive me, Julie."

"There's nothing to forgive."

"Will someone tell me what's going on?"

"My lips are sealed," Julie teased.

"Mine, too." Clara shared a conspiratorial wink with her daughter-in-law.

"At least let me know whom you're meeting with," Daniel pleaded as they walked to the car.

"Never."

"I could torture it out of you," he whispered seductively.

"I'll look forward to that." She slid an arm around his waist and smiled up at him. He looked so handsome that she couldn't resist stealing a kiss.

"What was that for?"

"Because I love you."

A brief look of doubt passed over his features. One so fleeting that Julie was almost sure she'd imagined it. But she hadn't. After everything that had transpired between them, her husband didn't fully believe she loved him. Time, she told herself, he only needed time. As the years passed, he'd learn.

On the ride home, Julie thought about how they'd traveled this same route so many times over the past six weeks that sights along the way began to blend into one another.

She sat upright. "Daniel?"

"Hmm?"

"Take a right here," she directed.

"Why?"

"There's a house on the corner that's for sale." They must have passed the place a thousand times. Julie had noted the Realtor's sign, but hadn't given it a second thought. Now something about the house reached out to her.

Daniel made a sharp right-hand turn and eased to a stop in front of the two-story Colonial home. The paint was peeling from the white exterior and several of the green shutters were hanging by a single hinge.

"Julie," he groaned, "it doesn't even look like anyone lives there."

Julie glanced around and noticed the other homes in the neighborhood. They looked well maintained. "All this place needs is a bit of tender loving care."

"It's the neighborhood eyesore," Daniel said impatiently.

"I'd like to see the inside. Can we contact the Realtor?" Already she was writing down the phone number.

"Julie, you can't be serious."

"But I am."

That evening they met the Realtor, Ryan Derek. "I'm afraid this place has been vacant for several months," he told them.

"What did I tell you?" Daniel whispered in her ear. "This isn't what we're looking for—"

"No," Julie interrupted as she climbed out of the car. "But I still like it. I like it very much."

"Julie," Daniel moaned as he joined her on the cracked walkway that led to the neglected house.

Ryan Derek hesitated and Julie sensed that his opinion of the place was similar to Daniel's.

"Can we go inside?" Julie asked.

"Yes, of course."

The moment Julie walked through the door she knew. "Daniel," she breathed, her hand reaching for her husband. "This is it. This is the house."

"But, Julie, you haven't even looked around."

"I don't need to. I can feel it."

The entryway was small and led to an open staircase with a mahogany banister that rounded at the top of the steps. To her right was a huge living room and to her left, a smaller room that would make a great library or office. Dust covered everything and a musty smell permeated the house. The hardwood floors were dented and badly in need of repair.

The formal dining room had built-in china cabinets and a window seat. The kitchen was huge with a large eating area. The main level had two bedrooms and the upstairs held three more. The full basement had plenty of room for storage.

"It doesn't have a family room," Daniel commented after their tour. "That's something you insisted on with the other house."

"This house doesn't need one," Julie insisted. She hoped that Daniel could see the potential of this house. "It's perfect. Right down to the fenced backyard, patio and tree house."

"Perhaps you'd see a few more houses before you decide," Ryan interjected.

Julie shook her head. "That won't be necessary."

She understood Daniel's doubts. This house would require some expensive repairs, but the asking price was reasonable.

"I feel you should be aware of several things." Ryan Derek's voice seemed to fade into the background as Julie moved from one room to the next, imagining how she would decorate. Two bedrooms downstairs were ideal. She could use one as a sewing area. The only problem she could foresee was having the washer and dryer in the basement. But the back porch was large enough to move the appliances out there. Of course, that would require some minor remodeling.

"Julie." Daniel caught up to her. "I think we should go home and think this over before we make our final decision."

"What's there to decide? If we don't go for it now, someone else will."

"That's not likely, Mrs. Van Deen," Ryan interrupted. "This place has been on the market for six months."

On the drive back to the Realtor's office it was all Julie could do to keep her mouth shut. Before she and Daniel climbed into their own car, Daniel and Ryan Derek scheduled another time for them to look at other houses.

"Why'd you do that?" she demanded when Daniel climbed into the driver's seat.

"Do what?"

"Set up another appointment."

"To look at houses—"

"But I've found the one I want," she declared. "Daniel, I love that house. We could look for another ten years and we wouldn't find anything more perfect."

"That house would be a nightmare. The repair costs alone would be more than the value. The roof needs to be replaced. There's dry rot in the basement."

"I don't care," Julie stated emphatically.

"I'm not going to fight with you about it. If we're going to buy a house then it has to be one we both agree on."

Julie had no argument. That house was everything Julie wanted. Hot tears blurred her vision. Something was definitely off with her lately. She couldn't believe she'd cry over something as silly as a house.

With Mrs. Batten's help, Julie ensured that Clara Van Deen's house was spotless the day she arrived home from the hospital.

The smile on her mother-in-law's face was reward

enough for the long hours Julie'd spent caring for her much-loved garden.

Mrs. Batten cooked a dinner of roast, potatoes and fresh strawberry shortcake, which had long been a family favorite.

"Is everything all right with you, dear?" Clara asked as they sat on the patio together in the late-afternoon sun.

The question surprised Julie. "Of course. What could possibly be wrong?"

Clara took a sip of tea. "I'm not sure, but you haven't been yourself the last couple of weeks. Has the house hunt got you down?"

"Not really." Julie straightened in the wrought-iron chair. "Daniel and I have more or less agreed to wait. There's no rush."

"But there was one house you liked?"

"We agreed to disagree." Julie changed the subject as quickly as possible. "Have you noticed how pink the camellias are?"

Deep in thought, Clara didn't answer. Daniel's expression was similar when he arrived at the condo an hour later.

Julie could tell something was wrong. "Is everything all right?"

"I thought we agreed not to take our disagreements to my mother."

Julie immediately understood. Clara had spoken to Daniel about the house. "We did," she admitted stiffly.

"My mother had a talk with me earlier."

"I know what it sounds like," Julie cut in, "but please believe me when I tell you that I only mentioned it. I tried to change the subject."

Julie watched as her husband's mouth thinned with impatience.

"I think I should have a talk with your mother," she continued. "She's going to have to learn that although we love her dearly, she can't get involved in our lives to the point where she takes sides on an issue. Okay?"

"Definitely."

Julie crossed the room, her arms cradling her middle protectively. They were walking on thin ice. Each desperately wished to maintain the fragile balance of their relationship.

Daniel cleared his throat and moved to stand behind her. "I can see that this house issue could grow into a major problem."

Julie shook her head. "I won't let it. It doesn't matter where we live, as long as we're together."

He gathered her in his arms. "I've been giving that house considerable thought."

"And?"

"I think we should be able to come up with a compromise."

"A compromise?"

"Yes." He pulled away slightly, his hands still linked at the small of her back. "We can buy that house if you agree to quit your job."

Ten

"Quit my job?" Julie repeated incredulously. "You've got to be joking."

"That house is going to need extensive remodeling. Someone has to be there to supervise the work."

"It isn't remodeling the house needs, it's repairs, most of which will have to be done before we move in." Julie walked to the far side of the room. "The house isn't the real reason you want me to quit—is it?"

"I want you to be my wife."

"And I'm not now?" she responded. "I enjoy my job. The problem is, you think I'm going to walk out on you again. It's almost as if you're waiting for it to happen."

"That's ridiculous."

"Is it?" she asked. "First you wanted a house that just happened to be an hour out of town. And now you want me to quit. Are you trying to close me off from the rest of the world?"

"I saw you with Jim Patterson last week," Daniel blurted out. "Will you tell me why you two found it necessary to have lunch together?"

"I can't," Julie replied defensively. "But I'm asking

you to trust me. Surely you don't believe Jim and I are involved in any way?"

"I've tried. A hundred times I've told myself that you must love me. You wouldn't have come back if you didn't."

"Of course I love you," she cried. "What makes you think I would even look at another man?"

Daniel lowered his gaze. "Sometimes I hate myself." The admission came with a bitter laugh.

"You don't trust me."

His expression confirmed her suspicions.

"I love you so much. I could never leave you," she said. "What will it take to convince you of that?"

Daniel couldn't meet her eyes. "I don't know. When I first saw you with Jim, I felt sick inside, then angry. Even though I'd heard you joke with my mother about some mystery meeting, I couldn't believe I'd see my wife and a good friend together. For two days I worried I'd wake up and find you gone."

"You actually thought I'd run away with Jim Patterson?"

"Why not? You ran away from me before."

"I haven't even thought about anyone else since I moved to Wichita."

"Why won't you tell me why you met him?" Daniel asked.

"I need you to trust me."

"I'm trying. Heaven knows I want to, but I don't know if I can."

"You don't look as if you slept at all last night," Sherry said when Julie walked into work the following morning.

"I didn't."

"Why not?"

When they'd gone to bed the night before, Daniel had stayed on his side of the mattress. He could have been on the other side of the world for all the warmth they shared.

"It's a long story," Julie answered. She got herself settled at her desk. "What would you say if I told you Daniel wants me to quit my job?"

"Does he?"

"Let's make this a hypothetical question." Julie wondered if, without knowing the background of her relationship with Daniel, Sherry would read the same meaning into his actions.

"Well, first he wanted to move to the boondocks," Sherry said thoughtfully, rolling her chair the short distance between their two desks. "And now he wants you home all day. My guess is that he's insecure about something. But I can't imagine why. It's obvious how much you love him."

"I wish Daniel realized that."

"You're not going to quit, are you? You've helped me so much with Andy. I'd really miss your friendship."

"No, I'm not quitting." Julie refused to give in to Daniel's insecurities. "Enough about my problems. How *is* everything between you and Andy?"

Sherry lowered her gaze. "Who would have thought wooing my husband would be so difficult?"

The phone rang and Sherry looked up. Suddenly pale, she motioned for Julie to answer as she rushed into the bathroom. Not for the first time in the past couple of weeks, Julie suspected her friend was pregnant.

Julie was off the phone by the time Sherry returned.

"Are you going to tell me or are you going to make me ask?"

"How'd you know?"

"Never mind that. Does Andy know?"

She began to cry. "No." She sniffed. "If we do get back together, I want it to be because he loves me. Not because of the baby."

"The divorce proceedings were halted, weren't they?"

Sherry nodded. "But only because Andy and I felt we needed time to think things through. We're not living together."

"You won't be able to keep this secret for long," Julie advised.

"I know. That's why I've given him three weeks to decide what he wants. If I'm going to lose him, then I'd prefer to face that now and be done with it."

"How does Andy feel about having an ultimatum?"

Sherry looked ashamed. "Andy doesn't know."

"Oh, Sherry," Julie groaned.

A tear slid down her friend's cheek. "I realize that sounds crazy, but I firmly believe I'm doing the right thing. If Andy found out about the baby and we reconciled then I'd never be sure. This way I can be sure that Andy really loves me and wants to make this marriage work."

The phone rang again and the pair were quickly thrown into their work.

That night, Julie taught herself to cook Daniel's favorite dinner.

"Did I miss something?" he teased, smelling the air as he entered the kitchen.

"Miss something?"

"It's not my birthday, is it? I've got it! You overdrew the checking account. Right?"

"Just because I made Stroganoff doesn't mean I'm up to something," Julie said.

"In my short experience as a husband, my immediate reaction is...you are!"

"Well, you're wrong. I've taken all your complaints to heart and bought a cookbook. I can't have my husband fainting away from lack of proper nourishment."

"Would you like me to demonstrate how weak I am?" he asked, slipping his hands under her shirt.

"Daniel, not now."

"Why not?" he moaned against her neck.

"Dinner will burn."

"That's never bothered you before."

"I thought you were hungry."

"I am. Come to bed and I'll show you how hungry I am."

Julie switched off the stove and fell into her husband's arms, relishing in the urgency of his kiss.

Dusk had settled over the city as they lay in bed an hour later. Daniel's hand caressed her bare shoulder. "I'll be happy when you're pregnant," he whispered.

"Why?" Julie asked.

"I thought you wanted a family."

"I do." But not before they were more secure in their marriage.

"Then why ask?"

"I want to know why you want a baby." Her greatest fear was that Daniel would see a child as a means of binding her to him.

"For all the reasons a man usually wants to be a father." He tossed aside the blankets and sat on the edge of the mattress. "And as I recall, we agreed that when you were pregnant, you'd quit your job."

Julie reached for her robe at the foot of the bed. She didn't know why he'd start an argument after they'd just made love. "I think you should know I've made an appointment with the doctor."

Daniel eyed her carefully. "So you think you might be pregnant."

"No," Julie said. "I want to make darn sure that doesn't happen."

As the days passed, Daniel threw himself into his work and Julie did her best to give the outward appearance that everything was fine. With Daniel not around much, Julie spent more and more of her free time with her mother-in-law.

The two women worked at getting Clara's beloved yard into shape. Julie tried to disguise her unhappiness, but she was convinced that her mother-in-law knew something wasn't right.

"I was pleased to see that old engagement photo of you and Daniel on the television," Clara remarked, working the border of the flower bed. Clara had recently visited the condo for the first time since Julie had moved in.

"We both look so young," Julie said.

"It's strange to remember you like that."

Julie got the impression Clara wasn't referring to looks. "We've all changed."

"Something's bothering Daniel," Clara commented, studying her daughter-in-law closely.

"Oh?"

"I saw him briefly the other day and was shocked by how worn-out he looked."

"He's been working a lot of extra hours lately."

"Is that necessary?"

"I...I don't know." Julie moved on to the next section of the flower bed.

"You look a bit weary yourself," Clara continued. "Is everything all right with you two?"

Settling back on her heels, Julie sighed. "Clara, Daniel and I agreed—"

"I know. Daniel told me. But I can't help worrying. You love each other and yet you seem miserable. Whatever the problem is, it can't be worth all this torment. Believe me, I know how stubborn my son can be. Just be patient with him."

"I'm trying," Julie whispered.

Back at the condo, Julie soaked in a warm bubble bath. She had no idea where Daniel was. Although it was Saturday, he'd left early that morning, before she was awake.

Julie had hoped the bath would raise her spirits. She'd been so tired lately. It was ridiculous. It seemed she was going to bed earlier and earlier and often had trouble getting up in the morning. Her appointment with the doctor was coming up; she'd mention it to him. It was probably a reaction to all the stress. She'd had enough of that to last a lifetime.

Abruptly, Julie sat up in the tub, causing water to slosh over the sides. It seemed so clear. She was pregnant. So much had been happening that she'd completely lost track of time. Julie leaned back and placed a hand on her flat stomach. Daniel would be pleased, and despite her misgivings, Julie was, too. Tears flooded her eyes. She cried so easily these days and now she understood why.

Julie climbed out of the tub and wrapped a towel around her body.

Sitting on top of their bed, she reached for the phone and dialed Daniel's cell. The phone rang twice before she hung up. What would she say?

Julie dialed a different number and waited several long rings. "Sherry," she said. "Congratulate me— we're both pregnant." With that she burst into sobs.

Eleven

"Here," Sherry said, handing Julie another tissue. "You're going to need this."

Julie glanced at the tissue, then back at her friend. "I'm through crying. It was a shock, that's all." Sherry had rushed over to the condo as soon as she'd hung up the phone.

"Discovering I was pregnant was a shock for me, too," Sherry said. "At first I was ecstatic, then I had so many doubts."

"A baby is exactly what Daniel wants."

"But for all the wrong reasons," Sherry assumed. "If Andy knew about me, I suspect he'd be thrilled. But again, for all the wrong reasons."

Julie nodded, feeling slightly ill. She hadn't eaten since breakfast, but the thought of food nauseated her.

"What did Daniel say?"

Julie winced. "He doesn't know yet."

"What are you going to do?"

"I don't know." Julie sighed. "He has to be told, but I don't know when. He's…hardly around these days."

"So he's pulling that trick again," Sherry huffed.

"He's working himself to death."

"That's what I thought about Andy. You aren't going to sit here and sulk. I won't let you."

"I'm not sulking."

"No, you're crying." She gave Julie another tissue. "Come on, I'm taking you out."

"Sherry, honestly, I appreciate your efforts, but the last thing in the world I want is to be seen in public looking like this."

Sherry giggled. "I'm going to let you in on one of life's important secrets."

"And what's that?" Julie asked.

"When the going gets tough, the tough go shopping."

"Sherry," Julie groaned. "I don't feel up to anything like—"

"Trust me, you'll feel a hundred percent better. And afterward, I'll treat you to dinner."

"But Daniel—"

"Did he bother to tell you he wouldn't be home for dinner the past three nights?"

"No."

"Then it's time you quit moping around and do something positive for yourself."

Julie realized her friend was right. "All right," Julie agreed, "I'll go."

It took the better part of an hour to make herself presentable, but Sherry was right, she felt better. Before they left, Julie wrote Daniel a short note, telling him her plans.

Sherry seemed intent on having a good time. First they hit the outlet mall, scouting out baby items and trying on maternity clothes.

Next they took in a movie, followed by dinner at an

Italian restaurant. On the way home, Sherry insisted they stop off at her house so Julie could see the baby blanket she was knitting.

"I think I'd better call Daniel," Julie said, sipping a cup of tea. The evening had passed so quickly. Already it was after eleven and although she'd left a note, he might be worried.

"Don't," Sherry chastised. "He hasn't called you lately, has he?"

"No," Julie admitted. They were like strangers who just happened to live together.

"I think I'll put on some music." Sherry reached for the stereo's remote.

The next thing Julie knew, she was lying on the sofa, wrapped in a thick comforter. Struggling to sit upright, she glanced at the clock. How was it light out?

"I was wondering what time you'd wake up," Sherry called from the kitchen. "How do you want your eggs?"

Julie was incredulous. "It's morning?"

"Right, and almost ten. You were tired, my friend."

"But…"

"I turned on the radio and within minutes you were fast asleep."

"Oh, no." Untangling the comforter from around her legs, she reached for her cell. "I'd better call Daniel."

As Julie dialed, Sherry handed her a small glass of milk and two soda crackers. Julie smiled her appreciation. Her stomach was queasy as it had been for several mornings. Julie had attributed it to nerves.

Several rings later, she hung up.

"No answer?" Sherry asked.

"No." Julie shrugged. "Maybe he was in the shower."

"Maybe," Sherry echoed. "Try again in five minutes."

"At least he knows I'm with you. If he was worried he would have called."

Sherry turned back to the stove. "He didn't know."

"I left a note."

"I stuck it in my pocket before we left. I'm sorry. I didn't know you were going to fall asleep. I thought if Daniel worried a little, it would be good for him."

"Oh, Sherry."

"It was a stupid thing to do. Are you mad?"

Julie shook her head. Sherry had no way of knowing that she'd walked out on Daniel once before or that he was worried she'd do it again.

"No," Julie said. "He doesn't appear to be concerned at any rate." For all she knew, he could've come home late, crawled into bed and not even noticed she was missing.

Fifteen minutes later, Julie was back home. The condo was dark so she walked across the living room to open the drapes.

"Julie?"

She swiveled around to find Daniel sitting on the edge of the chair, leaning forward, his elbows braced against his knees.

"Hello, Daniel." He looked as though he hadn't slept.

He stood, jamming his hands into his pockets. "I suppose you came back for your things."

"No." Somehow she managed to let the lone word escape. His clothes were badly wrinkled and his hair was askew. The dark stubble on his face was so unlike the neatly groomed man she'd lived with all these months.

"Well go ahead and get them," he said. "Don't let me stop you."

"You want me to leave?" she asked, her voice shaking in disbelief.

"I won't stop you."

"I see." Not knowing what to say, Julie took a step toward the hallway.

Daniel jerked his head up as she moved. His face was deathly pale.

"Julie," he called out.

She turned back expectantly. Tears filled her eyes and she wiped them aside with the back of her hand.

"I don't blame you for walking out on me," he spoke at last. "I drove you to it. I pushed you out of my life the first time and blamed you for it. I can't do that again." He took a tentative step toward her. "I lived for three long years without you and I won't go back to that. Julie—please—don't leave me. Let me make up for all the unhappiness I've caused you."

Julie flew into his arms and Daniel buried his face into her hair, taking in deep breaths as he refused to let her go.

"It doesn't matter why you saw Jim or any other man. I was a fool to think everything would be solved by having you quit your job."

"Daniel, listen—"

"Moving into the country was just as ridiculous," he interrupted. "I love you, Julie. You're the most important person in my life."

"Would you please listen for one minute? I'm not leaving and never was. I was with Sherry. And as for my job, I plan to work for another six months or so and then I'll think about quitting."

"Why six months?"

"Because by then the baby—"

"The baby?" Daniel repeated, completely stunned. "Julie, are you telling me you're pregnant? How? When?"

Julie laughed and lovingly ran her hand along his jaw. "You don't honestly need an answer to that, do you?"

"No," he said sheepishly. "All these weeks I'd hoped you would be. I wanted a child to bind you to me. I realize how wrong that was. You've always been with me."

When his mouth sought hers, Julie responded enthusiastically.

The doorbell chimed and Daniel glared at it irritably. "I'll get rid of them," he promised, kissing the corner of her mouth.

He opened the door to find a man Julie didn't recognize. "I'm looking for Julie Van Deen," the man said.

Julie looked at Daniel and shrugged. "That's me," she said, joining them in the front hall.

"Excuse me for intruding on you like this," the man continued. "I'm Andy Adams. Sherry's husband."

"Of course." Julie smiled. "I've heard a lot about you."

"Yes." He cleared his throat. "I'm sure you have. Sherry has mentioned you on several occasions, as well."

"Please come in. Can I get you something to drink?"

"No, thanks. If you don't mind, I'd like to ask you a few questions." He stepped inside, closing the door behind him.

"Is this about Sherry?" Julie didn't want to get

caught in the middle of her friend's marital problems. That could get messy.

"Yes, it is," Andy said. "I hope that's okay."

"I know that she's decided to stop seeing you and—"

"But why?" he asked. "I don't understand. I love my wife. I always have. It wasn't me who wanted that stupid divorce. Sherry seemed to need space and I figured the best thing I could do was give it to her."

"But then you decided to taste a little of that freedom yourself," Julie supplied.

"It was all a game. I knew Sherry was going to be there that night. By that point, I was desperate. I thought a taste of her own medicine would help."

"It did," Julie confirmed, recalling her friend's reaction.

"A little too well," Andy admitted. "We were to the point of moving back in together when—whammo—Sherry announces it's over and she doesn't want to see me again."

"I thought you were the one who—"

"No," he said forcefully. "It's true I thought we should take things slow. I wanted Sherry to be sure of her feelings."

"Andy, I want you to think about something. When you and Sherry separated, she went off her birth control pills. Does that mean anything to you?"

Silence hung between them. "I'm going to be a father?"

Julie nodded happily.

"I'm going to be a father," he repeated as a smile lit up his face. "Why didn't she tell me?"

"I think that's something you're going to have to ask Sherry."

"I will."

"Good." Julie felt relieved.

"Thank you, thank you." Andy shook her hand then Daniel's. "I've got to talk to Sherry. I can't thank you enough." He opened the door and left, nearly tripping in his rush.

"I know exactly how he feels," Daniel said, taking his wife in his arms. "Like a fool who's been given a second chance at happiness. Believe me, this time I'm not going to blow it."

"We're home," Julie announced as her mother-in-law rocked her three-month-old son. Daniel had bought the house of her dreams and made extensive repairs. Most of the work they'd done together during Julie's pregnancy.

Clara had spent the evening with little Ted while Julie and Daniel attended a banquet at the Country Club.

"Was Jim surprised to be Man of the Year?" Clara asked, passing the baby to Julie.

"No more than I was last year," Daniel answered with a chuckle. "But then last year was a very good year."

"It was indeed." Clara smiled. "I was given a new lease on life."

"So was I." Daniel slipped an arm around his wife and leaned over to kiss his sleeping son.

"Was he good?" Julie asked.

"Not a peep. He's so sweet. So small. Theodore August Van Deen seems such a big name for such a tiny baby."

"He'll grow," Daniel said confidently. "And be joined by several more if his mother agrees."

"Oh, I'm in full agreement."

The baby let out a small cry.

"It isn't feeding time, is it?" Clara looked to Julie.

"Not yet," Julie assured her. "Don't worry, Grandma. Babies sometimes cry for no reason."

"Teddy-boy, Grandma's joy." Clara took the baby from Julie and placed him over her shoulder. Gently, she patted his tiny back.

Daniel wrapped Julie in his arms. "I love you, Julie Van Deen."

"And I love you," Julie said. She lifted her face to kiss him, perfectly happy to finally have the family she'd always hoped for.

* * * * *

The latest installment of irresistible
Virgin River novels from
New York Times and *USA TODAY*
bestselling author

ROBYN CARR

Available now!   Coming March 2012   Coming May 2012

Welcome to Virgin River, where everyone in town
has a stake in seeing love survive…and thrive.

Available wherever books are sold.

REQUEST YOUR FREE BOOKS!

2 FREE NOVELS
FROM THE ROMANCE COLLECTION
PLUS 2 FREE GIFTS!

YES! Please send me 2 FREE novels from the Romance Collection and my 2 FREE gifts (gifts are worth about $10). After receiving them, if I don't wish to receive any more books, I can return the shipping statement marked "cancel." If I don't cancel, I will receive 4 brand-new novels every month and be billed just $5.99 per book in the U.S. or $6.49 per book in Canada. That's a saving of at least 25% off the cover price. It's quite a bargain! Shipping and handling is just 50¢ per book in the U.S. and 75¢ per book in Canada.* I understand that accepting the 2 free books and gifts places me under no obligation to buy anything. I can always return a shipment and cancel at any time. Even if I never buy another book, the two free books and gifts are mine to keep forever.

194/394 MDN FELQ

Name	(PLEASE PRINT)

Address	Apt. #

City	State/Prov.	Zip/Postal Code

Signature (if under 18, a parent or guardian must sign)

Mail to the **Reader Service:**
IN U.S.A.: P.O. Box 1867, Buffalo, NY 14240-1867
IN CANADA: P.O. Box 609, Fort Erie, Ontario L2A 5X3

Not valid for current subscribers to the Romance Collection
or the Romance/Suspense Collection.

Want to try two free books from another line?
Call 1-800-873-8635 or visit www.ReaderService.com.

* Terms and prices subject to change without notice. Prices do not include applicable taxes. Sales tax applicable in N.Y. Canadian residents will be charged applicable taxes. Offer not valid in Quebec. This offer is limited to one order per household. All orders subject to credit approval. Credit or debit balances in a customer's account(s) may be offset by any other outstanding balance owed by or to the customer. Please allow 4 to 6 weeks for delivery. Offer available while quantities last.

Your Privacy—The Reader Service is committed to protecting your privacy. Our Privacy Policy is available online at www.ReaderService.com or upon request from the Reader Service.

We make a portion of our mailing list available to reputable third parties that offer products we believe may interest you. If you prefer that we not exchange your name with third parties, or if you wish to clarify or modify your communication preferences, please visit us at www.ReaderService.com/consumerschoice or write to us at Reader Service Preference Service, P.O. Box 9062, Buffalo, NY 14269. Include your complete name and address.

DEBBIE MACOMBER

(limited quantities available)

TOTAL AMOUNT	$	_____
POSTAGE & HANDLING	$	_____
($1.00 for 1 book, 50¢ for each additional)		
APPLICABLE TAXES*	$	_____
TOTAL PAYABLE	$	_____

(check or money order—please do not send cash)

To order, complete this form and send it, along with a check or money order for the total above, payable to MIRA Books, to: **In the U.S.:** 3010 Walden Avenue, P.O. Box 9077, Buffalo, NY 14269-9077; **In Canada:** P.O. Box 636, Fort Erie, Ontario, L2A 5X3.

Name: _____
Address: _____ City: _____
State/Prov.: _____ Zip/Postal Code: _____
Account Number (if applicable): _____
075 CSAS

*New York residents remit applicable sales taxes.
*Canadian residents remit applicable GST and provincial taxes.

www.Harlequin.com

MDM0112BL